ROCK BOTTOM

Hayden Nicholas

First published by Dog Ear Publishing
4011 Vincennes Rd
Indianapolis, IN 46268
www.dogearpublishing.net

ISBN: 978-1-4575-5678-4

This book is printed on acid-free paper.

Printed in the United States of America

THANKS:

First and foremost to Jesus Christ, my lord and savior who guides my hands throughout my lifetime.

To my wife and son, Diane and Colton, for all their love and encouragement. Thank you for being my family.

To my parents, Jim and Beth, for their unconditional love throughout their lifetimes.

To Clint Black for his brotherly love and endless insight and support over the decades.

To Johanna West for her artwork and editorial contribution.

To Dick Gay and Jake Willemain and all my brothers on the road.

To Randy Warmuth, Mac Richard, Steve Dalbey, Gary Rose, Bryan Austin, Mia Westbrook, and many others for their spiritual guidance over the years.

And special thanks to Ray Rodgers and Jonni Hartman for all their love, encouragement, and hard work in support of me and my writing endeavors.

This book is dedicated to you, Jonni . . .

ROCK BOTTOM

Hayden Nicholas

1

1971

The caped man opened the bedroom door, letting a rectangle of light shine onto the staircase leading downstairs. He descended the stairs and entered a room barely illuminated by a small table lamp next to a tattered sofa. Traces of pot smoke still lingered in the air as a Led Zeppelin LP played on a stereo turntable. He heard soft moans and observed his captives, all with their hands and feet bound by shackles and chains while lying prone on the thick shag carpet floor. All three were still unconscious. During the evening of pot smoking and beer drinking he had laced their beer with a high dosage of dissolved methaqualone, eventually causing the three musicians to pass out.

The caped man set a leather pouch containing a variety of knives on a coffee table near the sofa before examining his bound captives. From questions asked earlier, he learned that all three were in their early twenties. Two of them were still living at home with their parents while pursuing dreams of becoming rock stars like their heroes in Cream, Grand Funk Railroad, the Jimi Hendrix Experience, and a host of other rock acts finding success in this new musical genre. The caped man had recruited the rockstar wannabes easily; finding them in a local nightclub and promising them paying gigs if they formed a band with him. Encouraged by the marijuana he offered in the back of his VW van in the nightclub's parking lot, and the free beer promised to them back at his house in the country, he drove them all into the Texas countryside to an old two-story house in the middle of nowhere.

The caped man adjusted the hood of his cape over his long hair and unrolled the leather pouch, revealing six knives with jade-studded handles, each in its own pocket inside the pouch. He chose an exotic-looking knife with a curved blade and examined it in the dim light of the room. The knife's handle had been carved into the shape of a serpent wrapped around a pole, its eyes decorated with small pieces of jade.

The caped man replaced the knife into the pouch and grabbed a stone effigy pipe carved into the shape of an eagle's head. With a wooden match he fired the substance in the pipe and drew deeply, letting the acrid smoke expand in his lungs until exhaling with a heavy sigh.

One of the musicians, a drummer, was starting to regain consciousness but the caped man seemed unconcerned. He set the pipe next to an ancient-looking stone mortar and pestle sitting on the table. He removed the heavy pestle and examined the contents in the mortar. The stone bowl contained a mixture of tobacco and a very precise amount of a Datura plant root that had been harvested and prepared according to instructions given to him by an American Indian shaman from New Mexico. According to the shaman, ancient sorcerers of Meso-America had been using similar methods for thousands of years in order to contact various plant spirits that offer the user power and protection. The caped man loaded the pipe with the last of the ground tobacco and Datura root remaining in the mortar.

"Hey, man," the bound drummer slurred, realizing through his drugged stupor that he was shackled with chains. "What's up?"

The caped man fired the final bowl of Datura. He began to chant something under his breath, ignoring the bound drummer on the floor.

"Get these chains off, man!" the drummer protested. "This ain't cool!"

The caped man continued his chanting. He was beginning to feel extremely light-headed. He sensed a change in the room.

The bound drummer was starting to panic. "Let me go, man! Come on! I promise I won't tell anyone!"

The caped man continued chanting for several minutes while the bound drummer's pleadings had turned into sobs and whimpers.

The caped man suddenly heard a distant buzzing in his ears before a black form seemed to appear from a dark corner of the room. He stopped his chanting. The mass of darkness swirled slowly until morphing into the rough shape of a person. A low rumbling emanated from the black form before the caped man heard a gruff voice in his head: *"Why do you call me?"*

"For your power," answered the caped man.

The black form seemed to grunt in reply while hovering in mid-air.

"I offer you life energy," the caped man said while gesturing to his bound captives on the floor.

"Who you talking to?" the bound drummer cried out. "You nuts or something?"

The caped man removed the serpent-handled knife from the leather pouch and approached the bound drummer on the floor.

"What are you doing?" the bound drummer shouted, his voice full of terror. "Please! Stop!"

One of the other bound musicians was regaining consciousness. He seemed oblivious to what was going on as the drummer screamed and yanked on the chains securing his arms and legs.

The caped man, with knife in hand, lowered himself to straddle his bound captive on the floor. The drummer's eyes opened wide when the curved blade pierced the soft flesh of his abdomen. His screams sounded like a wild animal as the caped man began working on the drummer's stomach with the serpent-handled knife blade.

Outside, an owl in a large oak tree began hooting frantically as the inhuman screams coming from inside the house increased in intensity, until ceasing abruptly . . .

2

2016

The live music nightclub, La Zona Rosa, stood where the bend of 4th street turns toward 6th street in downtown Austin. 6th street was famous for its bars and live entertainment, assisting in giving the city its moniker of 'Live Music Capitol Of The World.' Of course, this boast was claimed by many cities around the world but Austin's claim was supported by its hundreds of nightclubs and performance venues, not to mention the three hundred-plus bands that played them on a regular basis.

The Zeniths were rocking the joint. La Zona Rosa had two stages: the small one on the club side reserved for intimate performances, and the larger side of the venue offering a big stage with sound and lights. This side was usually reserved for premier bands and entertainers that drew larger crowds, many of them national acts. The Zeniths were playing on the big stage. The Zeniths got the gig at the last moment as a replacement for a popular band out of Denver that couldn't make the show. Many ticket buyers didn't show up but about three hundred did. And they all seemed to be enjoying the Zeniths.

The Zeniths. A local band. That always made a difference. Being an out-of-town act always seemed much more exotic, making the audience think they were part of something more special than just watching local musicians jam on stage. But the audience this night truly enjoyed the Zeniths with their vintage sound reminiscent of bands like Yes and ELO. Led by Gordon Lawler on keyboards and vocals, Trent Masters on guitar and vocals, Billy Stokes on bass and vocals, and Vince Crowley on drums, the band was tight, exciting, and innovative.

In the back of the room behind the mixing console was a slight man in his twenties with long black hair pulled back into a ponytail. His dark olive complexion revealed his Middle Eastern blood although he had been raised in Austin and had only visited his parents' homeland in Egypt once when he was just a young boy. His full name was Bashshar

Nadir but he'd gone by the nickname of *Bash* ever since middle school. He thought the name sounded more like a rockstar's name than Bashshar (unless the incorrect pronunciation *Basher* was used) but he preferred Bash. And Bash had wanted to be in a rock band ever since he was eleven years old.

When Bash was nineteen he had been one of the new guitarists to watch out for in Austin, no subtle feat in a city of thousands of guitarists who wanted to be noticed. Friends used to tease Bash that one day there would be a statue of him at Auditorium Shores, a statue bigger than the one of Stevie Ray Vaughn, the guitarist reared in Dallas who performed in the Austin club scene for years virtually unnoticed. When Vaughn became world famous in the early 1980s, Austin then began touting him as one of their own—especially after his tragic death in a helicopter crash in 1990.

But Bash was mixing sound for the Zeniths, not playing guitar for them. He turned knobs and slid faders with his left hand. His only hand. Or arm, really. His right shirt sleeve hung loosely over what was left of that arm; now an appendage extending about six inches below his shoulder. The motorcycle accident occurred a year and a half earlier. Back then Bash rode a used Honda PCX, more of a scooter than a motorcycle, but with a 125cc engine it got him where he needed to go. His friends and fellow musicians were always bugging him about buying a car, telling him that cars were a lot safer, but mainly they bugged him because they were tired of always having to haul his gear around when he had gigs.

Bash had been driving on the feeder of I35 while trying to get to a soundcheck at Antone's where he and the Tommyhammers were playing that night. It was a fill-in gig for Bash. Brendan Rowe, the Tommyhammers regular guitarist, had to go out of town for a funeral so Bash was filling in. The gig would be easy. Bash knew most of their material which consisted mainly of traditional blues and R&B numbers from the sixties. The Tommyhammers had secretly tried to hire Bash to replace Brendan many times but Bash wasn't interested. He was bored with that style of music—a musical genre that he felt had been overdone in Austin, especially after Stevie Ray had been killed. But Bash could always use the cash, all two hundred bucks, which he knew was more than they were paying Brendan.

Bash wanted to do something different with his music. To make his own mark. To blend the many styles he'd learned over the years and release them in a new and fresh way. What that blend was exactly, he wasn't sure, but he was working on it all the time.

Bash was actually thinking about this while driving his Honda PCX down the I35 feeder when a large, double-axle pickup truck came off the exit ramp at a high rate of speed. Bash kept his eye on the pickup, moving as far away as possible into the right lane of the feeder but the pickup's driver never saw him. The driver slammed on his brakes to keep from hitting the vehicle in front of him and turned sharply into Bash's lane. The impact to the Honda PCX sent it careening out of control, causing Bash to hit the pavement and roll under the pickup truck, his right arm getting tangled between the two rear axles. He was dragged a distance before the pickup truck finally came to a stop. Bash never lost consciousness during the accident. His helmet probably saved his life, a fact he came to regret while recovering in the hospital. During those early weeks of recovery, he wished he had died instead of being left with just one arm.

Bash endured multiple injuries: a concussion, a broken collarbone, and several fractured ribs, but his right arm had been mangled beyond repair. When the paramedics treated him at the scene Bash caught a glimpse of his destroyed arm. It looked like it had gone through a meat grinder. A short while later, mercifully, he lost consciousness.

When Bash awoke for the first time the following day and turned to look at his arm, he only saw empty space. He was now an amputee. And just like that, his dreams and plans were over. *I'll never play the guitar again . . .*

While in the hospital he thought about something someone had told him years ago: *You know what makes God laugh? Humans having plans.*

† † †

The Zeniths finished their encore. As the crowd left, Bash began coiling audio cables on the floor of the stage with his one arm while stagehands began breaking down the monitor system under his guidance. While the band partied backstage with their mainly female guests, he dutifully got the band gear together to make the load-out into the Zeniths' Ford van.

Ricky Rhodes, legendary Austin drummer and Bash's roommate, suddenly appeared on the stage. Ricky was there that night to watch the show but also to help Bash with the load-out. Ricky and Bash had been friends for years.

Bash greeted him with a smile. "How was the mix?"

"Great!" Ricky replied enthusiastically.

They both laughed. Most road musicians and crew members know that after a show when anyone asks the soundman how the show sounded out front, there was only one answer for the soundman to give, regardless of how the show actually sounded. *Great!*

Ricky Rhodes had been quite a figure in the 6th street music scene for years. His wild onstage and offstage antics, accompanied by lots of booze and loose women, were legendary among Austin's nightclubs and musicians. Most of the nightclub owners had grown weary of his wild, ego-charged, Keith Moon-style of behavior, some even banning him from their premises. But Ricky had cleaned up his act two years earlier, leaving all those indulgences behind and "giving himself to the Lord," as he liked to say. Nowadays he played the drums better than ever and was much easier to get along with, his priority being focused on his role as music director for a large church on the west side of town.

After Bash's motorcycle accident, Ricky came to the hospital practically every day, often bringing Bash junk food in his backpack, and always bringing plenty of good cheer to get Bash through the ordeal. It was Ricky who helped organize a benefit for Bash at the Saxon Pub, an event that raised thousands of dollars for the hospital bills, although the figure didn't even come close to paying the full amount owed. Since Bash's major-medical insurance had only covered a portion of the debt, some local business owners offered financial help after hearing the tragic story.

When Bash was finally released from the hospital, Ricky brought Bash into his condo as a roommate and eventually found him the soundman gig with the Zeniths. To Bash, Ricky had saved his life—or at least what was left of it.

"Why aren't you backstage partying with the band?" Bash said while piling some coiled audio cables on the stage.

"Because I'm here to help you, remember?" Ricky said. "Besides, I've already seen enough wannabe rockstars in my lifetime. The more

Jaegermeister they swallow the worse it gets. They wouldn't notice me anyway because of all the girls that flocked back there."

Bash smiled, thinking back to a time when girls flocked to him after gigs. He even remembered a gig three or four years ago when Trent, the Zeniths' lead guitarist, was backstage after a show where Bash and his band, Nadir, had just performed. Trent was all giddy about getting to meet Bash, showering him with compliments and how one day he was going to play like Bash and have his own band. Bash could still see the look of admiration and envy on Trent's face when two girls in miniskirts came up to Bash, each taking one of Bash's arms. One of those arms was gone now. The smile left Bash's face.

Ricky sensed the mood change. "Can I give you a hand?"

"Sure," said Bash. "How about a *right* hand."

"Ha-ha," Ricky replied in a deadpan voice while helping to coil cables. "You wanna grab a bite after we're finished?"

"Yeah, sounds good."

Trent Masters, the Zeniths' lead guitarist, suddenly arrived on the stage with a drink and cigarette in one hand. A starry-eyed, twenty-year-old blonde held his other hand. She looked uncomfortable in her short skirt, tight halter top, and high-heeled pumps.

"You gotta remember to coil my guitar cable on top of my amp, dude!" Trent said to Bash with a slight slur in his voice. "When we start the show I can't find it in the dark!"

That's not all you can't find in the dark, Bash thought to himself. Bash knew Trent's little authority routine for the girl's sake was influenced by the booze. Trent was usually too lost in the world to rub anyone wrong. Bash believed he had a big heart and felt a twinge of pity for him. "Sure, Trent," Bash said. "Sorry about that. I'll remember that in the future."

Trent turned to Ricky who was now disassembling the drum kit to help Bash prepare for the load-out. Trent's eyes looked glazed over. He took another gulp of Jaegermeister and stared at Ricky for a long moment before turning awkwardly and staggering down the stage steps with the blonde in hand.

"He's no Bash Nadir," Ricky said after Trent and the girl left, "but you have to admit he's a pretty good singer and showman."

"When he's sober," said Bash.

"I agree."

"If they have head-bobbing contests in the music biz," Bash added, "he's sure to win."

"They do have those contests," Ricky said with a smile. "They're called award shows, you know. MTV? Grammys?"

"That was a long time ago," Bash said. "Rock is dead, remember?"

"Maybe it's just sleeping," Ricky said with a smile, hoping to get a smile from Bash in return.

"Nowadays," Bash said, ignoring Ricky's little joke, "it's mainly about outlandish wardrobe and dance moves."

"Yeah, like Madonna," added Ricky.

"Madonna?" Bash guffawed. "That was decades ago! I'm talking about all these current *artists* which are nothing more than professional Karaoke singers with their prefab recordings, fake drums, and auto-tune software."

"Yeah, but look at their wardrobe!"

"Whatever happened to artists writing songs and playing real musical instruments?" Bash ranted, ignoring Ricky's attempt at humor.

"They're out there."

"Yeah, but where? The public doesn't care anymore. They swallow whatever is spoon-fed to them by the suits running the business."

"Hasn't it always been that way?" Ricky asked, not expecting an answer.

An hour later, with help from the local stagehands, the van was loaded with the Zeniths' gear and ready to leave. Bash and Ricky climbed in the van with Bash behind the wheel. "Magnolia?"

"Where else?" Ricky replied.

They drove to the Magnolia Cafe on Lake Austin Blvd in West Austin, not far from Gordon's house where the equipment was stored between gigs. The Magnolia Cafe—a Bohemian style of restaurant popular with old hippies and college students for the last thirty years—served a unique blend of breakfast, lunch, and dinner items twenty-four hours a day. It definitely beat Denny's or IHOP.

Bash and Ricky entered the Magnolia Cafe, past the front door and its '*Sorry, we're open*' sign, and sat at a booth against the back wall. Ricky ordered cheese enchiladas and Bash chose migas: eggs with tomatoes, onions, bell peppers, tortillas chips, and jack cheese all scrambled together. "Would you like the Love Migas instead?" the attractive red-headed waitress asked.

"Which are?" asked Bash.

"Migas cooked in *love* butter," she answered, putting special emphasis on the word love. Before Bash could ask, she said, "Fresh garlic and serrano."

"I'll have the migas without the *love*," Bash said, using the same emphasis on the word love while handing her his menu with a frown on his face.

The waitress lost her playful grin and walked away.

"Boy, you're a real ladykiller," Ricky said.

"Yeah, you ought to see their faces when I take off my shirt and show them my nub."

Ricky leaned over the table and said in a low voice, "When are you going to let go of this self-pity thing?"

Bash said nothing.

"This is going to destroy you," Ricky added. "You gotta find a positive outlook for your life. You've got a lot going for you."

Bash felt his anger rising. "Like what? Being a sound engineer? And the backline tech? And the equipment driver? And the babysitter for a bunch of spoiled wannabe stars? You're right! I do have a lot going for me! I'm the whole crew! A one-armed crew!" His voice began to rise. "Hey, Bash, I heard feedback at the top of the intro, don't let that happen again! Oh, Bash, next time make sure my cables are coiled on top my amp! Hey Bash, make sure to wipe down my strings after we finish! Hey Bash, go give that hot blonde in the first row a backstage pass!"

Ricky waited for Bash to finish his rant. When sure it was over he said, "It's life, dude. People don't always treat you like you should be treated. And by the way, during live performances, the soundman of a band is as important as the players on stage. Same goes for the rest of your roles within the band. It's a team."

Bash was still too angry to listen to Ricky's encouragement. "I guess my life mission now is to be a step-and-fetch slave!" Bash said in a loud voice. "A slave for moronic prima donnas who can't find their guitar cables in the dark!"

A few patrons nearby turned their attention toward Bash.

"Okay, dude," Ricky said in a soft voice. "Just chillax."

"Chillax?"

"Yes."

"You and your made-up words."

"Who says they're made-up?"

"Chillax? That's not a made-up word?"

"No!" Ricky said. "It's a combination of chill and re—"

"—I know how you combined the words," Bash interrupted with a smile of resignation. After taking a deep breath he said, "You are too much, Yogi."

"Smarter than the average bear, Boo-Boo."

Bash could never stay mad for long when Ricky was around.

After the waitress brought their food, and Ricky said his silent prayer, they both dug into their food and finished their meal in silence. When the waitress came with the check, Bash and Ricky both grabbed for it at the same time. Bash was faster. "Beaten by a one-armed man," he teased Ricky. "Tsk, tsk."

"I let you win."

"Yeah, right."

Soon they were back in the van on the way to Gordon's house. Bash's frustration had subsided. "Sorry about my outburst back there," he said.

"You don't need to apologize to me," Ricky said. "You just need to forgive yourself."

"Forgive myself?" Bash asked in a surprised tone. A moment later he said, "Okay, I forgive myself for my outburst at the Magnolia."

"I'm not talking about your outburst at the restaurant," Ricky said. "I'm talking about forgiving yourself for the accident that cost you your arm."

"What?"

"I think you're still blaming yourself for the accident," Ricky explained. "For not preventing it somehow. Which is a natural thing to do under the circumstances."

Bash didn't respond. While steering with his knees he grabbed a stick of *Juicy Fruit* chewing gum from his shirt pocket. He unwrapped the gum between his thumb and index finger and popped it into his mouth.

"Things are going to get better for you, Bash," Ricky said. "It's gonna take a little time, though. And a lot of faith."

"Faith in what?"

"In the one who made you and the rest of the universe."

"You mean the one who made me wreck and lose my arm and took away my only passion in life?"

"Why do people blame God for everything bad that happens?" Ricky said. "You know, there is another force in the world at work."

"Oh, yeah," Bash said sarcastically. "The devil."

"Call him what you want."

"Well if God created everything," Bash said, "then God created the devil. Right?"

"Yes, that's right."

"So that means God created evil."

"No, that's not right," Ricky said. "God created the angels, and like us humans he gave them free will. Free will is the ability to choose. Perhaps the most powerful of those angels—who is commonly referred to as Satan or the devil or whatever other name you like—*chose* to rebel. A third of the angels followed him, *choosing* to rebel along with him. Without God's living creations having free will there would be no such thing as real love. Without free will we would all be a bunch of robots." Ricky mimicked a monotone robotic voice. "We . . . love . . . you . . . God. We . . . love . . . you . . . God."

Bash smiled at the robot impersonation before yawning. It was almost three in the morning. He turned onto Gordon's street.

"I heard that Einstein had a great take on it," Ricky said. "He argued with a professor in Germany that according to the First Law of Thermodynamics, cold is only the absence of heat. Einstein also said that darkness is only the absence of light. Therefore, evil is the absence of God. Score one for Al Einstein."

"Al?"

"To his friends, yeah," Ricky said. "Albert to everyone else."

"I never knew that."

"And now you do."

"So you were a friend of his?"

"Sort of."

"Didn't he die like over a half century before you were even born?"

"When I say I knew him," Ricky continued, "I meant metaphorically."

, Bash yawned again. "You should've been a lawyer."

"No thanks," Ricky said. "Mr. Equipment Driver? Please take me to my Toyota. I'm ready to go home and get some sleep."

Bash turned into Gordon's driveway where they locked the van inside the garage before taking Ricky's Toyota pickup truck back to Ricky's condo. Once inside the condo, each man went to his own bedroom and collapsed on their mattresses. Ricky's loud snoring soon filled the condo but Bash didn't notice because he too was fast asleep.

Bash dreamed of white pickup trucks and winged angels hovering over him as he lay on the feeder road, this time with no arms or legs, just a torso writhing on the pavement. In the dream he heard one of the angels tell another angel, "We goofed up! He was only supposed to lose one limb!" He saw an angel scouting the accident scene, picking up Bash's limbs wherever he found them. Bash wondered how they were going to reattach them when the dream shifted to him trying to mix sound with a stick in his mouth. He hovered over the sound console from a hanging contraption that dangled his limbless body from above, allowing the stick in his mouth to reach the console. It was at a huge concert. He wasn't mixing for the Zeniths but for the Rolling Stones. Things were out of control. Mick Jagger's microphone was squealing loudly and the audience started booing as Bash frantically tried to make adjustments he couldn't make fast enough with the stick. The audience grew angrier, everyone looking at him with rage in their eyes. Mick and Keith were suddenly leaping from the stage and marching toward him. Mick wielded his microphone stand like a weapon as Keith did the same with his guitar. Defenseless from stopping the blows, Bash could only scream as they cursed him and beat him. He felt like a human piñata. He screamed and screamed and screamed until he . . .

Awoke. Bash heard Ricky snoring in the other bedroom. He got up and walked into the bathroom. He opened the medicine cabinet and grabbed a bottle of pills. He swallowed an Ambien and washed it down with tap water from the sink. After climbing back in his bed, he stared into the darkness of the bedroom while waiting for the sleeping pill to kick in. He thought about his mother and father, both killed in a car accident when he was eighteen; a head-on collision with a young driver too drunk to drive. She survived. Bash's parents did not. Bash's brother, Terry, whose birth name was Tarik, was fifteen at the time. Bash and Terry moved into their own apartment, living on the money from their parents' life insurance and meager savings and equity drawn from the sale of the family home.

A few years later, Terry, after finishing high school with most of the money gone, moved to Oregon to live with his father's brother, Walid Nadir. Walid was a devout Muslim and since 9-11 had become a devoted radical. *A jihadist,* Walid liked to call himself. Terry had been totally devastated by the loss of his parents. Walid blamed western culture, trying to turn Terry's grief into an intense hatred for America and all it stood for. Bash and Terry argued bitterly over this. Bash had made it very clear that under no circumstances was he going to go live with Walid and warned Terry that it was a bad idea for him to go. But Terry was eighteen by then and had made up his mind. Terry had always felt a connection to God stuff although his parents and Bash did not share those feelings. Bash had never been interested in religion. Period. Walid had explained to Terry that Bash had let his mind become polluted by western thinking, partially their parents' fault, which made Bash want to bash Walid in the nose. Of course, that was when Bash had two fists.

For a while Bash and Terry talked over the phone every month or so but the gap between calls grew wider over time. Gradually, the two brothers quit communicating altogether. Bash hadn't spoken to Terry in over five years. He wondered if one day he would see Terry's mugshot on TV after some terrorist attack Walid had organized and somehow pulled off. Uncle Wally, as Bash had once called him, had always been an opinionated blowhard in Bash's mind. Bash doubted if he could ever do a tenth of the things he threatened to do to the Big Satan—America. *But you never know for sure.* Walid now had money. Bash's grandfather, Walid's father, had died in Egypt shortly after Bash's parents were killed. Walid had received a sizable inheritance while Bash and Terry received absolutely zero. Bash believed Uncle Wally had convinced their devout Muslim grandfather to cut them out of the will.

Bash continued to stare at the ceiling of the dark bedroom in Ricky's condo. Memories of his lost family flashed in his mind; moments of happier days when he and Terry played soccer in their family's backyard, took vacations with their mom and dad, had picnics at local parks, made homemade ice cream, and watched cartoons on Saturday mornings in their pajamas. Bash wiped the tears from his eyes, and thanks to the sleeping pill, he soon fell asleep—a sleep wonderfully devoid of dreams . . .

† † †

3

*T*he Zeniths and their manager sat at a long table inside the County Line Bar-B-Q on Bee Caves Road. Bash had also been invited to the lunch although he didn't know why. This was a meeting between band and management and he was just a crew member. Actually, he *was* the crew. Although being the house sound engineer was an important role, along with performing all the duties expected of a full crew, Bash knew that regardless of his multiple roles he was still not a band member. *And never will be,* he reminded himself. *Bashman the soundman. Bashman the backline tech. Bashman the driver. Take your pick. I'll never be accepted as an equal to the band.*

A waiter came around and took drink orders first. Most of the guys ordered sodas or iced tea. Gordon Lawler, the keyboardist, vocalist, and founder of the band sat at the head of the table. His stylishly cut blonde hair complimented his handsome face. He sat proudly in his chair with confidence oozing from his pores.

Billy Stokes, the bass player, fiddled with his cell phone. He was short and stocky with dark hair cropped close to his scalp and a tiny gold ring in his left ear. Billy went with the flow, adding the high harmony vocals when needed throughout the Zeniths' repertoire. Although no one could say that Billy was the sharpest blade in the drawer, he was always upbeat and seldom criticized anyone's behavior.

Vince Crowley, the powerhouse drummer, was the threatening one in the band. He was six-foot-five in his flip-flops and powerfully built. His shaved head and multiple tattoos had earned him a moniker from Gordon: *Mr. Clean From Hell.*

Trent, the lead guitarist and vocalist, his long brown hair bordering a chiseled face, was the popular one with the ladies. Not only was he extremely handsome but he had a boyish quality that attracted many of both sexes. Trent seemed to be the lighthearted one in the band and he was easy to like by most who got to know him.

Trent asked for a Bud Light which earned him an unhappy look from Gordon. He sheepishly changed his order to a Diet Coke. Bash and Billy traded looks. Trent's drinking had become an issue over the last few weeks so there must have been some new rules put into play.

The band's manager, Timothy Permenter, had been born and raised in London. He wore thick-lensed eyeglasses that magnified his eyes as he spoke about future bookings and other band business in his proper British accent. He had many ideas for marketing their next CD on their website. He congratulated them on their increasing merchandise sales of ball caps, tee shirts, bandanas, and the last CD they had recorded.

Timothy then turned his attention to Bash. Everyone at the table did the same.

Uh-oh, Bash thought to himself. *This is where I get fired—what Ricky calls 'getting a hot dog and a roadmap.'*

"And Bash," Timothy said in a stern voice which was difficult for him since he was about five feet tall and had the voice of an English schoolboy, "we all have a bit of news for you, I'm afraid."

Bash raised his eyebrows, not sure if he cared or not about getting fired. He appreciated the job but it would not be the end of the world if they fired him. A band was either a brotherhood or it was not a brotherhood. He wasn't sure which category the Zeniths were in but it really didn't matter because Bash was not a band member and never would be. If they wanted him in the periphery of their brotherhood, great. If they didn't, there was nothing he could do about it so he would just move on to the next chapter in his life.

Everyone at the table stared at Bash with serious expressions on their faces. "Due to your performance as house engineer, stage manager, and backline tech, not to mention our equipment driver," Timothy said, "we have unanimously decided to . . ."

Everyone remained silent.

" . . . give you a raise."

Everyone broke into laughter, giving Bash high-fives from across the table. Trent raised his Diet Coke in salute. "To the Bashman, all for one and one for all!"

"I can't tell you how many compliments I receive on the sound quality of the shows," Timothy went on, "but compared to the bloke before you it is significant. Well done, mate. We want you to stay on with us."

Bash was surprised. All along he'd been thinking that no one in the organization had appreciated his busy role or even wanted him to continue with them after the first of the month. Bash shot a look across the table at Billy who winked at him. "Congratulations, Bash," Billy said in a sincere voice. "You deserve it."

Maybe the Zeniths would be a brotherhood Bash could grow into. "Thanks," Bash said, not knowing what else to say. "I'm speechless."

"Good," Gordon said in a joking way. "We don't wanna hear any of your speeches anyway."

After ordering lunch, Gordon leaned forward to address everyone. "Timothy has some good news," he said. "He's found a place we can move to. A house for all of us to live in and rehearse without problems from neighbors. This includes you, too, Bash."

"Okay," was all Bash could say as everyone turned their attention toward Timothy.

Timothy began to explain. "It's old but it's quite big. Also, it's in the country but not too far from town. So no complaints from neighbors about the noise when you rehearse or party, but close to civilization, if you know what I mean."

"Where?" asked Trent, a look of concern consuming his face.

"Near 290," Timothy said. "West of town. Under an hour from downtown Austin."

Trent didn't reply.

"And besides," Timothy continued, "we're going to be playing more out of town gigs in the very near future. Living in Austin proper won't be that vital."

Gordon made eye contact with Trent, knowing why the guitarist seemed hesitant. "Don't worry, dude," Gordon told Trent. "You can bring your babes out there if you like."

Everyone laughed.

"Yeah," Billy said, "and don't forget to bring some for us, too!"

More laughter.

"We can go look at it after lunch if you like," Timothy said. "I got the keys from the owner. He and his wife are big fans and they want to help out."

Everyone nodded their heads in agreement.

Bash and the band crowded into the Ford van with all of its bench seats removed except for one behind the driver and passenger seats to allow enough room to carry their band gear. Bash drove while following Timothy's used BMW onto loop 360 and eventually Highway 290. Everyone was in great spirits, laughing and joking with the windows rolled down. It was a beautiful March day in Texas.

Timothy turned onto a numbered ranch road where they drove a distance before turning again onto a dirt road that cut into the countryside. A rusty, worn-out sign stood at the junction of the two roads. It read: 'Rock Bottom Road.'

"Let's hope the name of the road isn't an omen for the future of this band," Gordon told the others inside the van.

Bash didn't say it but he was thinking the same thing.

"I like the name," said Billy. "After all, we are a *rock* band and I supply the *bottom*."

Gordon and the others in the van snickered.

"I meant *bottom* as in the bass," Billy said, picking up on their response. "I wasn't talking about my butt."

More snickering.

Oaks and cedars bordered the dirt road as the terrain began to ascend. They rolled up their windows in the van because of the plume of dust raised by the BMW. When they reached the top of a hill and started to descend on the other side, Gordon's phone beeped as a text message came in. "Tim says that it's not far," he said. "On the left." Everyone craned their necks to look out the windshield. They saw the house in the distance: a large two-story which appeared to be over a hundred years old. It was the only house they had seen on the road.

"There it is!" Billy said eagerly. "Hello, Rock Bottom!"

"Rock Bottom is the name of the road," Gordon said, "not the house."

"Yeah, but a lot of big houses have their own names," Billy said. "So I think the name is perfect!"

"Okay, okay," Gordon said with a smirk. "Hello, Rock Bottom!"

To Bash, Rock Bottom looked like it had needed a paint job for at least a half a century. It sat alone in a large prairie spotted with mesquite brush, cactus, and wild grass. Oak, juniper, and other tree varieties bordered the property, occasionally revealing a winding creek that meandered through the terrain. A few large live oaks offered shade for the old house, as well as a wide front porch that would provide some relief from the relentless Texas sun.

The dirt road came to an end near the house which stood off the side of the road. They parked alongside the BMW in the front yard which was a mixture of dirt, weeds, and dried grass worn down through the years of use. They piled out of the van and met Timothy at the porch. He unlocked the door and they followed him inside. He flipped a light switch which illuminated the large foyer and its old wooden staircase. The air inside smelled old. To the right of the staircase was a cozy room Timothy called a parlor. Next to it was the downstairs bathroom. To the left of the staircase stood a huge room. There was still visible evidence that a wall had been removed between two rooms which had turned the space into one large room. "How's that for a rehearsal room, boys?" Timothy announced.

"Awesome!" Billy said.

"It looks good," Gordon added.

"Not bad," Trent said. He seemed to be warming to the idea of living there with the band, away from the city and all its nightlife and perks—the perks mainly being women.

Bash kept his thoughts to himself. All in all, the place was in decent shape. It looked like someone had done some major work on the interior maybe fifteen or twenty years ago. There weren't as many bathrooms as most modern homes but there were plenty of bedrooms upstairs.

After examining the rest of the interior everyone stepped back out onto the porch. Bash noticed a horizontal white tank supported by a concrete foundation not far from one side of the house. "What's the tank for?"

"Propane," Timothy said. "Instead of natural gas. The house has central air, put in some years ago. Propane for heat, hot water, and cooking. Electricity for lights and cooling. Also, you have cable and internet. That's huge for being way out here."

"So how much cash will it cost us?" asked Trent.

"We can do a year lease," Timothy said. "First and last month up front and all very cheap."

"How cheap?" asked Vince, finally having something to say.

"Fifteen hundred a month," Timothy said, "which is *way* under market value for a place this size. We pay for the electric and propane but the property has its own water well. The pump house is that little shack next to the propane tank."

"What about when summer arrives?" Vince asked. "These old places are usually not insulated too good. What will the electric bill run then?"

"Probably a few hundred if we keep the thermostat on a reasonable setting," Timothy answered. "I plan to keep you boys busy touring so you won't be here all the time."

Everyone seemed satisfied by Timothy's answers.

"At any rate," Timothy said, "it won't start getting really hot until June."

"Except for Trent's bedroom," Billy joked. "It'll always be hot in there."

This drew chuckles from everyone, including Trent.

Bash thought the place was great and he looked forward to a new situation, not that he had a problem living with Ricky but it just seemed exciting to be a part of a band with everyone living together and making music all the time. *Besides, rent will be free!*

"Well, what do you think, mates?" asked Timothy.

Everyone nodded their approval. "Let's do it!" Gordon announced.

"Okay," Timothy said. "I'll take care of the paperwork today. We should be able to move in by the first of the month."

"Awesome," Billy said while giving Bash a left-handed high-five.

They all loaded back into the vehicles. Timothy drove back to his downtown office as Bash drove the Ford van back to the County Line BBQ where the band had parked their cars. They set a rehearsal time at Gordon's house for the following day in preparation for their two South By Southwest gigs. The SXSW festival started in a few days and was Austin's premiere showcase opportunity for hundreds of bands and entertainers from around the world. The Zeniths were hoping for some new contacts and bookings through the event.

After leaving the County Line BBQ, Bash drove the Ford van to Gordon's house where Ricky met him to take him back to the condo. Once in Ricky's Toyota pickup truck, Bash explained about the new situation with the Zeniths. Bash told him about the old house in the country, even revealing that they gave him a pay raise, but Ricky didn't seem too happy for him.

"What's the problem?" Bash asked. "It can't be about you losing rent money because I haven't been paying any rent."

"Yeah," Ricky said with a smile. "I've noticed that."

"Is something wrong with the house?"

"How would I know if something's wrong with the house?"

Bash shrugged. "Then what's wrong?"

"It's not the house," Ricky said. "It's the house *thing*."

"What do you mean?"

"I don't know, Bash," Ricky said with a hint of resignation in his voice. "All I know is that everyone playing music together is different from everyone living together."

"We'll still have our own space."

"I know," Ricky said, "but the Monkees thing only works on TV."

"The Monkees?" Bash said. "Man, you *are* old."

"Hey, Hey, We're The Monkees . . ." Ricky began singing.

Bash sang the rest of the line. ". . . You Better Stop Foolin' Around . . ."

"Well, I hope it all works out," Ricky said as they got closer to the condo. He couldn't resist adding, "There will definitely be more peace and quiet around my pad!"

"Ha-ha," Bash said. He was already starting to think about the room they would be rehearsing in at Rock Bottom. He planned in his head where to place the musicians and where to place the monitor mixing console within the room. Everything needed to be planned in advance so he could have the gear set up perfectly when the Zeniths were ready to start rehearsing at the new location. He smiled to himself. He finally had something he belonged to. A brotherhood . . .

† † †

4

Things began to change after the Zeniths moved into Rock Bottom. Any pretense of maintaining sobriety during the daylight hours quickly evaporated. Because of Rock Bottom's remote location they could play their music as loud as they wanted and anytime they wanted. This newfound freedom quickly escalated their open drug use without the fear of law enforcement suddenly arriving because of noise complaints. Late-night partying became commonplace. An attitude of *anything goes* grew gradually within the band. It wasn't uncommon for Bash to find half-naked girls roaming the hallways in the early morning hours during any day of the week. Although Bash didn't involve himself with the girls, he definitely did his share of beer drinking and pot smoking. Privately, he justified his behavior with the excuse of getting rid of a headache or dealing with the emotional pain caused by his physical handicap.

As the weeks went by, the Zeniths began traveling more extensively as Timothy booked them for more out-of-state club dates, concert openers, and large music festivals. With a larger budget for expenses, they now leased a forty-five-foot Prevost tour bus for the longer runs. The aftershow partying continued in the band's hotel and motel rooms but with less intensity than the gatherings at Rock Bottom.

On one occasion, in the early morning hours after a club gig in Baton Rouge, Louisiana, local police arrived at the motel where the Zeniths were staying. Apparently, a city official had filed a complaint when his underaged daughter arrived home after her curfew and confessed to participating in a little hanky-panky with one of the musicians. The police convinced the motel clerk to contact the band's manager in his room to have him come to the lobby in order to find the identity of the guilty musician. Timothy argued in his diplomatic tone and proper British accent that "none of his bandmates would do such a thing." The confrontation ended when the police sergeant in charge got a call on his cell phone to "halt all proceedings," as Timothy explained to the band later. The police left with a warning for the band to never come to Baton Rouge again unless they wanted "to leave in ambulances." The next morning as the band arrived on the tour bus to leave town, Trent was missing. Timothy explained to the band about the police the night before, and without being told everyone knew that Trent was the "guilty musician." They were becoming more and more fearful that the cops had something to do with Trent's absence. They were trying to decide what to do next when Billy looked out the bus window and saw Trent exiting a taxi. "Look who's here!"

Trent entered the bus looking sleepy and disheveled. "What's up, guys?" he said while heading to his bunk in the rear of the bus, blissfully unaware of the previous night's activities with the police. "I'm bushed. Gonna catch up on some Zs."

Everyone looked at each other and shook their heads in disbelief.

"He's the Inspector Clouseau of rock and roll," Gordon said.

"Who's that?" asked Billy.

Gordon gave him a condescending look before saying, "Clouseau, from the classic *Pink Panther* movies? The character Peter Sellers portrayed?"

"Oh," Billy said, acting like he remembered. He didn't watch many classic movies.

In the days that followed, everyone had a good laugh about the *missing Trent affair* in Baton Rouge but Timothy and Gordon soon made changes to their touring schedules. From now on, despite complaints from Trent, the bus would leave town *after* the gigs to avoid any similar situations in the future. And as the fatigue of travel grew, things calmed down a bit at Rock Bottom, especially after a particularly long run on the road.

During one quiet evening at Rock Bottom with everyone crashed in their bedrooms, Bash awoke to strange sounds coming from somewhere outside his bedroom. He inspected the upstairs hallway but found nothing out of the ordinary. He wrote it off as mice in the walls or the wind playing tricks. *Old houses always have their share of strange sounds,* he told himself before going back to bed.

Bash awoke a few hours later to distant music coming from somewhere in the house. It sounded like *Whole Lotta Love,* the Led Zeppelin song. *Is someone listening to music in their bedroom in the middle of the night?* But it sounded to Bash like the distant music was coming from above . . . in the attic. He climbed off his mattress again and entered the hallway, aiming his hearing toward the ceiling above him. He heard nothing. The music had stopped. Bash returned to his bed to finish sleeping.

Late morning the next day after everyone was awake, Bash was in the rehearsal room running cables and moving amps around while preparing for a rehearsal session that afternoon. Gordon was also in the rehearsal room programming his keyboards. Billy, Trent, and Vince were upstairs, standing at the door of a hallway closet.

"I'm telling you," Billy said to Trent. "You can hear voices inside."

Vince, playing along, stepped inside the dark closet and craned his big neck like he was listening. He stepped back out. "Yeah, I can hear them."

"What?" Trent said in a tone of disbelief.

Earlier that day, Billy had opened the closet door, causing the old-style doorknob on the inside of the door to fall onto the hardwood floor in the closet with a loud clank. He opened the door and replaced the doorknob, making a mental note that it needed to be repaired but also getting an idea to play a trick on Trent.

"I told you, man!" Billy said while casting a knowing look toward Vince.

"Let me see," Trent said while leaning into the closet, not willing to step inside.

That's when Billy gave Vince the signal and they both shoved Trent into the closet. Billy slammed the door shut and heard the doorknob fall to the hardwood floor in the closet with a loud clank. Billy snickered while hearing Trent grabbing for a doorknob on the door that wasn't there anymore.

"Real funny!" Trent said. "Now open up!"

"I think there are ghosts in there . . ." Billy said in his best ghostly voice impersonation. "And they have you all to themselves!"

Vince didn't say anything but his expression revealed that he was enjoying this.

Trent's voice began to rise in pitch and volume. "OPEN UP!" he shouted while pounding and kicking the door. "LET ME OUT! LET ME OUT!"

The door was bulging with every blow as Billy and Vince smiled at each other.

Trent's pounding was getting louder and more forceful.

Surprised by Trent's escalating violent reaction, Billy grabbed the exterior doorknob and tried to open the door. The door wouldn't open. "Hang on!" Billy shouted.

"GET ME OUT OF HERE!" Trent screamed. "PLEASE! PLEASE!"

Billy began yanking on the doorknob with all his strength. Vince pushed Billy aside and tried to open it. Even with Vince's brute strength, he couldn't budge the door open.

Trent's screams were frantic now, sounding like a wounded animal inside the closet. Vince was still tugging on the doorknob when it suddenly flew open and Trent came falling out onto the floor of the hallway.

"Dude! You okay?" Billy asked.

Trent curled into a fetal position on the floor outside the closet, obviously traumatized. He didn't respond to Billy's questions.

After hearing the commotion, Gordon and Bash came running up the stairs into the hallway. They saw Trent weeping on the floor. "What happened?" asked Gordon.

"I was just messing around," Billy said while leaning over Trent.

Trent jerked away from his touch.

"It was just a little joke," Vince said, trying to hide a smile. "Then he started freaking out. Practically kicked the door off its hinges before I could get him out."

Billy began rubbing Trent's back. "Come on, buddy," he said in a low voice. "I'm sorry. I didn't mean anything by it. Just a little joke."

Gradually, Trent started to regain his composure. His sobbing started to slow and his inhalations became short and quick. He raised himself to a sitting position.

"Dude, I'm so sorry," Billy said. He really felt bad and his expression showed it. "I was just goofing around."

Trent stood to his feet and saw everyone staring at him. He looked embarrassed. He walked past them and into his bedroom before shutting the door behind him.

Bash gave Billy a curious look. "What happened?"

"I don't know," Billy said. "I was just playing a little joke on him."

"Explain," Gordon said, his word sounding like a command.

"I came up here earlier and found that the inside doorknob was loose and came off easy," Billy explained. "We shoved Trent inside. I was just playing a little joke but . . ."

"But what?" asked Gordon.

"I don't know, man," Billy said. "When we tried to open the door it wouldn't budge."

Gordon looked to Vince.

"Yeah, it wouldn't open," said Vince.

"Maybe Trent was holding it from the inside," Bash suggested.

"With King Kong here pulling on it?" replied Gordon.

Vince's expression revealed that he didn't like being called King Kong.

"There wasn't anything for Trent to grab on to," Billy said. "The knob inside fell off when we slammed the door shut behind him."

"Then why wouldn't it open?" Gordon asked.

"I don't know, dude," Billy answered, "but it was like some force was holding it shut."

Vince nodded in agreement.

"When I tried to open it," Billy continued, "there was like some type of suction or something holding it shut."

"You're joking," said Gordon.

Billy and Vince exchanged looks. "No, we're not," said Billy.

Gordon walked over to the closet. He took a cursory look inside. "Cool," he said with a grin before heading downstairs.

"Cool?" Billy mouthed to Vince before both men began following Gordon downstairs, leaving Bash standing outside the closet door.

Bash reached down and grabbed the interior doorknob from the closet floor. He examined it for a moment before taking a look inside the dark closet. He set the doorknob back on the closet floor and grabbed the small flashlight clipped to his belt. The closet was totally empty. There didn't seem to be any cracks or openings in the walls, things that could cause a draft that might suck the door shut. He opened and closed the door several times. He didn't notice any pull on the door. Sometimes if an exterior door on the bottom floor was open, the wind could cause suction in other parts of the house. But no doors or windows were open and the closet interior seemed sealed. There was no logical explanation for the door being held shut by suction.

Bash headed back downstairs. He would grab a screwdriver and some screws later to reattach the doorknob. It was an easy fix but right now he had more important things to do. The guys wanted to run some tunes at four that afternoon and he still needed to set up the mixing console and monitors before tweaking everything to be ready on time.

As Bash reached the bottom of the stairs and headed back into the rehearsal room, sun rays beamed through a window on the upstairs landing. A Texas turkey vulture flew in a wide arc past the window, soaring gracefully through the blue sky while circling some dead animal it had spotted from a distance. Some of the branches of the gigantic live oak on that side of the house swayed in the breeze that blew across the rolling prairie. Rock Bottom creaked and groaned as old houses do. Then the wind died. The branches stopped moving and the interior of the house became deadly silent as the upstairs closet door began closing slowly . . . until it shut tight . . .

† † †

5

*T*he Zeniths were driving back from Houston after their performance at a large outdoor music festival on the outskirts of the city. They were just one of the opening acts for the headliner that evening, Bruno Mars, but the huge audience had responded with loud applause. The band was pumped up after the experience. The gig had been the result of the festival's promoter seeing one of their SXSW performances in Austin.

Timothy had driven his BMW to Houston for the show and Gordon and Trent rode back to Austin with him. Billy rode in the Ford van with Bash behind the wheel. Ricky also rode in the van, having accompanied Bash to the show to help out where he could. Vince was staying in Houston overnight with friends—friends that reminded Bash of characters from a *Walking Dead* episode.

Bash thought the performance went well. He was glad that Ricky had come along to help. But despite the success of the evening, Bash was getting one of the headaches he'd suffered since the accident. He wished he had some Ibuprofen.

"I'll tell you what was awesome," Billy said from the bench seat behind the driver and passenger seats. "Hearing my bass thundering through that giant sound system."

"I hear you," Ricky said from the passenger seat. "Vince's floor toms sounded like thunder!"

"That was me making them sound that way," Bash said with a smile.

"That goes without saying," Ricky said, "but the player has a lot to do with that. You know, it's the Indian, not the arrow."

"But without the bow," Bash added, "the Indian or the arrow has little effect."

"Oh, so I guess you are the bow?"

Bash had to smile. "You got it, Yogi."

"I wish we could get that kind of sound on all our gigs," Billy said, not understanding the bit about Indians, arrows, and bows. "You know, like in the smaller rooms we play."

"We could," answered Bash.

"How?"

"There are good systems out there," Bash said. "Some of the venues we play provide good ones but many don't. We could have a good system for every show if we bought our own. If you guys are willing to spend the bread."

"How much bread?" Billy asked.

"Thirty grand or so," Bash casually replied. " Maybe twenty. Retail."

"Ouch," Billy said.

"Yeah, ouch," Ricky agreed.

"Well," Bash said, "there are such things as bank loans, you know."

"No way," Billy said. "When Gordon put this band together we all agreed to not get into debt. We would build it up from the grassroots and grow as we go. Timothy was serious about that, too."

"I understand and respect that," Bash said, "but there comes a time when you got to expand to keep the thing moving forward."

Billy reached into his sock and removed a joint from three he had stored there.

"There's also great deals out there if you know where to look," Bash continued. "If we could score something really good for say twelve or fifteen grand, it would pay for itself in no time."

"What do you mean?" Billy said while lighting the joint and taking a big hit.

"Hey, man!" Ricky said. "Don't do that!"

"Chill out, dude," Billy said with a lung full of smoke.

"We're all going to reek!" Ricky complained.

"Then roll down your window, dude!" Billy fired back. "This van is owned by the band and I'm a band member, you know!"

Ricky ignored Billy's reminder of who was in the band and who was not and rolled his window down all the way, causing a blast of warm air to blow through the van like a tornado.

"So you were saying it would pay for itself?" Billy said to Bash, having to shout to be heard over the torrent of air blasting through the window.

"Yeah," Bash shouted back. "I mean, I know what we dish out for rentals on the gigs that don't provide sound. It adds up, man."

"Yeah, I hear ya," Billy replied. He offered the joint to Bash, forgetting he needed his one and only arm on the wheel. He raised the joint to Bash's lips so he could take a hit.

"Oh, great," Ricky said with an exaggerated frown. "You know, Bash, when you go to jail you'll need both arms to defend yourself."

Bash wanted the headache to leave. He took several puffs off the joint and held in the smoke. He finally let it out, the smoke disappearing in the cyclone condition inside the van. "If we go to jail," Bash said with watery eyes, "I know you'll be there to protect me."

Ricky shook his head, a pitiful smile on his face. "You know, I don't like going to jail for something I'm not guilty of," he said. "I might have to rat on you guys."

"Cops won't buy it," Bash said before taking another hit from the fast dwindling joint in Billy's fingers. "They smell weed and everybody goes down."

Billy offered the joint to Ricky. "You see? If you're going to pay for the crime, you might as well enjoy the crime!"

Ricky lowered his head in resignation and took the joint between his fingers. He acted like he was going to take a hit when all of a sudden he tossed it out the window.

"Hey, man!" Billy shouted. "Don't do that! That cost some serious money!"

Bash and Ricky traded looks. Bash started laughing uncontrollably which got Ricky going, too. Even Billy couldn't resist as he joined in the laughter. "You're still one crazy dude, Ricky," he said while fishing another joint from his sock.

Ricky was rolling up the window when he saw what Billy was doing. He jumped from the passenger seat and went for Billy's leg with the sock full of joints. Billy fell backward while trying to get away as Ricky grabbed at Billy's ankle, both of them giggling like schoolboys. With all the band gear behind the bench seat there wasn't anyplace for Billy to go.

While they wrestled, Bash came up with an idea. "Hey, chill!" he shouted. "We're getting pulled over!"

This got Billy and Ricky's attention immediately. They stopped wrestling and looked out the rear windows of the van where they only saw darkness.

"Dude!" Billy sighed. "You scared the crap out of me!"

Ricky climbed back into the front passenger seat. "Good one, Bash."

"I'm surprised you fell for it," Bash said.

"Once upon a time," Ricky said, "I wouldn't have cared if we were getting pulled over or not. And if I had been loaded enough I probably would've blown pot smoke in the cop's face when he came to the window."

"I know," Bash said. "I'm thankful you're not like that anymore."

"Thank God," Ricky said. "It was all his doing, not mine."

Billy thought about lighting up another joint but then he would have to risk the crazy drummer throwing it out the window. He decided to wait.

"What you were saying earlier makes sense, Bash," Ricky said, grabbing some bottled waters in front of his seat and passing one to Billy, then opening another for Bash and setting it into a cup holder mounted on the dash especially for Bash. "I know a guy who might be able to help you guys out. He buys all kind of things at auctions. He usually gets stuff for pennies on the dollar. I know he found some cymbals one time years ago and gave them to me for practically nothing. I'll put the bug in his ear and see if he comes up with anything."

"That's a good idea," Bash said.

"Yeah, every once in a while I act like someone smart."

"You are smarter than the average bear, Yogi."

"Yeah, and you are stoned, Boo-Boo," Ricky countered. "You don't need that stuff. Why do you do it?"

"I don't *need* it," Bash said in his defense, not willing to use the headache excuse with Ricky. "I just like to get high sometimes."

"Well, let me know when you wanna get a real high," Ricky came back.

Bash decided to let it go right there. He was stoned from the weed and the last thing he wanted to do at that moment was discuss religion with Ricky.

They drove onward with the CD player in the van turned up loud, pumping out the classic Yes song, *Roundabout,* as Bash followed Timothy and the BMW's taillights.

Billy said something from the back of the van. Ricky turned down the CD's volume. "Ten bucks says," Billy repeated, "that Trent will come up with an excuse to not unload the gear tonight. They'll probably drop him off somewhere once we get in Austin."

Bash thought for a moment. "What if we say we're going to unload tonight but we don't do it until tomorrow? When he backs out with some excuse for tonight, he'll be trapped into helping out tomorrow."

"That's a great idea!" Billy said.

"You guys . . ." Ricky said while shaking his head. "Don't you think you should leave him alone? He's pretty sensitive, you know."

"I can't believe what I'm hearing," Bash said. "You? The king of the practical jokers? Telling us we're being too hard on him?"

"*Former* king of the practical jokers," Ricky corrected him. "I think Trent's got some self-esteem issues. He needs help instead of everyone ganging up on him."

"Ganging up on him?" Bash had to laugh.

"Yeah, that's what I said," Ricky said. "I had a little talk with him a few days after the closet episode and he confided in me about things that happened when he was a kid."

"Like what?" asked Billy.

"Like I said," Ricky continued, ignoring Billy's question, "he has some issues to work out from his childhood. He's carrying a lot of baggage."

"Aren't we all," said Bash.

"True, but some feel the weight more than others," Ricky said. "Their bags may seem light to you but to them they are heavy."

"Wow," Bash said. "That's pretty heavy philosophy coming from a drummer!"

"Yeah, dude!" Billy chimed in. "That should be in a song!"

Bash and Ricky made quick eye contact and chuckled.

"What about you?" Bash asked Ricky. "You still have issues?"

"Are you kidding me?" Ricky replied. "I got more issues than *Playboy!*"

Bash laughed harder than normal, probably because of the weed. "Now *that* should be in a song!"

"I don't get it," Billy said.

33

"You know? *Playboy?* Magazine issues?" Bash said.

Billy still didn't get it.

"*Playboy* has released more magazine issues than any other magazine," Bash added.

"Oh," Billy said although he still seemed confused.

"Anyway," Bash said, returning his attention to Ricky. "I thought since you are *saved* and all, things were straightened out for you."

"Many things are straightened out for me," Ricky said. "Little things like where I will be spending eternity, but it doesn't mean I don't struggle with the same issues everyone else struggles with. It also doesn't mean I'm expected to be perfect because I'm saved. What it means is actually the opposite: Jesus, in *his* perfection paid the price for *my* imperfection. Past, present, and future."

Billy nodded his head politely but Bash didn't respond.

"Any other smart-alecky questions you wanna ask me, Boo-Boo?" Ricky said with a mischievous look on his face.

"No, all done," Bash replied eagerly.

Bash followed Timothy's BMW into the Shell Food Mart near the Highway 71 exit off Interstate 10. Timothy needed gas so Bash decided to top off the van as well. As Bash started to pump gas into the van's tank, Gordon and Trent exited the BMW while Timothy filled his own gas tank. Trent was carrying a leather bag on his shoulder as he headed toward the store.

Gordon sauntered over to the van. "How are you feeling, Bash?"

"Pretty good," Bash said. "A little tired. It's been a long day."

"Yeah," Gordon said with a wide yawn. "Maybe we should unload the gear tomorrow. I think everyone's bushed."

"Fine with me," Bash replied while filling the van's gas tank. "There's no rush for tomorrow anyway. And it's not like we have to worry about burglars breaking into the van out in the middle of nowhere."

That seemed to clinch Gordon's decision. "Okay, tomorrow then," he said while starting back for the BMW. "Oh, by the way, Trent's going to ride the rest of the way with you guys. He needs to get dropped off at some chick's house in town. Me and Tim are tired and we don't want to go out of the way to make the stop."

"Sure thing," Bash said, even though he didn't want to make the stop either. He also had to drop off Ricky at his condo. Now there were two stops.

Bash leaned his head into the opened driver's window and informed Billy and Ricky about Gordon's decision to unload the gear the next day. "And you were right, Billy," he added. "We're dropping Trent off somewhere in town."

After a moment of thought Billy asked, "Does Trent know about us unloading the gear tomorrow?"

"I don't think so," Bash said. "He was inside the store when Gordon decided."

"Don't tell him," Billy said. "Let him think he's getting out of it tonight."

Ricky's eyes were shut but he wasn't asleep. "So he's actually *not* getting out of it."

"That's right!" Billy said eagerly. "He'll have to help unload tomorrow."

"How clever," Ricky said in a sarcastic tone.

Trent came out of the store while texting someone on his cell phone. He approached Bash and the van. "Hey Bash," he said. "I'm going to ride with you guys so you can drop me off at a friend's house. Gordon and Timothy are tired and they don't want to drive out of the way."

"Where's the house?" Bash asked, not mentioning to Trent that Gordon had already told him about the new plan. "I need to drop Ricky off at his place, too."

"It's off Ben White near Manchaca."

"Okay," Bash said. "I'll drop you off first."

"Thanks," Trent said.

Trent climbed into the van and sat next to Billy on the bench seat. A moment later Bash pulled away from the Shell Food Mart to follow the BMW back onto the highway. Highway 71 was practically deserted since it was approaching two in the morning. Ricky leaned his head against the window and tried to sleep while Billy listened to music through his earbuds. Trent traded texts with somebody on his cell phone.

Ninety minutes later they were driving into Austin's city limits. "Take the Manchaca exit," Trent said. "The house is not far. Just a few blocks north of Ben White."

Billy still wondered if Trent knew that the unloading of the gear had been postponed until the following day. He decided to find out for sure. "Hey, Trent," he said while removing an earbud from his ear. "What about unloading the gear tonight?"

"Sorry, dude," Trent apologized. "I'll help out next time. It's Lynn. She's by herself and all freaked out about something."

Billy seemed satisfied by Trent's answer. "Right."

"Who is Lynn?" asked Bash.

"This babe I met a while ago."

"The cute redhead?"

"Yeah," Trent said. "She's going through some hard times and begged me to come over as soon as I could. You know how chicks are."

No, I don't, Bash almost said.

"Well, you better get home early tomorrow," Billy said while trying to make eye contact with Bash in the rearview mirror, "to make sure your rig is set up. You never know when Gordon may call a rehearsal."

"Oh, I will," Trent said. "Promise."

"So I guess we'll just have to unload the van by ourselves tonight," Billy said with a smirk. "Right, Bash?"

"Right."

"Thanks, guys," Trent said while placing a call on his cell phone. "I'm really sorry. I'd rather be with you guys, I promise." A hesitation. Then, "Lynn? How ya doing, baby?"

"Yeah," Bash said in a low voice, knowing Trent wasn't listening to him. "I know I'd rather be unloading heavy equipment than hanging out with some hot babe."

The van reached the girl's address a short while later. "Thanks, guys," Trent said while getting out of the van. "I'll be back early tomorrow to help out."

"Sure you will," Billy muttered as Bash drove away.

Bash's eyes were getting very heavy as he continued driving to his next stop at Ricky's condo. Bash dropped him off, thanking his friend profusely for all his help on the entire trip. "You are the best, Ricky."

"Drive slow and safe," Ricky said while climbing out of the van. "You don't need to get pulled over with your red eyes and all. Not to mention Billy's socks."

"Okay, daddy," Bash said. "I'll be a good boy. Promise."

The van finally reached Bottom Creek Road around four-thirty in the morning. Rock Bottom loomed in the distance, a few interior lights already on. Bash drove the van up to the house and parked. Timothy's BMW wasn't there. *Timothy probably dropped off Gordon and headed back toward his condo in downtown Austin.*

Bash and Billy stepped out of the van and stretched. Their stretches were followed by long yawns as they lumbered up the porch to the front door. Bash expected it to be unlocked. He was surprised that it wasn't. He used the key on the van's key chain and unlocked the door. He entered with Billy following behind. "Hello?"

Silence answered.

"Gordon?" Bash tried again. "You here?"

"Maybe he's planning on scaring us," Billy said.

"I think he was too tired for that," said Bash. "Maybe he's already asleep."

"I'm not so sure," Billy argued. "He seems to be enjoying ragging on me lately."

Bash turned on the ceiling light in the rehearsal room. It was basically empty except for a small sofa and some small tables. They searched the kitchen, then the room next to the kitchen which was used for storage of the equipment road cases. They headed back to the foyer and climbed the stairs. The light in Billy's bedroom was on. They checked the room and found it empty. "Did you leave your light on this morning?"

"No, I don't think so," Billy said with a frown.

"Let's check his bedroom," Bash said while leaving Billy's room. "We're going to feel really silly if he's in his bed asleep."

Bash leaned his head into the dark bedroom. "Hey, Gordon. You awake?"

Nothing.

Bash switched on Gordon's ceiling light. The bed was still made and everything in the room looked tidy and neatly organized. Bash took a few steps across the bedroom and opened its closet, looked inside, then exited the room into the hallway with Billy in tow. They searched the other bedrooms. There was no sign of anybody or anything out of the ordinary.

"Maybe he went home with Timothy," Bash finally said. "They would've reached Timothy's condo much quicker than having to drive way out here."

"Yeah, maybe so."

Bash and Billy went back downstairs and into the kitchen which was now pitch dark. Bash flipped on the ceiling light. "Didn't I leave the light on?"

"I'm not sure," Billy said, his attention focused on his cell phone. "I'll call Gordon."

Bash checked the door in the kitchen that led outside to the back of the house while Billy waited for Gordon to answer his cell phone. The kitchen door was still locked from the inside. Bash had a bad taste in his mouth. *Probably from the pot earlier.* He grabbed a stick of Juicy Fruit from a drawer they used for candy and sweets. As he chewed the gum he thought about Timothy and Gordon having a car accident. *They could be in a hospital emergency room right now,* he thought. *Or worse.* He knew how fast your life could change. *In less time than it takes to change lanes in a vehicle.*

Billy ended his call. "He's not answering. This is creepy, dude. What's up?"

Bash just shrugged, not wanting to share his fears of a car wreck being the reason Timothy and Gordon were so late.

Billy grabbed a can of beer from the fridge. They both sat down at the old Formica kitchen table Timothy had given them. "Sun will be up in a few," Bash said in an attempt to make idle conversation while waiting to hear something about Timothy and Gordon, hoping that talking would help him stay awake. "I can barely keep my eyes open."

A loud sound came suddenly from upstairs, sounding like a door being slammed very hard. Bash jumped from his chair and ran toward the staircase. "Come on!"

Billy didn't seem eager to investigate. "I told you!" he said in an excited voice. "Gordon's trying to scare us!"

When Bash got to the top of the stairs he saw that all the doors in the upstairs hallway were still open. All except for one. The closet door. It was latched shut. Bash was positive it had been open earlier because he remembered glancing inside the closet before heading back down to the kitchen.

Billy arrived upstairs and joined Bash at the closet door. "Dude, wasn't that just open when we were up here?"

Bash didn't answer as he reached for the closet doorknob and jerked it open quickly. The closet was empty.

Billy looked relieved. "If Gordon is here, where would he be hiding?"

Bash was about to say that he didn't believe Gordon was in the house when they both heard car doors shutting outside. By the time they got downstairs Gordon and Timothy were coming inside the house.

"What happened?" Bash asked. "I thought you would've beat us here by an hour."

"We got pulled over, man!" Gordon said in an angry tone, not stopping on his way to the kitchen.

"Yes," Timothy said. "We got one of those gung-ho type of policemen. Got us out of the car and searched us like we were common criminals! Without any probable cause or search warrant! Kept us standing outside my car for almost an hour!"

"Where did you get pulled over?" asked Bash. "I can't believe we didn't see your car and the patrol car lights on the side of the road."

"Leaving a Denny's where we stopped for a bite," Timothy said in a calmer tone.

Too tired to drop off Trent but not too tired to stop for food? "That's why I didn't see you," Bash said. "Even though I fell behind when I dropped off Trent and Ricky."

"It's a good thing you dropped them off!" Gordon shouted while marching out of the kitchen with a beer in his hand. "You could've been pulled over instead of us!" He glanced at Billy on his way up the staircase. "And you guys would be in jail right now. Right, Billy?"

Billy wondered why he was being singled out for the pot smoking since Gordon and everyone else did their share. "They didn't find your stash?"

Gordon stopped on his way up the stairs. He turned to look at Billy and shook his head in disbelief. "No, they didn't find my stash! They didn't find my stash because I would never be stupid enough to carry my stash in a car on a late night trip home! And if I had, I would be in jail right now!"

"I guess that's a good thing," Billy said reluctantly. "Since you guys got pulled over and all."

Gordon rolled his eyes while storming to his bedroom. "Putz!" he shouted while slamming his door shut.

Timothy avoided eye contact with Billy. "I'm going to crash in Vince's bedroom," he said, obviously embarrassed by Gordon's rude behavior toward Billy. "I'm too exhausted to drive. I'll see you blokes tomorrow."

As Timothy trudged upstairs Billy said, "I'm going to have another beer. Want one, Bash?"

"No, thanks," Bash said. "I'm hitting the hay. By the way, Billy. Gordon was out of line. You're not a putz."

"Thanks, Bash."

Bash headed upstairs toward his bedroom. He removed his shoes and collapsed onto the mattress on the floor. He didn't care about band infighting, noises in the house, or anything else at the moment. He was asleep in seconds.

†

Trent arrived at Rock Bottom the next morning around ten. He went into the kitchen and poured a glass of orange juice. He sat at the kitchen table and drank it while studying some website on his cell phone.

Timothy came down the stairs a few minutes later, still buttoning the shirt on his tiny frame. "Morning, mate! How was your night? Better than ours, I hope."

"What do you mean?" asked Trent.

Timothy told him about getting pulled over and hassled by the police. "We didn't get here until nearly sunrise."

Trent nodded absentmindedly while returning his attention to his cell phone.

"I need to have a meeting with everyone, Trent," Timothy said, "regarding an offer about some out-of-state shows in the fall. Gordon and Billy are going to be sleeping for a while. Vince won't be back for a few hours. We can have our meeting a bit later. Let's go out for breakfast. I'm buying. What do you say?"

Trent shrugged. "Okay."

Timothy sent a text to Gordon's phone, informing him of taking Trent to breakfast. A minute later they were out the door.

†

Bash was playing guitar in his dream, performing for a large audience in a huge concert setting. He was an established star. Many in the audience were waving signs with his name printed on them in bold fonts. Bash was captivating the crowd with his electric performance while moving rhythmically and confidently along the edge of the stage as dozens of hands—mainly female—reached for his legs. But what intrigued him most about the performance were the musical phrases and passages he improvised on his guitar; licks and techniques he'd never even thought of before, not to mention actually played.

As Bash drifted into consciousness he became aware that it was just a dream. He wasn't disappointed, though. He was excited about the new guitar licks and eager to try them on his guitar. When he opened his eyes, still remembering one of the guitar licks, the sobering truth fell on him like a ton of wet blankets. He stared at the ceiling, wondering if he would ever find true joy and happiness again.

In a moment of anger Bash yanked the sheets off his body with his single arm and sat up quickly. He lumbered out of his bedroom, hearing snoring from Billy's bedroom. He took a shower in the upstairs hallway bathroom and dressed in fresh clothes before walking downstairs. He took a quick glance at the nearly empty rehearsal room before heading into the kitchen. He felt better than he had immediately after the dream. Maybe one day he wouldn't care anymore that his guitar playing days were over. *I doubt it.*

Bash found some bacon and eggs in the fridge. Within minutes the powerful aroma of sizzling bacon filled the house. *This will wake them up,* he told himself.

And sure enough, Billy staggered into the kitchen in no time. "What's up, Bash?" he said while plopping into a kitchen chair.

"Just me."

"I guess Gordon and Timothy are still asleep," Billy said with a big yawn.

"I guess so."

Bash finished with the bacon and started scrambling a half dozen eggs.

"You're better at that with one arm than I am with two," Billy said, immediately wishing he wouldn't have said it. "Sorry, Bash."

"For what?" Bash replied. "I take that as a compliment." He brought a plate of bacon to the table and returned to the eggs cooking on the stove.

Billy nibbled on the bacon.

"Coffee's ready," Bash said, pointing toward the coffee maker with his chin.

"Man!" Billy said. "Would you marry me?"

Bash gave him a serious look, acting like he was trying to decide how to answer the question. "No," he finally said with a smile.

Billy chuckled. "That's okay, Bash. I still love ya."

Gordon sauntered into the kitchen. He looked freshly showered and dressed for the day, the way he always looked. He was studying texts on his cell phone. "Timothy and Trent left here a while ago and went to a restaurant for breakfast."

"Trent got here early?" asked Billy.

"Yes," Gordon said. "Timothy said they ran into Lloyd Weber at the restaurant."

"Lloyd Weber?" Billy said. "Lloyd Weber the promoter?"

"Yeah," Gordon said while continuing to read the text. "He says here that Lloyd might have some big dates for us. He wants to hear us today so we need to set the gear up as quickly as possible. They'll be here in an hour."

"An hour?" complained Billy.

"You're joking," Bash said.

"No, I'm not," Gordon said. "So let's get ready. I talked to Vince. He's already in town. He'll be here any minute to get his drums set up. Now let's go! Chop-chop!"

Bash and Billy watched Gordon march out of the kitchen.

"Chop-chop?" Billy said to Bash.

Bash put the bowl of scrambled eggs on the table and wiped his hand on a towel stuffed in his belt. He was glad Vince would be arriving soon to set up the drums but he still had a lot to do. He grabbed a plate of warm tortillas and brought them to the table. "Better make a taco to go," he told Billy while heading out of the kitchen.

Five minutes later, Bash, Billy, and Gordon were unloading the van and carrying the gear inside the rehearsal room. They needed to set up the keyboards, guitar amps, monitor console with its power amps and speaker wedges, and the microphones and stands before wiring it all together.

As they rushed to get all the gear set up, Billy suddenly stopped with a look of astonished realization on his face. "He did it again," he announced to anyone in earshot.

"What?" asked Bash.

"He did it again."

"Who did what again?" Bash asked.

"Trent," Billy said with a frustrated smile. "He got out of unloading the gear again!"

Bash realized Billy was right. "And you know what?" Bash added.

"What?"

"He didn't even have a clue that he was getting out of it."

"I know," Billy replied. "That's the part that drives me crazy."

Gordon suddenly said, "Hey, Billy?"

"Yeah?"

"You know how Trent sets up his amp rig, don't you?"

"Yeah."

"Get his stuff ready to go," Gordon said. "Guitars tuned, too."

The look on Billy's face was priceless. Bash tried not to laugh.

"Here, Billy," Bash said while handing him some cables. "These are Trent's."

Billy took the cables with a frown. He looked up at Bash with an expectant look on his face.

"Sorry," Bash said, still trying not to smile. "I've got to get these mic lines set up and ringed out. I'd love to help out, though."

Billy muttered to himself. He began cursing and throwing cables angrily.

"If you have a problem helping out you can always find another job!" Gordon shouted in an acidic tone. "It won't bother me any!"

Billy looked mortally wounded. Tears were forming in his eyes as he began setting up Trent's guitar rig.

Bash thought Gordon's comment was totally heartless and unnecessary. He thought about what Ricky would say: *You see, this is what it's like when a band plays together and lives together, and this is just the beginning . . .*

† † †

6

*B*ash drove the van toward the location of the storage unit auction while towing a fifteen-foot trailer. He had a large manila envelope with almost four thousand dollars in mainly hundred-dollar bills below his seat—money the Zeniths gave him to make the purchase if the auction went their way. He had already picked up Ricky's friend, Kyle McCurry, from Kyle's office in town. Kyle sat in the passenger seat while Ricky sat in the bench seat behind them. Kyle McCurry was broad in the shoulders with a square jaw accenting his rugged face. His close-cropped hair reminded Bash of the stereotypical Marine drill sergeant's haircut. Earlier that day, Bash learned from Ricky that Sgt. Kyle McCurry, formerly of the Second Marine Division, had been deployed to Camp Fallujah, Iraq, part of the II Marine Expeditionary Force. Kyle looked the part.

Bash tried to keep his mind off of worrying about bidding on a storage unit without knowing for sure that a sound system was even inside. Kyle was confident, apparently having inside information about the unit, but Bash still worried. Timothy and Gordon had both talked to Kyle and seemed convinced it was worth taking the chance, which took some of the pressure off of Bash, but the idea of buying a sound system had been Bash's idea originally. Bash tried not to worry. "You see a lot of action in Fallujah, Kyle?"

"Yeah, plenty," was all Kyle had to say about the subject.

"So how many other bidders do you think will be there?" Ricky asked.

"You never know," replied Kyle. "Maybe a dozen or more but that doesn't mean they'll all be bidding on our unit."

"I bet it gets heated sometimes," Ricky said.

"It's usually not as dramatic as those TV shows," Kyle said, "but it's highly competitive, which is one of the things I like about it."

"I imagine no one is really going to intimidate you anyway," Ricky said with a laugh.

"Aw, I'm just a big pussycat," Kyle replied with a shy smile.

Yeah, right, Ricky thought. *A big pussycat with razor sharp claws and fangs.*

"I'm the only person who knows what's in this particular unit," Kyle said, "so winning the bid should be easy."

I hope you're right, Bash thought to himself, wondering how Kyle had obtained his inside information—a question Timothy and Gordon had asked but Kyle had not divulged to them either.

Kyle directed Bash to turn onto the road where the storage units were located. "We're a little early but that's okay," Kyle said. "It gives me a little time to size-up the situation."

They parked nearby and walked toward the units. Ricky asked Kyle, "So, do you bid blind or do they let you examine the units?"

"They let you take a look before the bidding starts," Kyle said, "but you can't go inside the unit." He stopped walking and lowered his voice. "Okay, huddle up."

Bash and Ricky stepped closer to Kyle.

"Once the bidding starts," Kyle explained in a low voice, "just hang back and watch."

Bash and Ricky nodded their heads.

"When we first see inside the unit," Kyle continued, "be cool with your response. If it looks valuable, don't let on or show any emotions. These other bidders are shrewd. Even if they know nothing about professional sound equipment they will see your reaction and decide to win the bid if they think it's valuable. Understand?"

Bash and Ricky nodded again.

Once the auction started they watched the bidding on several storage units until reaching one particular unit. Kyle whispered to them, "This is the one."

A man who worked for the storage facility used a pair of bolt cutters to cut the padlock on the unit, same as he had done on the previous units. He rolled up the unit's door as everyone peered inside. The dozen or so bidders took turns getting as close as they could to look inside. Most just saw stacks of big black boxes against one wall with protective road cases filling the rest of the unit. But Bash recognized a logo on several of the road cases that told him an Avid VENUE Mix Rack was part of the package. The other cases probably contained the speaker arrays, although how many, he didn't know. The road cases looked new, probably never being on the road but belonging to a big club or small concert venue at one time. Bottom line: if the Avid twenty-four channel mix console was there with even a small number of speaker arrays, software rack, and all the cabling and connectors, you were talking over forty thousand dollars retail back when it was brand new. Cut that price in half for used gear and it would still be a steal for four thousand bucks, their budget for the auction.

The auctioneer, a skinny old man with white hair and mustache, started the bid at two hundred dollars. A Hispanic man wearing a straw hat and sunglasses upped the bid. He looked like Carlos Santana to Bash. Another man raised that bid. It went that way for a while between the two until the bid reached seventeen hundred dollars. Apparently, the two bidders knew something or at least recognized the road cases inside the unit as being expensive sound gear. Kyle jumped in to bump it up to eighteen hundred, getting a surprised look from both bidders. The other man dropped out at nineteen hundred, leaving Kyle and Carlos Santana to battle it out. Carlos became irritated with Kyle every time he raised the bid, making sideways comments but making sure the big man couldn't hear him. When Kyle raised the bid to twenty-six hundred dollars, the Carlos Santana-looking dude hesitated to raise the bid. The auctioneer finally said, "Twenty-six hundred going once! Twenty-six hundred going twice!" A short pause then, "Sold, for twenty-six hundred!"

Carlos cursed and stormed away while Kyle shared high-fives with Bash and Ricky.

The group of bidders moved on to the next unit being auctioned while Kyle, Bash, and Ricky went inside their unit. They helped Bash roll one of the Avid cases out where they could open it. Once the top was removed, Bash began laughing. "Oh, baby!"

"Is it good?" asked Kyle.

"Yes," Bash replied, marveling at the twenty-four channel mixer inside. "What a steal! This is awesome, Kyle!"

Bash began examining the rest of the cases. The Adamson speaker arrays and subwoofers would be more than adequate for all the Zeniths' smaller and medium-sized gigs. Everything looked practically brand new. "All this must have come out of a big club or theater or something," he said. "It's too clean to have been on the road."

"You're right," Kyle said. "It was actually never used. It came from a nightclub in Dallas that went belly-up before it ever opened."

"No kidding?"

"The owner moved it here to Austin in order to open a new place."

"You knew him?" asked Bash.

"Sort of."

"Did he ever open up the new place?" asked Ricky.

"No," Kyle said with a soft smile. "He was murdered before he had a chance."

"Murdered?" Bash said.

"I can't prove it," Kyle said, "but I think certain investors found him and settled some debts they had, if you know what I mean. He hid the gear here so the investors wouldn't find it. Too bad for him they didn't find it, but found him instead."

"That's terrible," Bash said while pondering Kyle's story. "I feel like we're taking advantage of his bad luck."

"Well, don't feel too bad for him," Kyle said. "The guy was a pimp, drug dealer, and a ruthless killer himself."

Bash's expression revealed his surprise. *What am I getting involved in?*

Ricky took a softer stance. "Bash, if we didn't win the bid, someone else would have."

"That's right," Kyle said. "The unit was going to be auctioned regardless."

Bash knew they were right but he still felt uneasy with the circumstances. "We won't be in any trouble, will we?" he asked. "You know, possession of stolen goods or anything like that?"

"No, no," Kyle said. "The receipts were all in his name. He owned it legally. No next of kin. I did all the research a while back."

Bash shook his head, still in disbelief at their good fortune, despite the fact that it hinged with someone else's misfortune. "What a deal, Kyle," he said. "I can't thank you enough. The Zeniths thank you, too."

"Yeah, man," Ricky added. "Thanks, bro."

"My pleasure," Kyle said. "Maybe I can get you guys to play for a party I'm planning on throwing at the end of the year."

"I'll pass that on to Timothy," Bash said. "He's the band manager you talked to earlier."

"Okay," Kyle said. "You do that."

Bash and Ricky continued exploring through the cases, amazed at the good condition of everything they saw.

"I'm going inside to settle up," Kyle said. "Give me thirty-one hundred. There will be a few expenses added to the auction bid."

Bash removed the thick wad of money from the envelope and counted out thirty-one of the hundred-dollar bills into Kyle's opened palm.

After Kyle left, Ricky found a stack of cardboard boxes in a rear corner. He opened the top one and saw ledgers, rulers, pens and pencils, and other office related materials.

"Looking for anything in particular?" Bash asked while opening various road cases and examining the interiors.

"Yeah," Ricky replied. "Since the gear came out of a club, I was hoping they had one of those mirror balls. You know, the ones you hit with a laser light, creating hundreds of laser beams."

Bash chuckled. "You're kidding."

"I thought you guys could hang it in the rehearsal room at Rock Bottom," Ricky said. "And if ya'll didn't want it I might buy it from you."

"You're nuts," Bash said. "Besides, those mirror balls are big. They wouldn't fit in a cardboard box. You feeling okay?"

"Maybe there's a smaller one somewhere here."

Bash shook his head and continued looking through the road cases.

Fifteen minutes later, two stout-looking teenaged boys showed up. One of them was Kyle's son, Ryan, and the other big boy was his friend. The boys would help load the van and trailer before taking Kyle back to work.

Less than an hour later the boys had the van and trailer loaded. Bash and Ricky climbed into the van, ready to haul the prize to Rock Bottom to show the band. They saw Kyle standing a distance away in the parking lot, talking to the Carlos Santana dude.

A moment later Kyle started walking toward the van. He handed Bash a business card through the open window. "This is that guy's phone number," he said, pointing his chin toward the Carlos Santana dude who was walking toward a vintage, cherry-red, 1957 Chevy convertible parked in the parking lot. "He says if you find any idols, let him know. He says he'll pay top dollar for them."

"Idols?"

"That's what he said," Kyle replied. "I don't know. It's Austin. Keep Austin Weird."

"Okay," Bash said. "Idols. Got it."

Kyle handed Bash the auction papers along with a ten-dollar bill. "The bid was twenty-six hundred, but after paying the fifteen percent auction fee, and the hundred dollar clean-up fee, that brought the grand total up to three-thousand-ninety bucks."

"Great," Bash said, placing the ten-dollar bill and the auction papers into the money envelope. "Sure we can't buy you lunch?"

"No, thanks. I gotta get back to work. Thanks, though."

"No, thank you."

Kyle gave them a thumbs-up.

A few minutes later Bash was driving the van away from the storage facility.

"Let's stop and grab some burgers," Ricky said. "I'm buying."

"I'll buy," Bash said. "Or I should say, the Zeniths are buying. It's the least we can do, bro! What a score! Thank you!"

"It was all Kyle's doing," Ricky said. "I was just the middle man."

"Without you it wouldn't have happened."

Ricky thought a moment before asking, "So what does that make me? The Indian, the bow, or the arrow?"

Bash smiled while he thought about it. "The bow," he finally said. "I think."

"Yeah, I think you're right."

"I'm getting a little tired of the Yogi Boo-Boo thing," Bash said a moment later with a mischievous grin. "Maybe I could start calling you Ricky-bow? Get it? Indian? Bow?"

Ricky gave Bash a look. "Okay," he said, the gears in his mind spinning fast. "As long as I can call you Squaw-bash! Get it? Indian? Squaw?"

Bash shook his head in disgust. "You could spell the bow part cajun-style," he said. "You know, b-e-a-u-x? Ricky-beaux!"

Ricky didn't miss a beat. "You could have your own song!" he said eagerly. "The Squaw-bash Cannonball!"

"You need to stop thinking now," Bash said with a deadpan expression, "before you totally humiliate yourself." A pause. "Ricky-beaux."

"Squaw-bash."

Their good mood continued as they stopped at Dan's, a legendary Austin drive-in burger joint that sold old-fashioned burgers, french fries, and thick milk shakes. They bought a sack of food to go before continuing onward, the van pulling the trailer full of gear, this time with Ricky driving so Bash could eat his food. Some of the smaller road cases and cardboard boxes rode in the back of the van, most of them not opened yet.

Later they drove slowly down Bottom Creek Road toward Rock Bottom, the van and trailer trailing a plume of dust behind them. Bash couldn't wait to show the band the sound system. From his close examination back at the storage unit, the sound system looked brand new to Bash. He couldn't imagine any of it being defective, or at least unfixable. Sure, there would be glitches to deal with but that went without saying. Everyone expected as much with any professional system. He planned to set it up quickly on his own time, reading all the manuals he could find online, making sure all the software versions were up to date. He wanted to know his way around the console before the next rehearsal. The next Zeniths gig where they needed to provide sound reinforcement was over two weeks away, plenty of time to get it all together.

As Ricky turned off the dirt road and parked the van and trailer near the house, Bash smiled inwardly. *Sure, Ricky and Ricky's friend, Kyle, had made it all happen but it was me who first came up with the idea and proposed it to the band.* He was finally making a substantial contribution and he couldn't wait to celebrate with everyone. Maybe this would lift everyone's spirits at Rock Bottom . . .

† † †

7

*J*onni Windsor hustled out the kitchen door in back of the restaurant, her dark hair pulled back into a ponytail. As a waitress at Polvos, a frumpy, hippie-styled, Tex-Mex restaurant on 1st street, she had stayed a little late to help out a new waiter. She was moving fast, eager to get to her destination tonight, her first service call since arriving in Austin, Texas a month earlier.

A young couple had contacted her after talking to a local pastor that Jonni knew. The couple had worked with some paranormal investigators a few months earlier that not only confirmed that their house was haunted but had also used the help of a local psychic—a woman claiming to be able to cleanse *"bad energy"* using an ancient shamanic ritual of incantations and the burning of certain herbs. After the ritual the couple said things were better for a while but eventually the problems returned. Now things were worse than before. Typically, the couple's confusion regarding the paranormal—aided by many well-intentioned clergymen and paranormal investigators on TV—had made the problem worse rather than better. Jonni wanted to help the couple *see the light,* so to speak.

Jonni had started the waitress job at Polvos after moving to Austin from Nashville, Tennessee. Her friend, Mandy, a college student at UT Austin had set up the job at Polvos and had also invited Jonni to share her tiny apartment as well. Jonni was eager to begin helping people. Texas seemed to be a good place to start. Her Nashville experience was history, not in a bad way necessarily, but she was glad it was over. She had learned plenty from the experience. Now it was time to begin a new chapter in her life.

Jonni had been an orphan until shortly after her fifth birthday when her foster parents, Bill and Beverly Windsor, had adopted her. They were good people, raising her with lots of love and care. They were a bit older than most parents of girls her age but that had never been an issue with Jonni. She loved them dearly. Bill died of congested heart failure at seventy when Jonni was eighteen, five years ago. Beverly died just two years later.

Despite being left a hefty inheritance from her foster parents, Jonni never gloated over having money or even told anybody about the inheritance. She lived a simple life, not interested in material wealth, preferring to make her own way while she lived a modest lifestyle.

From the family home in Steubenville, Ohio, Jonni moved to Nashville on an academic scholarship just a year before her foster mother died. She attended two semesters at Vanderbilt University but she let her grades slip when becoming involved with a paranormal investigator named Greg Palin. Their relationship had initiated Jonni into the world of modern-day ghost hunters and how easily most of them were deceived.   After losing the scholarship, Jonni was soon booted out of Greg's little group of paranormal investigators due to what Greg called a *"conflict of interest."* Earlier, one of the other investigators, a college graduate named Susan, accused Jonni of evangelizing rather than truly helping the victims of hauntings. Jonni explained that the only way for someone to be truly free from demonic attacks was through the power of God. But Susan only guffawed, insisting that the spirits involved were those of the deceased still in existence on the properties they investigated. Susan went on to tell Jonni that religion was the real culprit with all its medieval superstitions regarding the occult. Jonni reminded Susan of their recent case of a violent haunting in a home outside of Nashville, explaining how the family's faith and her own cleansing method removed the evil entities plaguing the home. "And this was after you, Susan," Jonni told her, "brought in a psychic who used some obscure pagan prayers which did nothing but escalate the family's problem."

Susan responded by calling Jonni a certain four-letter word. Greg saw the anger rise in Jonni's face so he intervened, but it became instantly clear that he was siding with Susan on the issue. The next day he told Jonni that their romance was over. It was like rubbing salt into the wounds Susan inflicted. The coups d' grace came a few days later when Jonni found out that Greg and Susan had become romantically involved. That was it. Jonni was done with Nashville. She cried over the phone to Mandy, her longtime friend from Steubenville who was going to school at UT Austin. Mandy invited her to come to Austin to live with her and also arranged the waitress job for her. So Jonni moved to Austin, away from Nashville, away from Greg and Susan and their world of deception.

In her spare time Jonni worked at designing a website for her unique style of ministry—a paranormal investigative group with emphasis on God's healing—although at the moment the paranormal investigative group consisted of just her. She asked Mandy to join but Mandy just laughed. "I get frightened watching scary movies," she told Jonni. "I don't think I would be much help screaming all the time."

Jonni started searching far and wide throughout Austin and central Texas for any information regarding families plagued by paranormal activities. But it was a daunting task. Even when she made an occasional contact, the victims of the hauntings were often uncooperative or biased in their beliefs, much of it fostered from watching all the ghost hunting television shows which were so popular with many folks.

Jonni, with a video camera, digital audio recorder, and a Bible in her backpack, climbed on her bicycle and rode to the address in a south Austin neighborhood where the family and their *ghosts* lived. Pastor Mark, who had introduced Jonni to the family at his church, was not going to be there. Jonni knew that many pastors and various clergymen didn't believe in paranormal phenomena, but many did, including Pastor Mark. He declined to participate due to his busy schedule but Jonni had sensed something else in his voice when they discussed the matter: Fear.

Jonni arrived at the address and was welcomed warmly by the husband and wife, Aaron and Heather. Jonni felt a demonic presence as soon as she was inside the house but she said nothing. She questioned the couple about the unusual occurrences at the house while they all drank hot tea from china cups. Jonni had them start the story from the beginning. Aaron, a balding man in his thirties explained: "After moving in, things were normal for about two months," he explained in his Texas drawl. "Then things went downhill."

Jonni listened to him recount details of all the strange events happening in the house during the last year, all of them typical for most hauntings. The feeling of being watched, strange sounds, and moving shadows soon escalated to glasses and dishes falling from cabinets along with Heather often being touched by unseen hands while in bed. Heather pointed out a crucifix hanging on the wall of the kitchen. "At least once a week," she explained, "I'll find this on the floor even though the nail holding the metal loop on the crucifix is fixed tight to the wall."

"The falling crucifix always follows physical contact," Aaron added nonchalantly while lifting his shirttail from his lower back.

Jonni couldn't contain her surprise when she saw the three bloody scratches on his back, looking like they came from the claw of some type of wild animal. "How often does this happen?"

Aaron and Heather exchanged glances before Aaron said, "Every time . . . we are intimate."

Jonni asked, "Do you feel the scratches when they happen?"

"No," Aaron replied. "Only after."

"And we always find the crucifix on the floor after that," Heather added.

Jonni then asked some questions involving their relationship and beliefs. She began with, "Have things deteriorated between the two of you?"

Aaron and Heather hesitated a moment before Aaron said, "Well, I seem to be angrier and less patient than I used to be."

Heather nodded her head. "And sometimes thoughts form in my head from out of nowhere."

"Thoughts?" asked Jonni.

"Bad thoughts," Heather continued. "Angry thoughts about Aaron and how he's not treating me right. But then I realize that's not true and I wonder where those thoughts are coming from."

Jonni paused for a moment before saying, "I need to ask you both a personal question."

Aaron and Heather nodded their heads.

"Are you Christians?"

They seemed confused. "You know that we attend church," Aaron said, "where Pastor Mark preaches."

"That's not what I asked you," Jonni said. "I asked if you were Christians. That means you have accepted Jesus as your personal savior. Going to church is good but it does not make you a Christian . . . just like living in a garage doesn't make you a car."

Heather nodded in understanding but Aaron broke eye contact with Jonni. Jonni waited for him to respond.

"I don't know," he finally said. "I never thought about it like that. Now that you bring it up, I must admit I've had some doubts lately."

Heather was surprised by his admission. "Really?"

Aaron seemed to be ashamed. He hung his head. "Yes."

"It's okay to doubt," Jonni said in a gentle tone to Aaron. "Everyone has doubts. You're no different than anyone else."

Her words seemed to soothe him. "Thanks, Jonni."

"Take time to pray anyway," Jonni said. "Be honest. Tell God your doubts. He will strengthen you and your faith."

Aaron chose his words carefully. "I don't mean to be rude or anything," he said, "but what does any of this have to do with our problems here in this house?"

"It has *everything* to do with it," Jonni answered without hesitation. She had their full attention now.

"When the psychic lady cleansed the house," Jonni continued, "did things improve after that?"

"Yes," they both answered.

"But then the problems returned?"

"Yes," Heather said. "Worse than before."

Jonni already knew this but she wanted to walk the couple through so they would reason things themselves. "This is not unusual," she said. "Even if the peace lasts for years, the ousted spirits can return eventually if no real opposition is found on return. But besides all that, at sometime in the past, an entry allowed them to enter."

"What do you mean by *entry?*" asked Heather.

"It's not uncommon for people in your situation to discover that the previous owners or tenants were dabbling in the occult," Jonni explained. "You know, messing with Ouija boards, Tarot Cards, stuff like that."

Aaron looked like he had something on his mind. Heather noticed. "What?"

Aaron sighed and said, "It makes sense."

"What makes sense?" Heather asked.

"I never mentioned it before," he said, "but when we first moved in I was cleaning out the garage and I found some stuff."

"What kind of stuff?" asked Jonni.

"Oh, some boxes of black candles," he said, "and one of those Ouija boards you mentioned."

"You never told me that," Heather said.

"I didn't think anything about it," he said. "I thought it was harmless."

"That's most likely how the spirits were invited here," Jonni said. "Is the Ouija board still here?"

"No, I threw it away."

"Well, that's good," Heather remarked. She turned to Jonni. "Right, Jonni?"

"Yes," Jonni replied, "but the Ouija board was just the tool used for the entry. It's like an invitation to the spirits in their realm. Once invited, they have to be *uninvited,* which requires an intervention from God."

Jonni paused to sip her tea. Aaron and Heather waited for her to continue.

"Now you asked earlier what your faith had to do with your problem," Jonni said. "I can help both of you to drive them out of your home but only with your faith and belief will they *stay* gone."

Jonni noticed that it was nearly dark outside as she waited for her words to settle in with the couple. She removed her video camera and audio recorder from her backpack. "Now, as I told you a few days ago, I would like to walk through the house and get some video and audio. This will help me know exactly what I'm dealing with when I return tomorrow night. Okay?"

Aaron and Heather agreed.

For Jonni, collecting video and audio data wasn't about verifying the existence of spirit entities, the motivation behind most paranormal researchers. Jonni knew that these spirits existed, she just wanted to gather clues to help her understand the type of spirits involved in order to be more successful in ridding them from people's lives.

Soon all three were walking through the dimly-lit house while Jonni shot video with her camera. In the master bedroom, Jonni sensed the strongest presence but she kept silent, letting Aaron and Heather explain to her about various incidents that had occurred in the room. "Sometimes when I'm alone," Heather said, "I think I see an impression on the mattress. You know, like someone is sitting there. But when I put my hand on the spot I find nothing."

After shooting video in all the rooms, Jonni used her digital audio recorder. "I'm going to try to capture some EVP," she said. "You know what that is?"

"Yes," Aaron said. "Electronic Voice Phenomena. The lady here before did the same thing."

"Did she get any responses?"

Aaron shrugged his shoulders and turned to Heather. "Did she tell you anything?"

"No," answered Heather. "She never did say."

Jonni began by first stating the location, date, and time on the recording. She then began asking questions. "Is anyone in the room with us?" She paused for several seconds between her questions. "Who are you? Why are you here? What do you want from Aaron and Heather?"

Jonni ended the session in the bedroom and went to the kitchen to continue. The crucifix was still on the wall as Jonni asked more questions, concluding with: "Why do you make this crucifix fall from the wall?"

A short while later all three were back in the living room. Jonni replaced her gear in her backpack, not surprised that nothing unusual happened since she had been in the home. But she knew the spirits were there. Watching. Sizing her up.

"I'll call you tomorrow," Jonni said. "Before coming back."

"Thank you, Jonni," Aaron said.

"Yes," Heather added. "Thank you so much for helping. For *wanting* to help."

Jonni felt the sadness of the couple. From her experience, one of the worst parts of these situations was the feeling of loneliness the people endured. Most folks kept their dilemma secret, fearful that no one would believe them or think they were crazy.

Jonni pedaled her bicycle through the dark neighborhood backstreets while making her way back to Mandy's apartment. Although there were a few streetlights along the way, the overcast in the night sky created an especially dark night. Several times she felt as if she was being watched, or followed, which caused her to pedal faster. She recited Psalm

23 aloud. Then she thought about her foster mom's mother, Granny Arrabelle. Granny Arrabelle was the reason why Jonni was helping people like Aaron and Heather. When Jonni was eight years old, spending the summer at Grandmother Arrabelle's farm in rural West Virginia, she learned what *ghosts* really were.

On one particular day early that summer, young Jonni explored the attic of a nearby farmhouse with another girl her age who lived in the farmhouse. They both heard strange noises when up in the attic exploring an old wooden trunk. While sorting through some old linens found in the trunk, Jonni heard a woman's voice coming from somewhere in the attic. The voice sounded friendly. Jonni asked the girl if she heard the voice but the girl wouldn't answer. The girl was afraid and wanted to leave the attic. The event didn't scare Jonni, though. It just made her curious. From that day forward Jonni believed her calling in life would have something to do with the paranormal.

After returning back to her grandmother's farm after the incident in the attic, young Jonni told her ninety-five-year-old Granny Arrabelle what had happened. Granny Arrabelle was not surprised. She told Jonni that she too had an ability to peek into the spirit world but reminded the young girl to remain more cautious than curious. "Most folks can't see or hear these things that you and I can see and hear," Granny Arrabelle told her. "But these things ain't what you think they are, child. They like to pose as humans who once lived on the Earth but that ain't what they are."

"Then what are they, Granny?" Jonni asked.

"They are evil spirits, child. Part of the devil's army."

"But the voice I heard didn't sound evil."

"That's because they are working for the lie."

"What lie, Granny?"

"The lie that there's a good life after death that don't have nothing to do with God," Granny said. "Remember, child, their goal is to lead as many souls astray from Jesus as they can. Trust me, darling. I have many first-hand experiences in the matter."

"Tell me, Granny."

"Not now, child."

"Please?"

Granny hesitated before telling her one particular story from her own youth. "When I was young," Granny began, "not much older than you, some other gals and me did something really stupid. The oldest gal, Bonnie, took us younger gals to her secret place in the woods not far from here."

"What secret place?"

"An old cave," Granny said reluctantly. "But you find any cave around here you stay away, child. You hear?"

"Ye, ma'am."

"You promise me now!"

"Okay, Granny. I promise."

Granny calmed a bit before continuing. "Anyhow, Bonnie took us to her secret place and with a kerosene lantern she showed the rest of us something she found in the back of the cave. When I saw it I wanted to leave right away. It was a human skeleton. The bones of a child. By all the beadwork and a stone spear near the bones, I reckoned they belonged to an Indian boy. But now I think it all came from a group of people roaming these parts a long, long time ago. Anyhow, Bonnie had an idea. She told us we was gonna have a séance. You know what a séance is, child?"

"No, ma'am."

"That's where people gather in a circle and hold hands in order to speak to the dead," Granny explained. "Well, I'll tell you, I wanted nothing to do with that and started to leave that cave when Bonnie called me chicken. That's when pride rose up in me and I told her I weren't no chicken. So I stayed and we did the séance, Lord forgive me."

"What happened?"

"Nothin' at first," Granny answered. "But then it got real cold in there and a mist formed above us and then a face formed right in that mist. It seemed to glow, though the lantern light weren't what was making it glow."

"What kind of face?"

"The face of a boy," Granny said. "A dark-skinned boy with long black hair and a ring in one ear. For a long time he said nothin' but just stared at us. I think we all was scared, even Bonnie. Then the boy spoke. In English."

"He did? What did he say?"

"He told us he was grateful for us freeing him from his prison. That some adults had killed him and hidden him in the cave, not giving him proper burial, so he couldn't go into the light. But now he could because we freed him. He thanked us all. Particularly Bonnie since it were her idea and all."

"So he was nice, Granny?" Jonni said. "A nice spirit?"

"Let me finish, child," Granny said. "After thanking us, the face just disappeared in thin air. The mist was gone, too. We all sat there for a moment, wondering if what we saw had really happened when we all felt a big rush of wind blow out the cave. Bonnie said that the wind was the boy's spirit leaving the cave."

"Wow!" Jonni said. "That's a great story, Granny!"

"That ain't the end of the story, child," Granny said, "only the start. In the days and weeks that followed I noticed that Bonnie was getting gaunt and sickly. She didn't show up at school for a whole week. So one day I walked all the way to her family home in town. When I got there her mama and sisters all looked as bad as she did. There seemed to be an air of sickness and fear surrounding them and the whole house. When I got alone with Bonnie she cried and sobbed the whole time while telling me what had been going on. She told me stories about dark shadows roaming the house at night, dishes and what-not crashing on the floor, everyone in the house having nightmares every time they was asleep, and a big list of other bad things afflicting her entire family. I asked her if she thought this was because of the séance. She began bawling real loud then, saying she did believe it and that it was all her fault."

"So what happened?" asked young Jonni.

"I'm getting to it, child," Granny said. "Well, I went straight home and told my Grandma Fern, who was living at home with us in those days. You see, I was afraid to tell my mama or daddy about the séance in the cave, knowing I would have gotten a whippin' for doing such a thing. Anyhow, Grandma Fern put on her shawl and took me along in her Ford Model-A and rode us to Preacher Micah's parsonage near the Baptist church in town. Preacher Micah was old back then but still strong as an ox. He came from that older generation who were fighting men. When he was young he fought Indians down in Texas, but after receiving the Lord he figured he'd rather save folks than kill 'em, no matter what color their skin was. Anyhow, Grandma Fern and me told Preacher Micah all that had happened to Bonnie and her folks since that day in the cave."

Young Jonni watched Granny take a sip of water before continuing.

"Well, Preacher Micah didn't waste any time after he'd heard enough," Granny continued. "He set his jaw and puffed up his chest, and with me and Grandma Fern we all rode directly to Bonnie's house not far away. Bonnie and her folks were mighty surprised to see Preacher Micah at their doorstep but they let him in since he weren't the type you could say no to very easily. Well let me tell you, Preacher Micah opened his 1611 King James Bible and went right to work, reciting in a loud voice the part about powers and principalities in First Corinthians. He prayed and recited for an hour or so while walking through the entire house. It was nearly dark when he began calling out the spirit inflicting the home, taunting it to show itself. And all of a sudden, that mist we girls saw in the cave appeared out of nowhere, hovering right over the kitchen table. And a moment later, guess what face showed up in that mist?"

"The Indian boy?"

"That's right, child," Granny said. "The same face we saw in the cave. Then it started talking, saying 'what do you have in common with me, preacher man?' and other things like that."

"Did everyone in the room see it, Granny?" asked young Jonni. "Or hear it?"

"I don't believe so, child. I know Preacher Micah, Bonnie, and myself did, though. I remember Bonnie's daddy staring at the preacher and all of us like we was crazy. Anyhow, Preacher Micah kept on reciting scripture to it until all of a sudden the face in the mist began swirling around, becoming fuzzy-like, before it turned into something else, the face of a horrible beast with lizard-skin and eyes . . . Lord, those eyes. I'll never forget 'em. Eyes so full of hatred it causes gooseflesh to rise on my skin just thinking of it. Anyhow, in a low horrible voice it says, 'I have the right to be here!' And you know what, child? It *did* have the right."

"Why, Granny?"

"Because when we did that séance we invited it in," Granny said. She thought for a moment before chuckling. "But Preacher Micah was *uninviting* it, so to speak."

"So what happened?"

"Well, Preacher Micah stood right up to it," Granny explained. "He began preaching to it, commanding it to go in the name of Jesus. He did this over and over, making that demon angrier than a riled rattlesnake. Then, with a loud growl, the demon and the mist just vanished. You could feel the change in the room. It was lighter and brighter. Everyone felt it. Even Bonnie's daddy who had never darkened the door of a church in his life fell down to his knees and accepted the Lord on the spot under the guidance of Preacher Micah. So I think the Lord opened his eyes to see the demon when Preacher Micah was commanding it to leave."

"What happened after that, Granny?"

"We left in Grandma Fern's Ford to take Preacher Micah back to his parsonage," Granny said. "When he got out of the car, Preacher Micah told me to never get involved in a fool thing like a séance again or he would personally tan my hide. Then he went inside his house to eat his supper."

Jonni smiled at the memory of Granny Arrabelle as she pedaled her bike closer to Mandy's apartment, not knowing that someday she would be faced with a situation similar to the story of Preacher Micah and the spirit from the cave.

After arriving at Mandy's apartment, Jonni was anxious to review her video and audio data from the evening, although for some reason she was fairly certain she wouldn't find anything in the video. She poured herself a glass of cheap white wine while the data from her video camera loaded into the software in her laptop. While sipping the wine she played the video and looked for anything unusual in the footage. She did spot a few tiny balls of light near one of the rooms but they could have been the result of dust or reflections of light in the hallway.

Jonni downloaded the audio files from the digital audio recorder into her laptop, opened her audio program, and started reviewing the EVP session from the evening. The first few recordings showed some visible spikes on the audio graph of her software program but the sounds were so faint she could not detect any voices. But that changed after she heard her own voice on the recording ask the question: "Why are you here?"

Jonni heard something that followed her question. She played the section several times and listened closely. It sounded like a chuckle. Like a woman chuckling. Jonni continued reviewing the rest of the session. She heard her own voice on the recording ask, "Why do you make the crucifix fall from the wall?"

A gruff female voice answered on the recording. "Leave him alone, you tramp!"

Gooseflesh covered Jonni's skin. She rewound the program and heard the voice again on the audio file. She searched the file for more responses but there weren't any so she looped the section containing the angry voice. The spikes on the audio graph were steep and violent like the voice itself. "Leave him alone, you tramp!"

Leave who alone? Jonni thought to herself. *Was the voice talking to Heather? About the husband, Aaron?* She didn't think so.

"Who is him?" Jonni asked herself out loud. She wasn't really frightened but she was still glad no voice answered in the empty apartment. A moment later she heard keys rattling at the apartment door.

Mandy came in with a big smile on her face, the smile she usually wore. "Hi, honey. I'm home!" Mandy followed this with one of her trademark giggles. Mandy was a bit homely and chubby but with her warm personality she was as attractive to Jonni as anyone she had ever known.

"Mandy!" Jonni said eagerly. "Come here! You gotta see this! I mean, hear this!"

Mandy tossed her backpack on the floor and sat close to Jonni. "What is it?"

Jonni explained her evening with Aaron and Heather at their home, quickly covering the points leading up to the captured EVP. She started the audio loop and watched Mandy's expression. At first, Mandy thought Jonni was joking with her, then her expression turned fearful. "Jonni, are you kidding me?"

"I promise, Mandy," Jonni replied. "This is no joke."

"Aren't you even a little frightened?" asked Mandy. "I mean, that voice gives me the creeps!"

"Actually, it makes me angry at how much grief these things cause," Jonni answered. "But it also makes me curious."

"Curious?"

"Yes," Jonni said. "I believe that voice was talking to me, and it told me to leave him alone. Since there is no *him* in my life at the moment, I'm a little curious."

"You sure it wasn't talking about the husband at this home?" said Mandy.

"No, I don't think so."

"Any wine left?" asked Mandy.

"Yes, in the kitchen."

"Maybe it was talking about Greg," Mandy said while walking the few steps to the tiny kitchen. "You know, encouraging you to not go back to him."

"To Greg?"

"Yes."

"No problem there," Jonni said with a laugh. "I don't need any help with that!"

Mandy came back with a glass of wine in one hand and the bottle in the other. She kicked the loafers off her feet and sat near Jonni on the sofa. "I honestly don't know how you do this," she told Jonni. "I would be so scared I would never sleep again."

"There's nothing to be frightened of," Jonni insisted. "I have the power of the Lord guiding me every step of the way."

"It's still scary!" Mandy said.

Jonni nodded before storing the audio file in a separate folder to add to her website once it was online. It had been a long day. She was exhausted. A few minutes later she stood from the sofa while Mandy organized her homework for the next day's classes. "I'm going to bed now," Jonni said while heading to her bedroom. "I hope you sleep well, Mandy."

"Goodnight, honey," Mandy said while starting on her homework.

After finishing her homework, Mandy organized her papers and downed the last sip of wine from her glass. She glanced in the direction of Jonni's laptop, still opened to the audio program that played the EVP earlier. She stared at the colored graph of the audio signals. She could almost make out the shape of a figure in the graph. She leaned closer to get a better look. She couldn't see any figure but she had an overwhelming urge to play the recording on the laptop. She reached for the laptop, wondering which button to push to start the playback when she seemed to break her trance-like state. She pulled her hand away like it had been burned. She marveled at the sensation of tingles on her arms. She felt cold and hugged herself.

Mandy reached over quickly and shut the laptop, frowning at her own silliness when it came to scary things like the voice on Jonni's recording. *I just let things get in my head, that's all. I'm not really that big of a baby,* she told herself while walking to her own bedroom. *I just have an overactive imagination, that's all.*

Mandy turned on a small TV she kept near her bed and turned it to a *Friends* rerun on a local channel. Funny and lighthearted. As she drifted off to sleep she never heard the sound from the living room of Jonni's laptop playing the EVP audio loop. "Leave him alone, you tramp!" the voice said over and over and over . . .

8

*B*ash powered down the new sound system in the rehearsal room. The Avid console had operated flawlessly. The system software enabled him to program mixes, allowing him the freedom to concentrate on cues and other issues during the shows. This was not new technology but it was new to him. He couldn't wait to use the entire system at the gig next week. He nurtured this optimism because if he let go of it for just a second he could easily fall into depression. Deep inside, the fulfillment that came with the artistic release of creating music and playing guitar dwarfed any excitement he could conjure up while mixing sound for other musicians, on state-of-the-art gear or not. But such was his life these days—playing games with his own mind to keep his sanity.

Bash studied the rehearsal room. The Adamson speaker array was too much for the room but Bash had gotten goosebumps when he ran an 80 Hz test tone through the subwoofers earlier in the day. He'd backed off when it felt like Rock Bottom might rattle apart from the vibration.

Bash wiped some sweat from his brow. It was getting hot in the rehearsal room. The air conditioning seemed to be working but the old house was poorly insulated. *And it's still April,* Bash thought. Rehearsals would probably be very unpopular in the heat of the day once July rolled around.

The band had four days off so Gordon and Timothy left town to meet with some promotion team in Dallas. Trent and Vince were who-knows-where, probably hanging out with some girls somewhere in town, leaving Bash and Billy alone at Rock Bottom. Bash used the time to study the Avid manual and various websites on the subject but he spent most of his time behind the console, running and storing programs while going through an entire pack of Juicy Fruit chewing gum. He had done just about all he could do until the Zeniths played their instruments through the system. He felt prepared for their arrival and the rehearsals starting in two days, but he was still restless.

Wanting to keep focused and not let his mind wander, Bash straightened up the gear in the rehearsal room including rearranging the endless coils of cables so he could walk around the room without constantly stepping on them. He trashed a dozen empty beer and soda cans from the last rehearsal, noticing that the ban on alcohol for Trent's sake had only been temporary. Nowadays everyone seemed to be drinking more. And it didn't stop with drinking. Joints were getting fired up all the time in the rehearsals. Bash collected all the roaches and put them in one ashtray on top of Billy's bass amp. Some of the guys were becoming a little too regular with the nose candy, too, especially before and after the shows. It was starting to become one big party backstage at the clubs and festival-style gigs they were playing. Bash participated sometimes by having a beer or taking a couple of hits of reefer occasionally but that was only after he'd finished his work and never during the shows. He had enough issues to deal with while being a one-armed ex-guitarist on the brink of severe depression. He didn't need to add substance abuse to that list.

As Bash cleaned the rehearsal room he found a stack of three cardboard boxes that came with the storage auction. He peered into the top box and saw ledgers and other office supplies. Bash heard a knock on the front door before Ricky entered.

"What's up, Boo-Boo?"

"Not much, Yogi," Bash replied. "What are you doing way out here in Rock Bottomland?"

"I just dropped by to see if you wanted to go hang out in town," Ricky said. "I knew you were out here by yourself. I called but you never answered."

"Sorry," Bash said. "I've been busy. I still have a lot to do before rehearsals start."

Ricky nodded. "Did you find a mirror ball in any of this stuff?"

"You seriously want one of them, don't you?" Bash said while awkwardly trying to move the box of office supplies from the top of the stack using his one arm.

Ricky approached to lend a hand. "Yeah," he said while lifting the box from the stack and setting it on the floor. "When you hit them with a laser light it's truly awesome."

Bash looked in the next box and saw more office materials like rulers, paperweights, and boxes of unsharpened pencils. "A mirror ball," he said while searching through the box. "At least now I know what to get you for your birthday."

"My birthday was last month," Ricky said.

"I know," Bash said with a smile. "It'll take at least eleven months to save up the money to get you one for your next birthday."

"You are so awesome!" Ricky said sarcastically. "I'll remind you as we get closer!"

"Would you give me a hand hauling these boxes upstairs?" Bash asked. "I'm trying to clean up some of the mess down here."

Ricky grabbed the two heavier boxes while Bash carried the lighter one with his arm clenching it against his hip. Once they got upstairs Ricky followed Bash into his bedroom.

"Just set them on the floor," Bash said. "I'll sort through them later."

Ricky set his boxes on the floor, intentionally not stacking them to make it easier for Bash to search through them. "You sure you can't break away to go into town?" he asked. "I thought we could grab dinner together. I'm buying."

"Thanks," Bash said, "but I need to finish reading the Avid manual. If you would've called first I would've saved you the trip out here."

"I did call but you didn't answer, remember? Thought you might have croaked or something. Don't you check your messages?"

"Sorry. I don't get too many calls these days."

"No worries," Ricky said with a disappointed smile. "We'll get together some other time."

"Sounds good."

"Well, I'm going to clear out of here. Call me when you have the time," Ricky said in a mock rejected voice. "Maybe you will love me again someday."

"Okay, I will," Bash replied with a grin.

Bash wanted to finish reading the sound console's manual but the truth of the matter was he was trying to avoid spending too much one-on-one time with Ricky. Ricky was starting to preach to him all the time about the excess of booze and drugs and women at Rock Bottom, saying it was just a matter of time before everybody would end up in jail. Or the morgue. It was starting to annoy Bash. They were good friends but Ricky's constant warnings were getting on Bash's nerves.

Bash used his foot to scoot one of the boxes toward the mattress on the floor. He felt very lucky to have a friend like Ricky. It was Ricky who had supported him after the accident during his post-hospital depression. Ricky was also responsible for getting him the gig with the Zeniths. Ricky was his best friend. He just wished that Ricky would lay off his rant about all the *sinning* going on at Rock Bottom and the gigs.

Bash removed a ledger from the box and thumbed through it. The ledger was full of blank pages. He examined more ledgers from the box. Only one of them had any numbers written inside and that only covered about half of a page. After sorting through the second box he found nothing of interest, just desk items like a desk blotter, a pen set, a stapler, a letter opener, and several containers full of paperclips.

Bash used the letter opener to open the last box which was sealed with packing tape. He removed some objects wrapped in old newspaper. The first one was a stone carving about the size of a large egg, shaped into a fat figure with a monstrous head. The twisted expression on its face was sort of comical. The comical facial expression didn't make Bash want to laugh, though. Something about the figurine was just plain grotesque. He recalled seeing photos of similar figures in schoolbooks when he was still in school, figures representing the gods of the Aztec and Maya. He unwrapped two more figurines that looked slightly different but with the same maniacal expressions on their faces.

Bash began unwrapping the last object in the box which turned out to be quite different from the others. About a foot tall and carved out of some type of polished stone was the figure of a naked woman with jeweled eyes. A seductive smile was carved into the face. She also had talons for feet, just like a bird. Hanging wings protruded from the back of the figurine. The piece was expertly carved, lacking any signs of wear, like it had been made recently yet for some reason Bash believed it was old. *Very old.*

Bash set the figurine on the floor next to his mattress and stared at it. Despite the bird talons it was powerfully erotic and captivating. *I hope one day a lady will walk into my life and love me despite my missing arm . . .*

even if she has bird feet. With a smile from that thought Bash lowered his head onto the mattress and stared at the ceiling.

A few moments later Bash felt a wave of despair descend onto him. He couldn't divert his mind with thoughts of mixing consoles or software programs like he had somehow managed to do with his recent attacks of self-pity and depression. Fresh tears rolled slowly down his cheeks. He missed his mother. He missed his father. He missed his younger brother, Terry. He missed the life he had before the accident. *That stupid accident. How will I ever get used to this?*

After calming the panic trying to rise within him by counting backward from ninety-nine, Bash started to fall asleep. Within a few minutes he dozed off.

An hour later he stood in front of the mirror above the upstairs bathroom sink. He stared at his reflection in the mirror. The dream had felt so real. He'd had vivid dreams before but this one was different—so clear it was easy to accept as not being a dream at all but some type of separate reality reached through his dreaming. Long ago he'd read of such things regarding certain practices of American Indian medicine men. When dreaming, they supposedly had the ability to travel to other worlds or dimensions. Bash never really believed it but now he felt there might be something to it.

Actually, there wasn't much to the dream. In the dream he was standing in a stone-walled room with the floor covered in colorful rugs and pillows. A beautiful woman with long black hair wearing a leopard-skin robe entered from nowhere. She looked like a Mayan queen, or at least what he envisioned a Mayan queen would look like. She began lighting torches on one side of the room, all the while giving him curious looks as if she had expected him to be there but was now checking him out for the first time. She said nothing but gave him a look that made his heart pound. Then he awoke.

Bash finished washing his face and went downstairs to the kitchen. He heated some leftover rice and vegetables in the microwave and ate at the Formica kitchen table while studying the Avid manual. When finished eating he washed the bowl in the sink—a process which involved trapping the bowl against the side of the sink with his thumb while wiping the inside with a sponge clenched between his index and middle fingers.

Bash went into the rehearsal room and powered up the sound system. He loaded Donald Fagan's *Nightfly* CD into the console. The recording quality of the CD was superb despite the fact that it was around thirty years old. Bash played the first track, *I.G.Y.*, increasing the volume to a loud but reasonable level while trimming the equalization between the lows, mids, and highs.

When the song ended he suddenly heard a sound from upstairs. Not a big sound, but like something falling on the hardwood floor with a thud. He paused the CD and listened for a few moments, wondering if the thud had been caused by something falling off a shelf from one of the bedrooms, the result of the vibrations from the big speakers. He heard nothing else so he started the CD again.

Billy entered Rock Bottom through the front door. He sauntered into the rehearsal room and smiled at Bash as the music blared out the big speakers. Billy found the ashtray on his bass amp and dug out the longest of the marijuana roaches. He joined Bash behind the console while lighting the roach with a disposable lighter. While the song *New Frontier* played, Billy took a big draw off the roach and offered it to Bash. Bash shook his head while still playing with the console's EQ controls.

The song ended and Bash stopped the CD. "What's happening, Billy?"

"Not much, dude. Man, that sounds great!"

"It's a great CD."

"Yeah, but through these speakers," Billy said, taking another hit from the dwindling roach in his fingers, "it sounds so huge!"

"You feel like playing your bass for a few minutes?" asked Bash.

"Sure."

Billy grabbed his Rickenbacker bass guitar and turned on his bass amplifier. Bash connected a cable from the direct-out of Billy's bass amp, through a DI, then to the Avid console, combining the sound of Billy's bass speaker cabinet with the Adamson speaker arrays and subwoofers. Billy smiled from the low rich tones thundering through the house while playing the bass lines from the Beatles' *With A Little Help From My Friends*.

After a half hour of working with Billy's bass they decided to take a break and grab some refreshment in the kitchen. Billy grabbed a beer from the fridge and joined Bash at the kitchen table. "You want to do something tonight?"

"Sure," said Bash, sipping on a flavored water. "Whatcha have in mind?"

"I don't know. Maybe go see a movie?"

"At a theater?"

"Yeah, where else?" Billy said. "Big screen. Big sound."

Bash thought for a moment before saying, "We could bring Trent's Blu-ray and big flatscreen downstairs, then hook the audio outs to the Avid. Make our own theater."

"That would be awesome!" Billy exclaimed. "It'll sound like a movie theater!"

"Bigger than a theater," Bash said with a smile. "Let's go raid his bedroom."

They went upstairs to Trent's bedroom where Trent had a padlock on a hinged latch mounted on the door and doorframe. "Bummer," Billy said. "When did he put this on?"

"Doesn't matter," Bash replied while pulling a Phillips screwdriver from his back pocket. "He needs some lessons in basic security, though."

Billy laughed as he watched Bash unscrew the entire latch from the door and frame. The screws weren't even screwed in all the way. "That's Trent."

Bash removed the latch and opened the door. Trent had quite the bachelor pad: satin sheet covered mattress, 60-inch flatscreen, even a small cabinet with assorted wines and liquors arranged neatly on shelves next to rows of DVD and Blu-ray movies.

Billy began searching through the movies. "I wonder where he keeps the good stuff?"

"Good stuff?"

"You know, the triple X," Billy explained.

"Don't know or care," Bash said. "But if you find any I'm definitely not planning on watching any of them . . . at least not with you, I mean."

Billy blushed with an embarrassed smile. "I didn't m-mean that," he stammered. "I was just curious, that's all."

Bash hid a smile while pulling several Blu-rays from the shelf. "What do you think? *Star Trek Into Darkness* or *The Martian*."

"He's got *The Martian?*" Billy said while grabbing the Blu-ray box from Bash's hand and examining it. "Awesome!"

"Okay," Bash said. "Let's get the flatscreen downstairs then we'll come back up for the player and discs. He started removing the HDMI cable from the back of the flatscreen. "Unplug the power cord, will ya?"

The big flatscreen wasn't all that heavy to carry but it was awkward when one of the two carriers had just one arm. Billy led them down the steep steps while Bash positioned his body a bit sideways to provide balance and support from above. As they went downstairs one step at a time there was one precarious moment when they almost lost their balance. "Dropping this would be bad," Billy said as they descended the old staircase. "Real bad."

"Just watch your footing," Bash reminded him. "One step at a time."

They reached the bottom of the stairs and carried the flatscreen into the rehearsal room before setting it on top of a large road case on wheels. They went back upstairs to grab the rest of the items. "What if he comes back early?" Billy asked.

"You'll have to take the blame," Bash said while ascending the stairs. "Otherwise I could get fired."

Billy nodded his head reluctantly as he followed Bash back to Trent's bedroom. Billy grabbed the Blu-ray player and the HDMI and power cables. Bash handed him the two Blu-ray discs they planned on watching. A mild headache had been brewing in Bash's temples the last hour so he stopped by his bedroom where he kept a bottle of Ibuprofen in his chest-of-drawers. He held the bottle in his hand but decided not to medicate himself this time. *The headache is not really that bad,* he told himself. He had received a mild concussion from his motorcycle accident, but now he was starting to realize that he was using the accident as an excuse, especially for his drinking and pot smoking.

Bash put the bottle back in his chest-of-drawers and started to leave his bedroom. That's when he noticed the female figurine with the bird feet lying on the floor. He knew he had left it standing, but there it was, tumbled over on its side. He squatted and set it back upright. He suddenly remembered the noise he had heard earlier when playing the CD downstairs. *Strange,* he thought. The little statue was heavy and well balanced. He stomped on the wood floor next to it to see if it wobbled. It did not.

After returning downstairs and hooking up the necessary cables, they rolled the road case with the flatscreen in front of the small sofa in the rehearsal room. A quick test of everything proved it all worked good. The sound was huge. The lows vibrated Rock Bottom's entire structure.

Before they started watching *The Martian*, Billy fired up a joint and offered it to Bash. Bash refused Billy's offer. He was tired of the mind-numbing effect of the drug. He also wasn't sure that it even helped with the headaches. *Maybe it's causing them.*

Billy took several puffs from the joint before heading into the kitchen to microwave two bags of buttered popcorn. When he returned they started the movie and had a great time, laughing and making silly comments while munching the popcorn. The hours went by. Bash really enjoyed himself, having forgotten all about the headache, realizing the marijuana and Ibuprofen weren't necessary after all.

After watching *The Martian* movie, they started *Star Trek Into Darkness*. When the movie finally ended, Bash was ready to call it a night. Billy agreed with a wide yawn as Bash powered down the sound system and headed to his bedroom, peeling off his tee shirt and removing his jeans before collapsing on his mattress. The female figurine had toppled over again. Bash shook his head and stood it upright before switching off the lamp next to the mattress. He drifted off to sleep quickly.

She stared at him with that same seductive smile, approaching him wordlessly, moving close enough for him to smell a fragrance both foreign and familiar to him. He could now see that her leopard-skin robe was opened, revealing her smooth brown skin beneath. Keeping her eyes locked onto his, she placed her arms on his shoulders while running her fingers through his hair. He suddenly felt self-conscious about his missing arm, but then he found himself placing both his arms around her waist. She moved her lips toward his then stopped suddenly. She took his hand and started leading him to a dark corner of the room. As they neared, the darkness lifted and he saw a pallet of multicolored pillows made of bird feathers and various animal hides. She let go of his hand and stepped gracefully into the pillows, dropping her robe in one move before reclining and beckoning him with her eyes. Bash could feel his heart thumping in his chest. He started to lower himself to the pillows to embrace her when he suddenly saw something in the corner of his eye. When he turned to look, he saw his father, mother, and brother sitting in chairs against the wall. They stared back at him with unconcerned expressions on their faces as if they were simply waiting in a doctor's reception area for their names to be called. Bash looked back to the naked woman reclining on the pillows. He suddenly heard her voice although her lips didn't move: "What are you waiting for?"

He looked back to his family. His brother, Terry, stared at him. Terry raised his eyebrows with a look that said, "Well? What are you waiting for?"

Bash felt nauseous. He wanted to escape but he didn't know how to get out of the room. Terry suddenly stood from his chair, getting approving smiles from their father and mother. Terry approached the woman and lowered himself on the pillows next to her. She smiled at Bash while beginning to embrace Terry. Bash began wandering frantically through the darkness to find an exit but ended up back at the pallet of pillows. Now he saw that Terry and the woman were embracing fully. His parents looked on with bored looks on their faces. "NO!!!" Bash screamed, although no sound came from his mouth. Suddenly, the room began to change. He saw Terry lying on a dirt floor, moaning and squirming in pain. Bash started floating above the scene, rising higher and higher until passing through the ceiling. He noticed he was ascending from an old wooden shack in a rural area. He kept rising higher and higher, like the motion in a Google Earth map simulation. He saw the land surrounding the wooden shack getting smaller and smaller, then the continent, until he was above the Earth. Suddenly his motion reversed in an incredible burst of speed, bringing him all the way back into the wooden shack where Terry was now in even greater agony. Something was wrong. Bash had the sense that Terry was dying. He screamed out to his brother but no sound came out of his mouth. The scene faded and he was back in the room with the woman. The woman extended an arm toward Bash. She turned and looked at him and said: "Won't you join us?" Bash stared back for a second before seeing his parents stand from their chairs. They began removing their clothes. "PLEASE!!!" Bash heard himself scream. "NO!!!"

The scream brought him out of the nightmare. The sun was high in the sky out his bedroom window. He was glad to be awake. The bad dream seemed foggy and disjointed to him. He didn't remember many details and didn't want to either. All he remembered was something about Terry. Something bad. Something was wrong with his brother. He could sense it. He had to call and find out. He needed to find his Uncle Walid's phone number. *Is it stored in my laptop? Did I transfer the contact information from files on my previous computer?*

Bash jumped to his feet and quickly pulled on his jeans, his hand alternating from side to side while yanking and wiggling to get them pulled up his legs. He hurried downstairs to the rehearsal room and grabbed his laptop, almost dropping it as he went into the kitchen, still not used to doing everything with his left hand.

Bash powered on the laptop. While waiting for it to boot he poured himself some orange juice from the fridge. After a few minutes he found the phone number. He called the number on his cell phone and waited, wondering if Uncle Wally's number was still good. It had been a while since he'd last called. *Over five years ago,* he reminded himself.

Bash heard the ringing over his cell phone. Once. Twice. Three times. It continued to ring without an answer. He let it continue for several more rings, hoping to hear an answering machine or voicemail pick up the call. He ended the call and stared off into the distance, realizing how difficult it might be to find his brother. He dialed the number again and listened to the ringing. This time someone answered on the third ring. A woman's voice. "Alo?"

"Hello," Bash said, surprised that the phone was answered. "Uh . . ." he struggled to remember the few Arabic phrases he once knew. "Ezayko . . . uh . . . min fa Dlak. Kayfa Haaluka?

The woman giggled. "Hopefully you speak English," she said.

"I do," Bash replied eagerly. "Who am I speaking with?"

"This is Shadya. And who is this?"

Shadya. Didn't Walid have a young daughter with a name like that? "This is Bashshar Nadir, calling from Texas."

"Could this be our long lost cousin?" Shadya asked. "The musician who never calls or visits?"

"Little Shadya?" asked Bash.

"Yes, but I'm not so little anymore."

"You sound all grown up."

"That is because I am all grown up," she said with another giggle.

"Yes, I guess it's been a while since I've talked to you."

"Yes, it has," she said. "I suppose you want to talk to Tarik?"

"Yes. Is he there?"

"No."

"Is he okay?"

"Yes. He should be back later today."

"He goes to school?" Bash asked.

"No, he has a job," Shadya said.

"Doing what?"

"Performing with a band."

"Really?" Bash said. "What instrument does he play?"

"The bass guitar," she said. "He sings, too."

Still singing and playing the bass. Good for him. "Has he been sick lately?" asked Bash.

"No, not that I know of."

"Has he been in some type of trouble?"

"Tarik is usually in some kind of trouble," Shadya said, her smile coming through the phone, "especially with Father. But he is strong and healthy and seems very happy. Or at least he was when I saw him this morning before he left the farm."

"The farm," Bash said. "Is that what your father calls it?"

"Yes," she said. "What else would he call it?"

"I thought Walid ran some type of terrorist training camp or something."

Shadya giggled. "No, silly. It's a farm where you grow things. And you should not say things like that over the phone."

"Why? Is Homeland Security bugging your phones?"

"You are trouble," Shadya said with a laugh. "Tarik is similar."

"Well, we are cut from the same cloth."

"Yes, you are."

An awkward moment of silence followed before Shadya asked, "Are you a rockstar yet, Bashshar?"

"No," Bash said with a nervous laugh.

"Not yet, you mean?"

"Right," Bash said. "Not yet." He quickly changed the subject. "So what do you do on the farm, Shadya?"

"Most of the cooking and cleaning, unfortunately."

"Any boyfriend? Or boyfriends?"

Shadya giggled. "Not really."

Bash heard voices in the room with her. Male voices.

"Please call back then," Shadya said in a completely different tone of voice, suddenly anxious to end the call.

"Did Walid just enter the room?"

"Yes," she said. "Call back later."

"Okay, Shadya. I'll call back."

"Call precisely at six-thirty," she whispered. "I will be here by the phone to answer. If Father answers it might not be good."

"I'm that popular, huh?"

A small giggle. "It is just the way he is."

"I understand. Talk to you at six-thirty."

"Okay, goodbye."

"Goodbye, Shadya."

Bash ended the call, feeling relieved that Terry was okay, but wondering why Walid's unforgiveness toward him had not softened over the years. *Why does he hang on to his bad feelings toward me?* Bash asked himself. *Probably because I told him I didn't need him or his God.* Bash still remembered the silence that had followed that conversation before Uncle Wally hung up, ending the phone call without even saying goodbye. *But I was young. And had just lost both my parents. How could he be so cruel and insensitive?*

Bash did the kindergarten math for the time difference between Texas and Oregon. *I'll make the call at eight-thirty tonight,* he told himself, planning on setting an alarm on his cell phone for a reminder.

Billy suddenly ran into the kitchen. He was out of breath. "He's coming!" he shouted "Hurry! He'll be here any moment!"

"Who's coming?"

"Trent!" Billy said, practically hyperventilating. "He called me a little while ago! He can't find his house keys so he wanted to find out if anyone was here to let him in! I forgot about his TV being downstairs until just now!"

"When's he gonna get here?" Bash asked.

"He was on his way when he called!" Billy said while looking at his wristwatch. "Any time now!"

"Uh-oh!" Bash said while jumping up from the table and running into the rehearsal room where Trent's flatscreen and Blu-ray player sat on the road case.

Bash and Billy scrambled to get everything put back into Trent's bedroom, almost losing control of the flatscreen midway up the staircase. After replacing the flatscreen in Trent's bedroom, Billy sprinted back downstairs to get the player and discs while Bash removed the HDMI cable from around his neck and plugged it into the rear of the flatscreen. He was plugging in the flatscreen's power cord when Billy came storming into Trent's bedroom with the player and discs. "He's here!" Billy whispered loudly, unable to contain his panic.

"Where?"

"A car is dropping him off in front of the house," Billy said while replacing the Blu-ray boxes on the shelf. They hurried out of Trent's bedroom and shut the door. While Billy held the latch with its padlock still dangling from it, Bash screwed in the screws as fast as he could to secure the door. They heard Trent opening the front door in the foyer.

"Hurry!" Billy whispered.

"I'm going as fast as I can!" replied Bash.

They heard Trent's footsteps inside the house.

Once Bash had enough of the screws in and didn't need Billy to hold the latch in place, he whispered, "I got it! Get out of here!"

Billy ran into his own bedroom as Bash hurried to finish the last screw on the latch. He couldn't remember exactly how far it had been screwed into the door frame but time had run out. He heard Trent's footsteps on the stairs now.

Bash ducked around the corner of his bedroom just in time. He fell onto his mattress and acted like he was sleeping, giggling to himself like a small child that had been involved in something naughty. A few moments later he heard Trent working the combination padlock before hearing the door open and close. Trent was crashing. *Probably been up all night with some babe.*

Bash remained on his mattress. Images from the dream the night before tried to reappear. He dismissed them, choosing to think about his conversation with Shadya and his call later when he hoped to talk to Terry. *It's been too long since we talked. I can't wait!*

After going downstairs and running software programs on the Avid, Bash fixed a turkey sandwich for lunch before returning to work with the console for a few hours. A headache began brewing. *Maybe I should just lie down for a bit.*

Bash went back upstairs to his bedroom and collapsed on the mattress. He closed his eyes and recalled certain images from the dream. He remembered nothing in particular except for images of a hurt Terry and a beautiful woman dressed in a leopard-skin robe. He let go of the images and closed his eyes, planning on just resting a bit before returning downstairs to continue working on the Avid. He started to fall asleep. *Oh well,* he thought. *A short nap may help with the headache.* Soon, he was fast asleep.

†

Bash opened his eyes, wondering when this moment was taking place. The sky was dark outside his window. It came to him slowly. He had taken a nap after working on the Avid. He looked at his wristwatch and saw the time, remembering that he was supposed to do something. Then it came to him. *It's nine and I was supposed to call Shadya thirty minutes ago!*

He jumped off his mattress, searching frantically for his cell phone. *I must have left it downstairs!* He ran downstairs and found the cell phone where he'd left it in the rehearsal room earlier that afternoon. *I can't believe I slept so long!* Bash made the call and waited. The phone on the other end rang too many times. He was about to end the call when Shadya answered the phone.

"Shadya, it's me, Bash!"

"You are late," she said. "Hold on. He's here."

Bash heard voices in the distance over the line. A moment later he heard, "Bashshar!"

"Terry?"

"Bash! Is it really you?"

"Yes, Terry!" Bash said, overjoyed from hearing his brother's voice. "It's me!"

Terry laughed over the phone, the same laugh Bash remembered but more masculine and grown up. "I can't believe it!" Terry said. "How are you?"

"Good! And you?"

"I'm still alive and well."

"*Still Alive And Well,*" Bash sang, an old melody Terry would remember.

Terry hesitated before saying, "Oh, yes! The old Johnny Winter song we used to play! *Still Alive And Well!*"

Bash laughed. "Yes. You on bass and me on drums."

"That's right!" Terry said. "I will never forget!"

"We had fun," Bash said, "didn't we?"

"Yes," Terry said. "I always said you should *stick* with the drums. Get it?"

"Stick. Drums. I see your humor hasn't changed."

"You were actually very good on drums," Terry said. "By the way, how is your guitar playing going? I bet you are incredible now!"

Bash had been so concerned about Terry when he made the call that he had not thought about the obvious questions Terry would ask. "Ah, I don't know about that."

"My brother, Bashshar," Terry said. "Still the modest one."

"How about you, Terry?" Bash asked, hoping to change the subject about his guitar playing. "Are you still playing the bass?"

"Yes," Terry said. "I play with a local band. We mainly play parties and weddings for local Arabs. Sometimes we play at the nicer hotels around Portland. You haven't heard anything until you hear *Play That Funky Music White Boy* sung in Arabic!"

Bash laughed loudly. "That's great, Terry! I'm so happy you are still playing! And making money with it!"

"Well," Terry said. "It's not much money but it helps."

"That's great, Terry."

After a long pause, Terry said, "I had a dream about you, Bashshar."

Bash had nearly forgotten about his own dream involving Terry, the motivation for the long overdue call. "When? Last night?"

"Over a year ago," Terry said. "A nightmare. I dreamed that you were killed on a motorcycle. Obviously, it was just a dream."

"Yeah, obviously."

"I remember long ago when you wanted a motorcycle and Father wouldn't let you have one. That must have sparked the dream. You don't have a motorcycle, do you?"

"No."

"Good," Terry said. "Like I said, it was just a dream. But for a while, I wondered if you were dead."

Bash didn't know what to say.

After another awkward pause Terry said, "Why have you waited all this time to call, Bashshar? I've missed you so much."

Terry's words cut Bash to the bone. He felt a heat swelling in his chest and his eyes began to tear. "I missed you, too, Terry," he said, his voice cracking a little. "And actually, I did call. Several times."

"When?"

"The year after you moved. I left my phone number with Walid but I never heard back."

"He never gave it to me," Terry said. "He never even told me you called."

"Of course he didn't," Bash said. "I knew he wouldn't tell you. So I should've been more persistent. I'm so sorry, Terry." Tears were now flowing down Bash's cheeks.

Terry exhaled loudly. "It's okay, brother. I don't know why I just let it go. I should have been more persistent with Walid."

Bash wiped his eyes, trying to stabilize his voice. "I don't know if that would have done any good," Bash said with a forced laugh, "with Uncle Wally being the way he is."

"That's funny," Terry said. "Uncle Wally. I forgot about us calling him that name!"

"Is he there now?"

"He's in his office, I think."

"Does he know you are talking to me?"

"No," Terry said without hesitation. "But it doesn't matter. He's ignoring me these days as if I do not exist."

"Why?" asked Bash.

"It's a long story," Terry said. "But it has to do with who I choose as friends."

"Ah," Bash said. "That doesn't surprise me."

"But my stay here is only temporary," Terry explained. "My friend, Khalid, has invited me to move in with him and his brother, Ishaq. They share a flat in Portland."

"Sounds like you have lots of friends," Bash said. "I'm glad for that. I have so many questions to ask you."

Terry said something away from the phone. Bash heard other male voices speaking Arabic. Terry came back on the line. "I have just a few more minutes," he said. "Someone needs to use the phone."

"Terry . . ." Bash said, trying to find the right words. "We need to stay in touch."

"Yes," Terry replied. "I had my own cell phone but I got behind on the service payments. But I'm getting a new one soon."

"Okay," Bash said. "You have something to write with?"

"One second." A moment later. "Okay. Go."

Bash gave Terry his cell phone number. "I really want to see you, Terry," he added. "I don't know when it will be possible for me to afford a trip up there, though."

"I know. I would like to come see you but I am in the same situation with finances. But one day . . ."

"One day," repeated Bash.

"Hey!" Terry said, just realizing something. "Khalid has a computer at his flat. He has a program called Skype. Have you heard of it?"

Bash knew all about Skype but hadn't had a reason to use it until now. "Skype is free," he said. "We could use it today. Do you have a laptop, Terry?"

"I did but it got stolen from my backpack," Terry replied. "Shadya has one but there is no internet available for us here at the farm. Walid has something in his office but he doesn't share it with us."

"Of course he doesn't."

"But I will ask Khalid the next time I'm at his apartment if I can use his computer."

"Okay," Bash said, not wanting to end the call yet.

"I must go now," Terry said. "I will talk to you soon, though. I am so happy you are back in my life!"

"Me, too, little brother. Me, too."

"Goodbye."

"Bye."

Bash sat there in the kitchen with the cell phone still held to his ear. He felt a peace he had not felt in eons. He heard someone coming into the kitchen. He set his cell phone on the table and quickly wiped his eyes.

Trent rounded the corner into the kitchen and saw Bash at the table. "Hey dude," he said while heading to the fridge.

"You just wake up?" asked Bash.

"Yeah," Trent said while pouring some V8 juice into a small glass. "I got here earlier today. I needed to get back to get some rest. This Jennifer chick is wearing me out."

"That bad, huh?"

"You wouldn't believe it," Trent said while heading back out of the kitchen. He stopped at the doorway. "Hey, nobody's been in my room, have they?"

Bash was surprised. He thought fast. "You have a lock on it, don't you?"

"Yeah," Trent said with a confused look on his weary face. "It's just that I went to put a disc into my Blu-ray player and a movie was already in. *Star Trek Into Darkness*."

"Yeah?"

"Yeah and I can't remember ever watching it," Trent said. "Weird, huh?"

"Yeah, weird."

"I tell you, man, there's some strange stuff going on upstairs."

"Like what?"

"Just some weird sounds and stuff. Sometimes I have creepy dreams, too."

This hit a chord with Bash but he didn't say anything.

"Anyway," Trent said as he started to leave, "I just thought I would ask. I guess I'm the only one going crazy here."

Bash watched Trent leave the kitchen. He felt guilty for not being honest with the guitarist. *But what would I have told him? That we broke into his room and took his flatscreen and Blu-ray player without asking permission?*

Several minutes later Billy entered the kitchen. "I'm heading to the store for some beer. Want anything?"

"Nah, I'm good."

As Billy left Rock Bottom to drive to a convenience store an inconvenient distance away in the band's Ford van, Bash went back upstairs to his bedroom. He grabbed some fresh clothes to put on after a shower. He saw the female figurine with the bird feet on its side again. He ignored it this time as he headed to the shower at the end of the hall.

As he showered, he thought about the conversation with his little brother. *Why have I waited so long to contact him?* He couldn't come up with an excuse. There was no reason other than him being so self-centered that he put his own depression in front of the love he had for his brother. But that was the past. Terry was now back in his life.

Nothing is going to bother me tonight. Not any headache. Not Ricky. Not any member of the Zeniths. Not some statue of a woman with bird feet that keeps falling over for no reason. The only thing that mattered now was Terry, and how soon they could be together again in person . . .

9

The relentless Texas sun bore down on Rock Bottom. The hot temperature had already reached the mid-nineties, not that uncommon for the middle of May in central Texas. The air conditioner was working hard but the rehearsal room was still sweltering hot.

The Zeniths were rocking hard despite the heat, blasting out tune after tune as their giant drummer, Vince Crowley, attacked the drums with flair and precision. Bash had to admit the guy was an awesome player although a jerk most of the time. Actually, everyone had been uptight and moody over the last few weeks. Of course, the drugs and booze weren't helping matters much. Bash had noticed a big change with the Zeniths' leader, Gordon, who seemed angry and depressed much of the time, complaining that his playing was deteriorating instead of improving as it should.

The Zeniths ended the song. "Let's break," Gordon said over his microphone. "I need an attitude adjustment."

"Amen to that," Billy said, eager to take a few tokes or whatever else would be offered by Gordon.

As Trent and Billy joined Gordon in the kitchen to *adjust their attitudes*, Vince made some mechanical adjustments on his cymbal stands. He looked toward Bash and said, "I still need more bass in my wedge."

"You got it," Bash said before making the adjustment on the console.

"I like to get what I ask for the first time I ask for it," Vince added.

Bash raised his eyebrows and stared back at the big drummer. "I gave you more bass," he said, "although I didn't know how much you wanted."

Vince's sweaty face darkened as he set his sticks down on his snare. "Well it's your job to know how much, right?"

"I'm not telepathic."

Vince locked eyes with Bash, his stare icy and cold. "No, you're just *monoplegic*," he said after thinking about his response, obviously already prepared to use the word on Bash when he got the chance.

Bash couldn't believe how fast this was going downhill. "Actually, a monoplegic refers to someone who has paralysis of a limb," he told Vince. "I'm an amputee. Now do you understand the difference?"

Vince's face revealed the rage building in him. "Yeah, I understand you are a punk!" He stood from his drums in a threatening way just as Gordon, Trent, and Billy returned from the kitchen with happy looks on their faces. By all the sniffing going on, Bash knew they had just snorted some cocaine. Billy was smoking a joint.

"Are we finished for the day?" Bash asked Gordon.

Gordon just shrugged. "Maybe. Why?"

"I'm expecting a phone call," Bash said. "I don't want to miss it."

"I'll let you know," Gordon said dismissively while walking to the small sofa.

Bash went into the kitchen and grabbed a bottled water. He looked at his wristwatch, wondering when Terry would actually call. Bash and Terry had talked five or six times over the last few weeks, ever since Terry had moved into Khalid's apartment, but so far Terry had been unsuccessful at using Khalid's laptop for any Skype sessions. Every time they tried to plan a session Terry informed Bash that Khalid had either taken his laptop and left town for a trip or the internet service was out of order. It had become obvious to Bash that this Khalid person wasn't very eager to loan his laptop to Terry.

Despite no computer for Skype, Terry had still been able to talk on the phone with Bash at least every three or four days. Terry always talked about his Arab dance band and Walid's unrelenting behavior toward him, and Shadya, his younger cousin. He also told Bash more than once about a popular band in Portland he might get to audition for sometime soon. *At least Terry is out on his own now*, Bash thought. *Away from Uncle Wally and his seventh-century tyranny.*

While standing in front of the fridge and drinking his water, Bash thought about the dreams he'd been having regularly for the past three weeks. After each dream he recalled a few images but he still didn't remember many details, only that Terry and a woman wearing a leopard-skin robe were involved. He'd told Terry about having dreams of him but without revealing anything about the woman.

Bash's cell phone began to vibrate in his pocket. He was pleasantly surprised to see Khalid's home number on the display. "Terry! How's my baby bro today?"

"Very well. How are you? You rehearsing your band today?"

"Yes," Bash said while stepping outside through the kitchen door to the back of the property, "but we just took a break."

"Should I call back?" asked Terry. "I know I'm early."

"No, I'm glad you called," Bash said. "Perfect timing, actually."

"Good."

Bash had been trying to decide when he would confess to his brother about the motorcycle wreck that took his arm, the event that ended his musical aspirations. He had come close to telling Terry about the accident the last several times they talked but he never went through with it. He had told his brother about working with a band called the Zeniths, about them all living in an old house together, but he never told Terry that he was the soundman instead of the frontman guitarist Terry assumed he was.

"How are rehearsals going?" Terry asked.

Bash hesitated to answer. "Okay, I guess," he finally said.

"That doesn't sound very positive," Terry said. "What's up?"

"Ah, nothing really," Bash said. "It's just this drummer. He's a brute and I think he dislikes me, to put it mildly."

"So what?" Terry replied. "Fire him. You are the band leader, aren't you?"

"Uh, no. Actually, the keyboard player is the leader."

"Yes, well, this keyboard player surely knows how valuable you and your guitar are in the band," Terry said. "I can't believe he would risk losing you over this drummer. You need to be firm with everyone in the band, Bash."

Bash chuckled. "You sound like Uncle Wally."

"I'm serious, Bash. Don't let them walk all over you."

"Okay, Terry," Bash said with a smile. "I'll try."

"There's something else I want to tell you," said Terry.

"What?"

"I've been having dreams," Terry said, "about you and me and some woman."

"Really?"

"Yes," Terry said. "The woman is wearing a robe made from a spotted animal like a leopard or something."

Bash was stunned by Terry's description of the woman's robe. "What color of hair does she have, Terry?"

"Black," Terry said. "Why do you ask about her hair color?"

"Uh, just curious," Bash replied, realizing how lame that sounded as soon as he had said it. "Sorry, go on."

"Well," Terry resumed, "she is very beautiful but there's something wrong with her. Something very wrong."

"What's wrong with her?"

"I don't know," Terry said. He seemed to be struggling for the right description. "She seems . . . dangerous."

Dangerous was how Bash felt about the woman in his dreams. *A beautiful but dangerous black haired woman wearing a leopard-skin robe. We are dreaming about the same woman! How is that possible?*

Bash heard the kitchen door open. "Hold on," he told Terry.

Billy was standing there. "We're gonna jam a bit and we need a few tweaks in the monitors."

Bash nodded and went back to his call. "I gotta go, brother."

"Okay," Terry said. "Oh! I almost forgot. Khalid will be back in town in two days and he promises I can use his laptop for the Skype session."

"Great!" Bash said. "I'll call you then and we'll set it up."

Bash hustled into the rehearsal room after ending the call. The Zeniths were already jamming on an energetic, jazz-fusion chord progression. He jumped behind the console and started scanning their faces, looking for gestures indicating they needed changes in the monitor mix. No one gave him any gestures until he looked at Vince. The big drummer pointed his stick angrily at Billy, suggesting he needed less bass guitar. Bash decreased the bass signal to the drum wedges in 1/2 db increments until Vince nodded. Vince then pointed at Gordon with a stick, gesturing for Bash to turn up the keyboards. After changes were made to the keys and Trent's guitar level in Vince's mix, Vince started back with Billy's bass level again, eventually going over everyone's signal levels several times, sometimes reversing the changes he'd made earlier. At one point Vince became especially frustrated and faked a stick-throw toward Bash.

Bash played the game without showing any emotion. He could turn the knobs as much as Vince wanted and it wouldn't bother him. At least he was doing something instead of just sitting behind their old monitor console and keeping an eye on everybody. Besides, Bash's job with the Zeniths was mixing Front-Of-House sound, not stage monitors. Monitor levels were tweaked during soundchecks and if Vince needed something changed in his audio mix, Gordon would have to do it since the monitor console sat next to his keyboard rig onstage. Bash doubted that Vince would be making any angry faces or throwing sticks at Gordon, the band leader. But Bash made a promise to himself: *If he ever throws a stick at me I will take my one arm and throw the stick back so hard that he will be wearing it in his eyeball . . .*

10

*T*he image on Bash's laptop screen was slightly jerky but the color was excellent. Bash stared at the screen with a smile growing on his face. They were two thousand miles apart but here they were, face to face, for the first time in more than five years.

"Look at you!" Terry exclaimed. "You look the same!"

"You look older," Bash said with a laugh, making sure the laptop's camera centered on his face and not his upper body. "And more handsome."

"Well, I am older since you last saw me," Terry said, "but I don't know about the handsome part."

"I bet you are a big hit with the ladies," Bash said. "Look at that face. You should be a movie star."

Terry looked embarrassed. "And what roles would I portray?"

Bash stared at Terry's image on his laptop and rubbed his chin with his left hand, acting like he was deciding, "Well they make a lot of movies these days about terrorists. You could play the handsome terrorist bad guy."

Terry laughed and shook his head. "You are too much, Bashshar!"

Bash could hear faint music playing in the background. "Is that a radio I hear?"

"That is Khalid's cassette tape player," Terry said. "A real antique. He has quite the collection but probably nothing you have ever heard."

"No Van Halen?"

"No," Terry chuckled. "Mainly traditional Egyptian artists. People like Moustafa Al Amri. Khalid likes him a lot."

"Is Khalid there now?" Bash asked after seeing a figure walk past the background behind Terry.

"Yes," Terry said. "He's in his bedroom working on his English studies. I boast about you all the time to him and his younger brother, Ishaq. I've played them that cassette tape you made me long ago and I tell them you must be even better now. Now that we are using Skype, maybe you could play something live for us. What do you think?"

Bash stared back with a smile frozen on his face. He could just put it off and not explain or he could deal with it now. He didn't want any secrets between him and Terry now that they had established a relationship again. It would be easy enough to hide his armless sleeve but he needed to be truthful with his brother. "Terry," he began, trying to gain his courage. "There's something I need to tell you."

"Yes?"

"About a year and a half ago," Bash said, his voice calm and unwavering. "I had an accident."

A long pause.

"On a motorcycle," Bash added.

Terry blinked but said nothing.

"I didn't die like in your dream," Bash said while reaching behind his neck and grabbing the back of his tee shirt, "but for a long time I wished I had." Bash yanked the tee shirt over his head and sat back to give Terry a full view of what was left of his arm.

Terry stared with a blank expression on his face. "My God," he muttered under his breath.

"So you see, my brother," Bash went on, relieved that it was over, "my dreams of being a rock star, or even just a guitar player are long gone."

Terry's eyes became watery but he kept control of his reaction. "I wished I would have known," he said. "I would have found a way to come home and be with you."

Bash shook his head. "I didn't want anyone with me after the accident," he said. "I just wanted to die."

Another long pause.

"But God had other plans for you," Terry finally said, dabbing at his eyes with a finger.

Bash didn't comment as he placed the tee shirt over his head and wiggled his arm back up the sleeve.

"There's a reason God allowed you to live, Bashshar. You know that, don't you?"

"And what would that reason be, Terry?"

"You are a talented musician," Terry said in an insistent tone. "It is not just about the guitar. If you had picked up the saxophone I am sure you would have been great."

"You still need two hands to play the saxophone, Terry."

"I'm not talking about the saxophone. That was just an example. What I'm saying is, you are capable of doing so much in life, even if you don't know what that is right now."

Bash appreciated his brother's optimism but he didn't know what to say.

"Do you remember what everyone said when you first started playing the drums?" Terry asked.

Bash thought for a moment. "No, not really."

"Everyone thought you were incredible! That's all I ever heard!"

"I don't remember that," said Bash, "but what's your point?"

"My point is, you were immediately good on the drums," Terry explained. "I used to get on them when you were not at the house and try to play them but I was horrible. I didn't have the coordination. But you were awesome. Even Father thought so. We all thought you would become a great drummer until you decided you wanted to play guitar. And then you became good at that! Better than good! God gave you the talent to do all of it!"

"I still don't get what you're trying to say, Terry."

"I'm trying to say that you are very talented musically," Terry said. "You're not just talented on the guitar. Maybe you should think about taking up the drums again."

"Terry? Are you crazy? You need both arms for playing drums as much as you need them for playing guitar!"

"That's not true," Terry said. "Don't you remember the drummer from that rock band in the eighties? What was their name?" A few seconds later. "Def Leppard! Remember their drummer?"

Bash suddenly remembered. It was as if a magical bell tinkled in his head. "Yes," he said. "Rick Allen. He lost his arm in a car wreck." Bash hadn't thought of that in ages.

"Right," Terry said. "And he learned how to play using pedals or something."

Bash remembered that Allen had built a drum kit using pedals that allowed him to use his left foot for what he did before with his left arm. "You're right, Terry. I totally forgot."

"What I'm trying to say," Terry said, "is that your options in life are still open. It's up to you. Your greatest obstacle is not your missing arm. It is your attitude."

Bash smiled. He touched Terry's image on the laptop's monitor screen.

"So this band you told me about," Terry said. "Was all that made up?"

"No," Bash said in a firm voice. "I mix sound for them. My friend, Ricky Rhodes, encouraged me after the accident to work behind the sound console. He actually got me the job with them."

"Ah," Terry said with understanding. "And this drummer in the band . . ."

"Vince."

"Yes. Am I right that you have no real say whether this Vince goes or stays because you are not a band member?"

"It's not so much that I have no say," Bash explained. "It's just that he treats me differently than he treats them. They see a great drummer, which he is, but they don't see the other side of him."

"Not yet," said Terry. "But they will one day."

"Yeah, you are probably right."

"I am."

Bash changed the subject. "How are things between you and Uncle Wally?"

Terry hesitated before answering. "Not good. But then when have they ever been good?"

"What's happening?"

"He doesn't like my friends," Terry said. "Especially Khalid and Ishaq."

"Why?"

"He accuses them of being apostates."

"Accuses them of being what?"

"Apostates."

"What's an apostate?"

"Someone who has left Islam," Terry explained, "to convert to another faith. A faith like Christianity."

"Have they converted?"

Terry hesitated to answer. "They have hinted to me that they have." Another hesitation. "But they seem to be remaining very secretive about it. And for their own safety, I suppose they have a good reason."

"Terry," Bash said. "This is America. People can believe what they want to believe!"

"I know," Terry said, "but many in the world of Islam disagree. And you know how Walid is."

"Yes, I know how Walid is," Bash said angrily. He thought for a moment before asking, "Does he think you're an apostate, too?"

Terry shrugged his shoulders on the computer screen. "Who knows? Anyway, I don't care what he thinks anymore."

"Are you?"

"Am I what?"

"An apostate or whatever."

Truth was, Terry had confessed his dissatisfaction of Islam with Khalid and Ishaq many times, even admitting to them about his recent unexplainable interest in Jesus Christ, a subject Khalid seemed very interested in. Of course, all this remained a secret between the three of them. "Yes, maybe I am."

"Watch out for Walid, Terry," Bash warned.

"I'm not worried about him."

"Maybe you should be," Bash said. "I don't trust him."

"You sound like Khalid."

"What do you mean?"

"Khalid is always asking me about Walid's business dealings," Terry explained. "He wonders if Walid is involved in extreme Islamic activities and he wants to know what I know, which is nothing." Terry knew that was not entirely true but he hadn't mentioned to anyone about the conversation from Walid's office he'd accidentally overheard.

"Khalid could be right," Bash said. "Watch your back."

Now it was Terry's turn to change the subject. "I really hope I can see you one day in person, Bash. I miss you."

"I miss you, too, Terry. It will happen soon."

Terry looked at his wristwatch. "I hate to end this session, Bash," he said, "but I promised Khalid I would run some errands for him and I need to go now."

"Okay, let's talk soon," Bash said. "Call me anytime."

"I will."

"I love you, brother."

"I love you, too."

They ended the Skype session. Bash felt like a huge weight had been lifted from his shoulders after coming clean about his accident. He went downstairs and grabbed a bottled water from the fridge before walking out the kitchen door to the back of the house. There was an old bench-style picnic table sitting outside under the shade of a giant oak tree. He sat down and sipped the water, reviewing the entire conversation with Terry as he gazed at the countryside surrounding Rock Bottom. He thought about Walid trying to dominate Terry's life. He knew Walid had always been slightly nuts but he wondered if the man had become dangerous with his constant preoccupation with the whole jihad thing.

Bash finished his water while turning his thoughts to the Def Leppard drummer and the pedal system that allowed the drummer to play with only one arm. *I could do something similar,* he told himself. *Maybe a hybrid kit; part acoustic and part electronic.*

Bash went back inside through the kitchen and headed toward the rehearsal room where the Zeniths' band gear sat in silence. The Zeniths were in Dallas visiting a few radio stations and having meetings with some concert promoters. Bash was all alone in the house. He walked over to Vince's drum kit and sat down on the drum stool. He grabbed a stick and hit the high-hat, then the snare. His right foot stomped the kick drum pedal on the one and three count while hitting the snare on the two and four count with his left arm. It felt awkward using the left foot to stomp the eighths on the high-hat instead of using a stick with a right hand. His meter sounded awkward. Of course, he hadn't played drums in years, which probably accounted for most of the awkwardness.

Bash toyed with the drum kit for a few more minutes before going back upstairs to retrieve his laptop. He ended up back in the kitchen, heating up some leftover spaghetti in the microwave for dinner while surfing the web. He found a few YouTube videos showing Rick Allen of Def Leppard playing his specially designed drum kit.

Bash started drawing on a blank piece of paper. He sketched a simple design for a kit with an acoustic kick drum, real cymbals, several high-hats in various configurations (closed, partially opened, and opened), and pedals to trigger electronic toms and snares. *Maybe I should just start with an electronic kit at first,* he thought. *That would make everything simpler until I make some progress. Then I could start working on a more complicated design of combining acoustic and electronic drums.*

Bash noodled on the paper while eating the spaghetti leftovers. *This could work,* he told himself. He felt his pulse rise a bit as he thought about it. *I could be playing music again!* he thought. *And it was all because of Terry!*

A while later Bash decided to take a jog down Rock Bottom's dirt road, something he had started a week earlier. He needed to let go of the energy churning inside him. As he ran, the sweat poured from him, ridding his body of all the toxins he'd been filling himself with for too long now. He had decided to replace beer with juice or water and to lay off the weed completely. His mind needed clearing as much as his body needed it.

The night ended with Bash surfing the web for prices on electronic drums and the hardware needed to make a pedal system for his specialized kit. He nodded off several times while reclining on his mattress with the laptop on his stomach. He finally ended his web surfing and set the laptop on the floor near the female figurine with the bird feet. He fell asleep quickly but slept fitfully through the night, having dreams of the woman in the leopard-skin robe. His parents were not in the dreams anymore but Terry was still in them. He tried to make contact with Terry in the dreams but it was impossible. Every time he attempted to get Terry's attention the same thing happened: *Bash would see Terry asleep in some other setting, then Bash would ascend through the ceiling, maintaining his bird's-eye view perspective as he went higher and higher until reaching Earth's atmosphere where he descended rapidly back to Earth, back to the dirt floor where Terry lay, then back to the scene in the dream with the woman in the leopard-skin robe. She never seemed to notice Bash's ascent and return to the room which Bash thought was strange.*

Of course, Bash remembered little of the dreams when he awoke, mainly just disjointed images which left him restless in the mornings. He couldn't explain why, but he instinctively knew that a big change was coming into his life . . .

† † †

11

"Because I don't feel like going," Jonni insisted. "That's why."

Mandy stepped back into the bathroom, studying her face in the mirror while applying eyeliner. "Come on," she pleaded. "We'll have fun."

"Doing what?" Jonni said from the kitchen, which stood about ten feet from the bathroom. "Parading around in front of a bunch of wannabe rock stars with too much ego and testosterone? No thanks."

"It won't be that way, Jonni. A lot of people I know from school are going."

Jonni didn't reply as she finished making a bowl of cereal with bananas on top, still thinking about her follow-up visit at Aaron and Heather's home not too long ago. There had been no supernatural events like the house shaking or loud unearthly moans heard in the movies, but as she prayed throughout the house she could sense that the spirit or spirits infesting the home were truly afraid of her; not of her exactly but afraid of God who owned her heart and empowered her to 'do even greater things.' When she had left Aaron and Heather's home, Jonni believed the home was clean but she knew the spirits could return if Aaron and Heather didn't allow themselves to be filled with the Holy Spirit. Jonni remembered the scripture where Jesus told his disciples that when a person is cleansed of an unclean spirit, the spirit will wander in waterless places until returning to its previous abode. There, finding it swept clean, the unclean spirit will bring seven unclean spirits more evil than itself to take up residence, leaving the human in a worse predicament than before. Jonni had swept the place clean but the rest was up to Aaron and Heather.

"What are you afraid of?" Mandy continued. "You're not afraid of ghosts but you're afraid of boys?"

"Ghosts aren't as dangerous," Jonni replied while eating her cereal.

"Look," Mandy said, "I know you are not interested in meeting any-one right now because of your breakup with Greg but some of us might like to meet someone."

"Us?"

"Well, Ginger is going, too."

Jonni had to chuckle. "If Ginger goes none of us will get any atten-tion."

"I thought you didn't want any attention?"

"I don't but . . ." Jonni decided to drop it. She didn't want to hurt Mandy's feelings by going on about Ginger's gorgeous looks, implying that if Ginger goes along no one will pay any attention to Mandy. *Or to me.*

Mandy came into the kitchen and grabbed a Diet Coke from the fridge. "Come on," she said. "We'll have you home in time to watch *Golden Girls.* Don't worry."

Jonni had to laugh.

"It'll be fun," Mandy pleaded. "Please?"

Jonni rolled her eyes. "Okay, I'll go," she mumbled with a mouth-ful of cereal.

"What?"

Jonni swallowed. "I said okay, I'll go."

"You will?"

"Yes! I'll go already!"

"Great! We'll have fun!"

"Yeah, right."

After finishing her cereal and taking a quick shower, Jonni dressed in a pair of tight black jeans and a blue silk blouse. She brushed her jet-black hair away from her face and applied a tiny amount of makeup, mainly to cover some small blemishes.

Ginger arrived with her short red hair and perfect figure, looking stunning as usual. Jonni believed Ginger could win a beauty contest wearing a potato sack.

"Hi!" Ginger said, her personality as bubbly as always. "I love that blouse!" she told Jonni. "You look great!"

The three young women chatted and primped another twenty min-utes or so before leaving the apartment and climbing into Mandy's tiny

Ford Fiesta, heading to a party at a house in the country hosted by a popular local band named the Zeniths.

†

The place was packed. Cars were parked everywhere around the old two-story house and along the dirt road approaching it. Music blasted from the speakers in the Zeniths' rehearsal room; music from the Zeniths' last CD. The room was clear of band gear so people had plenty of room to gather. The kitchen was crammed with people as well. Bash leaned against the side of the fridge, watching a group of girls hover around Gordon and Trent, asking questions with longing looks.

Bash had been talking to two male college students, Carl and Jeremy. The two followed the Zeniths when the band played in the area. They explained how they use to follow Bash before he mixed sound for the Zeniths, back in the days of his own band, Nadir. They explained what an incredible guitarist he *had* been; someone who *had* played circles around people like Trent. Bash knew they were trying to be nice and that they didn't realize they were placing his life in the past tense.

The one named Jeremy gave him an insurance salesman's business card with a YouTube address written on back. "I think you'll find this interesting," was all he said.

"Thanks," Bash said, placing the card in his pocket, not knowing if he should be thankful or not.

A dark-haired girl entered the kitchen and joined the girls hovering around Gordon and Trent. But her attention was not on the musicians. She gave Bash a pleasant smile before looking around for something.

"Can I help you?" Bash asked.

"Where's the trash can?"

Bash took the empty Diet Coke can from her hand and tossed it into a large plastic-filled trashcan in the corner.

"Thanks," Jonni said.

"Your welcome. You want another?"

"Sure."

Bash went to a large cooler across the room and grabbed another Diet Coke for her. "Here you go."

"Thank you."

101

"You're welcome."

"You with the band?" she asked.

"I mix sound for them."

"So you live here, too?"

"Yes."

She stuck out her left hand. "I'm Jonni Windsor."

Bash shook her hand and said, "Hi, Jonni Windsor. I'm Bashshar Nadir. But you can call me Bash."

"I like that name," she said with a genuine smile.

They continued to chit-chat while watching some girls flirt with Trent. Trent seemed very interested in one of the girls.

"Check it out," Bash whispered to Jonni. "The hunt has begun. His name is Trent."

Jonni saw a handsome guy with long hair practically drooling over Mandy's friend, Ginger. "You talking about the one ogling the redhead in the black halter top?"

"Uh-huh."

"That's Ginger," Jonni said. "She has that effect on lots of guys."

They watched Trent flirt with Ginger as she played it friendly but cool with him.

"If he gets any more excited," Jonni said, "his puppy dog tail may start wagging."

Bash laughed heartily. "That's good! He is a puppy, isn't he?"

Bash and Jonni made eye contact for an awkward moment.

"So how did you lose your arm?" Jonni suddenly asked.

Her forward attitude caught Bash off guard. He stared at her for a moment and said, "Motorcycle accident."

Jonni nodded. "When did it happen?"

"Over a year ago."

They both turned their attention back toward Trent and Ginger when all of a sudden Vince the drummer came storming into the kitchen with a maniacal look on his face. A small group followed him while chanting his name. "Vince! Vince! Vince! Vince!"

Vince brought a can of beer to his open mouth while leaning his head back. He squeezed the beer into his mouth and swallowed the can's contents in less than two seconds. He took another can of beer someone handed him and did the same. After four more beers chugged in the same manner, Vince beat his chest like King Kong.

"Who is that?" Jonni shouted in Bash's ear.

"That's Vince," Bash said, having to raise his voice to be heard over the applause and shouting in the kitchen. "The drummer."

After Vince the drummer let out a loud belch Jonni said, "You want to go outside for some fresh air?"

"Yes," Bash said with a smile. "We need some fresh air now."

They exited through the back door of the kitchen and walked to the picnic bench beneath the old oak tree. The full moon illuminated the area like a distant spotlight from the heavens. They sat on the bench seat facing away from the house. "So what do you do, Jonni?" Bash asked.

Jonni gave him a short synopsis of her arrival from Nashville into Austin not long ago, leaving out the part about Greg and the ghost hunting team that fired her. She talked about her website and interest in the paranormal field, feeling totally comfortable in Bash's presence.

"So have you ever encountered a ghost?" he asked.

"Many times," she said before taking a sip of her soda. "Haven't you?"

"No," Bash said. He paused before asking, "Can you prove it?"

"I'm not trying to prove anything," Jonni said. "I just want to help people get rid of them. To force them to leave, actually."

"Really?"

"Really."

"What if the ghosts don't want to leave?" Bash asked, not believing in anything as silly as ghosts but enjoying Jonni's company.

Jonni laughed. "Believe me, they never want to leave. And by the way, I don't refer to them as ghosts."

"No? Then what are they?"

"Demonic entities."

Bash loved her straightforwardness. "So they are demons?"

"Uh-huh."

"So there's no such thing as friendly ghosts?" he asked with a smirk. "No Caspers?"

"No," she replied with her own smirk. "But they often pose as being friendly spirits in order to fool people, especially people who start out not believing that there is a spirit realm. You see, once people experience this other realm for themselves, they have to process it in a way they can understand. So they are easily fooled."

"That's interesting," Bash said, still not believing any of it but impressed by her knowledge of the subject. "I've never heard that before."

"What have you heard?" asked Jonni.

Bash thought for a moment before saying, "That ghosts are the spirits of departed souls unwilling to move on . . . to the next plane of existence."

"Do you believe that?" she asked.

"No, I don't," he said, "but I could be wrong. I've been wrong about plenty of stuff in my life."

Jonni nodded her head in an approving way. "That's an honest answer. I like that."

"I guess I'm the type of guy who has to see it to believe it," added Bash.

"Yeah, I hear that from a lot of people," Jonni said with a twinkle in her eye. "But maybe the truth is the exact opposite."

Bash thought about that for just a brief moment. "You mean you have to believe it to see it?"

A big smile grew on Jonni's face. "Most people don't get it that fast," she said. "You're quick." Her next statement came out before she had time to think about it. "And you're handsome, too." She regretted saying it immediately. *Did I really say that?*

Bash blushed. "Ah, you probably say that to all the one-armed men you meet."

"You are the only one-armed man I've ever met," she said, still kicking herself for the *handsome* comment.

"You see? I was right."

Jonni's laugh was infectious. Bash couldn't remember feeling so comfortable with anyone before, especially someone he had just met.

They sat in silence for a while, staring into the darkness surrounding Rock Bottom, feeling totally relaxed in each other's company.

Bash broke the silence. "I may have seen a ghost once," he said before correcting himself. "I mean . . . a *demonic entity.*"

"Really? Tell me about it."

"Well, when I was young," Bash began, "I was camping with my family near Fredericksburg, not too far from here. It was almost sunset and I was roaming around a short distance from the camp, looking for arrowheads, when a movement in the trees caught my eye. I watched for a while and then saw a horse and rider moving through the trees. They were moving slowly, as if on a narrow trail. The strange thing to me was how they appeared to be almost transparent. I thought I could see through them. Then they vanished, as they say, into thin air."

"And that was it?" asked Jonni.

"No. I kept watching, thinking they were hidden by the trees and I might see them again. And I did. Except they were back where they started when I first saw them. I moved a bit closer to get a better view, maybe fifty yards from them. I saw more detail even though there was still a transparent quality to them. The rider was wearing a buckskin loincloth, his long black hair in braids, sitting on a blanket instead of a saddle. The horse was brown with white spots, a little smaller than most horses you see nowadays."

"A Native American from the past," said Jonni.

"Yes," Bash said, "but that's not the strangest part. What I was seeing seemed to be repeating itself, like a video loop repeating over and over. The horse and rider moved a few paces before turning in the opposite direction and going uphill as if ascending a steep trail. The head movements of the rider were identical each time. After the fourth or fifth time, I shouted, 'Hey!' but the horse or rider didn't respond. Like I said, it was if I was watching a video loop. Then it was over. The horse and rider were gone."

"Was that the end of it?"

"Well, I walked to the spot to get a better look," Bash explained, "to look for the hoof prints on the trail. But guess what? There was no trail. And the terrain in the area was flat. There's no way they could've been ascending a rise in the trail because there was no rise or trail. Yet I clearly saw them ascending uphill once they made the turn. Weird, huh?"

"Residuals."

"Pardon me?"

"Residuals," Jonni said again. "Or place memory. That's what some paranormal researchers call it. It's a type of paranormal event where the phenomena are unaware of you or any observers. Like somehow, a moment of time is replaying itself. Like you said, a video loop."

"That's interesting," Bash said. "So they aren't ghosts or spirits or demons? Just an image of the past replaying itself like a movie clip?"

"Something like that," Jonni said, deciding not to go further into the subject at the moment. "So you see, you have witnessed a paranormal event."

Bash smiled but he seemed to be in deep thought. He finally asked, "You think spirits or whatever can visit you in dreams?"

She knew his question had a personal ring to it. "Yes, I do," she answered. "You know someone dealing with this?"

Bash didn't respond immediately. "Yeah, sort of. Actually, it's me."

"Can you explain more?"

Bash seemed reluctant to continue.

Jonni got right to the point. "Look, you can tell me if you want to," she said. "Who am I to think you're crazy? I'm the one here who believes in the paranormal!"

Bash smiled. "I don't know where to start."

"How about from the beginning?"

As Bash explained about the recurring dreams of the woman in the leopard-skin robe, he began remembering more about the dreams. He decided to leave out the erotic components, though. He didn't want Jonni to think he had erotic dreams because he was a lonely one-armed pervert that had no love life. He told her that the dreams were occurring more frequently. "I can't explain, but they seem so real. More real than any dreams I've ever had."

Jonni studied his face for a long moment. *God, he's gorgeous,* she thought before chastising herself. *What am I thinking? I'm not ready to fall for anybody again!* "Can I ask you something kind of personal?"

"Yes."

"This woman in your dreams . . . does she make sexual advances toward you?"

Bash was surprised that Jonni knew. He hesitated but eventually nodded his head.

"How long have you had these dreams?"

"I don't know," Bash said. "Maybe a few months. Ever since I moved here."

Jonni nodded before asking, "Have you or any of the other band guys experienced any strange occurrences since moving in?"

"Yes."

"Like what?"

"Well, there was a strange thing that happened in an upstairs closet right after we moved in," Bash said, explaining the incident where Trent got locked into the closet when the doorknob had fallen off and Vince and Billy couldn't force it open. "There's also been strange sounds now and then, not that uncommon for an old house, though."

Jonni waited for more.

"And I have something weird that happens all the time," he continued. "I have this little statue on the floor in my bedroom. It's heavy, you know, being carved from stone and all, but it keeps falling over on its own. At first, I figured vibrations from the rehearsals were knocking it over but it's happened even when there's been no rehearsals."

Jonni nodded her head in understanding. "I felt a presence as soon as I walked in," she said. "I can always tell when there's activity."

"You think the house is haunted?"

Jonni didn't answer the question. "I want to hear more about this statue you told me about. What is it a likeness of?"

Bash described the female figurine with the bird feet.

"Is she naked?"

Bash nodded, feeling a little self-conscious about admitting he had a figurine of a naked woman in his bedroom.

"How long have you had it?"

"Not too long," he said, realizing where Jonni was heading with her questions. "You think it has something to do with my dreams?"

"Yes, I do," she said without hesitation. "Where did you get it?"

Bash told her about the storage auction and the box with the carving of the woman and the other stone figurines. He suddenly remembered Kyle telling him to call the Carlos Santana-looking dude if he found any idols in the stuff from the auction. "Are they idols?"

"To some people," she answered.

When Bash described the features of the other figurines, Jonni's facial expression changed into an expression of real concern. "Bash. Those figurines are demonic. I don't know what demons they represent but the woman with the talons for feet sounds like Lilith, a very well known succubus."

"A what?"

"A succubus," Jonni repeated. "Going back at least as far as the Roman Empire, people believed that evil spirits could enter men's dreams and have sex with them. They also believed these spirits can change gender. Incubus, the male form. Succubus, the female."

An awkward pause.

"Have you—"

"—No," Bash said quickly. "Of course not. I can't remember all the details but I know I haven't. There's something very wrong about it in my dreams . . . so I resist."

Jonni nodded, glad to hear his answer. "You have to get rid of all those figurines, Bash."

"And that will get rid of the dreams?"

"I hope so."

"What should I do with them?" he asked, thinking again about the Carlos Santana dude wanting to buy any idols they found in the storage items. "Maybe I could sell them. They might be worth something."

"You don't want to pass this curse on to someone else, do you?"

Bash shook his head quickly. "No, I guess not."

Jonni thought for a moment. "You need to bury them," she said while staring at the large field behind the house. "Out there. Then I'll pray over them. You have a shovel?"

"Should be one somewhere around here."

Jonni followed him around the side of the house where a small wooden storage shed stood. He reached inside the dark shed and sorted through several long-handled tools until he found a shovel. He leaned the shovel against the shed and said, "Come on, follow me."

They went back inside the kitchen. She followed him through the crowd of people, getting weird looks from Mandy as they continued upstairs and eventually to Bash's bedroom. Jonni saw the female figurine with bird feet lying on its side on the floor next to a mattress.

"See," Bash said. "When I was up here earlier it was standing."

The figurine seemed to glare at Jonni. It gave her the creeps.

Bash slid a box from his closet floor using his foot. He knelt on the floor and opened the box. The small figurines were still inside where he'd left them. "These are the other ones I told you about." He started to grab one of them.

"No," she said. "Don't touch them."

"I touched them when I first found them," he admitted.

"Well, don't touch them again."

Bash leaned toward the female figurine lying on the floor. "Does she look like this Lilith person you mentioned?"

Jonni studied it for a moment. "I don't know," she said. "It has bird feet like Lilith. But her facial features look more American Indian than Mesopotamian."

"Maybe Aztec or Mayan," Bash offered, "like the other figurines in the box."

"Yes, maybe," she said. "You have any tongs?"

"You mean flip-flops?" he said with a mischievous grin.

Jonni pursed her lips together. "Tongs," she corrected him while trying to resist from smiling. "Not thongs. And you're the first person I've heard in a long time that calls flip-flops thongs."

"I don't think we have any tongs," Bash said. He removed the flip-flops on his feet and handed one to her. "You'll have to help me," he said as he started scooting the figurine with his other flip-flop toward the box.

Jonni laughed out loud as she and Bash tried to squeeze the heavy figurine between the flip-flops to lift it into the box with the other figurines. The female figurine was too heavy and slippery for them to get any grip or balance to lift it. They laughed hard. "This is like some weird TV game show!" she said.

Mandy suddenly poked her head into the room. "Jonni?"

Jonni looked up, realizing how preposterous the situation looked with her and some guy kneeling on the floor of his bedroom, both trying to grab a figurine of a naked woman with a flip-flop in each of their hands. It made Jonni laugh harder. "Hi, Mandy," she managed to say. "Whatcha doing?"

A smile of uncertainty grew on Mandy's face. "Are you all right, Jonni?"

Jonni couldn't quit laughing. "Yes! Fine!"

"Hi," Bash said to Mandy before returning his attention to the figurine. They finally had it balanced between the grasps of the flip-flops when it fell the few inches to the floor, causing them both to break into even harder laughter.

"Okay," Mandy said with a puzzled smile. "I'll be downstairs if you need me."

Jonni could barely breathe because of her laughter. "Okay, Mandy!"

Bash and Jonni finally turned the box on its side and scooted the figurine inside it with the flip-flops. She lifted the box while Bash replaced the flip-flops on his feet and grabbed a flashlight from his chest-of-drawers. "Okay, let's go," he said. "We'll go through the front door so we don't have to go through the kitchen again and draw any attention."

"Good idea," she said while carrying the box and following him downstairs.

They walked through the foyer past the groups of people gathered in the rehearsal room. They exited Rock Bottom through the front door and walked around the house to the storage shed where they had left the shovel.

Vince had been in the rehearsal room with some other people and saw Bash and the girl carrying the box out the door. He followed them from a distance. He peered around the corner of the house and saw them heading across the field behind the house, the flashlight beam sweeping left to right as they walked into the darkness, the girl still carrying the box but also something with a long handle in her other hand.

Vince continued to the back of the house and stood near the picnic table. He saw Bash and the girl in the middle of the field. Vince pulled a piece of paper from his pocket and unfolded it. Using the long fingernail of his little finger, he scooped up some cocaine in the fingernail and brought it to his nostril. He snorted the white powder into each nostril while staring at Bash and the girl, maybe a hundred yards or so away. He wadded up the now empty fold of paper and tossed it away before entering back in the house through the kitchen door.

Bash and Jonni found a spot beneath a small copse of Spanish oak trees standing alone in the prairie to dig their hole. Bash broke the ground first before Jonni took over and shoveled out a hole wide and deep enough to bury the box. The soil was dry and rocky but it didn't take long to finish. It was a warm night but a steady breeze blew through the creek bed and rolling prairie surrounding Rock Bottom. When they finished burying the box, Jonni said a brief prayer over the burial site before they walked back toward the house with Bash balancing the shovel on his shoulder.

After dropping off the shovel at the storage shed, Bash and Jonni went back into the house through the front door. No one seemed to notice them except for Vince who watched them from his squatting position on the floor next to a girl with almost as many tattoos as him. They drank Jaegermeister straight from a bottle, his eyes glassy and angry-looking as the drugs and liquor worked their magic on him.

Bash and Jonni hung out in the kitchen for the next hour. She introduced Bash to Mandy and Ginger and the four of them visited for a while until Trent came over to Ginger with a beer in each hand; one for him and one for her. Ginger seemed to be softening to his advances as the night wore on.

Jonni, Mandy, and Ginger decided to leave a short while later, which disappointed Trent tremendously. Bash and Jonni traded contact info while walking to Mandy's car. Jonni gave him a quick kiss on the cheek before saying goodbye.

Bash walked back inside Rock Bottom with some extra pep in his stride. He felt funny. No girl had ever had an effect on him like Jonni. He felt like they had known each other all their life. *How strange!*

When Bash passed the rehearsal room, Vince called out with slightly slurred speech. "Hey, lover boy!" he shouted. "Did she already dump you?"

Bash kept walking. Nothing was going to ruin the good feeling rushing through him at the moment. He made his way up the stairs and entered his bedroom before closing the door behind him. He reclined on the mattress on his floor, reliving the moments and conversation with Jonni. He held the paper in his hand that had her phone number and email. Soon he fell asleep with a smile on his face for the first time in a long time. That night he slept peacefully without any dreams of the woman in the leopard-skin robe. As a matter of fact, the next morning he had no recollection of having any dreams at all. All he thought about was calling Jonni.

Jonni.

Even though Bash had just met her, he felt Jonni would be the one he would share his life with, something he never dreamed could happen so quickly . . .

† † †

12

*B*ash and Jonni agreed to meet at a small sushi restaurant in downtown Austin. Ricky had agreed to pick up Bash from Rock Bottom, eager to give him a ride when he heard that Bash was actually going to meet a girl at the restaurant.

When Ricky stepped out of his Toyota pickup truck at Rock Bottom, he heard drums playing inside the house. *Could that be Vince? No way.* He'd seen Vince play many times. Vince was good. Whoever was playing inside was struggling a bit.

Ricky walked inside and followed the sound of the drums into the rehearsal room. He saw Bash sitting at the kit, trying to use his left hand to play both the snare and hi-hat. Bash saw him and stopped playing immediately.

"Is Vince already fired?" Ricky said, wincing instantly as he realized Vince may be in earshot.

"No one's here," Bash said, perceiving Ricky's concern about being overheard.

"Sounds pretty good, Boo-Boo," Ricky said. "How long have you been practicing?"

"Not long enough," Bash said while standing from the drums. "I stink but thanks anyway for the compliment."

"You play better with three limbs than a lot of dudes with four," said Ricky, noticing that Bash was wearing new jeans and a freshly pressed collared shirt.

Bash ignored Ricky's encouragement as he grabbed his cell phone from a table.

Ricky saw that Bash looked anxious. "What's wrong?"

Bash shrugged. "I don't know," he said. "I guess I'm just a little nervous about meeting Jonni today."

"Come on, Romeo," Ricky said while patting Bash on the back and leading him outside to his Toyota pickup truck. They drove out of the front yard and onto the dirt road leading away from Rock Bottom.

"I guess I need to get a car," Bash said after they had been driving a few minutes. "Especially if her and I start seeing each other on a regular basis."

"Wow," Ricky said. "*Her and I* instead of *me and her*. This sounds serious."

Bash didn't reply but it was written all over his face. He was smitten with Jonni. He was also nervous. He grabbed a stick of Juicy Fruit chewing gum from his shirt pocket.

"So tell me all about her," Ricky said in a goofy voice. "What's she like? What movies does she like? What's her favorite books? What's her favorite color? You know, her whole personal history . . . but keep it short, okay?"

"I don't know much about her," Bash said, ignoring Ricky's attempt at being humorous. "Not yet, anyway."

"Not yet," Ricky said. "Yep, it's serious."

"No, it's not."

"Yes, it is."

"No, it's not," Bash repeated while stuffing the gum in his mouth.

"You still chewing gum all day?" asked Ricky.

"Yep."

"Gonna rot your teeth."

"I don't think so."

As they drove down the dirt road, Bash's nervousness began to subside a bit. Being around Ricky often had that effect on him. He marveled at the countryside and blue sky out the window. Everything seemed more alive than usual. He hadn't felt that way in a long time. Maybe ever.

Ricky turned up the volume of his speakers when he heard *You Wreck Me* by Tom Petty on the radio. "I love this drum groove!" he said.

"Yeah, me, too," Bash agreed.

"What makes the groove is the shaker and tambourine in the mix," Ricky explained. "You don't really hear the shaker because of the high-hat but you would miss it if it wasn't there."

"That's common in a lot of Petty's drum mixes," Bash said. "So simple and small but it makes the whole groove work in an incredible way."

"You've got a great ear, Boo-Boo."

A moment later the song ended and a DJ began babbling enthusiastically, causing Ricky to turn down the radio volume. They drove in silence for a few minutes before Bash said, "Thanks for everything you do for me, Ricky. You're amazing."

"My pleasure, bro," Ricky said. "I'll always help out if I can. You know that."

"Well then," Bash said with a smile, "will you join the band so they'll get rid of Vince the Terrible?"

"That bad, huh?"

"For me at least. Although he is a good drummer."

"Yes, he is."

"Not as good as you, though."

"No, of course not."

"To tell you the truth," Bash said, "I don't know how long I'll be able to hang around as long as he's in the band."

Ricky thought for a moment before saying, "A guy like that is a bad influence on others. If the rest of the guys aren't careful he'll drag them down to his level. I hear he's into some nasty stuff. Gordon. too. I don't know that for sure so keep that between you and me."

"What do you mean?"

"I don't know," Ricky said, "but I've heard that they're involved with some cult group here in Austin."

"What kind of cult?" Bash asked.

"I don't know," Ricky said. "Witch stuff. New Age. Doesn't matter. It's everywhere these days."

"Gordon, too?"

Ricky just shrugged.

"Well, it doesn't surprise me about Vince," Bash said after a moment's thought. "Along with his wonderful personality, he has a lot of tats of skulls and serpents. Has 'Satan' tattooed on his right knuckles. But his hatred toward me, I don't understand."

"There's nothing to understand," Ricky said. "He thrives on hate and anger. He can't treat Gordon or the band that way or they'll fire him. But they've seen it even if you don't think they have. It's amazing to me how people choose to be blind when it's convenient for them."

"Yeah, I agree."

"Just remember this," Ricky said. "We don't know what kind of world Vince was raised in. Inside, maybe he's crying out for something he never had, and he responds the only way he knows how to respond, which is a bad way to respond. Such is life without God's guidance. I know. I was there once."

"Yeah, but you were never the jerk he is."

"Maybe not to you."

"So I'm supposed to just start liking him?"

"Just hate the sin," Ricky said. "Not the sinner."

"Well, it may not matter for long," Bash said, "because I won't be hanging around if he keeps ragging on me."

"You have plans for what you'll do once you leave?"

"Not really," Bash said, not being completely honest. He decided to tell Ricky about his idea. "You remember Rick Allen? The drummer of Def Leppard?"

"Of course."

"Now don't laugh," Bash said, "but when I was a kid I played drums for a while before taking up the guitar."

"I remember."

"How could you remember?" Bash said. "I didn't even know you then."

"I remember before your accident when sometimes you would get behind my drums," Ricky explained. "You were good. I didn't tell you that at the time because I didn't want your big head to swell any bigger than it already was. I guess I was a little jealous."

"You're joking."

"I'm not."

"You're just saying that to build me up."

"Build you up for what?"

"For this little plan of mine that is probably a really stupid idea."

"I don't even know what your little plan is!"

"Well," Bash started, "Rick Allen had this pedal rig that—"

Ricky butted in, "—allowed him to play his left hand parts with his left foot."

"So you know all about him."

"Of course I do. I'm a drummer, you bonehead!"

"Anyway, I've been toying with the idea of doing something simi-lar."

"I think that's great!" Ricky said eagerly.

"My right foot still plays the kick," Bash continued, "so the left foot has to operate a pedal system that does more than just opening and closing the hi-hat."

Ricky nodded enthusiastically. "I hear ya, bro."

"I need to design the pedal system," Bash said. "Any ideas would be appreciated."

"Yeah, let me see what I can come up with."

Bash smiled and asked, "Are you sure you're not worried?"

"Worried about what?"

"Worried that I'll become a better drummer than you?"

Ricky had to laugh. "That wouldn't be that difficult to do."

"Yes, it would," Bash argued. "You are awesome and you know it. Actually, I don't think I have what it takes to be half as good as you on the drums, even with some elaborate pedal system, no matter how long I practice."

"Look," Ricky said in a serious tone. "Even if I was that good, which I'm not, I couldn't take any credit for it. Talent is a gift from above. And if you put God first, there's no limit to what you can become. On guitar, or drums, or whatever."

"You know what, Yogi?"

"What Boo-Boo?"

"I think you are an excellent example of what a Christian should be."

"Well, thank you, bro, but if that's true, I can't accept any credit for it. Any new improvements in my behavior is the result of Jesus, not me."

"Can I ask you a question?" asked Bash.

"Of course."

"Why are so many Christians such hypocrites?" Bash asked. "You know, Christianity doesn't have a great reputation among us sinners."

"We're all sinners."

"You know what I mean."

"I do," Ricky said, "and there are real answers to that question but first I want to ask you a question. There are many medical quacks in this country, right? So does that mean you will never go to a doctor when you are sick? That there are no good doctors in modern medicine?"

Bash started to say something but changed his mind.

"Most serial killers are white males in their thirties with very ordinary lives," Ricky continued. "Does that mean that all thirty-something white males with ordinary lives are serial killers?"

"Of course not."

"Well, that's the kind of thinking that leads people to believe that Christianity is phony. Also, anybody can say 'I'm a Christian.' But that doesn't make them one. Many are outright phonies."

"True."

"It's headline news when a Christian pastor cheats on his taxes or has an extramarital affair," Ricky went on, "but the thousands of good deeds and charities performed by thousands of Christians every day won't get printed on the last page of your local newspaper."

"But what about those preachers who cheat and have affairs?" Bash asked. "What's up with that?"

"They are human beings," Ricky answered, "and like all of the human race, they are imperfect and make mistakes. They get tempted and they fall for the temptation. Now some are total phonies. Wolves in sheep's clothing. They use the profession to gain wealth and power, saying the right things and looking the part to fool their followers. Like in all wars, the enemy does the most damage by infiltrating their enemy's camp. Right?"

"Yeah, I guess."

"But you want to know the main reason the world sees Christ followers as hypocrites?"

"Why?"

"Because when anyone steps into the faith," Ricky said, "the Lord accepts you just as you are. Let's say, a thief addicted to drugs sincerely accepts Jesus into his life. A process begins which starts changing his life. It doesn't mean he wakes up the next day free of his addiction, but the change has started, regardless of others seeing it or not. Let's say he goes to rehab, gets out clean, but then is tempted by someone to get high again and then he succumbs to the temptation and gets high. Others who know he is a Christian look at him and say 'hypocrite!' You see, the world thinks that if you are really a Christian you wouldn't sin again, which means you would have to be perfect, which negates the whole reason why Jesus came in the first place."

Bash nodded his head but said nothing.

"There are also people who think that God couldn't love them because they are too messed up," Ricky added. "Which leads them to believe they have to first perfect themselves on their own before God will accept them. Which is the exact opposite of the truth. Does that make sense?"

"Yeah," Bash replied. "It does. Good speech. A little long and wordy but still good."

Ricky gave him a look and faked a punch in Bash's direction.

Bash smiled. Once the smile faded away he said, "I haven't been able to reach Terry in over a week. I'm starting to get worried."

"You've called his cell phone?"

"He doesn't have one. I've been talking to him on a phone in the apartment where he lives."

"Have you talked to your uncle?"

"Walid?" Bash guffawed. "He wouldn't talk to me if I got down on my knees and begged."

"Maybe Terry has moved out of town," Ricky offered.

"But he would have told me."

"Maybe he hasn't gotten around to it yet," Ricky said. "You said he doesn't have a cell phone."

"That's true," Bash said. Good old Ricky. Always looking at the bright side of life. "But if I don't hear from him soon I may have to go looking for him."

"I'll help you any way I can," Ricky said. "You know that."

"Thanks, Yogi."

"Your welcome, Boo-Boo."

They drove in silence for a while until Bash said, "I hope she's not disappointed when she sees me. In broad daylight."

"Huh?"

"I said," Bash began with a slightly irritated tone in his voice, "I hope she's not disappointed when she sees me again."

"Hope who's not disappointed?"

"Jonni! You know, the girl you're taking me to meet?"

"Oh, her."

"Yeah, her, you louse!"

"What about her?"

"I was just saying . . . oh, never mind."

"You're giving up on her already?"

"I'm giving up on you."

"How sad," Ricky said, trying to hide a smile. "And after all the nice things you said about me just minutes ago."

"I'm just anxious about seeing her," Bash said. "What if she is disappointed when she sees me in daylight?"

"If this girl is disappointed because of your physical appearance then you need to move on. It's not complicated. It's not easy to do the right thing but it's not complicated. Just walk away."

"Just like that, huh?"

"Look," Ricky said. "She knew you were missing an arm when she gave you her number, right?"

"Right."

"Then quit worrying about it. You're a handsome guy no matter how many arms you have."

Bash smirked and said, "You think I'm handsome, huh?"

Ricky caught the look and chuckled. "Don't go there, Boo-Boo."

A short while later they were driving into downtown Austin. Bash was starting to act nervous again.

"Relax," Ricky said. "You're probably a rock star in her eyes."

"You mean a soundman."

"What's the difference?"

A few minutes later Ricky stopped his Toyota pickup in front of the sushi restaurant. Bash could see through the tall glass walls of the restaurant that there were only a few patrons inside. "She's not here," he told Ricky.

The sign of a dentist office hung on the wall next door to the restaurant. "Maybe you should get your teeth cleaned while you wait," Ricky said. "They look a little yellow."

Bash yanked the rearview mirror toward his face and grinned wide to check his teeth. "White as milk," he said before pursing his lips together and acting like he was going to give Ricky a kiss.

Ricky leaned away as far as he could and said, "Get out of here. Call me when you're ready to head home. Ricky's taxi service, always fast and free."

"Bye," Bash said while climbing out of Ricky's pickup truck.

Once inside the restaurant, Bash ordered a Diet Coke and sat at a table to wait for Jonni, thumbing through a website on his cell phone but not able to concentrate on it. *What if she doesn't show up?* a voice inside him asked. *Then I'll eat lunch by myself. Spend the whole day by myself if I have to. Oh, boy. How exciting.*

He saw Jonni locking a bicycle on a rack outside the restaurant. She came popping inside a few seconds later. She saw Bash and smiled at him before bouncing toward the table. "Hi! Sorry I'm late but I ran out of gas on the way here!"

Bash stood from the table. "Your bicycle runs on gas?"

"I was talking about me, silly!" she said. "*I* ran out of gas. My energy level has been low all day. I think I need to eat something."

"Well," Bash said. "You've come to the right place."

"How did you get here?" she asked while sitting down in the chair he offered her.

Bash sat back down in his chair and said, "I just walked right in."

"All the way from the house?" she asked in a tone of disbelief.

"No, just through the door," he said with a smirk. "A friend gave me a ride."

She gave him a warm smile.

Bash gave his own warm smile back. "Glad you came."

"Me, too."

Time flew by as they sat and talked while sipping on Diet Cokes. Almost an hour later they finished eating their custom-designed sushi rolls along with a bowl of edamame covered in some exotic spice. They discussed their opinions of various events occurring around the world. When Jonni enquired about his ethnic heritage, Bash said, "Both of my parents were Egyptian. My father was a doctor and my mother a nurse. They were both educated in America and obtained citizenship long before I was born. As a family, we made a trip once to Cairo to visit relatives, but my brother and I were raised here in Texas. I was born in Houston and Terry was born in Austin shortly after we moved here when my father set up his practice." *Quit talking so much!* he scolded himself.

"Are your parents still living here?" she asked.

"No. They were both killed in a head-on car crash when I was eighteen. That's when Terry moved to Oregon to live with my uncle's family." *Slow down! You're giving too much information too quickly!*

"So you're alone," she said.

"I have friends."

"But no family living here in Texas."

"No."

"Same with me."

"Your parents?"

"I never knew my real parents," Jonni said. "I was adopted by wonderful foster parents when I was young but they have since passed on."

"Any brothers or sisters?"

"Not that I know of."

Our situation is similar, Bash thought.

They decided to leave the sushi restaurant and take a walk outside. Bash paid the bill although Jonni insisted on paying her half by placing some folded bills in his shirt pocket. They walked toward Caesar Chavez street and beyond where they joined the nature trail bordering Lady Bird Lake, the section of the Colorado River that wound its way around downtown Austin. Joggers and cyclists crowded the trail but there was still plenty of room to just walk and enjoy the beautiful day.

"So I heard you used to be quite the guitarist," Jonni suddenly said.

"Who told you that?" Bash liked how she didn't mince words or beat around the bush but he was still surprised by her forwardness.

"Mandy's friend, Ginger, told us on our way back home from the party."

Did Trent tell this to Ginger? No way. He would never talk about another guitar player when trying to impress a girl.

"Yes," Bash finally said. "I played the guitar."

"She said that the guy in the band eyeing her at the party . . . what's his name?"

"Trent."

"Yes, Trent," Jonni said. "Trent told Ginger you were a local legend destined for fame and success."

Bash had to laugh. "Fame and success as a musician in Austin means being able to pay rent. Maybe."

"He told her you were great but then you lost your arm in the accident."

"And my dreams."

"All of them?"

Bash didn't respond right away. "No," he finally said, "I have some dreams."

"Any ones you would like to share?"

"Well, the most important one at the moment is to get back with my brother."

"In Oregon?"

"Here," he said. "Preferably."

Jonni smiled. "That's so sweet."

"Sweet?" Bash said with a chuckle.

"Yes. It shows you have a good heart."

Bash smiled. A moment later he said, "I have an idea to maybe start playing drums, but it's just in the idea stage."

"Really?" she said with lots of surprise in her voice.

Bash explained about the pedal system for the drum kit he wanted and about the Def Leppard drummer who did something similar many years ago.

After he'd finished explaining, she said, "That is truly awesome, Bash! That takes so much courage to keep your focus on all the things you *can* do instead of what you *can't* do. I'm impressed."

Bash laughed. "Well, don't be too impressed yet," he said. "I don't know if I'll be any good at it."

"I know you will."

"Oh, yeah? How do you know that?"

"Because I sense your strong spirit," she answered. "Just by overcoming your handicap, people will flock to see you no matter how good you are."

Bash realized that was probably true. People would be curious about the novelty of it and all, but he still had to be good at it before anyone would ever see him perform. His rules, not theirs.

"You're going to go far, Bash," she said while looping her arm around his arm. "I just know it."

Bash wanted to recite the quip: 'with the right woman behind you, you can go to the top,' but he knew it was too soon in their relationship. He scolded himself. *What am I doing? I barely know her and I'm thinking about spending the rest of my life with her? Am I crazy?*

After strolling for nearly an hour they headed back to the sushi restaurant where she had left her bike. "I've got to head to work now," she said while unlocking the chain around her bike.

"What's the name again?"

"Jonni," she said with a curious expression on her face.

"I mean where you work."

"Polvos," she said with a smile. "On South First."

"Right," he said. "My favorite Mexican restaurant."

"Really?"

"It is now."

Jonni smiled again.

Bash smiled back.

"Come on by," she said while mounting her bike. "I'll give you a free bowl of chips."

"Doesn't everyone get free chips?"

"Yeah, but not with the same amount of enthusiasm," Jonni said before riding away on her bike. "Talk to you soon!"

Bash stood there and watched her ride out of view. He decided not to call Ricky yet. He would first take a walk onto 6th street and visit some of his old haunts; clubs he used to hang out at before the motorcycle accident. He walked with a brisk gait, feeling lighter and happier than he'd ever felt before. *You're in love,* a voice inside told him.

"I know," Bash said as he nearly bounced on the sidewalk. "And it is *very* scary . . ."

† † †

13

ince found the shovel inside the storage shed. He grabbed it and marched across the open field behind the house, approximating the distance where he saw Bash and the girl burying something the night of the party. He studied the ground, looking for broken earth. It didn't take him long to find the spot beneath a group of small trees. He began shoveling the rocky soil out of the recently dug hole.

When his shovel made contact with something, Vince squatted and scooped out the rest of the dirt with his large hands, revealing the cardboard box with a gash on top where the blade of the shovel struck it. He removed the box and noticed it had some weight to it. He opened the flaps and saw the figurines inside. He examined each small figurine before lifting the female figurine out and holding it before him. *What is this stuff? Why did they bury it?*

As Vince ran these thoughts through his mind, the female figurine with the bird feet began feeling better and better in his hands. When he started to replace it back into the box, he stopped, suddenly not wanting to let go of it. He began fondling its smooth surface until an urge to get high consumed him. It was barely noon but he didn't care. *I can do whatever I want whenever I want,* he told himself. In some strange way, the female figurine seemed to agree with him.

Vince carefully replaced the figurine back into the box before taking it inside the house and into his bedroom. After removing the little figurines from the box and setting them on his bedroom floor, he grabbed the female figurine and held it in his hands. He felt an energy emanating from it that penetrated the core of his being. As he stroked its smooth stone surface, thoughts began to form that didn't originate from his own mind.

Vince stood the female figurine on the floor next to the other figurines and grabbed a plastic baggie full of cocaine hidden under his mattress. He poured out a large pile of the white powder on an empty plate before sorting the pile into three-inch-long rows with his fingernail. Using a rolled hundred-dollar bill as a straw, he inhaled the powder into each nostril with loud snorts, sounding like a raging bull about to charge.

A moment later he decided to call Cass, one of his girlfriends that was very much into cocaine, which he obviously had plenty of.

When Cass arrived at Rock Bottom and saw the figurines she became very excited. Covered in tattoos and body piercings, Cass drew a circle on the floor with a dark crayon before lining the circle with small black candles she had brought in a leather backpack. She set the figurines inside the circle, then lowered herself into a cross-legged position next to them. Vince put a Pantera CD into a portable boombox he kept in his bedroom before joining her in the circle. After snorting several lines of coke and smoking a joint, they soon fell into a trance-like state while Pantera roared from the boombox. Cass began speaking in some language Vince had never heard before. Despite not understanding the language, her words, mixed with the violent music filling the room, gave him chills from head to toe. Soon they were on his mattress where they stayed for hours. Time seemed to stand still. He remembered little of it when he awoke alone the next day nearly twenty-four hours later.

†

The next morning, while Vince was still asleep, Gordon left his bedroom and stared at the ceiling of the upstairs hallway. He could still hear faint music coming from above, music that awoke him just minutes earlier. The music sounded familiar. *Is that Cream? Yes, I think so.* He recognized the African-inspired drumbeats of Ginger Baker's drums and Eric Clapton's unmistakable guitar riffs. He began scanning the ceiling for an entrance into the attic. At the far end of the hallway he found a trapdoor-like contraption in the ceiling but there was no cord or rope attached in order to lower it.

Gordon found a stepladder and some narrow rope in the storage shed. He returned to the upstairs hallway and set the stepladder under the trapdoor. He climbed up and examined the metal eye attachment designed for a cord. He looped the long narrow rope through the attachment and tied a knot before climbing down and setting the stepladder aside.

After grabbing a flashlight from his bedroom, Gordon stood below the trapdoor, still hearing faint traces of music from above. He pulled hard but the trapdoor wouldn't budge. He used his weight and pulled harder, eventually hearing the spring-loaded contraption creak and moan before the trapdoor began opening like a jaw welcoming dinner. A folded wooden ladder was mounted on the inside of the trapdoor, exactly as he had expected. A cloud of dust and a moldy smell wafted out of the attic. The music coming from the attic was louder now. The dust particles danced to the music in the ambient sunlight coming from the upstairs hallway window. *"I've Been Waiting So Long, To Be Where I'm Going, In The Sunshine Of Your Love . . ."*

Gordon reached up and began unfolding the wooden ladder which probably hadn't been unfolded in decades. A moment later the ladder was fully extended. He put his foot on one of the lower steps to make sure it would hold his weight. It seemed sturdy enough. He grabbed the flashlight in his back jean pocket and began climbing up.

Once his head was inside the opening, Gordon aimed his flashlight beam around the attic, marveling at the size of the room. The music was still playing from somewhere across the wide expanse of the attic as he looked for a light switch or lightbulb fixture. He proceeded up the final steps and studied his surroundings, still not finding any interior lights. The high temperature in the attic was oppressive and smothering.

The Cream song ended. He waited for another song but nothing came. Examining the area around his feet, he noticed that a plywood floor covered most of the attic with only a few sections bare from any flooring, leaving just wooden supports with old fiberglass insulation stuffed between. He began walking carefully toward the opposite end of the attic, toward the area where he thought the music had been coming from. The plywood flooring creaked in protest as he proceeded slowly through the dark attic.

In the beam of his flashlight, Gordon saw a light switch mounted on a rafter. He flipped the switch and was surprised when two bare lightbulbs about ten feet apart came on, revealing the back portion of the large attic, casting deep shadows on the objects scattered about against the rear wall: a framed mirror, a tall hatrack, a chest-of-drawers, a set of folding chairs, stacks of cardboard boxes, and other various items covered in dust that appeared to be nothing but junk.

Gordon aimed the flashlight at the shadowy objects and there it sat on the floor: an old portable phonograph with attached speakers. The player was covered with cobwebs and he could see in the beam of the flashlight that the power cord was coiled loosely on the dirty floor, the power plug not even connected to a power source. *Where had the music been coming from?*

Next to the phonograph was a cardboard box full of vinyl LPs. He squatted to get a better look, lifting one of the albums into the light of his flashlight to get a better look, hoping he wasn't inhaling too much dust and mold that probably covered everything. He recognized the name 'Deep Purple' on the cover. He looked through a few more of the old LPs: 'Ten Years After,' 'Jethro Tull,' 'Santana,' and many others. Some he recognized, some he did not. *Where had the music been coming from?*

Gordon stood to his feet and wiped his hands on his pant legs. He turned his attention toward one particular cardboard box with some large rolls of paper sticking out. He grabbed one of the papers from the box and unrolled it, revealing an M.C. Escher black and white poster of characters seemingly descending steps that are actually ascending. *Or vice-versa,* he thought. The box was full of rolled psychedelic posters, most of them painted in fluorescent colors that glowed brightly when illuminated by a blacklight. He had an uncle who still owned a collection from the 1970s, displaying them proudly under a blacklight mounted in his man-cave basement.

Gordon returned the posters to the box and went to the chest-of-drawers nearby. *Maybe someone in the band is playing a joke on me,* he told himself. *Maybe they hid an old mp3 player somewhere, trying to lure me up here before jumping out of the dark to scare me.*

While using the flashlight, he opened the drawers one at a time, hoping to find a device responsible for the music heard earlier, but all the drawers were empty except for one. He found an old cigar box secured with a rubber band in one of the bottom drawers. He removed the cigar box, noticing a thin softcover book beneath the cigar box. He removed the book, and in the beam of his flashlight he saw a crude black and white illustration of a plant printed on the cover without a title or name of an author. He thumbed through the book and saw printed text and more drawings of plants with captions explaining how to cultivate and harvest them.

Gordon turned his attention to the cigar box. The rubber band securing the box's lid broke immediately when he began to remove it. The first object in the box that grabbed his attention was a stone pipe. The pipe's bowl was carved into the shape of an eagle's head. He lifted the bowl to his nose but detected only an earthy smell of old smoke. Next to the pipe were two dirty plastic baggies with some type of dark substance inside. An ancient packet of Zigzag rolling papers sat alongside the baggies. *Wow!* he thought. *Somebody's stash! How long has this been here?*

Temporarily forgetting about the music he'd heard earlier, Gordon carefully unrolled one of the baggies and aimed his flashlight at the contents inside. Darkened and dried-out by time, the substance was definitely marijuana, although primarily leaves and stems with plenty of seeds settled to the bottom of the baggie. He sniffed the contents but couldn't detect the familiar smell of weed. *Too old,* he told himself, realizing that along with the music LPs and the psychedelic posters that the weed must be from the sixties or seventies.

Gordon turned his attention to the other baggie. The substance in this baggie was very dark and coarse, reminding him of dirt. A thought came to mind: *Grave dirt.* He almost gagged when moving the opened baggie toward his face. The smell was rotten, like something dead. He rolled up the baggie and replaced it into the cigar box. He stared at the book and cigar box for a moment before deciding to take them downstairs so he could get a better look. With the box and book in one hand, and the flashlight in the other, he shoved the drawer closed with his foot. The drawer made a loud hollow sound as it slammed shut.

After switching off the attic lights, Gordon walked carefully toward the square of light in the attic floor with its unfolded wooden ladder descending to the floor below. His entire body tensed when his cell phone began to ring and vibrate in his jean pocket. He dug the phone out of his pocket while awkwardly holding the flashlight between his teeth. The ringing and vibrating stopped as he read the phone display with its message: 'Unknown Caller.' He replaced the phone back in his pocket and pulled the flashlight from his mouth before hearing a loud thumping sound from behind him. He turned quickly, his flashlight shining on the area with the cardboard boxes and chest-of-drawers. He told himself that something must have fallen. *Maybe one of the boxes fell to the floor. Or maybe a rat I disturbed knocked something over. Yeah, that had to be what happened.*

Gordon turned and started once more toward the attic's opened trapdoor. Although dripping with sweat from the heat in the attic, he suddenly felt a cool mass of air pass by his face. He was thinking about this strange phenomena when another sound came, causing his body to jolt in surprise. He turned and aimed his flashlight beam at the boxes and chest-of-drawers. The loud sound was definitely familiar since he'd just heard the same sound a few moments earlier when he slammed shut the bottom drawer of the chest-of-drawers with his foot. He could feel his heart pounding in his chest. "Who's there?" he said in a weak voice, relieved when there was no answer. He gained some courage. "Very funny, dudes!" he shouted. "You think you're going to scare me? Well, nice try! You can come out now!"

Gordon listened to the silence in the attic, the wheels in his brain spinning fast as he tried to rationalize the circumstances: *If one of the guys was trying to spook me, why did they wait until now? Why not jump out and scare me when I was looking through the drawers?* "If I find out who's doing this you're going to pay!" he shouted into the attic.

More silence answered him.

If anyone is hiding up here, how did they get up here without me hearing them? That trapdoor contraption was extremely loud when I opened it. Maybe they tiptoed up the ladder after I was up here? That's a lame idea. "I'm leaving now so good luck getting out! I'm gonna nail the attic entrance shut so I hope you enjoy your time up here!"

Gordon lost his balance when the shaking started. The attic floor seemed to be elastic as he struggled to keep from falling. The flashlight fell from his hand and rolled away as he stumbled toward the light of the opened trapdoor. He heard heavy thuds approaching him as he reached the steps and jumped into the opening, his feet landing about midway on the wooden steps of the trapdoor's ladder. Another jump and he landed in the hallway floor on his backside. He stared up at the opening in the attic. The loud thuds and shaking were gone.

He seemed amazed that he still had the book and cigar box clasped in his hand.

Gordon set the book and cigar box on the floor while quickly replacing the trapdoor's ladder back into its folded position. With one hefty shove, and help from the spring apparatus, the attic trapdoor slammed shut with a loud bang. Gordon listened to the silence around him while staring at the closed trapdoor. The rope he'd attached swung gently back and forth.

With a newfound courage and a bit of indignant anger, Gordon marched toward the first bedroom door he came to. He opened the door and saw Vince sprawled face-down on a mattress on the floor, his heavy snoring filling the room, sounding like a hibernating bear in the dead of winter. He closed the door and went to the next bedroom. He turned the doorknob and kicked the door open, causing it to smash against the wall with a loud bang. Billy almost jumped out of his bed, his eyes still trying to adjust from being suddenly awakened. "What's up, dude?" he said in a croaky voice.

"You've been sleeping this entire time?" Gordon barked.

Billy seemed confused as he rubbed his eyes and tried to focus on his wristwatch. "Yeah, man. It's only ten. What's up?"

Gordon stared at Billy, his angry expression softening a little. "You've been in here the entire morning?"

"Yeah," Billy said. "I didn't get back from downtown until about four. What's up?"

"And you didn't hear anything just now?"

"Hear what?"

"It sounded like a roaring freight train was racing through the house," Gordon said, unable to keep the frustration out of his voice. "And you heard nothing?"

"Sorry."

Although he didn't want to admit it, Gordon now believed that Billy had been asleep and had not heard anything. "Never mind," Gordon said angrily while leaving the bedroom. "Go back to sleep."

Gordon approached the next room, Bash's bedroom. While opening the door he suddenly remembered that Bash was staying at Ricky's condo for the next few days until rehearsals began later in the week. Gordon closed the door and went to the last bedroom, knowing already that Trent was shacking up with some chick in town. The sight of the padlocked latch on Trent's door confirmed it. Gordon grabbed the book and cigar box from the floor of the hallway. He took a glance toward the attic trapdoor before heading downstairs to the kitchen to make some coffee.

A short while later Gordon was sipping on his coffee and perusing through the book with the plant drawing on its cover. The contents of the book dealt with the cultivation and harvesting of one particular plant root used by Native American shamans, the Datura plant, also called Jimson Weed, Devil's Weed, and a host of other names. The unnamed author explained in detail how to prepare and ingest the plant's root, mainly by drying and pounding it into a coarse powder before mixing it with another substance, preferably dried tobacco leaves, then smoking it in a pipe. The author explained that partaking of the Datura in this fashion was an actual gateway to a spiritual realm where powerful entities existed; entities that could empower the individual or kill him.

Gordon closed the book and turned his attention to the cigar box. He examined the baggie containing the smelly coarse powder. *This has to be Datura,* he told himself. The supernatural connection enticed him. He unrolled the baggie and smelled the substance from a distance. *Maybe it tasted better when smoked?* The smell in its raw form made him want to gag.

Gordon removed his cell phone from his pocket to google Datura and remembered the call he received while in the attic. The phone still displayed 'Unknown Caller.' He checked for a voicemail. There was none. He opened the browser on his phone and was surprised by the amount of information about Datura, both scientific and spiritual. One thing was clear from most of the writers on the web: partaking of Datura in any manner could be very dangerous, even deadly.

With the phone still in his hand, another call came in. He stared at the display. 'Unknown Caller.' He answered quickly. "Hello?"

No voice response. But there was something else. Something barely audible but there nevertheless. Music. Cream. *Sunshine Of Your Love.* "Hello?" he repeated, not expecting and not getting an answer. He ended the call. A sharp bang from upstairs caused his body to jolt.

Gordon hesitated a few moments before leaving the kitchen and slowly ascending the stairs, his senses on high-alert for any sounds of movement. He suddenly remembered dropping his flashlight before fleeing the attic when the shaking began. He spent good money on that flashlight. *Maybe I should go back up there and get it. Yeah, right.*

As Gordon reached the upstairs hallway, he stopped in his tracks and stared at the attic trapdoor in the hallway ceiling, his mind unwilling to accept what he was seeing. He tried to ignore the dangling rope he'd attached to the trapdoor contraption. It swayed gently back and forth. But the movement of the rope was not the issue. The issue was the perfectly knotted hangman's noose tied into the dangling rope.

†

Hours after Gordon left Rock Bottom in the van, Vince finally awoke and lumbered downstairs wearing nothing but a pair of boxers, his multiple tattoos almost completely covering his large muscled body. He filled a glass of tap water at the sink and swallowed a handful of aspirin to soften the throbbing of the headache raging in his head. He plopped down in a chair at the kitchen table and rubbed his temples. He saw the cigar box. He opened it and began examining the contents. One of the baggies seemed to have some really cheap weed inside, and the other baggie contained a substance unknown to him. He became especially fascinated with the stone pipe. *An effigy pipe,* he told himself. He rolled it around in his meaty palms for a few moments before noticing the book on the table. He opened it and immediately began reading despite the throbbing headache still thumping away in his skull.

Billy appeared in the kitchen a short while later. "Hey, Vince," he said in the middle of a yawn while heading straight to the fridge.

Vince only grunted in reply as his attention was captured by the contents of the book.

Billy grabbed a can of beer from the fridge, popped the top, then sat down across from Vince at the table. He sipped on his beer for a few moments while staring at Vince. Billy couldn't remember ever seeing the big drummer read anything.

Vince finally felt Billy staring at him. He raised his bloodshot eyes from the book and stared back at Billy. "What are you staring at?"

Billy shook his head. "Well excuse me," he said in a testy tone. "I guess everybody woke up on the wrong side of the bed today."

"Who's everybody?"

"Well," Billy said. "Gordon woke me up this morning all bent out of shape. Something about me not hearing some big noise or something."

"What big noise?"

"Exactly," Billy replied. "Did you hear anything?"

Vince shook his head.

"He said it sounded like a train was going through the house," Billy said. "He was mad that I didn't hear it."

Vince changed the subject. "Who's stuff is this?" he asked while gesturing to the cigar box and book in his hand.

"I don't know," Billy said while sliding the cigar box closer across the table. He opened it and began inspecting the baggies. He grimaced after smelling the baggie of dirt-like substance. "Wow! That smells awful!" He examined the other baggie and made a face. "That's some bad weed. Where did all this come from?"

"That's what I was asking you."

Billy noticed the stone pipe on the table. "Cool!" He reached for it but Vince snatched it away.

"That's mine," Vince said.

"Okay, chill out!" Billy said. "I was just gonna check it out."

"I said it was mine!"

Billy lost his patience. He stood from the table abruptly and downed his beer before tossing the empty can across the kitchen into the sink. "I'm out of here!" he said while storming away. "Have a great day!"

Vince smiled at Billy's little tantrum. He replaced the stone pipe into the cigar box before taking it and the book upstairs to his bedroom, never noticing the rope attached to the attic trapdoor entrance—a rope that hung loosely without any trace of a tied hangman's noose . . .

† † †

14

*B*ash played a basic drum pattern on Vince's drum kit in the Zeniths' rehearsal room. He stomped the kick drum with his right foot on beats one and three while playing eighth notes on the hi-hat with the stick in his left hand, hitting the snare on the two and four with the same stick when those beats arrived in the count. Rehearsal wouldn't start for another hour. He beat on the drums to let out some tension building inside him. It had been a while since he'd talked to Terry. Bash had been trying to reach him but without success. His concern was now turning into worry.

Bash began syncopating the beat; doubling up on some kicks while putting the snare on the upbeat occasionally. He had a good groove going when all of a sudden he was yanked backward by his hair. He fell on his back and saw Vince towering over him, a slurry of profanity exploding from the big man's mouth. "No one plays my drums! Ever!" Vince kicked Bash in the ribs with his boot. Bash tried to squirm away. Vince kicked him again. Bash lost his breath but he kept crawling away. Another blow came to the back of his head and Bash literally saw stars as he felt himself drifting into unconsciousness.

"HEY!" Billy shouted while running into the room. He jumped on Vince's back, holding on to the big man with a chokehold around his neck. They both went tumbling to the ground, taking a cymbal and one of the floor toms with them. "WHAT'S WRONG WITH YOU, MAN!" Billy screamed at Vince.

Vince stood with a dazed look on his face. His forehead was bleeding where the cymbal had cut him.

Billy rushed to Bash who was still conscious but wheezing loudly as he breathed.   Gordon suddenly appeared. "What happened?"

Vince backed against a wall. He looked scared and confused.

"Maybe we better call nine-one-one!" Billy said.

"What happened?" Gordon asked again.

Billy turned to Vince. "You jerk!"

Gordon saw Bash on the floor. He brought his gaze slowly toward Vince. "You did this?"

Vince looked like he was about to cry.

Bash started to move. His eyes opened with a flutter.

"You okay, buddy?" asked Billy.

"Yeah, I think so," Bash said before wincing with pain when he tried to get up. He tried again, holding his right ribcage as he awkwardly stood to his feet. He felt around the ribs with his hand and took a deep breath. "I don't think they're cracked. Just bruised. I'll be okay."

Gordon's anger was now in full force. He marched toward Vince and pointed his finger at him, berating him with much profanity.

"I'm sorry, man!" Vince whined. "I-I just lost it! I think I took some bad stuff or something!"

"What bad stuff?" Gordon asked in a suspicious tone.

Vince shrugged his shoulders while Gordon glared at him.

Billy helped Bash up the stairs to his bedroom. Bash sat down on his mattress and leaned against the wall. He took a deep breath and relaxed, closing his eyes for a few moments at a time to see if he was dizzy when he reopened them. No dizziness. That was good. He didn't need another head concussion.

"You feeling alright?" Billy asked in a sincere tone.

Bash patted Billy on the shoulder and smiled. "You came to my rescue, bro. Thanks. You're a hero in my book."

Billy seemed really affected by the whole incident. "I can't believe he did that," he said. "That ain't right, dude. That ain't right."

"Would you get me some Ibuprofen, please?" Bash asked. "There's some in the bathroom, I think."

Billy brought him the tablets with a glass of water from the sink in the upstairs bathroom. "Anything else you need?"

"Nah, I'm good. I'm gonna rest for a few."

"Okay. I'll check on you in a little while."

Bash laid his head on his pillow and closed his eyes.

Downstairs, Gordon was still interrogating Vince. "You're the one who stole my stuff!" he hissed at Vince.

Vince shook his head. "I don't know what you're talking about."

"You're the one!" Gordon said. "I should have known!"

Vince wouldn't make eye contact with Gordon.

Gordon lowered his voice a bit. "Did you actually smoke some of that stuff? Do you know what that stuff was?"

Vince sighed in defeat. "Yeah, I knew. Datura. I read about it in that book."

"So you did steal it!"

"I didn't steal it," Vince said. "I just . . . borrowed it."

"How much did you smoke?" Gordon asked. He was now more curious than angry.

"Just a bowlful," Vince said. "In that pipe from the box."

"Was this today?"

"No, a few days ago."

Gordon hesitated before asking, "So what happened after you smoked it?"

"I don't know," Vince said.

"You don't know?"

"I don't remember."

"You remember nothing?"

A look of agitation grew on Vince's face. "Just some dreams," he said. "Nightmares, actually."

"That's it?"

"That's it."

Gordon knew he wasn't getting all the truth. "You should've just asked me if you wanted to try it. You didn't have to steal it."

"I didn't steal it," Vince said in an angry voice. "You did."

Gordon didn't like the look in Vince's eyes. He suddenly felt afraid of the big drummer. "I did?"

"Yeah," Vince said with a smirk. "It didn't belong to you."

Gordon didn't know what to say. He took a step backward to create some distance.

Vince's smirk turned into a smile. "But I did you a favor and returned it to the attic. And to *him*."

"Him?"

Vince didn't respond. He just stared at Gordon with a menacing look on his face.

Gordon decided to exercise his authority despite the fact that Vince might physically attack him. "Maybe it's time you start thinking about leaving this band," he said in an even tone. "We don't need this crap."

This seemed to break Vince's defiant stand against Gordon the bandleader. His demeanor totally changed. His expression now resembled a young boy sorry for his naughty actions. "Hey, come on, man!" he whined. "It won't happen again! Promise!"

A haughty look of superiority grew on Gordon's face.

"Really!" Vince continued. "I'm sorry!"

Gordon was glad he had gained the upper hand of the situation without getting beaten to a pulp. "Tell Bash you're sorry, not me."

"Okay, I will!" Vince said eagerly.

Gordon marched from the rehearsal room and into the kitchen. He grabbed a cold beer from the fridge and walked out the back door. He needed to be alone where he could think. *What happened back there? How did Vince know I got that stuff from the attic?* He wondered about the *him* Vince mentioned. Since the incident in the attic, Gordon had dealt with it all in denial, rationalizing that it had all been a dream or maybe an LSD flashback. After returning to Rock Bottom the day of the event in the attic, he had searched the kitchen but didn't find the book and cigar box where he had left them on the kitchen table. He told himself that the whole experience in the attic had never happened so he never questioned any of the band members about the whereabouts of the book and cigar box. Even the rope and stepladder he left in the upstairs hallway had been gone when he'd returned to his bedroom that evening.

But the exchange with Vince just moments ago confirmed that the attic experience had not been a dream or flashback. *It was real.* Which meant that the force behind it all was also real, the force that Vince said was a *him*. The hair on the back of Gordon's neck stood on end. He vowed to never stay alone in Rock Bottom again.

A short while later Bash was on his feet, searching the opened top drawer of his chest-of-drawers. He had a bad taste in his mouth—both literally and metaphorically. He grabbed a stick of Juicy Fruit from the drawer and removed the foil wrapper with his thumb and forefinger. He began chewing the gum while looking for a hairbrush in the drawer when his door opened.

Vince stood in the doorway. "Hey, man," he said. "I just wanted to tell you I'm sorry."

Bash just stared back.

"Well," Vince continued, "I just wanted to let you know that I'll make it up to you. Are you feeling alright?"

"I'll live."

Vince lowered his eyes. "Well, I just wanted to tell you that," he said before closing the door and walking away.

Bash let go of the heavy flashlight he gripped in the top drawer, ready to use it as a weapon in case the big drummer made a move toward him.

What a psycho, Bash told himself. *I knew he was bad news but this is ridiculous.* Bash made a vow to keep something on his person anytime he was alone around Vince, something like the heavy flashlight or maybe a hammer. Vince had gotten him with a sneak attack. There wasn't much Bash could have done to prevent the beating but from now on he wouldn't turn his back on Vince. If the big man came at him again he would stop him somehow, using whatever weapon he could find.

The Zeniths got through the rehearsal that evening although everyone was in a somber mood, sobered by what had happened to Bash earlier. The band largely ignored Vince who really went out of his way to be nice toward Bash, although Bash felt that it was all a show for the band's benefit. By the time the weekend rolled around, everyone had forgotten about Bash's beating, pretending like it had never taken place. Bash would have forgotten too except for the lightning bolt of pain he felt in his ribs when he leaned over or stretched the wrong way.

†

Terry stood at the airport pay phone and listened to Bash's voicemail recording on the other end. He almost left a message but changed his mind, deciding to keep his trip secret, surprising Bash when he arrived in Austin in a few days. He wished he could let Shadya know. He had been trying for days, ever since he got the new gig, but no one ever answered the phone at the farm. He felt bad that she didn't know where he was.

An Egyptian man was standing a few feet away, an impatient look on his face. "Come on, Tarik," he said in his Arabic tongue. "The hotel shuttle is waiting for us outside."

Terry hung up the pay phone receiver. He grabbed his bass guitar in its leather gig bag and his one piece of luggage. He followed the man and the other band members outside the small baggage terminal to the waiting hotel shuttle.

A week earlier Terry had auditioned for Bit Tawfiq, a Portland-based band that were well known in Arab circles in the Pacific Northwest and Canada. He got the job for his adequate bass playing but mainly for his ability to sing without a heavy accent, something the previous bass player lacked. Bit Tawfiq had lots of gigs on the books, some even abroad like now. They had already completed several shows in Canada; one in Vancouver, and two in a row at a popular Toronto nightclub specializing in Middle Eastern bands. Now they had one more show in eastern Canada before flying to Dallas, Texas to perform at a private show for a company owned by a rich Turkish businessman. *What a stroke of luck!* he had told himself after finding the Texas date on the band's itinerary. *Dallas is two hundred miles from Austin!*

Terry had already changed his return flight in order to stay in Texas longer after the Dallas gig, their last gig of the run. Terry told the Bit Tawfiq band leader that he wanted to visit his brother in Austin before returning to Portland. The band leader saw no problem with that. Terry was excited about finally seeing Bash after so many years. Although he was making a living doing something he loved, singing and playing the bass guitar, his time with Bit Tawfiq so far had been a major disappointment. The band members treated the whole experience as nothing but a job. Having lurid affairs with anonymous women seemed to be the priority. But soon he would be visiting his older brother in Texas. *That makes all this worth it!*

As Terry and the other Bit Tawfiq members rode toward the hotel in the shuttle, Terry thought about the upcoming trip to Texas. He hoped his reunion with Bash would be everything he'd imagined. He also hoped that Walid wasn't capable of executing the violent plans Terry had accidentally overheard that night at the farm not so long ago . . .

† † †

15

The Zeniths were playing a show at Stubb's outdoor stage to a packed house of over eight-hundred. They played several original songs which hadn't been recorded yet but were scheduled for the new CD. The rehearsals for the last several weeks at Rock Bottom were centered around the new songs.

Bash had relaxed from tweaking the mix by the second song of the show. He was now just waiting to hit certain cues for instrument rides and drum fills in the Zeniths' set list, but still staying alert in case anything unexpected happened, like a malfunction in the Avid software or the speaker arrays. He suddenly sensed someone standing near him. He turned and saw Jonni standing there with a sweet smile on her face. He smiled back and extended his hand to her, offering her to stand next to him. He made a couple of exaggerated movements with his hand over the console, pretending to be turning knobs and hitting buttons rapidly. She giggled although you couldn't hear it over the loud music. Bash leaned over close to her at one point and said in a loud voice, "I'm glad you came!"

She mouthed the words: "Me, too."

After the show, Bash oversaw the stage hands packing the gear into a truck owned by a cartage company. Soon, Bash and Jonni were sitting in a quiet spot in the venue, sipping bottled waters and talking about nothing important. He didn't mention anything about the beating he took from Vince, and since he wouldn't be taking off his shirt in front of her, she would never see the large purple bruises on his side.

"Have you talked to your brother lately?" Jonni asked.

"No," he said. "I've called Khalid's apartment and no one answers. And every time I call my uncle's phone number no one answers. A young boy answered once. I guess he's Walid's youngest kid. Anyway, he was no help. When I asked to speak to Shadya he said something in Arabic I don't understand. Then he hung up."

Jonni nodded in a sad way.

Bash saw Vince talking to two girls in black Gothic apparel. The girls reminded Bash of vampires.

Vince made eye contact with Bash. The look he gave Bash was unnerving. It seemed to say: *Wait until I get you alone, little soundman. You'll wish you would've died in that motorcycle wreck rather than deal with me.*

Jonni caught the look. She didn't like it.

Bash wasn't backing down. He kept his eyes locked onto Vince's eyes, sending his own telepathic message: *Next time you won't see me coming because you'll be blind, you tattooed freak. After I bury your own drumsticks in your eyeballs you'll look like a baldheaded bug with wooden antennae coming out of your eye sockets!* The part about the drumstick antennae made Bash smile.

Vince saw Bash's smile and his face reddened with rage.

Jonni noticed that their staring-challenge was getting worse. "Is the band staying at Rock Bottom tonight?"

"I don't know," Bash said, holding his gaze on Vince. "Maybe."

"How are you getting home?"

"I'm not sure," he said. "Gordon took off with the van. I guess he forgot I rode to the show with him. It's no big deal. It's happened before. I'd call Ricky but I'm tired of bugging him. I guess I'll call a taxi to take me to his condo. I know where he keeps the extra door key."

Jonni was thinking fast. "I have an idea!" she said quickly.

Bash broke his stare with Vince and turned to Jonni with a smile. "What?"

"Why don't you stay with us tonight?" she asked, getting a surprised look from Bash. "I'll fix you a bed on the sofa."

"Uh, well, I don't want to put you guys out or anything."

"It won't put anybody out," she said while starting to use her cell phone.

Bash watched her explain the situation to Mandy over the phone.

Jonni ended the call and said, "Everything's set up. We can stop for a bite if you're hungry. There won't be much in our fridge, I can tell you that."

Bash smiled. "Okay, I'm sold." He wasn't going to pass up the opportunity to spend time with her, although he held no fantasy that •

something more than just sleeping on the sofa might happen. He wasn't against the idea of something more happening, it was just that he really liked Jonni and he didn't want anything to threaten their budding relationship.

As they started to leave, Bash took a last look toward Vince but the big drummer had disappeared, leaving the two vampire girls standing awkwardly by themselves. Their angry faces were only inches apart from each other as they argued about something Bash couldn't hear.

Bash and Jonni left Stubb's with Jonni driving the Ford Fiesta that Mandy had loaned her for the evening. Bash checked his cell phone and saw a missed international call. There was a voicemail left by the caller. He listened to the message. He could hear noise on the other end, like the mutterings of people in a crowded place, but no one left a message. He listened several times, rolling up the passenger window to hear better, but no one spoke. *Could it have been Terry, calling from somewhere out of country? Then why didn't he leave a message?* The time of the call had been during the Zeniths' show earlier in the evening. He made a mental note to listen again when he got to a quieter place so he could hear better.

Jonni drove to a Jack in the Box drive-thru where Bash ordered tacos, the only thing he liked or ever ordered from the fast food restaurant. "That's the only thing I ever order here!" Jonni said, amazed at their similar taste in food. "I remember when they called them Monster Tacos!"

"Well," Bash said, "I remember when they called them Super Tacos!"

"Wow," she said with a smirk. "That must have been a *long* time ago."

"Actually that was before I was born," he said with a smile.

They ate while they drove to her apartment, marveling at how good the tacos still tasted. "I can't believe I still like these," she said. "It's been so long since I've had one."

"What's not to like?" Bash said. "Greasy meat in a shell, with the whole thing deep-fried in oil? It can't get any better than that!"

By the time they parked the Fiesta in the apartment complex parking lot and entered the apartment, Mandy was already in bed. She had left a note in the kitchen, welcoming Bash and reminding Jonni of the pillow, sheet, and blanket at the foot of the sofa.

"Want some hot tea?" Jonni asked from the tiny kitchen. "I have some Sleepytime."

"Sure," replied Bash. "Is that a flavor?"

"I think it's just a name for a decaffeinated Chamomile."

"Okay," Bash said, not having a clue of the difference in teas.

A few minutes later they were sipping on their cups of steaming Sleepytime tea while sitting on the carpet and leaning their backs against the sofa. They talked about nothing in particular while listening to a smooth jazz radio station turned down low to not disturb Mandy. Bash felt his cell phone vibrating in his jean pocket. He quickly handed Jonni his teacup to reach into his pocket and retrieve the phone. He looked at it and saw the number displayed by the caller ID. "Hello?"

"Bashshar," Shadya said, her voice hushed and slightly strained. "I'm so glad I reached you."

"What's wrong, Shadya?"

"I think Terry is in trouble."

Bash felt his heart sink. "What kind of trouble?"

"I haven't seen him in days," Shadya explained. "He's not at the apartment. Khalid is gone, too. No one is there."

Jonni decided to give Bash some privacy and headed to the kitchen.

"Maybe they went on a trip," Bash told Shadya, trying to keep his voice quiet in the tiny apartment. "Are you sure Terry's not traveling with his band?"

"I don't think so," Shadya replied. "When did you last talk to him?"

"Over a week ago," Bash said, now on his feet and pacing the room.

"I'm afraid that Father has something to do with his disappearance."

"What are you talking about, Shadya?"

"Well," she said, "I believe Father began questioning Terry's loyalty not long ago."

"His loyalty to what?" Bash asked, suddenly recalling his conversation with Terry about apostasy. "Loyalty to Islam or just loyalty to Walid?"

"They are both the same to Father," she answered.

All types of crazy scenarios were running through Bash's mind. He tried to calm himself. *It's okay. He's alive. He's got to be alive.* "Shadya," he said. "Have you gone to Khalid's apartment?"

"Yes, Bashshar, but no one answers the door. I've been there several times."

"You said Walid was questioning Terry's loyalty," Bash said. "You need to be more specific."

Shadya hesitated just a beat. "I can't talk about that over the phone, Bashshar."

Bash frowned. He was trying to remain patient.

"I know you and Terry have been talking lately," she said. "Maybe he told you something I don't know about."

Bash remembered Terry telling him about Walid's suspicions of Khalid and Ishaq becoming apostates. Bash hadn't even known what the word *apostate* meant until Terry had explained it to him. Bash remembered becoming concerned about Terry during that same conversation. *What if Walid believes Terry has become one of these apostates?*

Bash decided not to mention this to Shadya. He didn't know her well enough to trust her. "I can't recall him saying anything about any specific problems with Walid."

"Are you positive?"

"Yes," Bash said. "Shadya, I got an international call tonight but the caller didn't leave a message. You think it could have been from Terry?"

"I don't think Tarik would leave the country without telling me."

"Have you thought of calling the police to report a missing person?

"No," she said.

"You should."

"That could be complicated."

Bash was getting angry but he tried to control it. "Then I guess I will have to call the police myself."

"No, not yet," Shadya said, her voice revealing plenty of panic. "Let me follow some other roads first."

"What other roads?"

Shadya didn't answer.

"Shadya, have you talked to Walid about Terry's disappearance?"

"No," she said, "but I know he would only tell me to mind my own business."

"I'll bet he knows something."

"Perhaps."

"I'm going to call him."

"He won't talk to you."

"I won't take no for an answer."

"He is stubborn."

Bash thought for a moment and said, "Then tell your father *I'm* going to call the police. Maybe he will become less stubborn then."

"Then he will know I have been talking to you."

Bash thought about how to go around that. "Then tell him I tried calling him but you answered the phone," Bash explained. "Tell him I'm very worried that I can't find Terry and I'm going to call the police. That should get his attention and maybe then he will talk to me."

Shadya didn't say anything for a long moment. "Okay," she finally said. "I will tell him but he will not like it."

"I don't give a flip what he likes."

Shadya said nothing, knowing she was not going to tell her father about Bashshar's threat under any circumstance.

"I appreciate your call, Shadya," Bash said, "and I don't want to get you in trouble with Walid, but I will do what it takes to find Terry. You understand?"

"Yes, I understand."

"Okay," he said. "Goodbye, Shadya."

"Goodbye, Bashshar."

Bash ended the call and stared at the wall in Mandy's apartment. Jonni came back from the kitchen and handed Bash a fresh cup of tea. "Bad news?"

"Not good."

Bash explained all Shadya told him. Then he said, "Let me play you something." He handed Jonni his cell phone so she could listen to the voiceless message. "Listen to this and tell me what you hear."

Jonni listened to the recording twice before saying, "It sounds like the caller is calling from a busy location, someplace with a lot of people."

"Did you hear someone say something from a distance?"

Jonni listened again before saying, "Yes, but it's very faint."

"In a foreign language," he said. "Maybe Arabic?"

She listened again. "Maybe," she said. "I don't know. Do you speak Arabic?"

"Only a little," he said, listening to the recording one more time. "I don't know. It's hard to tell but I think I can almost hear someone saying the word *Tarik*."

"Tarik?"

"Yes, that's Terry's given name."

"You think the call came from Terry?"

"I'm not sure," he said. "The caller ID says it was an international call."

Jonni listened to the message again. "I still can't make out any words."

Bash checked his wristwatch. It was two-thirty in the morning. "Hopefully Walid will call me tomorrow if Shadya actually gives him my message about calling the cops."

"What if he doesn't?"

"Then I'll call the police myself," he answered, "just like I told her I would."

"The police aren't always helpful to strangers over the phone," Jonni said. "Especially from someone out of their jurisdiction. Besides, Terry is an adult. All the police will do is file a missing-persons report. And I think they'll only do that after a certain amount of time has passed since the person has gone missing."

"Then what else should I do?" Bash asked her, his tone revealing his frustration.

"Tell me more about your uncle," she said.

Bash explained to her about Walid's political and religious beliefs, filling her in on his uncle's longtime hatred of America and the West in general.

"Do you think he could be involved in domestic terrorism?"

"It's very possible," Bash said.

"Have the feds checked him out?"

"I haven't a clue."

"It just seems that after nine-eleven," she explained, "that Homeland Security would be all over someone like that."

"Who knows? I've tried not to think about it in the past."

"What if you get nowhere with your uncle or the police?"

"Then I'll go to Oregon to find Terry myself."

"Alone?"

"Yeah, I guess."

"You'll need someone to go along with you," she said. "Someone who can help you."

"Someone?" Bash asked with a slight smile.

"Yes, someone like me."

"What about your waitress job? What about Mandy and this apartment?"

"I can always get another job," Jonni said. "And Mandy will be fine."

"Thank you," he said, "I'd like to take a trip with you. Preferably a fun trip, though."

"We make life what we make it," she said, leaning close to his face. "Positive growth comes from hard times, not easy times." She kissed him tenderly on the lips.

"I agree," Bash said before returning the kiss.

Jonni made the bed on the sofa and folded back the sheet and blanket so he could get in easier. She fluffed up a feather pillow and gave him a smile. "See you tomorrow," she said before heading to her bedroom.

Bash climbed between the sheets and tried to stretch out on the sofa which was an inch or two too short for him. But he didn't care. All he could think about was his little brother gone missing . . . and the tender kiss he shared with Jonni . . .

† † †

16

Rock Bottom was dark. A strong wind blew outside, making the old boards creak and groan, causing tree limbs to scrape the roof on the back side of the old house. Shadows floated across the interior walls from clouds moving through the moonlight outside the windows. One particular shadow, darker than the rest, blacker than black, floated through the upstairs hallway toward the bedrooms. Vince's snoring could be heard from his bedroom but the shadow kept moving, finally stopping at a door with an unlocked padlock hanging on its hinged clasp.

Inside the bedroom—lighted only by the ambient blue light created by the digital displays of a clock radio, a Blu-ray player, and a cable TV box—laid a tossing and turning Trent Masters. He moaned gently from a nightmare raging in his restless sleep. He awoke suddenly. While on his back he stared at the ceiling of his dark bedroom while trying to slow the rapid breathing caused by the nightmare. He knew he had felt bad before going to bed, probably from the mixed drinks Gordon had made earlier.

Trent began to calm and started to close his eyes when his large flatscreen TV came on suddenly. The light from the screen was bright and stark, making his eyes squint. The image on the screen caused him to freeze in terror. He knew the scene, had seen it earlier in his life when his older brother talked him into watching the movie with him one night. *The Exorcist.* It was the scene where the actress, Linda Blair, portraying a twelve-year-old girl named Regan, was lying in her bed, possessed by the demon, her hideous face as rotten as the pit of Hell. The scene had given him chills when he saw it all those many years ago but nothing like it was doing now. He could only whine when the Regan Thing growled at him, calling him by name. "Hi, Trent!" she said in a hoarse voice. "Can I come and play with you?"

Trent's mouth fell open. His eyes opened wide in horror as a whimper started somewhere in his chest.

The Regan Thing began laughing a cruel and twisted laugh. "Trent! I want you!"

Trent wanted to bolt from his bed, smash through a wall, jump out the window, anything, to just get away as fast as he could. But he couldn't move. His arms and legs were paralyzed. He watched in horror as the Regan Thing began climbing out of the flatscreen TV. She laughed and laughed as she crawled across the floor towards his bed, her demonic head spinning round and round. He could hear the sound of her filthy hair whipping against the bed sheets as she crawled upon his bed, the weight of her body pressing against his paralyzed legs. Soon she was on top of him, her decayed face and stinking breath just inches from his. Her soiled nightgown smelled like a grave, or at least what he thought a grave would smell like.

Her laughter died gradually and turned into something else; a growl so awful that his bladder let loose. He felt the warm wetness soak his underwear and the silk sheets beneath him. She began opening her mouth wide, the rotten smell of decomposition wafting from the dark cavern in her throat. He knew what was coming. He remembered the scene, the one referred to as the *pea soup scene*. But instead of vomit, a writhing snake-like thing began creeping out of her mouth. The thing was death gray and seemed to have a life of its own as it inched toward his face.

A loud swooshing sound, like a powerful gust of wind, suddenly blew through the bedroom. Trent darted his eyes away from the hideous thing hovering over his face to see where the sound had come from. The Regan Thing also turned her head while searching for the source of the sound. A bright flash of light. Then a scream from the Regan Thing. The Regan Thing disappeared a moment before Trent's door suddenly flew open.

Billy stood in his underwear in the doorway, staring at Trent's bed with a horrified look on his face. Trent was just now becoming aware of his bed jumping violently on its legs, the hammering sound on the wooden floor deafening in its volume. The rest of the furniture in the room was also shaking and banging on the floor.

Billy jerked Trent from the bed. The Zeniths' bass player had him by the arm as they both backed to the doorway where Gordon stood watching in disbelief. The shaking and vibrating stopped abruptly. The room was quiet. In the eerie silence, like an afterthought, Trent's flatscreen TV made a popping sounding as a small puff of smoke streamed upward toward the ceiling, creating the pungent odor of burning electrical insulation. All three stared into the now peaceful bedroom.

"Did you see it?" asked Trent, his breathing still sporadic.

"I saw it," Billy said. "I thought you were having an earthquake in your room. I still can't believe it."

"No," Trent said. "Did you see . . . her?"

Gordon and Billy exchanged looks. "Her?" asked Billy.

"Of course not," Trent said, more to himself than to Billy, remembering that the Regan Thing disappeared the moment before Billy had arrived.

"I heard something," Billy said. "It woke me up. I left my room and followed the sounds to your room." Billy turned to Gordon. "Did you see anybody?"

Gordon shook his head. He seemed lost for words.

"I saw your bed and everything else in here jumping around like it was all alive," Billy added. "I still can't believe it but I saw it with my own eyes."

"Yes," Gordon said, finally finding his voice. "Your bed, with you in it, was shaking and pounding, just like in that old movie."

The Exorcist," Billy suggested.

"It was on tonight," was all Trent could say.

Gordon and Billy shared a look but said nothing.

All three stood in the doorway in their underwear while staring at the quiet bedroom. That's when they heard the commotion downstairs. They bolted down the staircase before staring in shock at the scene in the rehearsal room.

Vince, completely naked, shouted while swinging a microphone stand like a battle ax. He smashed the toms mounted on his drum kit, screaming in rage as pieces of the wooden drum shells splintered into the air. He turned to the bass amplifier next to the drums and brought the heavy base of the microphone stand down onto the amp head.

"Hey!" Billy shouted while running toward Vince in a threatening way.

Vince turned toward Billy, showing no fear or surprise in his dark, glazed-over eyes. Swinging the microphone stand like a baseball bat, Vince barely missed Billy's head. Billy tripped on debris as he dodged another swing of the stand aimed at his head.

Billy and Trent spread out in the rehearsal room, shouting at Vince while keeping a respective distance from the swinging microphone stand. "I'll kill you all!" Vince growled. "I'll kill everybody!"

Gordon stood at the threshold between the foyer and the rehearsal room, watching Billy try to reason with the enraged drummer. "Come on, dude!" Billy shouted. "Please stop! Is this going to fix anything? If you got a problem, let's talk about it and work it out!" Billy's attempt at diplomacy was not working.

"Why are you doing this?" Trent pleaded. "We're your friends!"

Vince turned away from the nearly totally destroyed drum kit and focused his attention on Trent. He smashed objects in his path as he marched slowly toward the guitar player. He kicked away Trent's vintage Fender Stratocaster sitting on a guitar stand, one of Trent's pride and joy musical instruments.

"Stop!" Trent shouted. "Don't do this!"

Billy moved toward Vince from the other side of the room with his own microphone stand in hand, trying to divert the crazy drummer's attention. "Hey, Mister Clean!" he shouted while swinging the mic stand. "Over here!"

Vince turned and immediately started for Billy, allowing Trent a path to escape the room. Trent saw Gordon standing in the foyer with a dumbfounded look on his face.

"Call the cops!" Trent shouted at him.

Gordon seemed paralyzed.

Trent bolted past Gordon and up the staircase. He ran toward his bedroom, grabbed his cell phone, then back down the staircase while talking frantically on his phone, almost knocking Gordon off his feet as he bolted back into the rehearsal room to help Billy deal with Vince.

Gordon suddenly broke from his trance-like state. Realizing the reality of the police arriving soon, he ran upstairs to his bedroom and knelt on the floor. He removed a metal lockbox from beneath his bed. He quickly dialed the combination of the lockbox and opened it before fisting a bag of weed and a handful of mini-ziplock plastic bags full of cocaine. He then grabbed the most valuable of the articles in the box: an opened package of Spearmint chewing gum with five foil-wrapped sticks of gum inside. The sticks had been laced with a powerful concoction of rare hallucinogenics manufactured in Iran before Gordon had purchased them from a dealer in Austin.

Gordon left the opened lockbox on the floor and hurried to the hall bathroom, never realizing that one of the mini-ziplock bags of cocaine had fallen from his fist and landed in his opened dirty clothes hamper near his bedroom door. He wedged the package of chewing gum in the elastic waistband of his boxer shorts before emptying the weed and the mini-ziplock bags of coke into the toilet. He then ripped the empty bags into pieces and tossed them into the toilet before flushing and watching everything disappear down the toilet. He took a deep breath and left the bathroom to head back downstairs.

The sounds of destruction and loud voices were even louder than before. Gordon continued to the kitchen where he carefully placed the special Spearmint chewing gum package in a kitchen drawer full of candy and other packages of gum. He took another deep breath and returned to the foyer just outside the rehearsal room.

Billy continued to spar with Vince while trying to keep a safe distance away. At one point Billy got backed against debris on the floor left by Vince's carnage. Vince brought the microphone stand down from above his head in a huge arcing swing, missing Billy by inches. This gave Billy the opportunity to strike Vince with his own mic stand. The blow caught Vince on the shoulder but the big man showed no sign of the blow having any effect whatsoever. It only made him angrier and more persistent. Billy managed to leap over the debris to get away from the madman drummer.

"Did you call the cops?" Gordon shouted at Trent.

"Yes!"

"I'd flush anything you got in your room!"

"My room is clean," Trent replied, his attention still on Billy and Vince. He shouted across the room to Billy. "The cops are on the way, Billy! You got anything in your room?"

Billy didn't seem to hear as he focused on staying out of Vince's reach. The drummer seemed intent on killing him with the microphone stand.

In seemed like forever but was actually only about twenty minutes later when Trent saw emergency lights flashing and spinning through the windows near the front door. Several Hays County Sheriff's Department patrol cars parked in front of Rock Bottom. Trent flung open the front door, signaling frantically toward the rehearsal room inside the house.

Two deputies, followed by two more from a second patrol car, hurried into the foyer. They saw the big, bald-headed lunatic covered in tattoos smashing stuff in the rehearsal room with the metal microphone stand. While three of them tried to deal with Vince, the other deputy escorted Gordon and Trent outside to the porch.

More patrol cars arrived. One of the cars stopped behind the Ford van parked near one end of the porch, preventing any of the Zeniths from trying to slip away in it. As many as six deputies tried to convince Vince to drop the microphone stand. Billy had finally gotten out of the room and was now sitting with the others on the porch, talking with deputies in the light of their patrol cars' headlights.

A team of officers, some in uniforms, some in plain clothes, maneuvered through the rehearsal room while trying to trap Vince. One of the officers eventually got into a position where he could use his X26 Taser on the big drummer. The two darts carrying the fifty-thousand-volt current had little effect on Vince. He growled and collapsed to one knee. His body shook for several seconds but he managed to yank the darts out of his side while rising back to his feet. A second officer armed with another X26 also shot a set of probes into Vince's back, this time bringing him down to the floor where all the officers moved in like a swarm of wasps.

A short while later it was all over. Gordon, Billy, and Trent, having already given their statements, watched the officers escort a cuffed and subdued Vince (now wearing boxer shorts retrieved from Vince's bedroom) to one of the patrol cars. Gordon had already told an officer where the Ford van's keys were located in his bedroom. A pair of officers searched the van for a long time before giving the keys back to Gordon, satisfied that no drugs or weapons were in the van.

Two plain-clothed officers remained near Rock Bottom's front door, talking in hushed voices. They approached Gordon, Billy, and Trent on the porch.

One of the detectives wore jeans and a tee shirt with a badge on a lanyard. "I'm Lieutenant Erik Kocurek," he said. Kocurek had a large handlebar mustache and was apparently the officer in charge. "One of my officers went to retrieve some shorts for the big fella. He found this in his bedroom." Kocurek showed them the clear evidence bag in his hand. They could see a large baggie full of cocaine.

"He claimed the blow was his," Kocurek said, his eyes hard and penetrating. "I didn't have you boys searched because you ain't wearing nothing but underwear. I don't think you would've stuffed anything in your butts since you had plenty of time to stash it somewhere else. So my question to you three is this: if my officers search the rest of the house, are they gonna find more illegal drugs?"

Gordon, Billy, and Trent shook their heads like innocent little boys.

"Are you sure?" Kocurek asked. "I don't like being lied to."

"Yes," Gordon said before correcting himself. "I mean no. We don't use drugs."

Kocurek looked bored by it all. After a moment of talking to someone on his cell phone, he told them, "Tell you what, boys. If we don't find any drugs in your bedrooms, we'll call it a night and leave ya'll alone to clean up that mess inside."

The three musicians shot sidelong glances at each other, trying to read each other's faces, wondering what the cops may find.

Thirty more minutes went by. Gordon sat on the front steps of the porch, staring off into oblivion while Billy and Trent stood nearby, all of them surrounded by uniformed and non-uniformed policemen moseying around the property while smoking cigarettes and joking with one another.

Kocurek returned outside to the porch with another detective. The detective had an evidence bag in his hand. "Who lives in the room with the mattress on the floor?" Kocurek asked. "Not the big fella's room but another bedroom."

Trent and Billy looked at each other without answering but Gordon spoke up. "Our sound engineer," he said without offering Bash's name. "He's not here, though."

"And who lives in the bedroom with the fancy bed and big TV?" Kocurek continued.

Trent's expression collapsed. *They must have planted something,* he told himself. He knew he didn't have any drugs in his room. At least not at the moment. *Could I have left something stashed that I forgot about?*

"It's my room," Trent finally admitted with a forlorn face.

Kocurek nodded somberly. "Okay," he said. "There won't be any charges brought against you and your sound engineer. You're free to go." He turned to two uniformed deputies near him and said, "Cuff these other two and read them their rights."

"You got to be kidding!" Gordon complained, believing his bedroom was clean.

"Oh, man . . ." Billy whined. "For what?"

"Possession of narcotics," Kocurek said while walking to his unmarked car. "The reefer's no big deal. But the cocaine possession will probably put you two in jail for a while. I told you not to lie to me." He shut his door and started his engine as Gordon and Billy were cuffed and placed inside another patrol car.

All the police cars began leaving the area in chaotic fashion. In less than two minutes they were all gone, leaving Trent standing all alone in front of the house with the Ford van parked near the porch, the only light coming from the moon and some ambient light leaking from Rock Bottom's windows. He turned and stared at the old house. A shiver passed through his body. The house seemed to be sneering at him, teasing him that he was all alone. *Come on inside,* it seemed to say. *Let's play!*

Trent wondered if the van's keys were in the ignition. He remembered Gordon telling the cops where he kept the keys in his bedroom, and he saw the cops searching the van, but he didn't know if they gave them back to Gordon or not. He started walking toward the van to find out. The van's headlights and taillights flashed on and off by themselves. Trent stopped in his tracks. He stood motionless and stared at the van for about five seconds, knowing that under no circumstances was he going to get inside of it.

Trent turned around and started walking toward the dirt road, not bothering to return inside Rock Bottom to retrieve any belongings, not even his pants or shoes which were still in his bedroom upstairs.

As he walked onto the dirt road in his bare feet, wearing only boxer shorts, with his long hair falling over his shoulders, he suddenly realized that his hand still clenched his cell phone. He began scrolling for a number on the phone, never giving a backward glance toward Rock Bottom— or the rapid blinking of the van's headlights and taillights as the house shook and vibrated as if a roaring train was rushing through its walls . . .

17

*E*ven though the shows with Bit Tawfiq had become a big letdown for Terry, with the band only interested in meeting loose women to take back to their meager hotel rooms, Terry was excited about his trip to Texas. But despite his excitement of seeing Bash in a few days, he felt very lonely at the moment. He had no friends on the road. The band was cold and unfriendly toward him since he was not involved in their sordid behavior. Most of the audiences were just foreign businessmen that only wanted to drink and dance with dates who were not their wives. They were not interested in any performance values of the musicians.

Now, in a tiny hotel room in the town of St. John, the most populated city in the maritime province of New Brunswick, Canada, Terry picked up the phone receiver in his room. It was early morning. He and the band were flying to Texas later that day. He was becoming more and more accustomed to the idea of leaving the band after the Dallas gig and staying in Austin with his brother. The only thing he would miss back in Oregon was his cousin, Shadya, and his friends, Khalid and Ishaq.

Terry tried Walid's number again, using an international calling card he'd purchased before leaving Portland. Twelve-year-old Amin, Walid's young son, answered the phone. Terry spoke in Arabic. "Amin! It is Tarik!"

"I know," Amin said, sounding bored.

"Is Shadya there?"

"No."

"I've been trying to reach her for days!" Terry said, reverting back to English. "Where is she, Amin?"

"I don't know."

"Why does no one answer the phone?"

"How would I know?"

"Has she left town?"

"No."

"Look," Terry said, "it is important you tell her to call me. I need to give you a number where she can reach me. Do you understand?"

"Yes."

"You have something to write with?"

"Hold on."

Terry waited for Amin to return to the phone.

After a long two minutes, Amin finally came back on the line. "I'm ready."

Terry gave him the hotel phone number, then, realizing she would miss him in Canada if she didn't call back soon, he gave the boy the motel phone number in Dallas where he would be later that evening and the following day. He told the boy to repeat the numbers to make sure he'd written them down correctly. Then Terry said, "Promise me you will give her the phone numbers."

"I promise."

"If you keep your promise," Terry said, "I will bring you a gift. Understand?"

"What kind of gift?"

"I don't know. What do you want?"

"Call Of Duty: Infinite Warfare," Amin said without hesitation. "For Xbox One. It won't be out until November but I want it pre-ordered."

"A video game?" Terry said with a laugh. "Your father would never allow you to have that kind of symbol of America's decadent culture."

"No, you are wrong," Amin said. "I already have the game system and many other games. As long as they increase my combat and tactical skills, Father says it is good."

Of course he would, Terry thought. *Having shooting and killing skills was a good thing according to Walid, good for dealing with infidels.* "Okay," Terry told the boy. "Call Of Duty: Infinite Warfare it is."

"And I want the confirmation number for the preorder sent to Father's email."

"Amin," Terry said, "this is not a kidnapping case where I'm wiring the ransom money to a foreign bank account."

"No email, no deal."

"Amin! I'm traveling abroad! I will get you the game when I get back! I promise!"

"No deal then."

Terry's frustration was building. "How do I do this? I'm in Canada!"

They have Gamestops there."

"I don't have time for this, Amin," Terry said before calming himself and thinking of a way to sweeten the deal. "Amin, I promise I will get you *two* games when I get back."

"Promise?"

"Yes!" Terry said eagerly. He could hear the boy's smile over the phone.

"Hold one second," Amin said before setting the phone down.

Terry was wondering where Amin went when Shadya's voice suddenly came on the line. "Hello?"

Amin, that little rat! She was there the whole time!

"Shadya!"

"Tarik?"

"Yes!"

"I've been worried about you," she said. "Where have you been?"

"Traveling," he said. "I've been trying to call you. No one told you?"

"No."

"No, of course not."

"Are you okay, Tarik?"

"Yes. I took a job with a different band. Remember Bit Tawfiq?"

"Yes," she said. "You are playing with them?"

"Yes. We've been playing in Canada."

"I've been to Khalid's apartment looking for you," she explained. "Is Khalid with you? He hasn't been there, either."

"Khalid and Ishaq are visiting their other brother in Germany," Terry said. "They will be gone for a while."

"I thought something bad happened to you," Shadya said. "I thought . . ."

"Thought what?" asked Terry when she didn't finish her sentence.

Shadya hesitated, then lowered her voice. "I thought you might have had a confrontation with Father."

"What confrontation?"

"Please don't play dumb with me, Tarik," Shadya said in a low voice. "I saw you eavesdropping outside Father's office door not long ago. I think you overheard something."

"I wasn't eavesdropping!" Terry said.

"Tarik, I saw you."

"Shadya, is Amin nearby?"

"No. I think he is back in his room playing video games."

Terry paused for a moment before saying, "Okay, so what do you think I overheard?"

Now it was Shadya's turn to hesitate. "I have no idea."

"Then why do you think I overheard something?" Terry asked.

"Because I saw you listening at his door," Shadya said. "You could have heard something Father didn't want you to hear. This could be a problem for him. That's why I was worried for you."

"Shadya," Terry said. "I'm not interested in Walid's business or his obsession with jihad and the return of the twelfth Imam or whatever."

"Don't say that over the phone!"

"Don't say what?"

"What you just said!" she answered. "Those types of phrases can trigger monitoring devices the government uses to track people!"

"Well, I hope they are monitoring us!" Terry said, a bit angry now. "Then maybe Walid will get arrested and nothing bad will happen to innocent people!"

"Tarik," Shadya said. "You don't mean that."

"I don't want to see innocent people hurt," Terry said in a calmer voice.

"Who said innocent people will get hurt?"

Terry didn't respond.

There was a long moment of silence over the phone. "Where are you now, Tarik?" she finally asked.

"I'm in Canada," he said before his tone of voice became lighter and more upbeat. "But we will be flying out later today, heading to Texas. We have one more show in Dallas tomorrow. Then I'm going to visit Bash in Austin! I'm going to surprise him!"

"That's great, Tarik," she said. "But you need to call him. He is worried that he hasn't heard from you in a while."

"You talked to him?"

"Yes. Just last night. I called him because I knew you two had been talking lately and I thought maybe he knew where you were. He needs to know you are okay."

"I tried to call him last night, too," Terry said. "But I only got his voicemail. I almost left a message but then the idea to surprise him came to me."

"Yes, he told me about receiving an international call from someone who didn't leave a message," she said. "He seemed very angry at Father, thinking he had something to do with your disappearance. He is very worried, Tarik."

"I guess I made a mistake not leaving him a message," Terry admitted. "I didn't realize he had been worrying so much about me."

Shadya saw an opportunity to ease Bashshar's mind and his threats of calling the police. "Would you like me to call him back for you?"

"Would you?" Terry said, not wanting to lie to Bash about his travel plans in order to surprise him. "We will be traveling all day and it's not easy always getting to a phone. Besides, my calling card is almost used up."

"I would be happy to call him for you."

"Just don't tell him I'm coming to Austin," Terry said. "I want it to be a surprise."

"Then what do I tell him?"

Terry thought a moment before saying, "Just tell him I'm okay. Tell him I've been traveling with my new band, Bit Tawfiq. Tell him I've been busy with them but I will be contacting him soon."

"Okay," Shadya said with a giggle. *Honest Tarik who always tells the truth.*

"Amin has the Dallas motel number where we will be staying but I guess you won't need it now," Terry added. "He tricked me into buying him some video games to give you the number."

Shadya chuckled. "That doesn't surprise me."

Terry paused briefly before saying, "Sorry you were worried, Shadya."

"It wasn't your fault," she said, still thinking of their discussion about the eavesdropping incident. "Let's not talk anymore about Father and matters that don't concern us. Okay?"

"Okay, Shadya."

"Let me know when you finally see Bashshar," she said. "I want to hear all about your visit with him."

"I will."

"Have safe travels."

"Thank you."

"Goodbye, Tarik."

"Goodbye, Shadya."

Terry ended the call on his end, followed by Shadya hanging up the phone receiver in the farm's kitchen, followed by Walid hanging up the phone receiver in his office.

Walid stared at the piece of paper with the phone number; the number of the Dallas motel where Tarik would be soon. He handed a twenty-dollar bill to young Amin who stood patiently across the desk from his father. "Good work, Amin," Walid said in Arabic. "Allah is very pleased."

"Do I still give the phone number to Shadya?" Amin asked.

"If she asks for it," Walid said while copying the phone number onto another scrap of paper before handing the original back to Amin. "She has no need of it now. But do not mention anything to her about you giving me the phone number or me listening to their phone conversation. Is that understood?"

"Yes, Father."

As the boy scampered away with his money reward, Walid stared at the ceiling in silence. A moment later he removed an untraceable pre-paid cell phone from his desk drawer and punched in the number of an associate in Texas. The associate would help fix the problem with Tarik . . .

18

*B*ash's cell phone started ringing. He opened his eyes, squinting at the muted morning sunlight coming through the thin curtains of Mandy's living room. It looked cloudy and overcast outside. He sat up on the sofa and saw Ricky's name on his cell phone's display. Bash glanced at a clock on the wall while answering the call. "Why in the world are you calling me so early? You know I worked late last night."

"You haven't heard?" Ricky's voice said over the phone.

"Heard what?"

"So I guess you didn't stay at Rock Bottom last night."

"No, I stayed at Jonni and Mandy's apartment. Why?"

"Really?"

"I'm on the sofa," Bash said. "So get your mind out of the gutter. What happened?"

"Sorry," Ricky said. "I didn't mean anything like that. But listen. Rock Bottom was raided by the police last night."

"What?" Bash was definitely awake now.

"Yeah, they arrested Vince, Gordon, and Billy."

"For what?"

"Vince for assault and possession of narcotics," Ricky answered, "and Gordon and Billy for possession."

Bash exhaled loudly over the phone. "Were the cops staking out the house?"

"I don't think so. Vince, your friendly drummer, apparently went nuts and started tearing the rehearsal room to pieces. Billy, Gordon, and Trent confronted him but Vince tried to tear them to pieces, too. They called the police who showed up and finally managed to subdue Vince. The police then searched the house and found dope not only in his bedroom but also in Billy and Gordon's bedrooms, too."

"Pot?" asked Bash.

"And coke. They could be looking at time behind bars."

"Oh, no."

"Oh, yes."

"What about Trent?" asked Bash.

"They didn't find anything in his bedroom so they let him go."

"Just like that?"

"Just like that."

"I think Trent is the luckiest person I've ever known," Bash said.

"Well, hold on to that thought because no one has seen him since."

"What happened to him?"

"No one knows."

"You think he's still at Rock Bottom?"

"Who knows?"

"He's not answering his phone?"

"No," Ricky answered. "It goes straight to voicemail when you call. At least that's what Timothy told me."

"Timothy called you?"

"No, I called him at his office once I heard about the bust on the radio," Ricky said. "Right before I called you."

"So Trent hasn't contacted Timothy?"

"No."

"Maybe Trent's with one of his girlfriends."

"Which one?" Ricky asked. "Timothy doesn't know any of them by name."

"What else did Timothy say?"

"He said he's trying to raise bail for Gordon and Billy."

"What about Vince?" asked Bash.

"Timothy is very angry at him," Ricky said. "He blames Vince for everything. Vince is on his own."

"So much for band loyalty."

"Yeah, right," Ricky agreed. "Anyway, it's only a matter of time before the local media digs up more on the story. You know how they will love it. Popular local musicians. Drugs. Naked drummer fighting the police."

"Yeah, I suppose so," Bash said. "Reporters are probably already on their way out there."

"So what do you want to do?" Ricky asked.

"I wanna head out there and see if Trent's okay . . . and check out the damage."

"The Avid system was there?"

"No. It's in cartage. Vince's backup drum kit and some spare amps should be the only gear at the house. Maybe a few of Trent's guitars, I don't know. "

"So you want to go this morning?" Ricky asked.

"Yes, I do."

"Okay," Ricky said. "We should go now. Weatherman on the TV says possible flash floods today. Give me directions and I'll come pick you up."

Bash gave him directions to Mandy's apartment complex before ending the call and lumbering to the apartment's tiny bathroom. He splashed cold water on his face with his hand. He left the bathroom and saw that both bedroom doors were still closed.

Bash wrote a brief note to Jonni on a piece of notebook paper, saying that an emergency had come up and Ricky was picking him up to take him out to Rock Bottom. He stared at the note on the kitchen table. His writing appeared very childlike to him. He wondered if he would ever learn to write well with his left hand. He left the apartment a moment later to wait for Ricky by the fountain in front of the apartment complex. Dark storm clouds were looming overhead.

†

Bash and Ricky jumped out of the Toyota pickup truck next to the band's Ford van parked near one end of the porch. They ran up the steps leading to Rock Bottom's front porch to avoid the steady rain falling from the overcast sky. The front door was unlocked when Bash tried the doorknob.

"Maybe he's actually here," Bash said while entering the dark foyer with Ricky following. "Trent! You here? It's me, Bash!"

No response.

"I'll look upstairs," Ricky said.

While Ricky went upstairs, Bash searched downstairs, turning on lights as he went.

Bash was in the rehearsal room when Ricky came back down the stairs to join him. "He's not upstairs," Ricky said. "Rooms are a mess, though.

"Then he's not here," said Bash.

They examined the carnage left in the rehearsal room. The drum kit seemed to be the most destroyed item in the room. Trent's prized '68 Fender Stratocaster, the guitar he never gigged with for fear of theft or damage, was lying on the floor. The guitar appeared undamaged, though. Ricky set it on a guitar stand nearby. There were lots of dings and scratches on Billy's spare amplifier cabinet but most of the damage looked only cosmetic.

Ricky followed Bash into the kitchen. Most of the drawers and cabinets were open but the contents seemed in order. Bash reached into the candy drawer for some chewing gum. He looked for his favorite flavor, Juicy Fruit, but couldn't find any. He saw an opened pack of Spearmint. He removed a stick, peeled off the foil, and folded it into his mouth. "I want to clean up some of the mess in the rehearsal room. You mind helping?"

"Not at all," Ricky said. "Let's do it."

They spent a full twenty minutes cleaning up the mess in the rehearsal room and stacking the battered drums in a corner. The storm grew outside as they worked, the raindrops now pattering loudly on the windows. "Let's head upstairs," Bash said.

A loud peal of thunder shook the old house as they both lumbered up the creaky staircase. They entered Bash's bedroom and saw all his clothing and other items strewn all over the floor by the police search. They discussed what could have happened to cause Vince to go crazy while Bash gathered his clothing from the floor.

"Bad drugs will probably be his excuse," Ricky said. "At least for his legal defense, of fighting with the police and all."

"Yeah, he used that excuse after his surprise attack on me," Bash said, starting to feel a painful throbbing in his temples. He hoped a big headache wasn't arriving. He realized that the chewing gum had left a bad taste in his mouth. He leaned over a trash basket in his room and spit it out. He cleared his throat and spit into the trash basket.

Although he hadn't mentioned it to Bash, Ricky had been feeling extremely uneasy since arriving at the house. It felt different than on previous visits. Now, upstairs, something felt very wrong. Negative. Unclean.

More lightning and thunder. Rain was now hammering the roof and windows.

"Let's go check out the other bedrooms," Bash said in a strange voice.

Ricky noticed the change in Bash's voice but said nothing.

They entered Billy's room and saw debris all over the floor.

"The cops should clean up their mess," Bash said in an irritated tone. "I can't believe they can just ransack somebody's house and then leave it this way."

"Yeah, know what you mean," Ricky said.

"What?"

"I said I know what you mean."

Bash looked very angry, causing Ricky to give him a concerned look as they headed to Trent's bedroom. The rain was coming down even harder now.

"You smell something funny?" Bash asked once they were in Trent's bedroom.

Ricky began sniffing. "Yeah. It smells like something's burning."

"Maybe electrical," Bash said.

They both approached the TV.

Ricky traced the power cables leading from the TV and the other gear to a multi-plug power box. The power box cable was unplugged from the wall. "Can't be from any of this stuff," he told Bash. "It's not even plugged into the wall."

Bash leaned behind the TV. "I recognize that smell," he said. "That's burnt wire insulation."

"Maybe there was some kind of electrical short and the police unplugged it."

"Or," Bash said, "the cops caused the problem. Stupid hicks. They don't care about people's personal property."

Ricky didn't like the way Bash was talking. It didn't sound like the Bash he knew.

They left the room and headed to Vince's room. They peered in and saw the same mess. The negative feeling felt stronger in this room to Ricky. He noticed a crude circle scrawled on the floor with little statues and black candles lining the circle. *Satanic stuff*, Ricky thought to himself. Bash never commented or even seemed to notice the circle on the floor.

After inspecting Gordon's bedroom they headed downstairs. When they reached the bottom of the stairs Ricky said, "You ready to get out of here now? The sky outside looks pretty nasty."

"No, I'm gonna stay."

"What?"

"You heard me."

"But why?"

"Because this is where I live," answered Bash with plenty of sarcasm in his voice. "At least for the moment. I'm unemployed now, remember?"

They walked into the kitchen. The stormy sky out the kitchen window was so dark it appeared to be night although it was late morning. Bash turned on the ceiling light.

"So what do you think happened to Trent?" Ricky asked. "You think he called someone to come pick him up?"

"Probably," Bash said while grabbing a beer from the fridge. "He's helpless by himself."

"I thought you quit drinking," Ricky said.

Bash didn't respond.

"It's a little early for a beer, isn't it?" asked Ricky.

"Not for me."

Bash's strange behavior was really starting to bother Ricky. He didn't know what to do other than to keep initiating normal conversation. "I still can't believe Trent hasn't contacted anybody. Isn't that strange?"

"He's a dingbat," Bash said while plopping down in a chair at the kitchen table. He held the can of beer between his legs and used his fingers to open the pop-top.

"I hope he's okay," Ricky said, sitting across from Bash at the table. "Trent can go off the deep end sometimes."

"Why do you care so much?" Bash said. "You and him aren't friends."

"I still care about him."

Bash smiled cynically. "Righteous Ricky, the holy drummer."

"I know that Trent is overly sensitive about things," Ricky said, choosing to ignore Bash's remark. "Remember the episode in the closet the first day ya'll moved in?"

"Of course I remember," Bash said. "He acted like a big baby."

"Are you kidding me?" Ricky said, trying to remain calm. "What's come over you?"

"Nothing's come over me!" Bash shot right back.

"Look, Bash, something has happened to you since we've been in this house. I don't think you realize—"

"—Nothing's wrong with this house!" Bash shouted, cutting him off. "Maybe you are the one with a problem!"

Ricky just stared at his friend, not knowing what to say. He wanted to get Bash out of there as quick as possible. "Let's just get out of here," Ricky said. "We've checked it out and there is nothing else we can do."

"Maybe there's nothing else for you to do," Bash said before taking a gulp of beer.

"Come on," Ricky urged him. "Let's go hunt for Trent."

"You go hunt for Trent."

Ricky was breathing heavier now. "I want to get you out of this place."

"You're not my daddy!" Bash shouted and stood from the table, looking like he was ready to fight.

The surprise showed on Ricky's face. "No, I'm not," he said in a soft voice while rising from the table, knowing that in his old days his fists would have ended the matter.

Something dark registered on Bash's face. He glared at Ricky. "What's wrong with this house anyway?"

"I don't know," Ricky said, "but it's not good. It feels . . . evil."

"You Christians!" Bash said, practically spitting out his words. "When something happens that you don't understand it has to be evil! Satan at work! The Devil made me do it! You're all so superstitious!"

"Bash," Ricky began, "This is not–"

"—Just get out of here!" Bash said impatiently. "I don't need you! I don't need anyone!"

Ricky contemplated physically manhandling Bash out of the house and into his pickup truck. He wasn't going to discuss leaving anymore. Bash was not his normal self. That much was obvious. "I'm asking you one last time to leave with me. Please! As your friend!"

"No, thanks."

"Okay," Ricky said while starting out the kitchen. Once he was behind Bash he made his move. He grabbed Bash from behind in a firm bear hug, lifting him off his feet while trying to move out of the kitchen and toward the foyer. Ricky was more than surprised when Bash exerted a seemingly inhuman strength and threw them backwards into a wall with such force that Ricky thought his back was broken.

As he sunk to the floor, trying to regain his breath, Ricky looked up and saw Bash towering over him with a large stainless steel kitchen knife in his one hand. Even more horrifying was the look in Bash's eyes. *Inhuman*, Ricky thought.

Rick struggled to stand up, keeping his eyes on Bash and the large knife. Once he was on his feet he backed away slowly toward the foyer. "Okay, Bash," he said in an even voice. "You stay. I go."

The odd grimace on Bash's face turned into a sinister grin as he waved the knife menacingly in the air. Ricky backed into the foyer, not willing to turn his back toward the maniac holding the knife. Bash followed Ricky to the front door, the knife still waving in the air. Ricky opened the front door by reaching behind him. The sound of the raging storm gained in volume. He shut the door and ran down the porch steps toward his parked Toyota pickup truck.

Once inside the truck, completely soaked from his short exposure in the torrential rain downpour, Ricky started the ignition and turned on the windshield wipers. He stared at the closed front door, trying to stall the raging storm building inside of him. He let out a loud plea to God. "Lord, please guide me into doing the right thing!"

To the repetitive sound of the thumping wiper blades, Ricky thought about the situation. *If I call the police Bash would probably resist arrest in his current state, causing him to be seriously injured, or worse. What do I do?*

He prayed silently this time, keeping his eyes open and focused on Rock Bottom's front door through the whipping of the windshield wipers. A name suddenly entered his thoughts:

Jonni.

He shook his head in confusion. *What could she do? She could end up seriously hurt or killed if she confronted Bash in his present condition.* Ricky quietened himself and breathed deeply. The thought came again:

Jonni.

Ricky put the Toyota in reverse and backed out onto the dirt road which was already slippery with mud. As he drove through the heavy rain, Ricky realized he didn't know Jonni's phone number. Although he knew how to find the apartment complex, he didn't know her apartment number since he'd met Bash out by the complex's fountain earlier that morning.

I'll cross that bridge when I get there, he told himself.

Ricky also hoped he would be able to cross any natural bridges on the way since the storm looked like it was going to become a true Texas flood . . .

19

*J*onni called Bash's cell phone again. She had already left several messages but still hadn't heard back from him. The storm raging outside the apartment had not let up all morning. It was now almost noon and no end to the rain seemed to be in sight.

A voice finally answered Bash's phone. "Yeah?"

Jonni wasn't sure it was Bash. "Bash? Is that you?"

"Of course it's me. Who else would be answering my phone?"

Jonni was surprised by his abrupt answer. "I-I'm sorry. I didn't mean to bother you. I was just wondering if everything was okay. Your note said there was an emergency."

"Look," he said. "I'm a little busy right now. Maybe we can talk later."

Maybe we can talk later?

"Oh . . ." she said, trying not to show her hurt. "Okay. Sorry to bother you."

She expected him to apologize or try to explain his behavior but he just ended the call without even saying goodbye.

Jonni marched to the kitchen for a bottled water. She was glad that Mandy had already gone to school and hadn't heard what had just happened.

Jonni's anger subsided as sadness and self-pity moved in. *Why did he treat me that way? Everything was fine last night. Was he mad that we didn't sleep together?* She didn't know what to think. Maybe she didn't know him well enough. Maybe this was a side of him she needed to see, before things got more involved.

The doorbell rang. She hurried to the door and peered out the peephole. She saw a stocky guy that looked slightly familiar. "Yes?"

"Jonni?" the guy said. "This is Ricky Rhodes. Bash's friend. I need to talk to you. I think he's in trouble."

Jonni quickly unlocked the door and opened it. "Come in."

"Sorry that I'm soaked," Ricky said while stepping inside. "This storm is relentless."

"Let me get you a towel," she said while heading to a closet nearby.

"I didn't know which apartment you lived in," Ricky said while drying himself with the towel she gave him. "I picked up Bash this morning from the fountain in the parking lot. I had to convince the dude in the manager's office that I wasn't a psycho and really needed to find you. Your name is not on the lease but fortunately I remembered Bash mentioning Mandy's name this morning."

"Bash left me a note before he left," Jonni said, "saying there was an emergency and that you were picking him up. What was the emergency?"

"The police raided Rock Bottom last night and arrested some of the band," Ricky explained. "Actually, all of the band except for Trent. I'll give you more details later but right now we have a bigger problem." He paused, trying to gather his thoughts. "I don't know how to explain it."

"Just start from the beginning."

Ricky explained to her about the change in Bash's behavior once they were inside the house that morning, ending his story with the part involving the knife. "I felt like something wasn't right as soon as we entered the house," he said. "But how he became over the next hour is unbelievable. When I tried to manhandle him out of there, his strength resisting me was . . . . not human."

Jonni nodded, a plan already forming in her mind. "He sounded different when I talked to him on the phone."

"When was that?" asked Ricky.

"Right before you knocked on the door," she said. "I'd been calling him all morning but he wouldn't answer or call back. He finally answered. He wasn't himself. He sounded different. He was cold and he ended the call like he didn't want to talk to me."

"So what do we do?"

"We need to get out there to help," she said. "As quickly as possible."

Ricky showed some reluctance. "Jonni, he was extremely dangerous when I left."

Jonni cocked her head and asked, "So why did you come here?"

Ricky looked her squarely in the eyes. "Because I prayed for help. And I got a response."

"What was the response?

"Your name."

Jonni's eyes twinkled. "Then it's out of our hands," she said. "Let's go."

"I'm ready when you are."

Jonni went to her bedroom and grabbed a raincoat from the back of her closet. They left the apartment and ran through the pouring rain before climbing into Ricky's Toyota pickup truck, heading out of town toward Rock Bottom in one of the worst floods in Austin's history.

†

His mood was foul. He grew angrier and angrier with the cops for being so disrespectful in the way they trashed the house. "Stupid pigs!" he shouted as he walked slowly through the upstairs hall with the large kitchen knife still in his hand. He felt like destroying something. Anything. Or anyone. He only had one hand but with the long blade, it would be enough. With all the fury built up inside him, he would have no problem slashing them to the ground and stabbing them until they were nothing but bloody pulps, whoever *they* turned out to be.

Bash went into Vince's bedroom and walked straight to the female figurine standing upright on the floor. He sat down before it, staring at it in fascination. A smile grew on his face. A flash of lightning strobed outside the window, followed by a crack of thunder a second later. Bash didn't notice. He began drifting into the figurine's eyes, into a world far away from bands and cops and accidents where you lost limbs and loved ones. In this world, he felt special. Powerful. Invincible. Wanted.

He dropped the knife and grabbed her from the floor. With the figurine in his hand, Bash leaned back onto the mattress while holding her close to his chest. His eyes closed slowly as he became drawn to her. He could feel her heart beating along with his own heartbeat.

†

Two Austin Police Department patrol cars blocked Barton Springs Road, forcing vehicles to take the detour up a steep road through a confusing neighborhood layout where most of the cars were just following the cars in front of them, resulting in everyone becoming lost and ending up on dead-end streets. The rain came down in sheets, showing no sign of ceasing. Ricky had left the apartment complex using Barton

Springs Road to get to Loop 1, the Mopac, which would take them to 290 and eventually the long dirt road leading to Rock Bottom. But now the flash flooding was making it difficult if not impossible to just cross town.

Jonni called Bash's cell phone every fifteen minutes or so. Bash never answered. It was now early afternoon but the sky was as dark as night. Ricky kept his attention on the car's brake lights ahead of him, his wipers on high-speed, beating out a rhythm that marked the urgency of the situation. Suddenly, an overwhelming sensation overtook him, a sensation of knowing somehow that Bash was in serious trouble and needed immediate help. Jonni was using the map app on her cell phone, trying to navigate Ricky out of the neighborhood to get to the Mopac when Ricky pulled over and put the pickup in park. "I think we need to pray for Bash right now. Okay?"

"Absolutely," she replied. "Can I lead it?"

"Yes," Ricky said.

Jonni closed her eyes and prayed loudly, praying for strength and victory for themselves and Bash, regardless of what lay in store for them at Rock Bottom.

When the prayer was over, Ricky said, "Bash needs someone like you in his life."

"And someone like you, too," she added.

Ricky put the pickup in gear and drove back onto the street.

"Prayer is our most powerful weapon," Jonni said a moment later. "My grandmother taught me that prayer is the most important thing we can do before going into battle."

"Battle?"

"Yes," she said. "This is a spiritual battle we are involved in."

"Tell me about your grandmother," Ricky said while driving through the pouring rain, determined to stay calm in order to get them to Rock Bottom safely. He knew Jonni's soft voice would do the trick.

Jonni told him about Granny Arrabelle and her battles with the spirit world. How even in her elderly years Arrabelle had emptied neighbors' houses of unclean spirits by claiming authority in the name of Jesus. "Granny told me that ridding people of unclean spirits didn't have anything to do with men in white collars rattling rosary beads and sprinkling holy water all over the place," Jonni said. "Granny told me it came from faith. Faith in Christ. The power is from Christ."

"So you saw her deal with . . . unclean spirits?" asked Ricky.

"With my own eyes."

They drove in silence for a few moments as the heavy rain continued.

"Bash needs you in his life," Ricky suddenly said. "I'm glad he's so overtaken by you."

Jonni's eyes lighted up. "What do you mean?"

"I mean I believe he is head-over-heels in love with you."

"Really?" Jonni said, trying to hide her elation. Another thought dampened her joy a bit. "Well, he didn't sound like he was in love with me when I talked to him earlier."

"Like I said," Ricky said. "He was not himself. He was a completely different person."

The huge Texas thunderstorm was not letting up. Ricky struggled to see through the windshield as they inched through a traffic-clogged neighborhood, trying to reach a main thoroughfare to get to the highway.

"Bash hasn't told me much about you," Ricky said. "What do you do?"

Jonni explained about her own work in helping people plagued by the paranormal, an ability encouraged by her Granny Arrabelle. She told him about her plan of creating an organization with other like-minded individuals to help on a larger scale.

"That's a great plan," Ricky said. "I wish the best for you."

"Thank you," Jonni said. "You see, the mass of public opinion rests on the belief that these spirits, or *ghosts* as most folks call them, are the spirits of deceased people who are somehow stranded in a dimension between our world and the afterlife. They believe this because these spirits want them to believe that. But most of these spirits are only posing as those deceased individuals. Granny Arrabelle called them *familiar spirits*, a description from the Bible. But she also believed there are many levels of unclean spirits. Just like there are many levels of soldiers in an army. Familiar spirits may be the most plentiful, though."

"Familiar spirits, huh?"

"Yes," she said. "The Bible says there are demonic presences all around us in the unseen world, demons that are more *familiar* with us than we know. Granny Arrabelle believed that many of the supposed dead people haunting homes are really those people's familiar spirits appearing to us as the spirits of those people."

"I remember seeing some TV shows years ago where psychics contacted the deceased loved ones of people in a studio audience," Ricky said. "My instincts told me something wasn't quite right."

"That's not your instincts," she said, "that's discernment from the Holy Spirit. Without that discernment we are all fooled."

"Are you saying that these psychic mediums are phonies?" asked Ricky.

"Many are," she replied. "Although there are many genuine psychics."

Ricky thought about that. "So you're saying that the genuine psychics are being fooled? That they are not actually seeing and speaking to people's dead relatives?"

"That's right," she said. "They are seeing and speaking to spirits *posing* as dead people's relatives."

"Why are these spirits doing this?"

"To deceive," Jonni answered. "The demonic world supports the lie that the afterlife has nothing to do with God—especially the God of the Bible. This is seen predominantly in séances or what you described, where mediums contact deceased loved ones for clients. Many of these mediums are phonies but I personally know a few that I believe are not. The problem is, the genuine mediums are being deceived. These mediums accurately describe the *deceased* loved one's appearance to the *living* loved ones, giving them information that the familiar spirits are providing the medium. The spirits, through the medium, mention things that only the *deceased* loved one could know, like a pet name or secret known only by the *deceased* loved one and the *living* loved one when they were together in life. That sells it completely. In practically every case, the final message from the spirit posing as the *deceased* loved one says the same thing: *'Don't be sad! Everything is wonderful here!'* In other words, *'don't worry about not having a relationship with God. Just keep doing what you're doing and you will end up here with me.'* And that last part is the only truth of that message. Read First Samuel 28, where King Saul visits the Witch of Endor in order to contact the deceased Samuel from beyond the grave. That's a good example."

Ricky drove a while before saying, "Well, you definitely understand this stuff in a way I've never thought about."

"There's much I don't understand," Jonni admitted, "but I understand enough to not be fooled by their lie." Jonni studied the map on her cell phone. "Take a right at the next stop sign. It shouldn't be too far ahead."

"Okay," he said. "Thanks."

"Granny often prayed around the clock for days before attempting to cleanse a person or their home," Jonni continued. "She also used an army of prayer warriors to pray for her and the afflicted as well. These prayer warriors were men and women that had oodles of faith like herself. Prayer is the key."

Ricky thought for a moment before asking, "Do you think that these *familiar spirits* are causing the problems at Rock Bottom?"

"No," she said without hesitation. "I think a much more powerful level of unclean spirits are involved."

"So there are different levels?"

"Yes," she said. "There are many levels. Just like an army."

Ricky thought about that, wondering about the differences between the levels.

"The Mopac is straight ahead," she said while studying the map on her phone.

Ricky merged onto the freeway. They were now on their way.

As the seconds ticked by they drove through the storm in silence. Ricky remained in a constant state of silent prayer while Jonni did the same. She paused occasionally to call Bash on her cell phone but without success.

"Uh-oh," Ricky said while suddenly pressing on the brakes.

The traffic ahead came to a halt. All Jonni could see through the heavy rain was a sea of red taillights. The freeway was now a wet parking lot. "A wreck?" she said.

"Or flooding," Ricky said. "Or both."

They both fidgeted while the pickup truck advanced slowly, a few feet at a time. Between their constant prayers, Ricky glanced at his wristwatch while Jonni called Bash's cell phone. This trip was taking way too long . . .

20

*T*he room with its large cut-stone walls was full of colorful rugs intricately woven in the style of the Maya. Everything seemed alive with an awareness of its own. Bash was suddenly led by brown-skinned women wearing colorful feather-plumed apparel into a stone pool that looked to be made from a solid piece of jade. The pool was full of warm water and aromatic oils. The women never made eye contact with him but smiled in a mischievous way, hiding facial expressions that could be friendly or hostile. After soaking in the pool, a luxurious robe made of Jaguar fur was draped over him.

Then she came into the room. She glided toward him and brought her beautiful face close to his. Her eyes, dark as polished obsidian, searched his very soul and found the vulnerable parts, igniting his lust to a level he never knew before. They seemed to float into each other's embrace, toward the virtual sea of colorful rugs below them.

Then he heard a whisper close to his ear. It was actually felt more than heard. A gentle wind blew through him, interrupting the eroticism of the moment. He started to become aware that the scene wasn't what he thought it was. She sensed the change and her face began to change.

"No," Bash said, although his mouth did not move. He seemed to be answering someone's question. "I choose the light, not the dark."

A high-pitched scream grew from her throat as she morphed into something reptilian that writhed on the pillows, her appearance so hideous that Bash felt he would lose his mind. Some type of thin membranes that looked like wings began flapping before she hovered above him, the taloned claws of her feet flexing like a hawk preparing to grab its prey.

A gasp of air escaped Bash's lungs as he returned to reality, or at least some altered version of reality. The ceiling light in the bedroom was on. He breathed heavily. He suddenly realized he was holding a large kitchen knife, the tip of the blade pressed against his throat. He dropped the knife to the floor like it was a poisonous snake. He then looked down at the female figurine next to him on the mattress. Confusion overtook him. *Why is it here? We buried it out back! Me and that girl! What was her name?*

Bash stood from the mattress and gazed at all the debris in Vince's bedroom. His eyesight was clear yet everything seemed distorted in a bizarre way. He could see what he thought was the very fabric of matter with its cobweb design joined together by tiny tendrils of multicolored light.

Bash saw the other figurines, the ones that looked like Mayan deity idols, bordering a circle on the floor made with a black marker or crayon and lined with black candles. He grabbed a large shirt from the pile of clothing on the floor. He wrapped all the figurines inside the shirt, forming a cloth bundle that could be carried by his one hand.

A storm was raging outside. Bash had no idea of the time. *It must be late because it's dark outside.* He vaguely remembered sleeping on the sofa in some apartment a night or so ago but he didn't remember how he got to Rock Bottom or how long he had been there. A loud peal of thunder sounded nearby. The lights in the bedroom suddenly went off.

While carrying the cloth bundle of figurines into the dark upstairs hallway, he went into his bedroom for a large flashlight he kept in his chest-of-drawers. The lights came on but went off again. He walked downstairs and into the kitchen on his way out the back of the house. A lightning strike somewhere close to the property jolted his body as soon as he stepped outside into the pouring rain. The loud storm sounded like it was being processed by some special audio effect—like a flanger or chorused delay.

Bash marched toward the copse of Spanish oaks where he and the girl had buried the box of figurines the night of the party. Within seconds he was completely soaked. His hair lay in wet strands over his forehead as he stumbled through pools of water and thick mud. He finally found the hole they had dug. He aimed the flashlight at it. It was filling with water. The mound of dirt piled at the side of the hole was now a lump of mud. *Someone definitely dug up the box*, he told himself. *Was it me?*

Bash fell to his knees and set the flashlight on the muddy ground. He placed the bundle into the hole, then scooped the muddy pile over the bundle with his bare hand. He patted it all down firmly before grabbing the flashlight and standing to his feet.

Another flash of lightning illuminated a small clearing in the tree line a short distance away. He saw something he hadn't noticed before. Just a glimpse revealed by the flash of lightning. He aimed the flashlight toward the clearing and saw it. An old cemetery. Old tombstones. Probably a dozen. Some toppled over. They looked old. Maybe from a century or more ago. He saw something strange. He watched for it again. Then he saw it. The ground in front of one of the old tombstones undulated. He stared in disbelief as something began climbing out of the muddy soil of the grave. He saw another grave breaking open. Then another. He aimed the flashlight on one of the things crawling out of the graves. A corpse of a woman dressed in a filthy gown shuffled toward him, followed by more corpses of men and women climbing out of their graves. It was like a scene from a cheap horror movie. Bash laughed at the absurdity of it.

As the dead climbed from their graves and stumbled awkwardly toward him in slow-zombie-motion, Bash lumbered back to the house. He marched through the mud, careful not to fall, entering the kitchen and locking the door behind him in one single move. He peered out the window, holding the flashlight close to the windowpane to diminish the glare. He saw no corpses approaching the house. Nothing was moving outside except for the driving rain still coming down in sheets. *Am I losing my mind?*

The kitchen ceiling light came on. Bash set the flashlight on the counter near the kitchen sink before removing his wet clothes. He tossed the clothes in the sink and dried himself with paper towels. He suddenly felt like he was being watched. He turned quickly and saw someone sitting at the Formica kitchen table.

A young man with very long hair, wearing a Jimi Hendrix Experience tee shirt, sat at the table. Something wet matted the hair near his temple. *Blood?* The man smiled at Bash and began singing: "Rainy Day. Rain All day. Ain't No Use In Gettin' Uptight. Just Let It Groove Its Own Way."

"That's a Hendrix song," Bash said to the longhaired man. "And you're not real."

The longhaired man disappeared with a sudden flash of lightning from outside. Thunder rolled through the earth, vibrating Rock Bottom's foundation. The light in the kitchen went off and on again.

Bash walked out of the kitchen stark naked, heading toward the staircase and his upstairs bedroom. Music suddenly began blaring throughout Rock Bottom. The Hendrix song, *Rainy Day, Dream Away:* "Let It Drain Your Worries Away," Hendrix sang, "Lay Back And Groove On A Rainy Day . . ."

Once inside his bedroom, Bash put on a pair of boxers removed from his chest-of-drawers. Hendrix's wah-wah guitar was wailing. The music stopped suddenly. That's when Bash heard the sound coming from beyond his bedroom. He listened carefully. There was still a lot of noise coming from the storm raging outside but this sound had come from somewhere inside the house.

Bash started to grab a pair of jeans and tee shirt from a drawer when he heard a new sound. This one much closer. From just outside his bedroom. It sounded like fabric dragging on the old wood floor—a shuffling sound, creating a slow but steady rhythm. A wave of panic crawled up his spine. The lights in his bedroom and hallway were flashing on and off rapidly, creating a strobe effect as Bash stared at the open doorway of his bedroom, hearing the shuffling sound getting closer and closer. The lights quit flashing and stayed on.

Then it rounded the corner, a hideous smile on its rotten face. An old woman. An old dead woman in a see-through gown that was filthy and tattered, her saggy flesh dangling beneath it. She stared at him with malice radiating from her black eyes. A surge of gooseflesh climbed up the back of his neck as his attention was drawn to the bottom of the gown dragging on the floor. Beneath it, he saw talons. Bird feet. Old and gray and decaying like the rest of the woman. Her smell was so hideous that he gagged. Then he noticed she was clutching something in her shriveled hand; the female figurine with the bird feet that he had just buried. A name entered his thoughts: *Lilith.*

The dripping-wet dead woman jeering at him was advancing closer. He didn't notice that he had been backing away from her until his back reached the wall. He suddenly began looking frantically for something he could use as a weapon. A lamp stand. A hammer. A baseball bat would be good. But there were none of those things in the room.

Bash quickly sidestepped around the slow-moving dead woman and hurried toward the staircase, only finding to his horror that more dead people were slowly struggling up the stairs. The closest one was about halfway up the staircase. He was short and fat and dressed in an old-fashioned suit and tie that hung in shreds from his bloated body. The clothing looked scorched. A smaller one, perhaps a boy, followed the fat one. The dead boy-thing had melted-looking skin dripping from its face. Behind it was a female, this one taller than the others with singed hair and more scorched clothing. There were more dead people entering the staircase.

Bash ran toward Billy's bedroom and slammed the door shut behind him. He fastened the oversized deadbolt on the door before heading to the closet for the object he remembered being there. He grabbed the aluminum baseball bat from the closet and heard dull thumping on the bedroom door. The dead people were banging on it. The blows were weak but persistent. He approached the door, planning on sliding open the deadbolt before starting one-armed swings of the bat to knock the dead people out of the way so he could get down the staircase and escape the house. He reached for the handle of the deadbolt, slid it open slowly, but stopped from yanking open the door when he saw something sliding through the crack at the bottom. A shadow. A thin dark mass that seemed to never end. Bash jumped back from the door and stared at the mass on the floor as it began to transform into something else. A serpent. The serpent raised its head at least three feet off the ground, its expression flat and emotionless but with eyes that emitted extreme cruelty. The serpent seemed to be sizing him up, evaluating his weaknesses, staring at him with its cold reptilian eyes.

Bash changed his plans of escaping out the bedroom door. He made his move. He jumped over Billy's bed and reached the bedroom's window. He dropped the bat and unlocked the latch on the window, using all the strength in his one arm to yank upwards on the window. The old window probably hadn't been opened in years. It creaked with protest but it finally slid open. Wind and rain immediately began blowing inside as Bash climbed out as fast as he could. The shingles on the roof overhang were slippery with rain as Bash inched his way along the roof to find somewhere he could climb down without breaking a leg. Or maybe his neck.

Bash looked over his shoulder frequently to see if the large serpent was following him as he searched in vain for a way to get down. Nothing had followed him. He gave up on finding a spot to climb down so he squatted on a gabled section of the roof near the front of the house. A few minutes later he saw approaching headlights on the dirt road in front of Rock Bottom. The vehicle, a small pickup truck, turned toward the house. Bash squinted at the bright headlights as the pickup stopped and two people jumped out. A man's voice called up toward him. "Bash! What are you doing up there?"

Bash suddenly remembered the man. It was Ricky.

"Snakes!" Bash shouted back. "Dead people!"

"Stay where you are!" the voice of a woman shouted up at him.

It was Jonni. He now remembered her as well. *Jonni and Ricky. Here. To help.*

"Stay where you are!" Ricky shouted before running into the house.

Jonni stood by the pickup in the rain, hoping to keep Bash occupied so he wouldn't try something crazy and fall off the roof. "Just stay there, sweetie!" she shouted. "Ricky is on his way!"

Bash hardly heard the "Ricky is on his way" part because he was still thinking about her calling him "sweetie." "Okay!" he shouted back, his voice sounding very foreign to him. "How are you?"

Jonni moved closer to the house. "I'm fine!" she shouted. "Sorry we didn't get here sooner, but if you haven't noticed, we're having a little sprinkle!"

"Yes, I've noticed!" he shouted back with a laugh.

"Are you naked, Bash?"

"No, I've got boxers on!"

"Oh darn!" she joked, just wanting to keep his attention until Ricky reached him.

Ricky crawled out of Billy's opened bedroom window onto the roof overhang. He inched along slowly on the wet shingles while making his way to the front of the house. Bash turned when he heard Ricky approaching.

"Give me your hand," Ricky said while offering his extended arm. "The left one," he joked.

"Did you see them?"

"See who, Boo-Boo?"

"The dead people," Bash said with a crazed giggle. "And the angry snake."

"No dead people or snakes," Ricky said. "Now come on, let's go. I'm getting wet up here."

Bash stood and took Ricky's hand as they inched their way to the opened window. Ricky waited for Bash to climb inside before following him through the window. Bash realized he was in Billy's bedroom when he saw the aluminum baseball bat on the floor. Thankfully, he couldn't see the snake or any dead people.

Bash and Ricky dried themselves with towels from the hall bathroom before entering Bash's bedroom so he could dress. Bash lay prone on his mattress, going through the tedium of putting on a pair of jeans with one hand, a process involving jerking upwards on the waist of the jeans while wiggling his hips and legs. "You wouldn't believe it, Yogi," he said. "It was like *Night Of The Living Dead* around here."

Ricky studied his friend, wondering if Bash had been experimenting with some type of mind-altering drugs, which would explain his change in personality earlier and his running away from dead people and angry snakes. But the negative feelings Ricky experienced at the house earlier still nagged at him. "It's okay now," Ricky said, tossing a folded tee shirt at him. "Let's go check on Jonni."

Bash slipped on the shirt and bolted out the room and down the staircase where Jonni waited for him. They immediately embraced into a hug that didn't end. "I'm so glad you're alright," Jonni said while kissing his cheek.

"And I'm glad you're here," he said, giving her a soft kiss on the lips.

Ricky cleared his throat as he came down the staircase and passed them. "Come on, lovebirds," he said while leading them toward the door. "Let's get out of here. Bash, you got keys to lock up?"

"They're somewhere," Bash said. "Try the kitchen."

While Jonni escorted Bash to the pickup truck, Ricky went into the kitchen and found the door leading outside to the back of the house wide open. Bash's keys and cell phone were next to each other on the kitchen table. The bad feeling he'd experienced earlier that day was still there. He was anxious to leave and never return to the old house. He grabbed Bash's keys and phone from the table.

"I'm out of here," he said loudly before slamming the kitchen door shut and locking the deadbolt, never noticing the muddy streaks on the floor at his feet—streaks that looked like they were made by wet clothing dragging on the floor . . .

† † †

21

*T*he next morning they all awakened at Ricky's condo after an eventless evening and long night of sleep. After rescuing Bash from Rock Bottom to drive through the flooded streets of Austin, they stopped off at Mandy's apartment so Jonni could grab a fresh change of clothes. The rain had finally stopped but many areas of town were impassable due to the high water. They eventually made it to Ricky's condo without a problem. Jonni slept in Bash's old room while Bash slept on Ricky's large sectional sofa.

Jonni brewed some coffee and made toast from a loaf of bread she found in the kitchen, maybe the only food item there. Soon they were sitting around the living room with the window curtains opened wide. It looked beautiful outside. The sun was shining with not a cloud in the sky. They sipped on their coffees, glad that the stormy events from the previous day were over.

Bash checked the messages on his cell phone. Much of his memories of the freaky events at Rock Bottom were now foggy and distant. He couldn't remember much, but what he could remember was enough to give him chills. He knew he would never forget that day. The day of the storms—the storm outside Rock Bottom, and the storm inside.

Bash listened to his phone messages while Jonni and Ricky chatted over their coffees about nothing in particular. There were several messages from Jonni. It hurt him to hear her worried voice but he listened to them anyway. There was a long message from Timothy informing Bash to pick up his paycheck since he would be in his office all day. Timothy rambled on and on about canceled band bookings and unhappy promoters, information that Bash was not interested in. Timothy stated that Trent was still nowhere to be seen. Old news. Then Bash listened to a message from Shadya. It was very good news. She had talked to Terry. Apparently, Terry has been traveling in Canada with a band and would be contacting him soon. *What a relief!* The good news from Shadya had made Bash's morning.

"Terry is okay!" Bash announced, interrupting their conversation. "Shadya talked to him! She left me a message yesterday!"

"Where is he?" asked Jonni.

"In Canada!" Bash said, his voice full of excitement. "She told me he'd be contacting me soon!"

"That's awesome, Bash!" she said.

Bash went into the kitchen and returned with a fresh cup of coffee. "What do you say we go out for lunch?" he said. "My treat."

"What choice do we have?" Ricky said. "You've seen my empty cupboards."

"Yes, you're right, Yogi," Bash said. "I need to pick up my check from Timothy at his office then I'll take us out to lunch."

"You talked to Timothy?" asked Ricky.

"No, but he left me a long message. He's been looking for Trent without any luck. He sounds worried. He's dealing with all types of cancellations. He says there are lots of unhappy promoters."

"His worries are only beginning," Ricky said. "Especially now that three-quarters of his meal ticket are in jail, and the last quarter has disappeared from existence."

"Hey! What percentage am I?" Bash asked with a smirk.

"I'm afraid you have no percentage in the equation according to Timothy," Ricky said. "You are an expense. Something he has to spend money on."

Bash laughed in a defeated way. "What about all that stuff about being part of a family? A brotherhood? Remember?"

"Yeah," Ricky replied, "I remember *you* telling me that. And I remember me telling you that a band living together is different than a band playing together. Add sex and drugs to the rock and roll and look what happened."

Jonni cleared her throat loudly. "I think on that note I will go get ready."

After Jonni left the living room, Bash told Ricky, "I don't know what to think about what happened out there at the house yesterday. It feels like nothing but a horrible nightmare now. Like a bad acid trip or something."

"Don't take this the wrong way, Bash," Ricky said. "But did you take anything?"

"What do you mean?" Bash said.

"You know, something that could have caused you to hallucinate."

"No way," Bash said without hesitation. "I've never taken anything like that. A little booze and a little pot in the past but that's been it for me my entire life."

"What about unintentionally?"

"What do you mean?"

"Don't you take medication for your headaches?"

"Just Ibuprofen," Bash said. "But I don't remember taking any yesterday. You picked me up in the morning and took me to the house. I don't think I even ate or drink anything. I can't remember."

"Strange day."

"That's the understatement of the year."

"There's something else," Ricky said. "When we got to the house I felt something I can't explain."

"What do you mean?"

"I don't know. It just felt wrong in the house. Like a *super* bad vibe."

"Did you take anything?"

"Ha-ha," Ricky said. "It's hard to describe. But something gave me the creeps."

Bash saw that Ricky wasn't kidding.

"I actually told you how I felt when we were there," Ricky went on, "but you didn't seem concerned."

"Sorry, I don't remember that."

"Well, I remember being focused on leaving," Ricky said, "but you weren't interested in that, either. And . . . never mind."

"Never mind what?"

"Well, you were very angry," Ricky said, deciding not to mention anything about Bash threatening him with a knife. "Belligerent, might be a better word. I've never seen you like that, even when you were in the hospital after your accident."

Bash became lost in thought. He could hear Jonni using a hairdryer from the bathroom. "So you think something supernatural was happening, or what Jonni calls *paranormal*?"

"I don't know," Ricky replied. "I'm just trying to explore all the natural explanations before coming to that conclusion."

Bash heard the hairdryer stop.

"What do you think?" asked Ricky.

"I don't remember much," Bash began, "but I do remember some details I wish I'd forget. Like dead people coming out of graves."

Ricky didn't know what to say.

"If you rule out me being drugged," Bash added, "that only leaves the paranormal. But that just can't be true."

"Why not?" Jonni said while walking into the living room.

Bash smiled at her before answering, "Because things like that just don't happen in the real world."

"How do you know those things came from our world?" she said. "The *real* world."

Bash didn't know how to answer that. "They definitely *seemed* real but that doesn't mean they *were* real."

"Sometimes," she began, trying to choose her words carefully, "spirits can make a person experience what they want them to experience."

"I don't know what to think about that, Jonni," Bash said sincerely. "But even if that's true, does that make the experience real?"

"To you, yes."

"Right," Bash said. "But if someone else witnessed what happened yesterday at the house, would they have seen what I saw?"

"Who knows?" Jonni said. "All I know is that I've heard of spirits that can make people see what they want them to see."

"But that still doesn't make it real," Bash argued.

"It depends on how you define *real*," she said.

Ricky was staying out of this.

"So do you believe what I experienced was real?" asked Bash.

"Yes, I do," she said.

"Why?"

"Because I've seen things," Jonni said. "*Real* things that are believed by most folks to be impossible."

"Like what?" asked Bash.

"I don't want to go there right now," she said, "but let's say they were similar to things I saw last night before we left the house."

"What things?" Bash asked, his expression revealing his surprise.

Ricky was also interested in her answer. "What did you see?"

"Muddy streaks on the kitchen floor," she answered.

"What muddy streaks?" asked Bash.

"The muddy streaks on the floor near the *opened* kitchen door," she said in a casual tone. "The door you said you closed and locked after seeing the bodies come out of the graves."

Bash blinked his eyes but said nothing.

"The door was open before we left," Ricky said. "While you guys were waiting for me to grab the keys and phone, I saw the opened door before I closed and locked it. But I didn't notice any mud on the floor."

"I was a wet mess when I came inside," Bash said to Jonni. "How do you know the streaks weren't from my muddy feet?"

"Were you wearing a long dress or robe?" Jonni asked.

"What?"

"I'm not talking about footprints," she explained. "These streaks were made by something like fabric dragging along the floor. They probably blurred any footprints left by your bare feet."

Bash suddenly remembered the sound of dragging fabric before the dead woman entered the bedroom. But he didn't mention this.

No one said anything for a long moment.

Bash broke everyone from their trance. "Hey!" he said in a loud cheerful voice with a big smile on his face. "Enough of all that! Let's go into town for lunch!"

Ricky nodded in an approving way but he seemed lost in his thoughts.

Bash kept the smile glued on his face, but inside a storm brewed as he realized it was possible that everything he remembered happening at Rock Bottom really did happen. He knew he would have to return to Rock Bottom to check out the graveyard for himself, otherwise the event would plague him for the rest of his life . . .

† † †

22

*T*erry walked through the motel lobby and out the glass doors. When Bit Tawfiq landed at DFW airport the night before, dark storm clouds were looming in the sky. Their flight from Canada had been delayed by the storm but they finally made it to Dallas just a few hours late. Today was clear and sunny. The blue sky and hot temperature reminded Terry of countless days of his childhood in Austin.

Terry strolled through the parking lot toward the Texas Roadhouse restaurant a few hundred yards distant, noticing many puddles of rainwater from the storm the day before. Another lunch alone. At least this was the last show with the band. They didn't know this but he did. Soon Terry would see his brother, Bash, surprising him with his sudden arrival in town. Terry couldn't wait for the gig that night to be over and done. Then a short flight to Austin tomorrow. The band had a short setup and soundcheck at four in the afternoon in a fancy hotel ballroom where they would perform later that night for the Turkish businessman's private party. After lunch, Terry planned on practicing on his bass guitar for a while before showering and dressing. Transportation would arrive later at the motel to take him and the band to the fancy hotel and its ballroom.

As Terry strolled across the parking lot toward the restaurant, a dark van cruised up beside him. The side door slid open quickly, the sound catching Terry's attention. He saw several men, dark complected and of Arab descent like himself. They jumped out of the van and grabbed him. Terry tried to break free but the men overpowered him easily. They had him in the van in less than five seconds. The driver took off as the men tied Terry's hands and feet with plastic zip-ties. Terry shouted at them in Arabic. They slapped a strip of duct tape over his mouth as he continued to mumble his protests. The next thing he saw was one of them placing a dark cloth hood over his head. And just like that, Terry was a prisoner . . .

† † †

23

*T*imothy greeted them with a worried expression on his pale face. Bash sat in a chair across from Timothy's desk while Ricky stood nearby, examining the vintage rock concert posters Timothy had in frames on the walls.

Timothy searched his desk drawer for something and said, "You just missed Trent."

"What?" both Bash and Ricky said with plenty of surprise in their voices.

"Yes," Timothy said. "Caught me by surprise, I must say."

"Where has he been?" asked Bash.

Timothy just shrugged. "I don't know exactly where he's been staying," he said in his crisp British accent. "But I believe he has multiple choices, if you know what I mean."

Bash and Ricky nodded in understanding.

"Regardless," Timothy continued, "he said he was not going to be staying in Austin for long. He informed me that he is taking a bus to visit his dear old grandmother in St. Louis, Missouri."

"A bus?" asked Bash.

"He's afraid of flying," Timothy said before removing an envelope from his desk drawer. "Anyway, I think it's a good idea for him to stay gone for a while in case the authorities change their minds and decide to press charges against him." Timothy handed the envelope to Bash. "You might want to consider doing the same, Bash."

"You think they could still press charges against me?"

"I guarantee you that they can still press charges," Timothy said, "but who knows if they will."

"But they didn't find any drugs in my room," Bash said in his defense. "And I wasn't even there."

"I know," Timothy said with a shrug. "Just like Trent's room, but still . . ."

"Did he say anything about his stuff at the house?" Bash asked. "All the electronic stuff in his room. TV? Clothes?"

Bash's question reminded Timothy of something. He found a folded piece of paper on his desk and handed it to Bash. "Oh, Trent left this for you."

Bash was surprised. "For me?"

Bash unfolded the note and began reading:

'Dear Bashman,

Sorry I didn't get a chance to say goodbye. Also sorry for how things worked out. You deserve better. Anyway, I want you to have my 1968 Strat. You can do what you want with it. It should be worth a good chunk of change. Right now I think my rock guitarist days are over. I'm looking for something but I don't know what. Something better than I have now. Besides, I'll never be the guitar player you were so I want you to have the Strat. Keep it or sell it. It's yours. But don't take less than four grand for it if you sell it. Thanks for being so good to me—

Your friend,

Trent'

It actually didn't surprise Bash that Trent was thinking of quitting the business. Bash had been seeing a change in Trent for a while. But giving him his prized Strat? *Now that was a surprise!*

"Trent had a strange story to tell me," Timothy said after Bash finished reading the note. "Concerning the night of the arrests."

"What happened?" asked Bash.

Timothy explained Trent's story of waking from a nightmare and seeing his television coming on by itself where the movie *The Exorcist* was playing. "And then the possessed girl in the movie came out of the telly and proceeded to climb on top of him in bed," Timothy said, looking slightly embarrassed for saying it.

"He told you that?" asked Bash.

"Yes," Timothy said. "And when I visited the jail yesterday, Billy told me that he heard a commotion in Trent's bedroom and when he arrived he saw the bed shaking and jumping. He even compared it to a scene he remembered from a horror movie. Guess what movie?"

"The Exorcist," said Bash.

"That's right."

"Do you believe him?"

Timothy exhaled loudly. "I think both Trent and Billy *believe* what they saw," Timothy said. "Of course it might have been drug induced. Hallucinogens. I knew they obtained some a while back. Some kind of exotic Persian acid, I believe it was."

Bash and Ricky took a quick glance at each other.

"Did you see Gordon in jail?" Bash asked. "Or Vince?"

"Gordon has already posted bond," Timothy said. "He is meeting with his lawyer as we speak. I had the Ford van picked up from the house this morning so he will have transportation. In regards to Vince, his charges are more severe so he will not be going anywhere very soon. He can rot in there for all I care."

"What about Billy?" asked Bash.

"His father flew in from Arizona last night," Timothy said. "I talked to his father this morning. He should be out on bond sometime today."

"So Trent's just gonna leave all his stuff at the house?" Bash asked.

"No," Timothy said. "I will be keeping it for him. I'm sending someone out there tomorrow to get it."

"Except for the guitar," Bash said while handing Trent's note to Timothy.

Timothy read the note and handed it back. He didn't look pleased. "That was generous of him."

"Yes, it was." Bash replied.

Ricky was curious, of course.

"Trent gave me his 1968 Strat," Bash told Ricky.

"I don't think he should give up playing the guitar," Timothy said, pushing his glasses up his nose. "He is amazing and should continue with his career."

"He is amazing," Bash said. "He has a big heart. I don't really deserve his gift. I can't do anything with it anyway."

Neither Timothy or Ricky responded.

After a moment of awkwardness, Timothy stood, signaling them that the meeting was over. He extended his hand to Bash across the desk, then realizing he had extended the wrong one since Bash was permanently left-handed, he swapped arms awkwardly. "I'm glad you stopped by," he said. "I hope we can work together again, Bash. I have some new acts I'm looking at. Hopefully, you will be available."

Bash just smiled and shook Timothy's hand. "We'll see."

"I negotiated with the owners of Rock Bottom regarding the lease," Timothy added. "We have the house until the end of the month but you need to be out a week earlier to allow the maids time to come in and clean it."

It'll take more than maids to clean that place, Bash thought to himself. "I need to grab a few things out of there," Bash said, "but I won't be staying for long. I'll give you back my set of keys once I'm done."

After leaving Timothy's office, Bash and Ricky drove back to People's Bookstore on Lamar where they had dropped off Jonni before visiting Timothy. Bash opened the envelope with the check by using a process where he secured the envelope to his leg with his thumb while opening it with his forefinger. He removed the check and saw the amount. It was correct according to Bash's calculations of the number of shows and half-pay rehearsals he was owed.

They waited near the bookstore's entrance for Jonni. She eventually came out of the store with a bag full of books in her hand. They drove to the bank so Bash could cash his check, then drove to a restaurant on East 7th that advertised an 'asian fusion' cuisine. The food was supposedly great and inexpensive, one of the reasons it was so popular.

During the meal, the subject turned to Trent. "I still can't get over him giving you his Stratocaster," Ricky said.

"What's that?" asked Jonni.

"A guitar worth a lot of money," Ricky said.

"Why did he give it to you?" she asked Bash.

Bash waited to swallow his mouthful of food. "He wrote a note to me saying he was quitting the music scene," Bash said. "He said he wanted something better in life."

Bash went back to eating his spicy chicken bulgogi. Jonni had ordered the hummus roll and almond soy bubble tea while Ricky had the japchel—sweet potato noodles with curry, tofu, and sliced avocado.

"Do you think he's really going to quit playing?" asked Jonni.

"Yes," said Bash. "Otherwise, I can't imagine why he would give me the Strat. It was his pride and joy."

"Where is the guitar now?" she asked.

"It's still in the rehearsal room at the house," Ricky answered for Bash. "I know because I found it on the floor and set it on a guitar stand."

"Maybe we should go back out there and get it," she said, "before it gets stolen."

Ricky didn't say anything but he didn't look eager.

"Let's have dessert first," Bash said. "I'll order what this place is famous for."

Bash ordered three green tea ice creams which they all marveled over as they ate the unusual dessert.

"This is incredible!" Jonni said while taking tiny bites of the ice cream. "I admit it didn't sound all that good when you ordered it."

After finishing the desserts, Bash paid the tab and they all left the restaurant to climb back into Ricky's Toyota pickup truck.

"Are you sure you want to go back out there?" Ricky said after driving away from the restaurant.

"Yes," Bash said without hesitation. "Don't you?"

"I'm just concerned for you," Ricky said with a forced smile. "I don't want you getting freaked out or anything. Again."

"Don't worry about me," Bash said. "I don't want you to have to go back out there on my behalf, though . . . especially if you're afraid."

Ricky had to laugh. "Trust me, Boo-Boo," he said. "I'm not afraid of anything." He turned to Jonni. "Are you afraid of going back to the house?"

"No way," she said with a smile. "I'm ready anytime."

"Well," Ricky said, "I'm in for driving out there right now."

"Good," Bash said.

"As long as we're out of there before dark," Ricky added.

Bash and Jonni both laughed.

"No problem with that, Yogi," Bash said. "No problem at all . . ."

† † †

24

Someone yanked the hood from his head and left the room. Terry heard what he thought was a padlock being locked on the exterior of the door. He squinted to adjust his eyes. He was sitting on a dirt floor. Several holes the size of quarters were drilled into the top of one of the wooden plank walls. The holes let in beams of sunlight that twirled with dust from inside the dank air of his prison—an old wooden shack somewhere far away from the motel where he had been captured. The sunlight seemed extremely bright to him. The man who had removed the hood had also removed the plastic zip-ties from his wrists, apparently, so Terry could eat from the bowl of rice he now saw on the ground.

Terry shoveled down the bland food with a plastic spoon left near the bowl. A paper cup of lukewarm water was also on the ground. Terry gulped it down after finishing the rice. He didn't know how long he had been in captivity but he felt it had been at least a four or five hours. This was the first food he'd had since his arrival in Texas.

Terry knew without any doubt who had ordered his capture. He also knew why. *Walid somehow found out about me overhearing that conversation in his office. How did he found out? Did Shadya tell him? No way. But she is the only one who knew.*

Terry doubted that they would kill him because if Walid had wanted him dead he would already be dead. Which meant: Walid was just keeping him silent until the mission was completed. *But when would that happen?* Terry had no idea of when the attacks would happen. *Would they keep me prisoner until then? For months? Maybe years?* Terry also had a hard time believing Walid would follow through with any *suicide mission* involving him giving up his own earthly life. He knew Walid was capable of convincing others to perform suicidal acts in the name of Allah, but he doubted that Walid would participate in any suicidal act.

Terry prayed. *God, if it's not in your will to release me from this imprisonment then please help me through the ordeal.*

He thought of the positives. At least his captors had fed him. They hadn't tortured him or anything. That was good.

An hour or so later Terry heard rattling at the door of the shack. Two men entered. They said nothing as they proceeded to kick Terry in the head, stomach, and legs. Terry vomited up his rice and water as they continued the onslaught. He screamed for them to stop in both English and Arabic but it did no good. They had no mercy to give. The beating seemed to go on forever.

All of a sudden the two men stopped the beating on cue, as if they had been on a timer, neither tormentor saying a word to Terry or each other. They left the shack and fastened the padlock back on the door. Terry was sprawled on the dirt floor of the shack. He moaned. He couldn't see well. His eyes seemed to be swelling shut. He felt sharp pains in his ribs. He prayed again for God to pull him through. He didn't pray to Allah, the God of Islam, but to the one true God of the universe, the God he always knew existed despite what others said . . .

25

*R*ock Bottom looked harmless in the afternoon sunlight. Bash saw a car parked near the house. Then he saw a man with a camera loitering near the front porch. Ricky parked the Toyota pickup beside the car. They climbed out and Bash said, "Can I help you?"

The man with the camera was tall and thin with a shock of curly brown hair that looked like it hadn't been combed in days. "I'm Gary Barbin," he said. "Austin American-Statesman. Do you live here?"

"Yes," said Bash, "but not for long."

"Were you here when the arrests occurred?"

"No," Bash said, digging in his pocket for the house key. "So I can't tell you anything about it."

Ricky and Jonni accompanied Bash up the porch steps.

"Do you work for the Zeniths?" Barbin asked.

"Not anymore," said Bash.

"What did you do when you worked for them?"

"House sound."

"So you were their sound engineer," Barbin said.

"Uh-huh," Bash said while unlocking the door and stepping inside.

Barbin made eye contact with Jonni but turned his attention toward Ricky. "Did you work for them, too?"

Ricky smiled and shook his head as he led Jonni into the house.

"Can I get a photo inside?" Barbin asked Bash.

Bash was ready to close the door. "Gary, was it?"

"Yeah."

"There's nothing here for you to see, Gary," Bash said. "And I got things to do."

"I just need some pics for my column," Barbin said in a humble voice. "I won't use your name if you don't want me to."

Bash stared back at the reporter. He seemed to be an okay guy. Someone just trying to do their job. "Okay, but just in the rehearsal room. *Former* rehearsal room, I mean."

"Thanks," Barbin said. "Can I get your name?"

"Let's not," Bash said while leading Barbin into the rehearsal room.

Jonni went into the kitchen while Ricky grabbed the Fender Strato-caster on its guitar stand. He looked around the rehearsal room for its guitar case but didn't see it anywhere. "You know where he keeps the case for the Strat?"

Bash nodded. "In the storage area next to the kitchen."

Ricky left the room to retrieve the case with Trent's prized 1968 Fender Stratocaster guitar in his hand.

Barbin snapped shot after shot of the room and the destroyed drum kit stacked against one of the walls. "What do you think happened here?" he asked while photographing the room.

Bash thought for a long moment before finally saying, "You can use this if you want, Gary. But just don't use my name."

This got Barbin's attention. He stopped shooting photos and approached Bash. "I don't know your name," he said, trying not to appear too eager as he removed a pen and notepad from his shirt pocket. "Anonymous. No problem."

"And no descriptions," Bash continued. "Like how many limbs this *anonymous* person has."

Barbin grinned and nodded his head as Bash saw Ricky carrying the guitar case out the front door to load it into his pickup.

"This house is haunted, Gary," Bash said in a matter-of-fact tone. "An evil spirit possessed a band member and made him destroy the stuff in this room."

Barbin scribbled in his notepad, not showing any reaction.

"From what I hear," Bash continued, "it was like a scene from *The Exorcist* around here that night. And then the cops showed up and the *real* horror show began."

Barbin didn't hide his smile as he wrote down Bash's words.

"Okay, we're done now," Bash said while leading him back to the front door.

"Thank you," Barbin said while handing Bash his business card. "If you think of anything else please call the number on the back. That's my cell."

Bash nodded before shutting the door and walking to the kitchen where Jonni waited.

"He get his photos?" Jonni asked.

"Yeah," Bash said while tossing the business card in the trash beneath the sink.

"I heard you talking," she said. "What did you say?"

"I told him the place is haunted and an evil spirit possessed Vince."

"Really?" Jonni giggled.

Ricky entered the kitchen. "Funny," he said. "But he may print it."

"I don't care if he does or not," Bash said. "Regardless, he said I will be referred to as an anonymous source."

Bash started for the kitchen door leading outside to the back of the house. He stopped suddenly and looked down at the floor. "Jonni," he said. "I don't see any muddy smears."

Jonni joined him near the door. "They were right here," she said. "I remember clearly."

"Maybe someone cleaned the floor?" Ricky said while coming to see for himself.

"Without cleaning the muddy footprints that are still there?" Bash said. "*My* muddy footprints?"

Sure enough, the area near the door was covered in bare footprints but no muddy smears or anything remotely similar to what Jonni had described.

Jonni was frowning in confusion.

Bash noticed and said, "Welcome to my world."

All three walked out the kitchen door toward the back of the house. Bash led them across the prairie to a small mound under the copse of Spanish oaks. "This is where we buried the figurines the night of the party. Remember?"

"Yes, I do," Jonni said.

"I reburied them here during the storm," Bash added. He faced the direction of the small graveyard he had seen, or thought he had seen. "Follow me."

Jonni and Ricky followed without saying a word. The closer they got, the clearer it became. There was a graveyard for sure. Maybe a dozen graves. But the ground near the tombstones was not broken. Weeds and small brush covered the area. The graveyard looked like it had been abandoned for decades. Maybe longer.

"Well, there it is," Bash said in a casual tone. "But it doesn't look like like anyone has been climbing out of their graves lately."

Jonni examined the inscription on one of the tombstones. "Rebecca Margaret Flanders," she read out loud. "Born October 3, 1844, Davidson County, Tennessee. Died June 10, 1889, Hays County, Texas."

"You can find these old abandoned family graveyards in lots of remote locations here in Texas," Ricky said. "They're not that rare."

"Davidson County, Tennessee," Jonni said. "That's Nashville. Where I lived before I came here."

"Just a coincidence," Bash said.

"I don't believe in coincidences," replied Jonni.

"Welcome . . . home . . . Jonni . . ." Bash crooned in a ghostly sing-song voice.

Jonni laughed. "Stop it."

Bash began examining the other tombstones in the little graveyard. "They're all named Flanders."

"It's not only a family graveyard," Jonni said, "but look at the dates when they died."

Bash read the dates. He saw that about six of them had died on the same day: June 10, 1889. The others had died years earlier, some of them as far back as the 1850s and 1860s. "I wonder what happened to the ones that died the same day," he said. "That's unusual, isn't it?"

"Not really," Ricky said. "Diseases like Cholera used to wipe out entire families, even in rural areas."

"Yes," Bash said, "but dying on the same day? Same week or month, yes. But the same day?"

"Yeah, I see what you mean," Ricky said. "Maybe something else more violent happened. White settlers in these parts were often up against hostile Indian raiders. Apache. Comanche. They were known to massacre entire families, but they usually took the women and children as captives. But that was before the 1880s. I have an ancestor who was scalped before watching Comanches kill her husband. She lived into her nineties and always wore a bonnet to hide the bald spot on her head where she'd been scalped and left for dead."

"Really?" Bash said, giving him a strange look. "When did that happen?"

"In the middle 1800s," Ricky said. "Near Lockhart. Not far from here."

"The newest burial date in this cemetery is 1893," Jonni said. She glanced toward Rock Bottom. "I'll bet you that this house was built around then.

"How do you know when it was built?" asked Bash.

"The architecture looks like late 1800s or early 1900s," Ricky said in agreement with Jonni. "Definitely not 1850s."

Jonni pointed at two of the oldest tombstones. "These people died in 1856, probably long before Rock Bottom was built. Which means . . . there could have been another house here before Rock Bottom was built."

Bash thought for a moment before saying, "So the question is, if there was a previous house, what happened to it? Was it torn down to build this one?"

"I doubt if they tore it down to build a new house," Ricky said. "Back then, most people in this part of Texas didn't have the means or the money."

"Well," Jonni said, gesturing toward her surroundings. "The older house could've been built somewhere close by. It could still be out here somewhere. Or what's left of it."

"It's possible," Ricky said. "But unlikely. Most of the older homes around here, the ones built in the 1840s and 1850s, were dog-runs built out of log and mud. Most of them have since burned down. The Germans, being the incredible craftsmen and masons they were, built their structures out of stone, but very few of the old log homes are still around."

"Wow," Jonni said. "I'm impressed. You know your history. That's cool."

"Mainly Texas stuff," Ricky said, feeling a little self-conscious about her being impressed. "My family has been here since Texas was a Republic."

"What does that mean, Professor Know-it-all?" Bash asked.

"I mean when Texas was its own country, Boo-Boo," Ricky said, not missing a beat. "If you would've spent more time in school during your youth, you would know more of this stuff called *history*."

Bash ignored the remark and tilted his chin toward Rock Bottom. "There could've been another house built on the same spot," he said. "Maybe the original house burned down and someone built Rock Bottom on top of it. And maybe the fire that destroyed the original house killed the people living there, on that one day, June 10, 1889."

"I suppose that's possible," Jonni said.

"What made you think of a fire?" asked Ricky.

"Because most of my *so-called* hallucinations were burn victims," he said while turning and walking back toward Rock Bottom. "A whole family of them . . ."

26

"Because he needs someone to look after him," Walid said. "And that's all I have to say on the matter!"

Shadya turned and stormed away angrily. Her little anger act was for her father's sake, though. She didn't want to appear too happy about getting away from the farm for the summer, hoping Walid would give her extra money for the trip to sooth her anger. She would have to look after her little brother, Amin, while they were in Cairo but it probably wouldn't be too bad since her mother would also be there to help. She loved Amin but he could be a handful. He'd gotten even worse the last couple of years. More indolent towards women in particular. Her father had seen to that.

Shadya went to her sparsely furnished bedroom to begin packing her bags. She was getting excited about the trip to Egypt. She had been there only once before when she was around nine or ten but now she would be able to do some things on her own. And she would be away from all the cooking and chores her and her mother and aunts performed daily at the farm. Amin would be attending school at some mosque Walid had enrolled him in, hopefully giving her plenty of time to see the sights without her little brother tagging along and bothering her. Walid had said he may join them later in September or October but Shadya thought he was just saying that. She believed he was eager to be rid of them for a few months, which was fine with her. Shadya and her mother would enjoy the break from all the chores at the farm and Walid's relentless dominance of the family.

Shadya decided to make some notes of all the things she needed to do before leaving the country. First, she made a list of items she needed to buy for the trip, scribbling them all on a yellow notepad. She had been surprised that her father had given her and her mother a fairly decent budget for the purchases. He was usually very cheap when it came to giving money or gifts to the women in the family.

Shadya and her mother drove to a Portland mall in Walid's weathered Honda Odyssey van. She made a mental note to call Tarik and tell him the news about the trip to Egypt. He should be in Austin by now, experiencing his long-desired reunion with his older brother, Bashshar. She hoped they were having fun. She would call Bashshar's cell phone before she left. She had lots to do today . . .

† † †

27

$\mathcal{B}$ash and Jonni sat quietly on the edge of Mandy's apartment complex pool, their bare feet dangling in the water. It was almost nine at night. There was still some daylight left but the pool area was completely deserted. They had been in the water for over an hour, swimming laps and playing catch with a Frisbee. Ricky was now relaxing on a recliner nearby, checking his text messages, starting to feel like a third wheel. Since Bash and Jonni did not own vehicles, Ricky was also beginning to feel a bit like a taxi service. He would've suggested Bash use Uber or Lyft—the two main online transportation services in Austin—to get to Mandy's apartment complex, but both services had left the city after being voted out for not complying with Austin's city council demands. Actually, Ricky didn't mind driving Bash to see her. He was happy Bash finally had someone special in his life. He could have just dropped Bash off at the pool, his original plan, giving them some one-on-one time, but Jonni insisted that he too stay for a swim.

"You want to do what?" Bash asked her.

"I want to do a cleansing of the house," Jonni said again.

"Why don't we just hire some maids instead?" Bash replied.

"Ha-ha."

"Are you serious?"

"Of course, I'm serious."

"At night?"

"Of course at night."

"That's crazy."

"That's what I do, Bash," she said. "I've done this before. And always at night."

Bash turned to face Ricky on the recliner. "What do you think, Yogi?"

"About what, Boo-Boo?"

"About doing a spiritual cleansing of Rock Bottom."

"Sounds great," Ricky said, his attention still focused on the texts. "You and Jonni should work well together."

"You don't want to participate?" Bash said with a wide grin.

"No, thanks."

"Come on," Bash implored him. "It'll be fun!"

"Fun?" Ricky said, looking up from his cell phone. "Running from dead people will be fun? Maybe meeting up with Linda Blair for snacks afterwards?"

Bash laughed loudly. "Yeah, a pea soup snack!"

"You are nuts," Ricky said. "You shouldn't mess with this type of stuff. You're not qualified for it. Tell him, Jonni."

"Do I need a certificate of qualification or something?" Bash asked her.

"You'll be fine," Jonni said. She turned to Ricky. "It could be enlightening for him."

Ricky understood what she meant but he didn't respond. Maybe the situation would help lead Bash to the realization that there was more to the universe than he believed, but Ricky wasn't sure returning to Rock Bottom was the way to go about it.

"I'll go if you go," Bash told Ricky.

"Not interested," Rick shot back.

"You need to learn to face your fears," Bash said, unable to hide his smile.

Ricky wouldn't take the bait. "You two just want me to go because you need transportation," he said. "Maybe both of you should start considering getting some wheels so you can drive yourselves wherever you want to go. Think about it. There are probably hundreds of spiritually unclean locations around Austin. Maybe thousands. Demons galore . . ."

"So will you take us out there?" Jonni asked, unfazed by his remarks.

"Of course I will," Ricky said without hesitation.

Despite Bash's teasing and joking, Ricky could see that Bash didn't look very eager to return to Rock Bottom for *any* reason involving going out there at night, especially not for any spiritual cleansing. But Jonni wanted to do it and Ricky knew Bash had to save face. "You really want to do this, Bash?" Ricky asked him.

"I have some questions I'd like to get answered," Bash said, "but even if I didn't have any questions, I'm not going to let Jonni go out there by herself."

Jonni sighed. "I don't mind going by myself. I just thought it would be enlightening for you."

"How could it be enlightening for me?" Bash said.

"You might see that there really is a spiritual realm," she said, "an *unseen* world that doesn't obey or adhere to the rules of the *seen* world."

Bash wasn't sure if he wanted to know about this *unseen* world, especially if that's what he experienced the day of the storms. "So, when is the last time you performed a spiritual cleansing?"

"The week before I met you," Jonni answered without hesitation. "For a married couple in south Austin."

"And you did it on your own?"

"Yes," she said. "But teams are better. Especially when the teams are made up of believers."

"Believers of what?" asked Bash.

"Believers of God," she said.

Bash turned to Ricky with a big smile on his face. "Well, that leaves me out," he said. "I guess you'll have to go in my place, Yogi!"

Ricky didn't respond. A moment later a big smile grew on his face. "Hey!" he said. "I just thought of something!"

"That's a miracle within itself!" said Bash.

"You guys could get your own ghost-hunting TV show," Ricky said, ignoring Bash's remark. "You could call it the Jonni and Boo-Boo Show! Get it? Like *boo* when you scare someone! Bash, you could be the side-kick who is always getting spooked!"

Bash gave him a look.

"When you get really scared," Ricky continued, "the special effects people could tease and spray your hair to make it stand straight up!" Ricky broke up in laughter. "That would be hilarious! I'd watch every night the show came on TV!"

Bash tried to splash pool water on him. Jonni did the same.

Ricky left the recliner and joined them at the edge of the pool. "Are you sure about this, Jonni?" Ricky asked. "You sure you know what you're doing?"

"Yes," Jonni said. "I learned everything from my Granny Arrabelle, remember?"

"Yes," Ricky said. "I suppose you did."

"Ya'll have some little secrets I need to know about?" asked Bash.

"When Jonni and I braved through the floods to save you from the dead people and snakes," Ricky said, "we talked about her grandmother and her abilities."

"And what abilities are those?" asked Bash.

"She believed in Jesus," Jonni said. "And she used his name when she cleansed people's homes of evil spirits."

"I know you believe that," Bash said, "but I'm just being honest with you that I'm skeptical."

"Fair enough," she said, pausing for a moment before adding, "So if you don't believe what you experienced that day was caused by evil spirits, you must believe it was a result of a mental breakdown. Right?"

Bash started to argue her point but he realized she was right. It had to be one or the other. *I'm not sure which is worse: losing my mind, or the evil spirit thing.* He thought of something else. "There is another possibility."

"What?"

"Maybe I was drugged."

"Did you take anything that would cause you to hallucinate?"

"Like I said earlier," Bash said, "I don't remember eating or drinking anything that day. Ricky, do you remember me eating or drinking anything when we went out there that morning?"

"You had a beer from the fridge," Ricky said, "which I thought was strange for you since it was so early in the day. But you were already a different person by then. And the beer was unopened. I clearly remember you popping the tab on the can before you started gulping it down."

Bash stared at Ricky, not remembering anything about drinking a beer that day.

"Okay," Jonni said, "so you being drugged is a third possibility. Which if true, would give the spirits plenty to work with in causing you even more misery."

"Why do they want to cause anybody misery?" asked Bash.

"Because that is what they do, Bash," she answered. "They thrive on hate and anger, and wish nothing for the human race except for total destruction, spiritual and otherwise."

Bash shook his head. "It's just so hard for me to believe."

"Well," Jonni said, "the only way you will know for sure is by going out there with me to do the cleansing."

Bash knew she was right. Now he knew what she meant by him getting *enlightened*.

After a period of silence, Ricky spoke up. "If this stuff about evil spirits is not real, then why do so many people use the Bible to cleanse haunted locations?"

"Why do you care, Mr. He-who-is-afraid-to-go-out-there?" Bash said.

"Tell us what you think, Ricky," said Jonni, giving Bash a little punch in the ribs.

"Okay, you see all these paranormal investigators on TV looking for ghosts in people's homes," Ricky explained. "Most of the findings from these investigations report of negative spirits, hardly ever nice spirits. I've never heard of them claiming to have recorded a pleasant welcome EVP from Casper the friendly ghost."

"So?" said Bash, trying to suppress a smile.

"So most of the time these paranormal investigators conclude that there is something evil going on," Ricky continued, "so they call in a pastor or priest who blesses the house using prayers from the Bible. Since most of these paranormal investigators are agnostics or atheists, it appears odd that they go this route. They don't believe in God or the Bible but they believe that people who do can fix the problem. It seems to me that their logic is a bit contradictory."

"I see what you mean," Bash said, "but I think people expect that type of thing. These ghost-hunting shows are not meant to be educational. They are only meant to be entertaining. Ratings are everything. Scary is fun. You know, like in all those old horror movies where the hero uses crucifixes and holy water to defeat the vampire."

"Yeah but most people don't believe in vampires," Ricky said. "That's nothing but superstition."

"People say the same thing about the Bible," Bash shot back. "That it's nothing but a superstition."

Jonni listened without interrupting. She wanted to hear their thoughts.

"All I was saying," Ricky said, "was that for unbelievers to enlist the help of the Bible seems like a big contradiction to me."

"I get that," Bash said. He was starting to become annoyed. "But many people think the Bible contradicts itself, too."

"Yes," Ricky said, not missing a beat, "and I used to be one of those people. And like most of those people, I hadn't spent much time investigating my heart or the scriptures regarding those *supposed* contradictions. Spend some real time exploring what the Bible says and compare it to what the History Channel says and you might be surprised."

Bash tried to suppress his anger. Ricky was so stubborn on the matter. "Maybe those who believe that everything the Bible says is true are just focused on their own wishful thinking!" Bash said. "I don't mind getting into theological debates with you, Ricky. But with you, the debate always ends with 'the Bible is always right!' No matter what! How can I ever win?"

"Is that what it's all about?" Ricky said. "Who wins or loses a debate?"

Bash shook his head in disgust.

"The truth is the truth," Ricky added. "Regardless of what you think or what I think or what anyone thinks. The truth is still the truth. It's up to everyone to make their own choice, though. Hopefully, the right choice."

"I agree with that," Bash said.

"But here's a thought about the choices we make, Bash," Ricky said. "If you are right, then we are all in the same hopeless boat. We live. We die. That's the end. There is no more anything. So it doesn't really matter what we do or think because there is no eternity for us, good or bad. By the way, I believed that for most of my life."

Bash tilted his head and shrugged.

"But if you are wrong," Ricky continued, "and the God of the Bible is real, and all of us are eternal souls, and we refuse his offer of redemption, to turn back to him, where does that leave us?"

"I don't know, Ricky," Bash said, still feeling frustrated by the discussion. "Where does that leave us?"

"You have to determine that for yourself," Ricky said. "I'm not telling you what to believe, Bash. All I'm saying is that everybody owes it to themselves to *diligently* search their hearts and minds before making a rash decision that there is no God and that all this eternity stuff is foolishness. It's okay to doubt, but anyone would have to believe they know everything in the universe to come to that conclusion! Now to me, *that* is wishful thinking."

Well said, Jonni thought to herself.

For while they just sat there in silence, wading their feet in the pool.

Jonni finally broke the silence. "So . . . we go out there this weekend?"

"Yes, the lease on the house is good until the end of the month and I haven't given my keys back to Timothy yet," Bash said while staring into the pool, still thinking about what Ricky said about searching diligently before making a choice. *Have I searched diligently? No. I haven't really spent much effort searching at all.*

"I got gigs on Saturday and Sunday," Ricky said eagerly.

"How convenient," Bash commented.

"What about this Friday then?" asked Jonni.

Ricky exhaled before saying, "Your driver has no problem with that. He will be waiting patiently for you outside the house as long as you need him—in order to complete *your* spiritual cleansing."

Bash started making *cluck-cluck* chicken sounds.

Ricky jumped to his feet and wrestled with Bash, trying to push him in the water. They both fell into the pool, laughing and splashing each other like small boys.

Jonni watched and shook her head. *Maybe I should go alone . . .*

† † †

28

alid sat within a circle of men. Along with some of the older men, Walid wore baggy trousers and a traditional striped kaftan over a long shirt called a gallibaya. Some wore turbans. The only common feature shared by all were beards; some short, some long. They were all under a tree on the edge of a field at Walid's farm, sitting on a large blanket, drinking tea and chatting about the weather and crops for nearly an hour before the problem of Tarik—the focus of the meeting—came up.

An older man with a bushy gray beard and a penetrating stare, Abdul, continued the conversation in Arabic. "How can you be certain, Walid? He could have told anybody!"

"He has not," Walid said. "He has been interrogated extensively. I am convinced he has told no one."

Abdul shook his head in disgust. "Even though he talks with his brother frequently?"

Walid lowered his eyes. "With respect, Abdul," he said, "I have the situation under control."

Abdul raised his voice, "Walid, you should have taken care of this long ago! It is your duty to restore your family honor! Both definitions of murtadd—irtidad and ridda—apply here! The Quran, and the Hadiths, and Sharia all agree! Have you never read the commentary of Al Khazan?"

Walid could only stare back at Abdul, having no recollection of the commentary Abdul was talking about.

"The famous commentary of Al Khazan," Abdul continued, "used extensively in the Mohammedan University called Al Azhar where your grandfather studied, quotes from Malik ibn Anas, Ahmad ibn Hanbal, and others, and gives this interpretation: 'All the deeds of the apostate become null and void in this world and the next. He must be killed.' Can the issue be made more clear than this?"

The other men in the circle stared at Walid.

Abdul stood suddenly and said, "Allahu Akbar," and left with most of the men.

Walid sat under the tree with the two remaining men. He knew that under intense interrogation, Tarik had never mentioned anything about any plans of jihad to Bashshar or anyone else. But that didn't really matter anymore, as Abdul had pointed out. Tarik and Bashshar had brought shame to Walid and his family through their apostasy. When their father, Walid's brother, died years ago, paternal responsibility fell onto Walid. Since both siblings have rejected Islam—one for no religion and the other for a different religion—it was Walid's duty to kill them both, which would restore honor to the family.

"Abdul is right," Walid told the two remaining men. "It is my duty to take care of this myself. Allah is very clear on the matter."

One of the men said, "I do not believe this task is required of you, Walid. An option, yes. A requirement, no. Abdul is an old fool. Besides, it is risky for you to do this when we are so close to enacting our holy war."

"I'm not afraid of risks," said Walid.

"I know that you are not afraid of risks," the man said, "but I am talking about compromising the entire mission. We need you free and alive to ensure our success."

"It is my duty to deal with Tarik and his brother myself," Walid insisted.

The man stared at Walid with a patient expression on his bearded face. An idea had started to grow in his mind during Abdul's speech to Walid. He cleared his throat before explaining his idea to Walid. "There is a way for you to perform your duty, Walid," the man said, "and to keep you free and alive until our mission is completed."

"Explain this to me, Khalid."

"Send me and Ishaq down to Texas to *rescue* Tarik," Khalid said. "We both have Tarik's confidence. He will lead us to his brother and we will take care of them both. But *you* will actually pull the trigger, so to speak."

Walid looked confused. "How is that possible if I am not there?"

"It is very simple," Khalid explained. "Ishaq and I already have Tarik's trust. After we rescue Tarik from his captors, we will have his *complete* trust.

We insist we must reach his brother because he too is in danger. I know that Bashshar lives with musicians in an old house in the country near Austin. Tarik will lead us to this house."

"Then what?"

"We use explosives," Khalid said. "After securing the inhabitants, I will rig detonators triggered by a cell phone call. *Your* call. Problem solved."

"How will you secure them?" Walid asked. "What if there are too many of them?"

"That will be easy," Khalid explained. "Ishaq and I will handle it with no problem. They are musicians. Weaklings. We will scare them senseless before binding their hands and feet like helpless dogs."

Walid looked at Ishaq who stared back with a blank expression on his face—a face with cheeks covered more by stubble than a full beard.

"We will then shoot everyone in the head if you like," Khalid explained, "except for Tarik and Bashshar, saving them for you and your call that triggers the explosion."

Walid was looking more convinced.

"Can your friend in Texas provide the supplies I need?" asked Khalid.

Walid, in deep thought, began nodding his head slowly.

"The house is old," Khalid continued. "It will go up like a torch. We will be back here in plenty of time before the mission starts. Once the authorities in Texas make their connections to us, it will be too late."

Walid was now convinced. "Yes, we do this your way, Khalid."

"We will need cash," said Khalid.

"I'll supply all the cash you need," Walid said while rising to his feet. "And my Texas friend will supply the rest, including a car, weapons, and the explosives."

"I will need detonators," Khalid said. "And cell phones to wire to the detonators. Pistols will be adequate."

Walid said, "Follow me back to my office to make a list of everything you need. Then I'll make the call to Texas."

After making the list in Walid's office, Khalid and Ishaq walked back across Walid's field toward the area where they had parked their car. Khalid, with his arm around his younger brother's shoulder, said, "Can you believe it, Ishaq? We will only have to continue our play-acting for a short while longer! Then we will be back to complete our mission and join all the other martyred brothers for eternity! Just think of the virgins waiting for us!"

"Allahu Akbar!" Ishaq replied with a smile.

When Khalid turned his head away, the smile on Ishaq's face disappeared instantly.

Still in his office, Walid called his friend in Texas on one of the many untraceable pre-paid cell phones he owned to inform him of the new plan. His friend would make all the necessary arrangements to complete Khalid's mission. The problem concerning Tarik and his brother would be over in a few days, and Walid would actually perform the honor killings, even if he wouldn't be face to face when he did it. He would then be free to start the countdown—the countdown to the multiple suicide attacks on the Great Satan that Walid had been instrumental in organizing himself . . .

29

The Cedar Street Courtyard on 4th street was slowly coming alive. Bash sat at the bar, sipping on cranberry juice as he listened to the voice messages on his cell phone. He ran into several old musician friends while there. They wanted to hear all the gory details of the drug bust at Rock Bottom but Bash could only relay what he'd been told. They acted like they understood but Bash knew they believed he knew more but couldn't say for legal reasons. They asked if the guys were still in jail. They asked about Trent. They asked if the band was going to stay together. *Blah, blah, blah.* Bash had grown weary talking about it.

After listening to several messages on his voicemail regarding some potential work with a San Marcos band Timothy was signing, Bash heard Shadya's voice on a message. "Hello, Bashshar," her voice said, sounding upbeat and happy. "I bet you were very surprised! I know you two must be having fun together. I wish I could be there but guess what? I'm going to Egypt for the summer! I can't wait to hear about everything when I get back! Ciao for now!"

Bash tried calling the phone at the farm in Oregon but no one answered. No surprise there. Along with Shadya, Walid and his entire clan had probably gone to Egypt for the summer. Bash listened to Shadya's message over and over, trying to detect who she was talking about when she said, "I know you two must be having fun together."

She had to be talking about Terry.

He tried to explore other possible explanations: *Was she talking about Jonni and me when she referred to "you two?" No, I never mentioned Jonni to Terry or Shadya.* The only meaning he could get from Shadya's message suggested that Terry was supposed to be here in Texas. *Did Terry's plans change and he simply forget to call me?*

But now he couldn't reach Shadya or anyone in Oregon. The more he thought about the situation the more frustrated he became. He tried to look at the bright side: *Maybe Terry is on his way and will be surprising me with a call, telling me he is here in Austin. Yes, that's very possible.*

Bash looked at his wristwatch and noted the time. Jonni would be arriving any moment now. She had borrowed Mandy's car since Mandy was nursing a cold at the apartment. After work, Jonni had planned to meet him at Cedar Street where they were to go to dinner and a movie at the Alamo Drafthouse.

While he waited, Bash was quickly losing interest in the dinner and movie. All he could think about was Terry. He wasn't even thinking about the visit to Rock Bottom the next night. *What if he never shows up? How would I know what happened to him if someone doesn't call and tell me?*

Bash decided he would keep calling the farm in Oregon, hoping that someone left to look after the place would eventually answer. It was the only hope he had at the moment besides Terry suddenly showing up in Austin.

When Jonni arrived, Bash explained about Shadya's message before letting Jonni listen for herself. "There's no way of reaching her in Egypt?" she asked.

Bash shook his head slowly.

"Don't any of these people have cell phones?" she asked, obviously frustrated with what to do next.

"Terry said he had one but he lost it or something," Bash said. "Walid probably disapproves of them for his family. Western decadence and all that."

"Well, don't worry," Jonni said. "Terry may be planning a surprise visit. Maybe Shadya misunderstood what day he planned to arrive. Give him a few days."

"I hope so," Bash said with a sad smile. "Terry has always been the sweetest, most loving person you would ever know. And still is."

Jonni saw the emotion in Bash's face. She leaned over and kissed him on the cheek. "Don't worry," she said. "And hang on to your hope."

"Thanks, Jonni," Bash said. "You always lift me up."

"You're welcome. You still wanna go to the Alamo?"

"Yes," Bash said after a moment's thought. "I do."

After the dinner and movie at the Alamo Drafthouse, Jonni dropped off Bash at Ricky's condo. Bash had been calling Walid's phone every hour on the hour, even through the movie at the Alamo which was *Duck Soup*, part of a Marx Brothers festival.

Ricky was not at the condo so Bash found the spare key under a certain potted plant nearby and let himself in. He felt a bit queasy, maybe from the hamburger and all the candy and popcorn he consumed at the Alamo. *Probably my nerves, too.* As much as he tried to let it go, he couldn't stop worrying about Terry.

Bash headed straight to Ricky's spare bedroom, noticing Trent's Stratocaster guitar case leaning against a wall where Ricky had placed it. He flipped open the latches of the case and opened the lid. The guitar sat silently in its plush lining, reminding Bash of a corpse in an opened, velvet-lined coffin. He shut and latched the case before angrily pulling back the sheets on the bed with his one hand.

After undressing, Bash turned off the bedroom light and climbed between the sheets. He had difficulty falling asleep. He tossed and turned most of the night until waking up around three in the morning from a dream so vivid he thought it had really happened. He had seen Terry in a dark cell-like room. His brother was in a fetal position on the filthy floor, looking like he had been severely injured. Terry's eyes were blackened and swollen shut. He looked bruised and battered. At a certain point in the dream, Terry made eye contact with Bash for a brief second. Then the dream was over.

Bash went to the kitchen for a glass of water. He couldn't seem to shake the feeling that Terry was in serious trouble. While gulping down the water Bash stared at a magnetic Bible verse attached to Ricky's refrigerator door. 'Be devoted to one another in brotherly love. Be joyful in hope . . .'

Brotherly love. He definitely understood and felt brotherly love for Terry. *But be joyful in hope?* The concept was easy enough to understand but seemed impossible under the present conditions.

Bash went back to the bedroom and called Walid's number. No one answered but Bash *hoped* it had awakened someone. And he really *hoped* it had been Walid that was awakened. *Now that would bring me some joy!*

Bash was growing tired of this treatment from his mean-spirited uncle. And if Walid was behind anything bad that had happened to Terry, Bash was ready to wage his own jihad against Uncle Wally . . .

† † †

31

*T*erry had already made up his mind. After the last beating he decided to make an escape attempt even if it resulted in his death. He now believed his captors were planning on killing him. He'd overheard them talking outside the shack. One of them said something in Arabic about Terry's soul soon being in God's hands. Terry only hoped he had enough strength to run away once he got through the back wall. He'd already partially loosened one of the wooden boards in the wall hidden by a stack of hay bales. He planned on slipping out and making his escape under the cover of darkness. He had convinced his captors several days ago to undo the plastic zip-ties on his ankles. They complied, believing he was too weak to try anything, and also because it was difficult assisting Terry outside to relieve himself with tied ankles.

Terry thought of the dream he had last night. An image of his brother, Bash, had appeared to him in a misty form, like a spirit. The vision lasted for only a few seconds but it had somehow vitalized him—giving him hope and a will to survive.

Now it was near nightfall. Terry remained on the floor, waiting for his captors to check in on him as they always did around this time of day. They would enter the shack, and believing he was asleep, they would both leave and drive an old Jeep back over a hill. Terry had witnessed this routine through a crack in the boards several times. They wouldn't return until the next morning when the beatings and interrogation would resume. He presumed there was a house or some type of dwelling over the hill where they slept. He hoped he would find the keys in the Jeep when he finally made his escape from the shack. If not, he would have to make his way to safety on foot. He still had no idea of his location; only knowing it was in a remote area in the country two or three hours from Dallas.

During the interrogations Terry told them all he knew, which was not much. They seemed most interested in who he had talked to regarding the overheard conversation in Walid's office. Terry was worried about

Bash. He swore to his captors he hadn't mentioned anything to his brother, even as they shocked his privates with an old car battery and cables, but they appeared to not believe him. He had to escape if for no other reason than to warn Bash.

It was nearing sunset when Terry heard the Jeep park outside the shack. He heard the rattling of the padlock as they opened the door and entered. He wondered if this time things would be different—his captors simply entering and shooting him in the head.

Terry heard them mumble to one another as he pretended to sleep. Instead of another beating, or worse, they left and locked the padlock back on the door. He heard the Jeep drive away. Terry struggled to his feet. Although weakened by his lack of nutrition and injuries endured from the beatings, he hurried to the wall hidden by the bales of hay. He was glad they hadn't left his wrists tied. He dragged one of the bales away from the wall, revealing the board he'd already started loosening. One more night and the boards would be completely loosened and removed for his escape. He just hoped he survived until then . . .

32

*J*onni stored the Bible she had been reading back into her backpack. "I'm ready to go," she said while setting the backpack near the door in Ricky's living room.

"That's all the gear you use?" asked Bash.

"Yes," she said. "You think I'm missing something?"

"No," Bash said, "but I thought most paranormal investigators use a lot of electronic devices."

"How do you know what devices paranormal investigators use?" Ricky said while putting clean socks on his feet. His hair was still wet from the shower he took earlier.

"I've seen a few of those ghost hunting shows on TV," Bash told him. "They usually have video cameras and audio recorders and whatnot."

"First of all," Jonni said before taking a sip from a Diet Coke on the coffee table, "I'm not a paranormal investigator. I'm a paranormal *healer*. I use a video camera and digital recorder on initial visits but I don't need them in this case. As far as all that ghost hunting gear you see on TV— like motion detectors, EMF meters for measuring changes in magnetic fields, infrared probe thermometers, laser grid scopes, even full spectrum cameras that can detect visible, near-infrared, and near-ultraviolet light— I don't need them. On my budget, I can't afford any of it anyway."

Ricky smiled at Bash. "Is that the *whatnot* you were talking about?"

Bash narrowed his eyes at Ricky.

"The reason the producers of those ghost-hunter TV shows want all those high-tech gadgets," Jonni explained, "is because it is very appealing to the general public, even to those who don't believe in the paranormal, and especially to a generation dedicated to microchip technology in the same way ancients were dedicated to their idols of gods."

Bash's eyes reflected his admiration of this woman.

"Now I'm not saying that all of these paranormal investigators on TV are simply pandering to their producers," Jonni continued. "Many are using this technology willingly to gather and display evidence to reach their goals."

"And what are their goals?" asked Bash.

"To prove to themselves and the fans that another *realm* exists," she said. "I don't need to prove this. I know the realm with all its spirits exist. But gathering evidence can still be good in order to discern if a person or place is really being infected by unclean spirits, or is just a fraud, or a byproduct of someone's mental state, which is why I usually use a camcorder and digital audio recorder on my initial visits. But I already know that Rock Bottom is unclean. And I plan on cleansing it."

"How are you going to cleanse it?" Bash said, trying not to sound skeptical even though he was skeptical.

"You'll see."

Ricky looked anxious and nervous. "Ya'll ready to go now or do you guys want to philosophize the rest of the night?"

"Wow!" Bash said. "You actually know a word more than one syllable long!"

Ricky formed a fist and faked a punch toward Bash.

"Remember," Bash side with a smile. "I only have one arm."

"I only need one arm to take you down, Boo-Boo," Ricky replied.

"Oh yeah?"

"Yeah."

"Who says?"

"I do."

"Oh yeah?"

"Yeah."

Jonni rolled her eyes and headed toward the door. "I'll be in the car, kiddies."

†

"Man, it's hot in here," Ricky said. "The air seems so thick."

"Timothy probably turned off the air conditioner in order to cut the electric bill," Bash said. "I guess I can't blame him. His money source has suddenly dried up."

"Let's turn it on," Ricky suggested. "We can turn it back off once we're finished."

"We're not going to be here long enough for the place to get cool," said Bash.

"It'll help a bit," Ricky said. "I'm burning up."

"The upstairs thermostat is next to the bathroom," Bash said. "You turn it on and I'll get the one downstairs."

"You guys need to cut out all the mundane talk," Jonni said with her eyes closed. "Stay focused on why we're here."

Ricky headed up the staircase, glad that he knew where the hallway light switch was located at the top of the stairs. Even with the light, he had the uncanny feeling that he was being watched. He quickly found the thermostat and set the temperature to 74 degrees, a bit cooler than the 80 degree setting it had been set to. He bolted back downstairs to the *former* rehearsal room where Jonni still stood.

Bash returned a moment later. "Okay. The AC is on down here."

"Upstairs is on, too," Ricky added.

Bash and Ricky quietened when Jonni said, "Let's hold hands for a prayer before we start."

They joined hands as Jonni began a loud prayer, asking for success in driving out the unclean spirits from the house. She finished by asking God to prevent any unclean spirits in the house from following them once the three of them left Rock Bottom. Bash felt silly but he kept his feelings to himself.

Jonni removed the Bible from her backpack. She attached a small reading light on the back portion of the Bible with the reading light's spring operated clip.

Bash and Ricky watched Jonni walk throughout the rehearsal room while reading passages of scripture in a loud voice: " . . . that by his death he might break the power of him who holds the power of death, that is, the devil, and free those who all their lives were held in slavery by their fear of death." The rehearsal room was empty except for some cardboard boxes and the bedrooms' dressers and mattresses stored neatly against one of the walls.

Bash and Ricky followed her through the bottom floor of the house, resisting the urge to turn on lights since she requested they do the cleansing in darkness. Jonni kept reciting the Bible verses. Often, she voiced her words as if addressing someone specific: "The reason the Son of God appeared was to destroy the devil's work. You know that, don't you?"

While they were in the foyer, Jonni recited a passage from Philippians 2: "Therefore God exalted him to the highest place and gave him the name that is above every name, that at the name of Jesus every knee should bow, in heaven and on earth and under the earth, and every tongue acknowledge that Jesus Christ is Lord, to the glory of God the Father."

All three heard the music at the same time. Coming from somewhere upstairs. They listened. Bash suddenly said, "I know that song. That's Santana."

"Got A Black Magic Woman," Carlos Santana sang. "Got A Black Magic Woman . . ."

Jonni ignored the music and started up the staircase toward the second floor while reading from Colossians 2: "And having disarmed the powers and authorities, he made a public spectacle of them, triumphing over them by the cross."

Bash and Ricky followed her up the staircase. Bash switched on the upstairs hallway ceiling light once they reached the second floor.

"I don't need the light," she said. "I'm bringing a *new* light to this darkness."

Bash and Ricky didn't need the ceiling light, either. They could hear where the music was coming from.

The attic.

"I guess we're going up there," Bash said, trying to read Ricky's expression before turning off the ceiling light. "You up for that?"

Ricky didn't reply.

"We finish the bedrooms first," Jonni told them. "Then we go up."

When they entered Bash's old bedroom, Jonni recited a passage from Isaiah 59:19 from memory: "When enemies come in," she said in a loud voice, "like a flood the Spirit of the Lord will put them to flight."

Jonni continued with her cleansing in Billy's bedroom, then Gordon's bedroom. She recited scriptures in the bathroom and the hallway closet, too. The Santana song blaring from the attic came to an end. The attic was silent.

After entering Trent's bedroom they heard a loud thump from one of the bedrooms nearby. Jonni ignored the thumping sound, treating it as a distraction while she finished reciting her chosen scripture before leaving Trent's room.

As they entered the last bedroom, Vince's bedroom, they all stared in surprise at the object in the middle of the bare floor. The female figurine was there, in a crude circle drawn on the floor, lying on its side but still facing them. "Are you seeing what I'm seeing?" Jonni asked.

"Someone dug it up and brought it back inside," Bash said. "Again. I reburied it the day of the storm."

"Who?" asked Ricky. "Who would've dug it up?"

Bash shrugged, having no memory of the dead woman bringing it into his bedroom the day of the storm. "I don't know. Maybe Vince?"

"The last I heard," Ricky said, "Vince was still locked up."

"The day I took you guys to the old cemetery," Bash said, "I saw the mound where I reburied all the figurines. It looked undisturbed."

"Whoever did it," Ricky said, "could've just filled up the hole to make it look like it hadn't been disturbed."

"Never mind," Jonni said, stopping their useless speculation. "Let's finish."

Jonni said more prayers, focusing her attention on the female figurine in the circle. After finishing the prayer she led them out of the room into the hallway.

"Shouldn't we rebury it?" asked Bash.

"Leave it for now," she said. "We'll get rid of it later. *Permanently*, this time. Okay, you can turn on the hall light now."

Bash flipped on the hallway ceiling light. Jonni stared at the trapdoor leading to the attic. "Can one of you find some rope or something to attach to this attic door so we can open it?"

"There might be something in the toolshed," Bash told Ricky.

Ricky nodded unenthusiastically. "Okay."

"And a flashlight," added Jonni.

"There used to be one in the drawer next to the the fridge in the kitchen," Bash said, "if the drawers and cabinets haven't been cleaned out already."

"I've got a flashlight in my truck," Ricky said.

"Bring them both, please," Jonni said.

"We're also going to need a stepladder," Bash added. "It's in the toolshed, too."

Ricky nodded again. "Anything else, sir?"

"No, that will be all for now," Bash said, dealing with his nervousness in the same way Ricky was dealing with it—trying to make humor out of a tense situation.

Ricky headed downstairs. He felt uneasy walking down the staircase, still feeling like someone was watching him. Once he reached the front door he looked back over his shoulder. Nobody was there.

Ricky walked out the front door and headed to his Toyota pickup truck parked near the front porch. He opened the passenger door and reached into the glove box to remove his flashlight. *Bash said the toolshed was in the back of the house.*

Ricky walked around the side of the house, his flashlight beam illuminating the ground before him. The nagging feeling of being watched resurfaced, but he didn't look behind him this time as he continued toward the back of the house to find this supposed toolshed.

Ricky found the toolshed and pulled open the flimsy wooden door with a creepy-sounding creak. He aimed his flashlight inside and saw the stepladder leaning against a wall. He also saw a length of narrow rope hanging on a nail. He reached for the rope but became distracted by a strange noise coming from the area where they had discovered the old cemetery days earlier. He aimed the flashlight in the direction of the cemetery but the location was too far away for the flashlight beam to reach.

Ricky grabbed the rope and placed it around his neck. When he reached for the stepladder he heard the hiss. He aimed the flashlight toward the floor of the toolshed and saw a pair of glowing eyes staring back; eyes attached to a very angry-looking face baring its teeth. Ricky gasped and jumped back as the raccoon bolted out the toolshed with another hiss.

Ricky muttered under his breath as the critter disappeared from sight into the dark night. He grabbed the stepladder and started for the kitchen door in the back of the house, hoping it would be unlocked to save him a trip back around the house. It should have been locked since they hadn't opened it since being at the house, but he turned the doorknob and the door opened. That's when he heard another strange sound, like a low moan, coming from somewhere near the old cemetery. He quickly entered the kitchen and locked the dead-bolt behind him.

Ricky turned on the kitchen's ceiling light and leaned the stepladder against a wall. He found a flashlight among some other items in a drawer near the fridge. He glanced around and saw a toaster and coffee machine on the countertop. He opened a cabinet and saw that it was full of plates and glasses. Another cabinet was full of pots and pans. Obviously, the kitchen items had not been boxed and moved out yet.

Ricky suddenly heard something outside the kitchen door. He stared at the deadbolt above the doorknob, glad that it was still locked. Another sound. This time it sounded like someone was wiggling the doorknob, trying to get in. Ricky grabbed the stepladder and hurried out the kitchen toward the staircase in the foyer, annoyed by the fact that he was spooked like some little kid afraid of the boogyman. The gooseflesh on his arms and the back of his neck didn't help matters.

When Ricky arrived with the rope, flashlights, and stepladder, Jonni and Bash were staring at the attic trapdoor in the ceiling. More music was coming from the attic. Ricky stopped and listened, too. After a moment he said, "Tull."

"What?" asked Bash.

"Tull," Ricky repeated. "Jethro Tull, the rock band from the seventies. The flute is the giveaway. Besides, I've heard this song before. It's not one of my favorites."

They heard something else. It sounded like another voice had begun singing along in the attic with the vocalist on the recording. The music seemed louder now as they heard the lyrics clearly: "If Jesus Saves, Well He Better Save Himself, From The Gory Glory Seekers, Who Use His Name In Death . . ."

"Set the stepladder up, please," Jonni said.

Ricky propped the stepladder below the trapdoor and climbed up to attach the rope to the metal eyelet. "Oh Jesus Save Me . . ." the song went on.

Once the rope was attached they moved the stepladder out of the way while Ricky, his heart now racing, pulled on the rope. The attic trap-door creaked loudly in protest but it opened easy enough, revealing total darkness and absolute silence. No music. No sounds at all.

Ricky unfolded the ladder mounted to the trapdoor and stepped back.

"Let me have your flashlight, please," Jonni said to Ricky.

Ricky handed it to her reluctantly.

"Both of you can stay here if you want," she told them.

"No way," said Bash. "I've got to see for myself." He turned to Ricky. "You find the other flashlight?"

Ricky reached in his pocket and gave it to him.

"We probably won't see anything," Jonni said. "It's scared." And in a louder voice as she started up the trapdoor ladder, "It's too afraid to show itself!"

Ricky didn't say it but he was glad for that.

"You stay down here," Jonni told Ricky.

"No," Ricky protested. "I'll come, too."

"You need to stay down to open the trapdoor, Ricky," she said before raising her voice again. "In case *someone* gets cute and shuts it to scare us."

Bash frowned before following Jonni up the ladder into the dark attic, assisting himself on the steps with his one arm.

Jonni aimed her flashlight throughout the dark attic, aided by the wedge of light entering through the opened trapdoor. The heat in the attic was stifling. Bash came up beside her, shining his flashlight on the rafters nearby. "See any light switches or bulbs?" he asked her.

They both saw a light switch at the same time. Jonni flicked it on and off a few times but no lights came on. "Bulbs are probably burned out," she said while aiming her flashlight beam on various items stored on the far side of the attic. She noticed some furniture and piles of cardboard boxes among the items. "Hello?" Jonni suddenly said in a loud voice. "Where are you? You can't hide! In the name of Jesus, I command you to show yourself!"

Bash suddenly felt a wisp of cool air move by his face. He started to say something about it when they both heard the sound. A low groan. "You hear that?" Bash asked her.

Jonni ignored his question and shouted toward the spot near the back wall where the groan had come from. "I command you to show yourself in the name of Yeshua haMashiach!"

Bash suddenly stumbled on something on the floor. He aimed his flashlight near his feet and saw a small flashlight. "Look at this," he said.

Jonni picked up the flashlight from the floor and flipped its switch several times. "Batteries are dead."

Bash examined it in the beam of his own flashlight. "It's new. Someone's been up here recently."

Jonni handed it to him and continued toward the back wall. Bash pocketed the dead flashlight and followed her. She started reciting another loud prayer: "I have been given authority to trample on snakes and scorpions and to overcome all the power of the enemy . . ."

They heard another low groan.

"Show yourself!" Jonni shouted. "In the name of Jesus Christ!"

Bash stopped walking when Jonni stopped walking. He aimed his flashlight at the corner of the room where Jonni aimed her flashlight. He didn't see it at first. Then he did. A mass of darkness roughly the size of a large man. Bash's mind reasoned that it was a shadow being formed by their flashlight beams.

"I command you to leave this house," Jonni said, her voice firm and unwavering. "In the name of Jesus!"

Bash stared at the mass for several moments before noticing its subtle movements; movements that seemed to be similar to swirling smoke but in a way that lifeforms move, unlike a simple cloud of smoke swirling randomly. He couldn't make out any features, maybe something that resembled a head on some shoulders, but he couldn't be sure. One thing he knew for sure: it was no shadow caused by the flashlights. Then he heard it. The sound almost rumbled, like a low pitched voice, yet different somehow. Within seconds the low rumblings turned into a distinct voice, low but clear, the way Bash imagined a giant's voice would sound. The language was beyond foreign to Bash. It resembled no dialect he had ever heard.

The voice stopped speaking and Jonni spoke back, seemingly answering it. "Yes, I know you *had* permission," she said, "but by the authority of Yeshua haMashiach I revoke that permission! You no longer are allowed to dwell here! Now be gone!"

The growl from the mass was horrible, making the hairs on the back of

Bash's neck stand on end. Jonni seemed unfazed, though. "Whoever enabled the entry is gone now!" she shouted. "You must leave! By the authority of Jesus Christ, the son of the most-high God, lord of lords, creator of the universe! Go now! And take all your little underlings with you!"

Little underlings? Bash thought.

Leaning against the wall below the opened attic trapdoor, Ricky's entire body jumped when the trapdoor's ladder folded violently into its closed position with a loud bang, followed by the trapdoor slamming shut with an even louder bang.

"Bash!" he shouted while grabbing for the dangling rope. "Jonni!"

He pulled on the rope with all his strength, using his entire weight, but the trapdoor wouldn't budge. He heard more loud sounds coming from the attic. "Can ya'll hear me? Bash! Jonni!"

In the attic, most of the cardboard boxes and furniture shook and vibrated, creating enough noise that Ricky's calls were not heard. Jonni stood her ground although Bash was ready to get out of there. Even though he saw the mass with his own eyes and heard its frightening voice with his own ears, Bash's mind could not process any of it. The vibrating objects in the attic along with the trapdoor slamming shut joined the list of the impossible, although he was witnessing it himself. "The trapdoor shut!" he heard himself shout.

"I know!" Jonni shouted back. She raised her voice to an even louder volume. "Oh! That was so clever! I guess we are supposed to be scared now! Trapped up here with you and all your disgusting little helpers!"

The objects in the attic ceased shaking and vibrating.

Jonni stepped toward the mass, causing it to disappear and reappear a short distance away in a fraction of a second. She grabbed a wooden chair and faced it toward the mass. "I've got an idea!" she said in a cynical tone while sitting in the chair. "Since we are all going to be up here together for a while, I'm going to read us some scripture! But only for a few hours or so!"

Bash could only hope that wasn't true.

Jonni opened the Bible on her lap, her reading light helping her to see the words on the page. She began reading aloud from Mark 5 where Jesus called out the demons from a man who roamed the tombs in the area of the Gerasenes. The shaking and vibrating began again but Jonni ignored it while speaking in a loud firm voice. When she got to the part where the demons in the story begged Jesus to be sent into a herd of swine nearby instead of being cast into the Pit, her reading light went out. Bash's flashlight went off at the exact same time, leaving the attic in total darkness. Jonni tried her flashlight but it too was dead.

"Tired of storybook reading?" Jonni said. "Okay, I have another idea!"

Bash saw Jonni's smartphone light up her face as she opened the home screen. She searched through her apps while saying, "You like to play music up here, don't you? Well, I have hours and hours of music on my phone! How about this one?"

Music began playing from her phone, a song sung by a choir of small children: "Jesus Loves Me This I Know, For The Bible Tells Me So, Little Ones To Him Belong, They Are Weak But He Is Strong . . ." Jonni started singing along with the children: "Yes Jesus Loves Me, Yes Jesus Loves Me, Yes Jesus Loves Me, The Bible Tells Me So."

The song was in the middle of the second verse when her smartphone shut off suddenly, leaving the attic in darkness again. Bash pulled his own phone from his pocket and discovered that it too was dead. He could hear Ricky's voice calling their names from below the attic. "Tell him we're okay," Jonni told Bash.

"We're alright, Ricky!" Bash shouted over his shoulder. "We'll be back down soon!"

"The trapdoor is stuck!" came Ricky's muted reply.

"Just chill!" Bash shouted back. "We're good!"

Bash listened to Jonni's voice in the complete darkness of the attic. "So you don't like the music, either!" she said. "I guess I'll go back to reciting scripture! Don't worry, I have at least a hundred Bible verses memorized . . . since we're going to continue playing this little game of yours!"

Jonni began reciting Bible verses. Within seconds the shaking and vibrating started up again. She raised her voice to be heard over the noise.

A few minutes later the noise stopped suddenly and the cell phones came back to life along with two light bulbs mounted on the rafters. They both heard the sound of the trapdoor opening. Although still stifling hot, the air in the attic seemed lighter somehow.   Ricky's head appeared through the trapdoor opening. "You guys okay?" he shouted.

"Yes," Bash answered while staring at Jonni. "It's gone, isn't it?"

Jonni didn't answer. "Come on," she said while walking toward the trapdoor. "I'm thirsty."

Jonni switched off the attic lights before they both climbed down the steps.

Ricky stared at them for a long moment before asking, "What happened?"

Bash could only shake his head but his expression revealed he had witnessed something extraordinary.

"You want me to shut the trapdoor?" asked Ricky.

"It doesn't matter," Jonni replied. "Open or closed, she knows her private room is no longer private."

Bash was shocked that the entity was female. "That was a her?"

"Sort of," replied Jonni.

Ricky looked to Bash for clarification. He got nothing but a blank stare in return.

Ricky folded the ladder and heaved the trapdoor, its springs slamming it shut with a loud bang. He followed Bash and Jonni downstairs toward the kitchen.

In the kitchen, Jonni grabbed some sodas from the fridge and offered one to Bash. He shook his head. Jonni offered it to Ricky who took it from her hand, popped the top, and gulped half of it down. Bash sat down at the breakfast table and stared off into space as Jonni leaned against the sink and sipped on her soda.

"So what happened?" Ricky asked patiently, directing the question more toward Bash than Jonni.

"I saw it," Bash said.

"Saw what?"

Bash didn't respond.

"The dark entity running things here in the house," Jonni answered for him.

"You saw it?" asked Ricky.

"She talked to it," Bash said. "It talked back. I didn't understand it but I heard it."

Ricky was lost for words.

Bash began muttering nonsensical words in a low voice before saying, "That's what it sounded like to me."

"She said she had a right to be here," Jonni explained in her calm voice. "That she had permission. But I informed her that her permission was being revoked by none other than God Almighty, creator of the universe."

"I can't believe that was a *her*," Bash said. "I guess that doesn't matter much since it was not human."

"That's right," Jonni said. "It seems they can choose the gender they want to portray. So I guess they're actually not male or female. If that makes any sense. I don't know."

"I don't get it," Ricky said. "Something like that needs permission?"

"Yes," Jonni said. "People open the door in a variety of ways, which gives it the right to enter. Permission, actually."

"So what happened," Ricky asked, "when you revoked its . . . permission?"

"It didn't like it," Bash answered for her. "It tried to shake the attic apart to frighten us, I guess. You heard it."

"I heard a bunch of noise," Ricky said, "but I thought you guys were moving stuff around or something."

"It became angry," added Bash.

"It's always angry," Jonni said. "But it became scared, which made it even angrier."

"You scared it?" asked Ricky.

"The power of the Word of God scared it," she replied.

After a short pause, Ricky asked, "So is it finished? Is it gone?"

"I doubt it," she said. "Temporarily, maybe."

Her answer surprised Bash. "I thought you kicked it out?"

"You have to realize something," she said. "Entities like these are very powerful and won't go without a long fight. They've had the run of this house for a long time. I'm going to need help to rid them."

"What do you mean *them*?" Ricky asked. "There's more than one?"

Bash was curious, too. "Yeah, you mentioned others while we were in the attic. Little underlings or something like that."

Jonni glanced between both men. "That's right," she said. "There are many here."

Bash and Ricky stared back at her with blank expressions on their faces.

"But the one I dealt with was the boss of this domain," she explained. "Just like a captain, it has lieutenants and sergeants and foot soldiers that obey it."

"You saw them, didn't you?" asked Bash.

"I saw some of them," she answered.

"Why couldn't I see them?" Bash said.

"For the same reason you couldn't understand the words it spoke," she said.

"Why is that?"

Jonni seemed to be weighing her words carefully. "I was born with an ability," she finally said, "but I've also had lots of experience in these situations which has honed that ability." Jonni wanted to tell Bash that her ability also required plenty of belief and faith. She decided to say it in a different way. "The world says 'seeing is believing.' But the truth is the exact opposite."

Bash had heard that before. *Had it been from Jonni?*

"So they're still here?" asked Ricky.

"Not at the moment," she said, "but they could come back, although probably not while we're still here. That's why we need to stay for a while."

"What?" said Bash and Ricky at the same time.

"How long is a while?" Ricky asked.

"The longer we're here," she said, "the longer they'll stay gone."

"We can't stay here that long," Bash informed her. "The lease on the house is up soon, remember?"

"Not until the end of the month," she replied.

"That's nearly a week from now," Bash said. "I don't think Timothy is going to go for that. He said the maids need to come in and clean a week before."

Ricky nodded eagerly.

"You could ask him," she said. "Couldn't you?"

"Jonni," Bash began, "regardless of what Timothy says, I'm not interested in staying here any longer."

"Bash, even a few days could make all the difference," she said. "With us still here, they may not come back at all."

Bash didn't look convinced. Neither did Ricky.

"It's worth a try," Jonni went on. "I'm only thinking about the next poor souls who move here in the future. We owe them that much, don't we?"

Bash looked to Ricky for help but Ricky didn't know what to say.

"Well," Bash said in a tone of resignation, "I guess we could stay for a day or so but I still need to talk to Timothy. I'll call him tomorrow. Will that work?"

Jonni nodded her head. "Fair enough."

Bash made eye contact with Ricky who didn't look eager to stay for even five more minutes. "Ricky, if you are uneasy staying here with us, I understand. Don't we, Jonni?"

Ricky looked agitated. "And what? Just leave ya'll stranded out here by yourselves? Is that what you think I would do?"

"So you'll stay?" asked Bash.

Ricky narrowed his eyes, realizing Bash had played him. "Until tomorrow," he said. "I won't promise any longer than that."

"Good," said Bash.

Ricky exhaled in frustration. "So where are we going to sleep? If we get any sleep."

"We can use the mattresses in the big room," Jonni said. "I saw some sheets and blankets in the upstairs closet."

"Just like a little slumber party," Ricky said in a cynical tone. "Isn't that cute?"

Bash had to laugh. "Don't worry," he said. "I'll hold your hand if you get scared."

Ricky wasn't in the mood for jokes. "Whatever."

Jonni asked them both if there was a way to play music from her smartphone on bigger speakers.

"Not long ago that would've been no problem," Bash said. "But all that stuff is gone now."

"I've got a Jawbone Jambox in my glovebox," Ricky said. "Not sure if it's charged or not, though. It's fairly loud. Louder than your phone for sure."

"Great," she said. "I want to fill the house with some good positive music."

"Not the kiddie choir stuff again I hope," said Bash with a smile.

"No, of course not," she said in a sarcastic voice. "You guys are so grown up that I thought I would play something more on your level of maturity."

"You mean like MercyMe or Casting Crowns?" asked Ricky.

"I was thinking more like the soundtrack to the Spongebob Squarepants movie," she said with a smile . . .

† † †

33

*T*he sound of a vehicle arriving at the shack woke Terry up. *Just like clockwork,* he thought. Time for more beatings and torment. But something was different this time. It was still dark outside and the engine of the vehicle outside the shack was left running. His captors usually shut off the Jeep's engine when they arrived at the shack. *Maybe they're planning on putting a bullet in my head and ending the matter.*

Terry heard the padlock rattling on the door. He closed his eyes, pretending to be asleep, although he knew it would do no good. They usually delivered a kick to his ribs to wake him up.

The door opened. Terry opened his eyes and a flashlight beam blinded him. A familiar voice caused him to sit up quickly. "Tarik! You are alive!"

Terry saw a bearded man approaching him with a smile. "Khalid!" Terry exclaimed. "Is it really you?"

"Yes, my friend!" Khalid said. "This is your lucky day!"

"I must be dreaming!"

"No dream," Khalid said. "We are rescuing you."

Only then did Terry realize that another man was standing inside the doorway of the shack. It took him a moment to recognize the man. "Ishaq!"

Ishaq, never one to waste words, replied with a nod.

"But . . . how?" Terry mumbled. "What happened to—"

"—I'll explain once we are in the car," Khalid interrupted. "We have to be quick. The guards could regain consciousness at any moment."

Khalid and Ishaq helped Terry to his feet and to the waiting Dodge Intrepid sedan outside the shack. They opened the rear door of the sedan and helped Terry into the backseat. From the harsh glare of the Dodge sedan's interior dome light, Terry noticed a pistol in Khalid's belt.

A moment later Khalid was driving across an open pasture, following a faint trail left by the tires of countless vehicles over the years. They passed by a rusty mobile home with a few lights on inside while heading toward a gravel road in the distance. Terry saw the Jeep parked next to the mobile home.

Ishaq handed Terry a bottled water and a banana over the seat.

Terry devoured the banana and gulped down the water while glancing over his shoulder to see if they were being followed.

"Don't worry," Khalid said while turning onto the gravel road. "They won't be going anywhere soon. Ishaq threw the Jeep's keys into the trees. If they have a spare set they will be in for a surprise because Ishaq also disabled the motor. Right, Ishaq?"

"Right," Ishaq said while staring at the darkness outside the passenger window.

Terry didn't expect Ishaq to say much. He never said much. He had suffered a stuttering problem since childhood. One word at a time was what you usually got from Ishaq. "Walid is responsible for this, isn't he?" asked Terry.

"Of course," Khalid said, thinking to himself that Tarik would never know that Walid was also responsible for the rescue. "He thinks you know something about some big plans he and his radical friends are organizing."

"But how did you know they captured me?" asked Terry.

"Ishaq's childhood friend," Khalid said, giving his well-rehearsed response to the questions he knew Terry would ask. "What is his name, Ishaq?"

"Jamal," Ishaq said, the only word Khalid had required him to memorize.

"Yes," Khalid said. "Jamal is an old friend of Ishaq. Or I should say, *was* an old friend. Jamal was one of your guards."

"The shorter of the two?" asked Terry.

"Yes," Khalid said, knowing his answer made no difference since neither of the guards were named Jamal.

Terry thought for a moment. "So he told you about me, Ishaq?"

Khalid answered for Ishaq. "Yes. Jamal called Ishaq to brag about capturing you and holding you prisoner. Calling Ishaq was a very unwise move. But very good for you."

"But how did you know where they were keeping me?"

"Jamal told him," Khalid said. "And as luck would have it, Ishaq had been here before when he and Jamal were young. Jamal's uncle owns the property. Right, Ishaq?"

"Right," came the reply.

Terry noticed that Ishaq was more aloof than normal. Maybe Ishaq betraying his friend, Jamal, was bothering him. "So what did you do to this Jamal and the other one?" Terry asked.

Khalid hesitated to answer. "Well," he finally said. "We surprised them before they had a chance to respond. I think they were puzzled by Ishaq being there, which gave me the edge in taking control of the situation."

"You said they could regain consciousness at any moment," Terry said, knowing Khalid was carrying a handgun. "Did you strike them on the head with your handgun?"

"Yes, but we probably should have shot and killed them," Khalid answered, trying to steer the conversation in the direction he wanted. "They will be contacting Walid soon. As soon as they regain consciousness, that is."

"Your lives will be in danger now," Terry said. "You and Ishaq have risked your lives for me. I don't know how I will ever be able to repay you both."

"Forget that, Tarik," Khalid said, trying to stay patient. "Jamal told Ishaq that Walid is also after your brother. Bashshar's life is in danger, too, Tarik."

Terry already knew this but hearing Khalid say it made his stomach churn.

"Tarik," Khalid went on, "didn't you tell me that your brother lives with a band of musicians out in the country near Austin?"

Terry tried to remember if he had mentioned this to Khalid, but he must have since Khalid knew. "Yes, but I don't know the house's exact location."

"You need to call him," Khalid said while handing a cell phone over the seat. "Maybe this house in the country will be a good place for us to hide until we form a plan."

"Yes," Terry said. "I need to talk to Bash. What time is it?"

"Two AM," Khalid replied.

Terry realized he had probably only been asleep for a few hours before Khalid and Ishaq arrived at the shack.

"Hopefully your brother is at this house in the country," Khalid said. "Make the call, Tarik."

Terry felt his back pocket and shook his head. "I don't have his number," he said reluctantly. "It was in my wallet but the guards must have taken it."

Khalid turned on the interior dome light and handed Terry a leather wallet over the seat. "You mean this wallet?" he said with a smile.

"Yes!" Terry said. "Where did you find it?"

"I saw it sitting on a table before we left the mobile home," Khalid said. "I recognized it from before, when you would sometimes leave it out on the coffee table at the flat in Portland."

"Wow!" Terry said with a look of admiration on his bruised face. "You think of everything, Khalid!"

If you only knew, Khalid thought.

"Where did you get this car, Khalid?" Terry said while removing a folded piece of paper from his wallet.

"I rented it at the airport," Khalid said, the only truthful answer he had given Tarik.

"You've also spent a lot of money on me," Terry said while reading Bash's cell phone number on the folded paper. "And took great risks. I owe you so much. You, too, Ishaq."

Ishaq didn't respond.

"Forget that," Khalid said. "Just find Bashshar, Tarik."

Terry punched in Bash's number on the cell phone Khalid had handed him. "I'm calling him now."

Khalid turned off the interior dome light. He could only hope that Bashshar was at this house in the country, or even in town since he knew that most bands travel frequently. But if Tarik could reach his brother by phone, Khalid felt confident that Bashshar would come quickly to meet him, hopefully at this house in the country.

Terry waited as Bash's phone began ringing. It was the middle of the night. He hoped Bash would answer. Terry had planned on surprising his brother with a visit, but never under these circumstances . . .

† † †

34

*B*ash's cell phone began vibrating on the floor next to his mattress. The rehearsal room was dimly lit by a small lamp next to the mattress Jonni slept on. He grabbed his phone and saw a number and area code he didn't recognize. He noticed the time display on his phone. It was a little after two in the morning. They had been awake until shortly after midnight, listening to music on Jonni's smartphone played through Ricky's Jawbone Jambox. There had been no disturbances in the house. No visits from the dark mass or any of its *underlings*. Bash had fallen asleep quickly. He now wondered if it had all been a dream. A nightmare. But he knew it had not.

Bash answered the phone call. "Hello?" he said in a sleepy voice.

"Bash! It's me! Terry!"

After the surprise of hearing Terry's voice on the other end, Bash was now wide awake. He listened to Terry as a now awake Jonni and Ricky gave him curious looks from their own mattresses on the floor.

"Listen, Bash," Terry said. "We are in grave danger. Walid wants us both dead."

"What?" exclaimed Bash. He listened in disbelief as Terry explained his ordeal of capture and torture, and how Khalid and Ishaq had rescued him at great risk to themselves.

"If they hadn't rescued me when they did," Terry said, "I could've been dead by now."

After listening for another few minutes, Bash finally asked, "Terry, where are you?"

"On our way to Austin," Terry replied. "On Interstate 35. Near Waco. Bash, are you in town?"

"Yes!" Bash said. "I'm at Rock Bottom now!"

Terry suddenly remembered the name of the house from previous conversations with Bash. "Can we meet you there now?"

"Of course, Terry!" Bash said.

"Khalid thinks your house's location will be a safe spot for us to lay low," Terry explained, "until we figure out what to do next."

"I'll be here waiting for you," Bash said. He gave Terry general directions before saying, "Call me when you get on 290 and I'll guide you in from there."

After ending the call, Bash explained the conversation to Jonni and Ricky who were now sitting up on their mattresses, their full attention on Bash. Bash recounted what Terry told him but intentionally left out the part about himself being in danger as well.

"Why would your uncle do this to his own nephew?" Jonni asked.

"Terry didn't go into details," Bash answered, "but he told me that Walid believes Terry overheard him discussing something . . . something Walid didn't want him to hear. So Walid had him kidnapped and tortured to find out what Terry knew."

Jonni and Ricky could hardly believe what they were hearing.

"Do you think your uncle is involved in some type of criminal activity?" Jonni asked a moment later. "Selling drugs, stolen goods, something like that?"

"No," Bash said, his anger at his uncle growing by the minute. "Uncle Wally is too religious for that. He hates the West, especially America. Since nine-eleven he's applauded every terrorist attack here and abroad. An act of terror is more likely."

"Is he capable of that?" asked Ricky.

Bash shrugged his shoulders. "Depending on the act, I guess anyone is capable."

"Bash," Jonni said. "You could be in danger, too."

"Why would he be in danger?" asked Ricky.

"Because his uncle probably knows that he has been talking with Terry," Jonni said. She paused for a moment before adding, "Not only that, but if Walid believes Bash knows something about his . . . illegal plans or whatever, then Walid knows Bash could have told us, too. We could be in danger also."

Ricky shook his head in disbelief. "This is crazy."

Bash thought about Jonni and Ricky being targets along with him and Terry. "You're right, Jonni," Bash said while rising from his mattress. "You and Ricky need to get out of here now."

"I'm not going anywhere," Jonni said.

"Yes, you are."

"Forget it," she said. "You think I'm afraid of dealing with thugs? *Human* thugs, by the way."

Bash knew what she meant but he was still worried for her and Ricky. "I know you aren't afraid, Jonni. But I can't risk something happening to either one of you because of my family problems."

"I thought *we* were family," she shot back, her tone indicating it was a question.

Bash glanced at Ricky who nodded in agreement.

"We have a better chance of making good decisions if we stick together," Jonni insisted. "I'm a team player."

Bash began running his fingers through his long hair while pacing the floor. He knew Jonni was right about sticking together. "I don't know what to do at the moment," he finally said. "Just wait for them to get here then come up with a plan, I guess."

Ricky chose his words carefully. "Bash, please don't take this in the wrong way, but is there a remote possibility that Terry is just being over-dramatic? That his capture and torture and all the rest is being exaggerated a bit?"

Bash's eyes answered the question. "No way," he said. "Terry is not like that. Besides, I heard the emotion and weariness in his voice. Also, I know Walid. I think he has gone off the deep end."

Ricky seemed satisfied from Bash's response. "Then I think we should call the police," he said while rising from his own mattress.

"And tell them what, Ricky?" Bash asked. "That some Islamic terrorists are hunting us down and we need them to send a SWAT team out here for protection? Out to the same house where some drug crazed rock band was busted not long ago? With me being part of the drug crazed rock band?"

Ricky didn't say it but he thought, *Yeah, I see what you mean.*

Jonni watched Bash pace the floor. "How long before Terry gets here?" she asked.

"Hour. Hour and a half."

She stood from her mattress. "With all your brother has been through he will need some fresh clothes, food, and maybe even some medical care."

Bash hadn't thought of that. "Yes, you're right."

Jonni turned her attention to Ricky. "Is there a twenty-four hour Walmart anywhere close?"

"Yes," replied Ricky. "There's one out on 290."

"I'll make a list," she said while beginning to type into the text messaging window of her smartphone. "I'll text it to you when we're finished, Ricky."

"I'm going to take a quick shower," Bash said while reaching into his pocket and handing Ricky a roll of cash, mainly twenty-dollar bills. "Get underwear and socks. And some cheap jeans and a few shirts. Terry's probably a bit taller than me. I don't know for sure. Is that enough cash?"

"I'll cover it if it's not enough," Ricky said. "You need anything?"

"Yeah, get me some underwear and socks, too," Bash said. "Maybe a fresh shirt."

"Okay," Ricky said. "Now, please do us all a favor and go take your shower."

Bash tried to force a smile at Ricky's little joke but he could not.

"You need anything, Jonni?" Ricky asked her.

"I could use a few toiletries," she said. "I'll put them on the list. I've got cash if you need more."

"I've got it covered," Ricky insisted.

While Jonni made the shopping list on her cell phone, Bash headed upstairs for a shower, never even glancing at the rope still attached to the attic trapdoor, or noticing that it was swaying back and forth like the pendulum of a clock . . .

35

While Ricky drove into the darkness on his way to the Walmart he wondered what he'd gotten himself into. Bash was his good friend but things seemed to be getting out of hand. He didn't need all this in his life right now. A voice inside of him said, *Don't fear. I have you right where I want you at this exact moment in time.* More thoughts came to mind. *Is Bash's brother being truthful?* What if all this business about being captured and interrogated was just made up? An attempt to get attention from Bash or whatever. Ricky knew nothing about Bash's brother other than what Bash had told him. *But what if it is all true?* Then Bash and Terry were in danger. *Which means Jonni and myself could also be in danger.*

Ricky thought about the right course of action for the moment. His suggestion for Bash to call the police kept haunting him. But Bash's response made sense. *What could the police do? Or even the FBI or Homeland security or whatever? The situation would be the same. What evidence exists other than Terry's story of capture and torture under the orders of an Islamic terrorist uncle?*

As Ricky drove into the nearly empty Walmart parking lot, he thought of Bash's comment about a SWAT team. It reminded Ricky of his friend, Kyle McCurry, the man who took them to the storage unit auction. Kyle was not a SWAT officer or even a policeman but he had similar experiences from his experience in the Marine Corps while raiding buildings in Iraq. *Probably as much experience as many SWAT officers.*

Ricky found Kyle's office number in his cell phone and made the call, leaving a detailed voice message on Kyle's answering machine. It was early Saturday morning. Still Friday night in most people's thinking. Hopefully, he would hear back from Kyle sometime that day.

†

Bash let the hot water of the shower splash onto his face. The events in the attic only hours earlier seemed like a distant dream. He had never believed in the supernatural but he could not deny what he witnessed with his own eyes and ears, including his experiences when alone during the day of the big storm. *What if there really is another realm or world existing parallel to our own? What if there really is a God?*

Bash could not ponder any of these thoughts for long because of the new turn of events. Part of him was excited that he would soon be with Terry but the situation robbed him of any joy. The idea of Walid having Terry tortured made Bash's blood boil. He never liked Walid but now he felt a new emotion toward his uncle. Hatred.

Using an old bar of soap and a partially full bottle of shampoo found near the bathtub, Bash began to lather quickly, anxious to finish the shower to be ready for the call from Terry. He fantasized about creating an offensive plan instead of a defensive one—a plan that involved hunting down Walid and repaying him for everything.

†

In the light of the porch, Bash ran to the Dodge Intrepid sedan as it parked in front of Rock Bottom. Terry was slow to get out but managed to embrace Bash with a long hug while tears ran down his bruised cheeks. Khalid and Ishaq exited the car and stood nearby, giving the two brothers their space. Khalid stretched his back with a smile fixed on his bearded face as Ishaq stood as still as a statue. Jonni watched from the porch, noticing Khalid's pistol from the dome light of the car when he straightened the hem of his shirt to conceal the weapon.

Bash and Terry finally ended their embrace. "Bash," Terry said, "This is Khalid."

Bash reached for Khalid's left hand eagerly. "Thank you, Khalid!"

"You are quite welcome," Khalid said with a chuckle.

After shaking Ishaq's hand and repeating his thanks of gratitude for saving Terry, Bash led them all to the front door. Khalid kept looking back over his shoulder, seemingly checking the dirt road for cars while Ishaq just stared at the ground. When Bash introduced Jonni to Terry, she hugged his brother lightly, trying not to crinkle her nose at his foul body odor. She stuck out her hand for handshakes toward Khalid and Ishaq but they only nodded their heads politely instead of shaking her hand.

They all entered the foyer and Khalid checked out his surroundings in a nervous way.   Bash led them into the kitchen. "Sorry," he said, "except for a few mattresses and the kitchen table, there's no furniture left in the house."

"Are you and the band moving somewhere?" asked Terry as he sat gingerly in one of the chairs at the kitchen table.

"Uh, no," Bash said. "The band is no more. It's a long story. I'll fill you in later."

"So we are alone?" Khalid asked with the same smile he'd worn since arriving.

"Except for a friend of mine who went to the store for supplies," Bash said. "He should be back soon. He's buying some fresh clothes and toiletries for you, Terry."

Khalid lost the smile for just a moment.

"Thank you, brother," Terry said.

"Are you hungry?" Jonni asked.

"Not at the moment," Terry said, "but thank you. We grabbed a sandwich at a convenience store on the way here. I was starving."

Stopped for a sandwich? Jonni knew that Terry probably hadn't eaten in days but stopping for food while fleeing from terrorists didn't sound right to her. "When Ricky gets back," she said, "I'll prepare some breakfast. Is there anything else you need?"

"A bath would be nice," Terry said. "I'm sure I smell like a donkey."

"I'll fill the tub," she said while leaving the kitchen. "Hopefully there's soap."

"There is," Bash said. "Clean towels in the hall closet, too."

After Jonni left the kitchen Terry asked, "So she is this Ricky's girlfriend or wife?"

"No," Bash said. "She's a friend. Of mine. Of ours."

Terry smiled. "I see."

Bash blushed but he left it alone.

"So there are no other houses on this road?" Khalid asked Bash.

"No," Bash said. "I know it's strange but the road only goes to this house. It's a dead end."

A dead end! Khalid thought. *Well said!* "How many exterior doors are there?"

"Just the front door and this one," Bash said, gesturing toward the kitchen door.

"Are you expecting any visitors anytime soon?" asked Khalid.

"No," Bash said. "Just Ricky when he gets back from the store."

"The reason I ask," Khalid explained, "is because if anyone comes here, other than your friend who went to the store, we must assume they are our enemy."

"And then what?" asked Bash.

Khalid frowned at the question. "I have a plan," he finally said, "but I need to make a few calls first."

"That reminds me," Bash said. "I need to make a call myself."

This got Khalid's attention. "To who?"

Bash raised his eyebrows.

"I'm sorry," Khalid said. "I don't mean to pry but under the current situation I would like to know who knows we are here."

"I need to call the band manager," Bash said. "The lease on the house is in his name. I need to clear it with him regarding us staying here for a few days or whatever. It's nothing urgent that has to be done right away, though. It's Saturday. I'm sure he'll be sleeping until later in the morning."

"Okay," Khalid said. "So you can make the call later today?"

"Of course," Bash replied.

"I do not want anyone to know we are here yet," Khalid explained. "We may be out of here soon anyway. Maybe even today."

"I understand," said Bash.

No, you don't, thought Khalid.

†

In the beams of his headlights, Ricky saw a sedan and two men standing near Rock Bottom's front porch, staring at Ricky's pickup truck as it approached. One of the men was talking on a cell phone. For just a moment Ricky thought about doing a 180 and fleeing for help but realizing they must be the men that rescued Terry, he parked the Toyota pickup truck next to the sedan and got out. It was still dark so the porch light was on. Sunrise was still a few hours away. "Hi, I'm Ricky," he said. "Bash's friend."

A dark-haired man with a beard approached him with a wide grin. "Yes, Bashshar told us you would be arriving soon." He held out his hand for a handshake. "I am Khalid and this is Ishaq."

While shaking Khalid's hand, Ricky nodded at Ishaq and got a nod back. He began grabbing bags from his truck bed.

"Give us a hand, Ishaq," Khalid said while helping Ricky with the bags. "This is very kind of you bringing supplies. Tarik has nothing except filthy clothes that his captors left him in."

"I'm glad I was here to help out," replied Ricky.

"Very fortunate for us," Khalid said. *But very unfortunate for you.*

"How is Terry?" asked Ricky.

"He is better now," Khalid said as they brought the bags into the house. "Weak and a little bruised but he will be fine."

Bash met them at the door. "Food bags to the kitchen," he said while smiling at Ricky. "The rest in the rehearsal room."

"Yes, sir," said Ricky with a weak smile.

While Khalid took the food bags into the kitchen, Ricky and Ishaq set the other bags on the floor next to the mattresses. "So where's your brother?" Ricky asked Bash.

"Still in the bathtub," Bash said while removing some jeans and other clothes from the bags.

"Those are yours," Ricky said. "The darker ones are for your brother. There's also tee shirts, underwear, and socks in one of the bags."

"Thanks, Ricky," Bash said. "You are awesome."

"Yeah, I know," replied Ricky.

Bash took the bags and started for the staircase. "Jonni's in the kitchen," he said while climbing the stairs. "She seems excited to cook for everyone."

"I'm excited for that, too," Ricky said while turning his attention to Ishaq. He offered his hand. "Thanks for all you have done."

Ishaq turned his eyes away while shaking Ricky's hand. "Thanks."

After an awkward moment of silence, Ricky started for the kitchen. "Let's find out what's happening in the kitchen."

Bash changed clothes in one of the empty bedrooms before bringing the bag to Terry in the bathroom. He knocked on the door. "You need any help, Terry?"

"No, I'm almost done," Terry said. "I'm a little slower than usual."

"That's okay. Take your time."

Terry opened the bathroom door with a towel wrapped around his waist. "Come in." He removed the clothes from the bag in Bash's hand and began dressing slowly.

Bash saw the large bruises all over his back and sides. The anger at Walid swelled again. "You think anything is broken?"

"Just my pride," Terry said while grabbing a toothbrush from the bag.

The brothers made eye contact and embraced with a hug.

Tears were flowing down Bash's cheeks. "I'm so happy to be with you, little brother. I never want to be apart again."

"Yes, together now on," Terry said while trying not to weep. "Forever."

They began to laugh while wiping the tears from their eyes. "Your makeup will start to run if you don't stop!" Bash said.

After composing themselves, Terry said, "We will get out of this situation safely, Bashshar. I promise. God even promised me!"

"Yes," Bash said. "I believe you."

Bash left the bathroom to let Terry finish dressing.

Ricky was walking up the staircase. When he got to the top he asked Bash, "How's Terry doing?"

"He's okay," Bash said. "He's bruised up quite a bit."

Bash and Ricky saw Khalid stop halfway up the staircase.

"Everybody okay?" asked Khalid with the same grin he always wore.

"Yeah," Bash said. "Terry's getting dressed. We'll be down in a minute."

"Okay," Khalid said before turning and descending the staircase.

Ricky moved close to Bash. "He's starting to get to me," Ricky whispered close to Bash's ear. "I haven't been here for twenty minutes and he follows me everywhere. He seems to be watching me constantly."

"He's just paranoid," Bash whispered back. "And I think he has a right to be."

"Yeah, I understand. I just wish he'd quit staring at me all the time."

"Just chill out," said Bash.

Ricky started to tell Bash about leaving a message with Kyle when the bathroom door opened and Terry stepped out. Bash introduced him to Ricky. They shook hands eagerly.

"I've heard much about you," Terry said. "Thank you for all you have done for my brother. Especially for taking care of him after his motorcycle accident."

"I didn't do much," Ricky said.

"Yeah, he just reminded me daily of why I still needed to live," Bash said. "Visited me every day in the hospital. Raised money for me. Gave me a place to live. Got me a job. I decided if I didn't get better I'd never get rid of him!"

The three laughed as they descended the staircase, despite knowing that they were being hunted. If they would have known how close the hunters actually were, they wouldn't have been laughing at all . . .

† † †

36

"No," Khalid said in Arabic. "We keep to the plan. We do it before sunrise."

Ishaq said nothing while they stood in the darkness near the Dodge sedan parked in front of the porch.

"Someone could arrive once it is daylight," Khalid said. "We do it now."

Ishaq looked like he was about to vomit.

"The plan is perfect," Khalid continued. "Walid actually triggers the explosion with the call. The honor is still his, despite our assistance."

Ishaq still didn't say anything.

"We will be back in Oregon before anyone identifies the remains of the bodies," Khalid went on. "When they link us to this it will be too late."

Rock Bottom's front door opened. Jonni shouted, "Breakfast is ready!"

"Thank you!" Khalid said in English with a wide grin. "We will be right in!"

Ishaq exhaled loudly.

"I am hungry," Khalid told him, switching back to Arabic. "We eat breakfast first. You finish quickly. Then excuse yourself. Get the gas containers from the trunk and set them on the porch. Then bring the bags inside. After everyone is secured I will begin wiring the cell phone apparatus to the pressure cooker. Once we are out of the house, I call Walid and he makes the call that triggers the explosion. Understand?"

Ishaq nodded reluctantly before both men returned inside the house to eat their breakfast.

†

"This food is delicious!" Khalid said after swallowing his bite of scrambled eggs.

"Thanks," Jonni said while standing at the stovetop and stirring more eggs in an iron skillet. "Would anyone like more?"

"Yes, please!" Terry said as he grabbed more toast and bacon from a platter on the breakfast table.

"There's more if anyone is still hungry," she said.

Khalid made eye contact with Ishaq who stood with his back to the wall while nibbling on his plate of food. He had barely eaten any of it. "How about you, Ishaq?" Khalid said. "You want more food?"

"No," Ishaq replied, getting the message that it was time. "Excuse m-me, please," he said before setting his plate of food in the sink and leaving the kitchen.

"He's so polite and well-mannered," Jonni said while scooping the last of the eggs in the skillet onto Terry's plate.

"And shy," said Ricky who had already finished eating.

"Not shy," Khalid said, losing his smile.

"He has a stuttering problem," Terry explained while eating his second helping of eggs. "That's why he doesn't talk much."

"Yes, but he is improving," Khalid added while keeping eye contact with Ricky. "He is still nervous around strangers, though."

Ricky held his gaze. "No offense intended."

"None taken," Khalid said before his full smile returned.

Ishaq walked out the front door and stopped on the porch. He stared into the darkness, trying to calm the surge of panic stirring within him. He could just start running, eventually getting a ride to a bus station or airport. *But Khalid would find me.* Even if his brother didn't find him, where would he go? He would be a traitor. Walid and the others would never stop looking for him. He would die a horrible death once they caught him.

Ishaq went to the trunk of the car and removed two five-gallon containers of gasoline and set them on the porch next to the front door. He returned to the trunk and removed the backpack with the pressure cooker inside. The pressure cooker contained the detonator, wrench sockets, packaged explosive, and a bag of jellied gasoline that added an incendiary element to the explosion. The wire leads from the detonator inside the pressure cooker protruded from tiny filed edges in the lid, waiting to be connected to the cell phone apparatus that would initiate the detonation. Ishaq knew it would all function perfectly since Khalid was an expert in this design.

Ishaq placed a tote bag over his shoulder that contained some pliers, plastic zip-ties, the cell phone apparatus, and a Glock 9mm handgun. He carried everything into Rock Bottom and set the backpack on the floor just outside of the kitchen. He removed the Glock from the tote bag and entered the kitchen.

Khalid saw him and stood from the breakfast table. He removed the pistol from his waistband. "Everyone on the floor, please," he said in a calm voice.

Shock and surprise registered on everyone's faces.

"On the floor now!" Khalid ordered loudly while cocking the hammer on his revolver and pointing it at Ricky's head.

"What are you doing?" Terry protested.

"What should have been done long ago!" Khalid replied. "Now on the floor! Face down! Now!"

Bash and Terry rose slowly from the table and lowered themselves onto the floor while Ishaq held them at gunpoint. Ricky stood, and noticing that Khalid had lowered the gun from his head, elbowed Khalid in the nose with enough force to cause blood to spurt from the man's nostrils. Ricky went for the gun but was unsuccessful. Khalid struck Ricky on top of his head with the butt of the handgun. Ricky fell to the floor with a heavy thud.

Khalid cocked the revolver and pointed it at Ricky's motionless body on the floor.

"Stop!" shouted Bash. "Don't shoot! Please!"

"Why are you doing this?" Terry pleaded. "I thought you were my friends!"

"You okay, Ricky?" Bash said, getting no response.

Khalid calmed a bit since Ricky looked like he was out cold. He released the hammer on the revolver and told Ishaq, "Collect all their cell phones and place them on the table."

Ishaq did as he was told, removing the cell phones first from Ricky's pocket, then from Bash's pocket. He placed both of them on the breakfast table. He hesitated when approaching Jonni on the floor.

Jonni sensed his reluctance to reach into her pockets. "I don't have a cell phone."

Khalid cocked the hammer on his revolver and pointed the handgun at Ricky's motionless body.

"Next to the mattress in the big room," she told Ishaq.

"Go get it," Khalid told Ishaq while grabbing a towel to stop the flow of blood pouring from his nose.

Ishaq returned with her cell phone and placed it on the table with the other phones.

"Secure their hands behind their backs with the zip-ties," Khalid said in Arabic while grabbing the backpack from outside the kitchen and returning to the table. He unzipped the backpack and began wiring the cell phone apparatus to the leads protruding from the pressure cooker as Ishaq began looping the plastic zip-ties around their wrists.

"Let them go," pleaded Terry. "They haven't done anything. Do what you want with me but let them go. Please."

Khalid ignored Terry's pleading while remaining focused on the wiring of the pressure cooker bomb.

Bash looked over his shoulder and saw what Khalid was doing. *Oh, my God. He has a bomb. He's going to blow us all up.*

"Tie their ankles, too," Khalid told Ishaq. "No one escapes this room."

Ishaq didn't reply as he continued securing their wrists.

Khalid stood from the table and stepped over the captives on the floor. He began scooting the heavy stove away from the wall. Everyone on the floor—except for Ricky—turned their heads to see what Khalid was doing.

Khalid wedged his way behind the stove with two pairs of channel-lock pliers in his hands. Bash stared in horror as he realized that Khalid was tinkering with the gas connection between the wall and the stove. *This is it*, Bash thought. *He's going to fill up the house with gas before blowing everything to smithereens. Including us.*

Khalid climbed out from behind the stove a few moments later. "I am going to splash gasoline on the exterior with one of the containers," he told Ishaq in Arabic. "When you finish here, take the other container and splash the upstairs."

Bash lowered his face to the kitchen floor. He thought he could hear a faint hissing sound from behind the stove. He wondered if the gas filling the room would render them unconscious or maybe even kill them before the bomb detonated. *Probably not,* he told himself. *Maybe in the movies. But not in real life.*

Bash began to pray. It was the first time he had prayed since his accident. Back then he had prayed to die. Now he prayed to live. Jonni had come into his life. Terry had come back in his life. He had so much to live for. The prayer he released seemed to come from deep within him: *God, I want to believe that you exist. If you do, then I know you can save us. Let us live. Let Jonni and Terry and Ricky live and be a part of my life. And God, if you let us live, I promise that my number one goal in life will be to get to know you. I promise . . .*

†

Walid sat at the desk in his office and stared at a prepaid cell phone in his hand. Khalid should be calling again any moment, informing him that they were good to go before giving him the number of the detonator-phone which would trigger the explosion. The plan had gone perfectly so far, according to Khalid who had updated him less than an hour earlier. But Walid would save any celebration until after the explosion when he got the final report from Khalid himself. "Call me, Khalid," he mumbled to himself. "Call me."

The farmhouse phone on Walid's desk rang suddenly, startling him with its loud brash ring. Walid answered the phone and heard an operator's voice explaining about an international collect call from Cairo. "Will you accept the call?" she asked.

"Yes," Walid answered.

A moment later he heard Shadya's voice on the other end. "Father?"

"Hello, Shadya," Walid said with a sigh. "How are you?"

"Wonderful!" she said. "Cairo is such an exciting place!"

"Did you and your mother find the accommodations satisfactory?"

"Yes, very comfortable," Shadya answered. "Mother actually suggested I call to find out when you will arrive."

"I see," Walid said. "As I told her before, once I finish my business dealings, I will make preparations to join the family."

"So no time soon?" asked Shadya.

"When I am ready, Shadya."

Shadya was actually elated by the news that her domineering father would not be joining them right away. "Yes, Father."

"How is Amin doing in his school?"

"He doesn't start until next week," Shadya said. "Remember?"

"Oh right," Walid said, still distracted by the fact that Khalid hadn't called back yet. "Well, call me with a report once he begins."

"Yes, Father." *A report? How affectionate!*

"Tell your mother to watch her spending," Walid said. "There is more to do in Egypt than just spend money. Tell her to visit some of the many mosques that are numerous in the city."

"I will," Shadya said with her own sigh. "Goodbye, Father."

"Goodbye."

Walid hung up his desk phone and stared at the cell phone in his hand. "Call me, Khalid," he said aloud. "This is taking way too long."

†

Ricky was still unconscious as Ishaq secured his wrists behind his back.

Terry tried to reason with Ishaq. "Don't do this, Ishaq. You are not like Khalid. You don't have to—"

"—No talk!" Ishaq shouted while jerking the Glock from his waistband and pointing it at Terry.

Terry closed his eyes and began mumbling a prayer.

Ishaq replaced the Glock in his waistband and approached Jonni. Bash noticed the gun. He knew he had to act fast.

†

On the porch, Khalid removed a small flashlight from his pocket to guide his way. He took one of the gas containers and proceeded to the side of the house. He began splashing gasoline on the exterior wall, knowing it would help accelerate the inferno. While inching his way along the exterior of the house, splashing gasoline as he went, Khalid suddenly heard thumping sounds from above, apparently coming from inside the upstairs area of the house. He quit splashing the gasoline and listened. A moment later he set the gasoline container on the ground and aimed his flashlight toward the upper portion of the house. The sound ceased immediately. He detected the slightest of movements from just

262

outside the perimeter of his flashlight beam. He searched his surroundings with the flashlight, his ears still tuned toward the upper portion of
the house for more sounds. If one of the captives had escaped and fled
upstairs, surely Ishaq would have come running to inform him by now.

Khalid saw or heard nothing else unusual so he returned to his task
of splashing gasoline on the wall while working his way back toward the
porch in a methodical way.

†

Ishaq finished securing Jonni's wrists before kneeling down over
Bash. He looped a plastic zip-tie over Bash's wrist and hesitated, wondering how he would secure the single arm. Bash knew what was happening. He made his move. He jerked his arm from Ishaq's grasp and
went for the Glock in Ishaq's waistband. Ishaq fought for the gun but it
flew out of his hand and slid across the kitchen floor. Bash was on his
feet within seconds as Ishaq scrambled on all fours for the Glock. Bash
grabbed the heavy iron skillet from the top of the stove, and with all his
strength he brought it down hard on top of Ishaq's head, scattering rem-
nants of scrambled eggs across the kitchen. Ishaq flattened on the floor.
Out cold. Or dead. Bash didn't care. All he knew was that he still had to
act fast.

Bash grabbed the Glock and placed it in his own waistband before
grabbing a knife from a kitchen drawer. He started cutting the plastic zip-
tie on Jonni's wrist. The dull blade and the tough plastic made the task
difficult.

After Bash had freed Jonni, she grabbed a pair of scissors from the
drawer and freed Ricky who was starting to regain consciousness. Bash
cut the zip-ties on Terry's wrists. He listened carefully for any sign of
Khalid's return as he placed the knife in the sink and removed the Glock
from his waistband. "Head outside toward the trees!" Bash whispered to
them. "Hurry!"

Terry helped Ricky to his feet and they all started to exit through the
kitchen door leading to the back of the house. Bash began leading the
group through the darkness toward the trees across the open prairie
behind the house. Ricky was moving slow but Terry and Jonni helped
him as they trudged across the dark terrain, trying to reach the safety of
the trees in the distance.

Bash wished he had a flashlight, but as he thought about it, he realized it wouldn't be smart to use one. Once Khalid returned to the kitchen and saw that they had escaped, the man would easily spot a flashlight beam in the darkness of the outdoors. Even though Bash was now armed with Ishaq's Glock semi-automatic handgun, he didn't relish being shot at by Khalid. Gunfights in movies or TV shows were exciting to watch but Bash felt that in reality they were probably very unpredictable.

†

After Khalid finished soaking the porch with gasoline, he tossed the empty container aside. Before entering the house he noticed the second gas container still sitting on the porch. "Ishaq!" he shouted while entering the house. "What is taking you so long?"

Khalid entered the kitchen and saw Ishaq lying prone on the floor. He cursed under his breath. Ishaq's handgun was nowhere to be seen. Shock and anger consumed Khalid's face. He leaned over his brother to examine him just as Ishaq began to regain consciousness.

"What happened?" Khalid hissed in Arabic. "Get up!"

Ishaq struggled to clear his mind while Khalid forced him to his feet. Ishaq steadied himself by leaning on the kitchen counter while Khalid repeated his question. "What happened, Ishaq?"

"I d-don't know . . ."

Khalid wagged his gun near Ishaq's face. "Where did they go, Ishaq?"

Ishaq shook his head, trying to think.

Khalid glanced at the door leading to the back of the house. His anger grew. "Ishaq, you idiot!"

As Khalid started for the kitchen door, a series of loud thumps from upstairs stopped him in his tracks.

More thumps were heard, sounding like multiple footfalls.

A smile grew on Khalid's bearded face. "Let's go!" he told Ishaq. "Be vigilant! One of them has your gun!"

Khalid and Ishaq left the kitchen and started up the staircase, staying alert in case there was an ambush. Khalid entered the first bedroom which was illuminated by its ceiling light. The room was empty. He and Ishaq went to the next bedroom. Empty. His confidence of the captives hiding upstairs began to wane. *Then who made the noise up here?*

Ishaq still felt woozy from the blow on his head. A wave of nausea overcame him but he fought the urge to vomit. He staggered from room to room, following Khalid as he had all his life.

As Khalid and Ishaq exited the last bedroom and entered the hallway, they both heard thumps from the upstairs ceiling. Khalid's attention went to the attic trapdoor and its dangling rope swaying like a pendulum. A large smile grew on his face as a chuckle escaped his throat. "Tsk, tsk," he said. "Clever but sloppy."

Khalid and Ishaq approached the attic trapdoor. Khalid reached for the rope but Ishaq grabbed his arm. "My gun!" Ishaq warned in a loud whisper. "Th-they have it!"

"How could I forget?" Khalid whispered back, his voice full of disdain for his younger brother. Khalid aimed his revolver at the trapdoor. "This will get their attention."

"Wait!" Ishaq said in a panic. "The gas!"

"It will take a while for the propane to fill the house," Khalid said impatiently. "If we are able to quickly regain control of the situation, the situation your stupidity caused, then this house will be obliterated long before the propane will fill the house."

Ishaq calmed a little but fear still consumed his face.

Khalid fired two rounds into the trapdoor, the loud reports reverberating throughout the old house with all its empty rooms.

They both heard scuffling in the attic beyond the trapdoor.

"Trapped like rats," Khalid said while signaling Ishaq to open the trapdoor.

Ishaq grabbed the rope in both hands and pulled. The trapdoor opened with a loud groan. "Hello up there!" Khalid shouted into the dark attic. "This is only going to make things worse for you!"

Silence answered.

Khalid motioned for Ishaq to lower the folding ladder.

The attic interior remained dark and quiet as Khalid started up the trapdoor ladder, stopping when his head almost cleared the opening. He aimed his flashlight into the darkness, his other hand holding the revolver, ready to return fire. He saw no one but noticed plenty of hiding spots behind boxes, furniture, and other junk stored in the attic.

"Follow me," Khalid said while continuing up the ladder. "And stay alert."

It felt hot and oppressive once they stepped into the dark space. Ishaq's nausea was getting worse. He fought back the bile rising in his throat.

As Khalid scanned the large area with his flashlight, the size of the room registered with him. Clearing the attic would take time. *Time I don't have.* He devised a new plan. "Get the other gas container from the porch and bring it up here," he commanded Ishaq.

Ishaq descended the trapdoor ladder, moving a little slower than usual, as Khalid proceeded slowly toward the back of the attic, the revolver in one hand and the flashlight in the other. Khalid felt a cool patch of air move by his face. At the same time, he noticed movement behind some furniture, like a shadow, but he remained calm and deliberate as he moved slowly and patiently. "You are only making this worse for yourself!" he announced in a loud voice. "You could have had a quick and painless death downstairs! But now you will roast like meat in an oven!" He kept moving slowly, wiping the sweat from his brow with the back of his hand, ready to shoot anyone that appeared out of the dark shadows.

Khalid heard Ishaq returning up the ladder. Ishaq came to his side, out of breath, the container of gasoline in his hand. "Start with the walls," he told Ishaq in a voice loud enough to be heard by anyone in the attic. "Make sure to soak the boxes and furniture."

Ishaq began splashing the gasoline everywhere as Khalid kept a sharp watch for any movement. "Last chance to show yourselves!" he shouted as Ishaq finally emptied the gas container and tossed it aside.

Khalid's cell phone began vibrating in his pocket. He handed the flashlight to Ishaq before removing the cell phone from his pant pocket, keeping the revolver in his other hand. He glanced at the display on his phone: 'Unknown Caller.'

Khalid answered the call. "Hello?"

No reply.

Khalid ended the call and started to return the cell phone into his pocket when it began vibrating again. He answered the phone again. "Who is this?"

No reply.

It had to be Walid, Khalid told himself. *He's the only one that has received a call from this phone. Wrong number? Not likely, but possible.* The thought of a wrong number call to the other cell phone, the detonation cell phone, quickly crossed his mind but he dismissed the thought just as fast.

"Okay!" Khalid shouted while replacing the phone in his pocket, "Fun and games are over! You have made your choice!"

The attic trapdoor slammed shut so loudly and with so much force that the sound caused Khalid and Ishaq to jolt in surprise. Khalid instinctively turned to face the trapdoor while aiming his revolver at the same time. The beam of his flashlight revealed the ladder in its folded position on the trapdoor.

Ishaq slowly approached the closed trapdoor. Khalid followed while turning his head frequently to scan the attic with his flashlight, expecting an ambush.

Nothing moved in the attic.

Khalid focused his attention on the trapdoor, amazed by its folded ladder. *Obviously, the ladder had to be folded before the trapdoor could shut, but how is it possible we did not hear it being folded?*

†

Bash and his group finally reached the tree line bordering the property. They moved deeper into the protection of the woods before lowering themselves to the ground for a brief rest. Their eyes were now better adjusted to the darkness. Bash could still see the outline of Rock Bottom and a few of the interior lights through its upstairs windows.

Jonni squatted next to him. "Were they shooting at us? I heard two shots."

"I don't think so," he whispered back. "They sounded like they came from inside. But I don't know why. Maybe Khalid shot the brother."

Bash turned toward Ricky's dark silhouette. "How you doing, Ricky?"

"Better," Ricky said in a low voice. "I think I'm going to have a big lump on the top of my head, though. Thanks, bro. You saved us all."

"Let's save the congrats for later," Bash said. "We're not out of this yet." He noticed a hint of sunrise toward the east. "We really need to get to an area flanking the road before sunrise. Maybe we'll spot them leaving. Then we can make our way back to Ricky's truck to get out of here." *That's definitely wishful thinking,* he told himself.

Bash chastised himself for not grabbing his cell phone from the breakfast table. He could have called for help by now. *Stupid!* He continued to survey the area, realizing that thinking logically under stress wasn't as easy as it sounds. *I need to focus on what to do now,* he told himself. *Not what I should've done.*

A moment later Bash addressed his little group. "If we stay hidden behind the trees," he said in a quiet voice, "we could reach the road before sunrise. Hopefully, without being spotted."

"What if they spot us?" Terry asked.

"Then we'll have a shootout," Bash said. "I still have the brother's gun."

No one responded.

Bash was just as concerned as the others. He had only fired a handgun a few times in his life, and that had been with his right hand when he had a right hand. Now he wondered how accurate he would be with his left hand if he got into an exchange of gunfire with Khalid. In the dark. With bullets aimed toward him. *Probably not so good.*

†

Khalid was losing patience. "Open it!" he ordered Ishaq.

Ishaq lowered himself to his knees and leaned over the trapdoor. He pushed on it but the trapdoor wouldn't budge. He tried again, using all his weight, but it didn't move even a fraction of an inch. It felt like it had been nailed shut. The smell of gasoline, along with the oppressive heat in the attic, was starting to overwhelm Ishaq. A wave of panic threatened him. He fought the urge to let go of any self-control and start screaming.

"Get on top of it!" Khalid yelled, momentarily breaking Ishaq's panic attack. "Use your legs! We need to get out of here now!"

Ishaq stood on the trapdoor and extended his arms to grab hold of a rafter for a better grip. He stomped. And stomped again. And again. "No good!"

"Move out of the way!" Khalid hissed while jerking Ishaq away and placing himself over the trapdoor. He stomped but the trapdoor wasn't moving for him, either.

"Did they n-n-nail it shut?" Ishaq asked in a frightened voice.

Khalid shook his head in exasperation. "Did you hear any hammering, Ishaq?"

Ishaq started to say something but Khalid cut him off.

"—Shut up, Ishaq!" Khalid shouted. "This is all your fault! You are an idiot!"

Khalid tried to think but the claustrophobic condition of the attic was starting to threaten his sanity, too. The smell of gasoline was not helping. "Keep stomping, Ishaq!"

They both positioned themselves on the trapdoor and began stomping in unison. They stomped and stomped but the trapdoor was not opening. Sweat was pouring from both of their bodies. *How is this possible?* Khalid thought to himself. *They must have wedged something between the trapdoor and the floor below. But what? They just happened to have a ten-foot beam lying around, and then shut the trapdoor without me hearing them before wedging the beam in place?*

Khalid's cell phone suddenly sounded a text alert from his pocket. He retrieved the phone and read the text. It was only one word:

'Bye.'

Khalid shook his head in confusion while staring at the text.

Downstairs in the kitchen, the display on the cell phone detonation apparatus suddenly illuminated . . .

†

Bash and his group were moving slowly through the trees, skirting the open prairie while keeping an eye on Rock Bottom in case Khalid and his brother came in pursuit.

Jonni felt a low rumble in the ground before the massive explosion rocked the earth beneath them. They all stared in disbelief at Rock Bottom in the distance. Debris rained down from the sky, some of it landing on nearby trees. They heard a few secondary explosions, smaller than the original, as they watched a giant blaze begin to consume the old house. Rock Bottom was burning out of control.

No one said a word for a long minute. Then Terry said, "You think they were inside?"

"Maybe," Bash replied. The area surrounding the house was well illuminated by the huge flames. Nobody seemed to be running from the inferno.

"We need to get to a phone," Terry said.

"No one make a move," Bash said.

"He's right," Jonni added. "They may have gotten out before the explosion, thinking we were hiding somewhere. They could be watching from a hiding spot."

Ricky finally spoke up. "I don't get it. If they wanted to kill us, why not just shoot us? Why use a bomb at all? It doesn't make sense."

"It makes perfect sense," Terry said. "In their reasoning, that is."

"What do you mean?" asked Bash as he watched Rock Bottom burn.

"You saw what they were doing," Terry replied. "They had a phone wired to something in the backpack."

"I know," said Bash. "I think it was a pressure cooker bomb."

"Yes," Terry said. "Detonated by a cell phone call. They went to all that trouble so someone else could make the call that triggered the explosion. And I know who that someone is."

Bash tried to digest what Terry was saying. A moment later he said, "Walid."

"Yes," Terry answered. "It was an honor killing."

"A what?" asked Ricky.

"An honor killing," Terry repeated. "In Islam, the head of the family is responsible for the execution of his own family members if they become apostates."

"Apostates?" asked Ricky.

"Someone who leaves the Muslim faith," Jonni said.

"That's right," Terry said. "Someone like me. I began questioning Islam a while ago but I never admitted it to Walid or anyone else at the farm. But I did drop some hints to Khalid, who was posing as an apostate himself . . . and as my friend. I know now that he baited me. He was working with Walid the entire time."

"So why me?" Bash asked. "I'm not an apostate. I never believed in that crap from the beginning."

"That too is a form of apostasy in the eyes of Islam, Bash," replied Terry.

Bash could only shake his head at the insanity of it all.

"There's more," Terry said. "Walid was suspicious that I had told you something. Something that I actually never told you. This is the reason he had me abducted and questioned. To find out if I told you."

"Told me what?" Bash asked.

"About his plans."

"What plans?"

Terry hesitated before saying, "His plans of a major terrorist attack in the Northwest."

No one said a word as Rock Bottom continued to burn.

"How do you know this, Terry?" asked Jonni.

"Because I overheard him discussing it in his office," Terry said. "I didn't plan on spying on him. It just happened."

"How did Walid find out that you overheard him?" Jonni asked.

"I don't know," Terry replied. "I've been trying to answer that question since I was abducted."

No one said anything for a long moment as they watched the old house burn.

Bash broke them out of their hypnotic gaze. "Let's go," he said. "I want to get a view of the front of the house, to see if their car is still there."

They started off again while staying hidden by the trees. They had almost reached the dirt road when Jonni said, "Someone will surely see the fire soon. Fire trucks could be arriving anytime now."

"Another reason we need to get to the road," Bash said while starting to move again.

A moment later they scurried toward a spot near the dirt road about a hundred yards from the burning house. The sun was rising in the eastern horizon but the flames consuming Rock Bottom illuminated the entire sky. They now had a view of the front of the burning house. Bash saw that the upper story at the front of the house had already collapsed onto the front porch. Burning debris nearly covered both vehicles parked nearby. Bash felt fairly certain that Khalid and Ishaq were not going to be a problem anymore. "Sorry about your pickup, Ricky," said Bash.

"That's okay," Ricky said. "It's insured. We got out of this alive. That's the only thing important. What a miracle. Thank you, God."

Bash remembered his prayer earlier when on the floor of the kitchen. "Yes," he said. "Thank you, God."

Everyone was so focused on the burning house that they almost didn't see the approaching vehicle. "Look out!" Jonni warned everyone.

They lowered themselves to the ground, still partially hidden by brush and a few trees near the road. They watched a white Dodge Ram pickup truck slow to a halt in the middle of the road a short distance from their hiding spot.

"You think Khalid had others working with them?" whispered Jonni.

"I don't know," Bash replied. "Just keep down."

The driver's door opened and a tall man stepped out, his attention on the inferno.

Bash saw the short rifle the man carried in one hand.

Ricky suddenly stood up and began waving his arms. "Over here!" he shouted.

"Are you crazy?" Bash hissed while trying to grab Ricky. "You'll give us away!"

"It's okay," Ricky said before cupping his hands around his mouth and shouting toward the man, "Kyle!"

The man turned toward the sound and began trotting towards them.

Bash now recognized the man that had helped them acquire the sound system at the storage unit auction months earlier. *But what is he doing here?*

"Man, I'm glad you listen to your messages," Ricky said as Kyle McCurry approached them. The big man squatted next to them, glancing warily between his surroundings and the small group of weary individuals.

Bash stretched out his hand toward Kyle. "Good to see you, Kyle!"

Kyle had to switch the small assault rifle to his other hand to manage the left-handed handshake. "I guess I got here too late," Kyle said.

"I left a voicemail with Kyle when I went to the Walmart," Ricky explained to the others. "I told him what was happening at the time, with Terry being rescued from his captors, but I didn't expect this to happen when I left the message."

"So I take it that the bad guys arrived," Kyle said.

"The rescuers I told you about were actually the bad guys," Ricky said. "They tried to kill us all."

"They had a bomb," Terry said.

"They also released propane from the stove in the kitchen," Bash added. "Something must have gone wrong and caused the bomb to explode early. Thankfully, we had already managed to escape."

"Were they inside when it went off?" asked Kyle.

"I don't know for sure," Bash said, "but I think they were. If they made it out before the explosion I think we would've seen them by now. Their car is still there."

The sun was creeping higher over the horizon. "I'm going to move this beast off the road to make room for the calvary," Kyle said before starting back toward his pickup truck.

Calvary? Bash thought to himself.

Kyle parked his Dodge Ram pickup truck off the road between the woods and the weary-looking group, using the truck to block them in case the bad guys were still in pursuit, hiding in the trees somewhere. Sirens could be heard in the distance. He stepped out of the cab with an armful of bottled waters instead of the assault rifle. "I made a call earlier to my friend in the field office of the Austin bureau," Kyle said while handing out the waters. He saw their confusion. "FBI. Special Agent In Charge John Forrester."

Bash and the others listened carefully.

"When I mentioned to John the name Ricky left on my answering machine," Kyle explained, "John entered the database and discovered an open investigation involving this Walid Nadir character with both the FBI and Homeland Security."

Bash and Terry stared at Kyle with dumbfounded looks on their faces.

"Apparently, he's a major player in a terror cell up in Oregon," Kyle said. "That's all John would tell me. He'll be here soon. I also called 911 to report the fire when I first arrived." The sirens were getting louder. "It should be fairly crazy here shortly."

Kyle noticed the bloody patch in Ricky's hair. He removed a first-aid kit from the cab of his truck and began using a folded antiseptic napkin on Ricky's head wound.

Ricky started recounting all the events leading up to the explosion.

"Just relax, son," Kyle said. "Believe me, you'll be sick of telling the whole story before the day is over. I'll hear all about it soon enough." •

Several fire engines and EMS vehicles began arriving along with multiple Hays County Sheriff's Department vehicles. Within seconds, emergency personnel were swarming everywhere around the property. A couple of paramedics approached Bash and his group, seeing if anyone needed medical attention.

A while later, just as two detectives began questioning Bash and the others, an unmarked sedan arrived. Three men in suits exited the sedan and approached Kyle and the group. "Never a dull moment when you're involved, McCurry," one of the men said.

The man flashed his credentials to the detectives. "I'm Special Agent Forrester with the FBI," he told them. "I'd like to keep any media away until we are gone. Can you help with that?"

One of the detectives nodded somberly before punching in a number on his cell phone to request a patrol car to block the entrance of Bottom Creek Road.

"This is John Forrester from the FBI Field Office," Kyle told Bash and the group. "He's definitely interested in this case."

Agent Forrester glanced at the firemen hopelessly attempting to extinguish the raging fire. "Anyone need medical attention?"

Bash shook this head. "EMS already checked us out."

"I've got an SUV on its way to bring you folks to our office for questioning," Forrester said. "We'll get your statements then send you home for some rest. I also have a Bureau psychologist at the facility if anyone needs counseling."

No one answered Forrester.

Forrester scanned the group's weary faces. "Have any of you talked to anyone other than Kyle here?"

"All our phones were taken from us when we were abducted," Bash said. He gestured toward the inferno. "They are nothing but ashes and melted plastic by now."

"Good," said Forrester before correcting himself. "Not about your personal property but good you haven't talked to anyone."

Bash tried to smile but he could not.

Moments later a dark SUV arrived and parked near the FBI sedan. Agent Forrester and the two agents that had arrived with him escorted the group toward the SUV.

Terry, Ricky, and Jonni began climbing inside. Bash turned and took a long last look at the burning house. At that exact moment, the entire western wall of Rock Bottom collapsed in on itself with a loud rumble. As Bash climbed inside the SUV he could have sworn that he heard Rock Bottom moan in agony . . .

† † †

37

Walid Nadir had already vacated his farm and moved into a suburban location in the outskirts of Portland; a multi-room condominium used for the staging of the attacks. Walid was accompanied by six men who were trying to organize their backpack bombs for the multiple attacks planned later that day.

Although he knew no details, but since he never received a call back from Khalid, Walid was certain that Khalid and his brother had failed their mission. Now it was a battle for the clock. The Feds could very well be on their trail if Tarik was still alive and had somehow managed to get to the authorities. If Khalid and Ishaq had been captured, Walid felt confident that Khalid wouldn't reveal anything but the younger brother might be a problem. Walid knew beforehand that Ishaq wasn't as zealous as Khalid, one of the reasons he had hesitated to accept Khalid's plan.

Walid reassured himself as he watched his compatriots finish their preparations. *The attack will still be successful,* he told himself. *And I will escape capture as planned.*

A young Syrian man dressed in stylish corduroy pants and a wool sweater arrived at the condo. He handed Walid a folded piece of paper. Walid read the message which was written in Arabic. The note simply stated that Khalid had failed in silencing Tarik and that Khalid and his brother, Ishaq, had not survived an explosion in an old house located near Austin, Texas. More importantly, the note informed Walid that Tarik might be working with the authorities and that the entire mission could be compromised if the mission wasn't expedited immediately. The angry tone of the wording in the note was unmistakably Abdul. *Abdul, the old goat. How had he discovered anything about any government investigation of their plans?*

Walid—who had never been one of the intended martyrs for the suicide attacks, only an organizer—weighed his options. He already had plans for his escape when the mission was finished, plans that no one knew but himself, but now he needed to enact those plans immediately. There was only one question at the moment: *Can I leave the condominium without drawing suspicion from the others?* He thought quickly and made his decision. He turned to one of the men in the condo. "Give me the keys to your vehicle!" he said before placing Abdul's note into his pant pocket. "I have an emergency meeting!"

The man looked surprised but gave Walid the keys. "It's the tan Kia," the man said. "Parked next to the VW van."

Another man with a thick beard and the weathered look of a warrior overheard and approached Walid. "No one leaves!" the bearded man barked in Arabic. "You know that!"

Walid stared defiantly at the man. "Do you want to ignore a direct order from the old man?"

The bearded man hesitated while thinking. "Abdul ordered you?"

The young courier who had delivered the note spoke up. "I just delivered him the message."

"From Abdul?" the bearded man asked.

"Yes," the courier replied. "Abdul gave it to me himself! He said it was urgent!"

The bearded man nodded reluctantly as Walid started for the door.

"I'll return as soon as possible!" Walid said. "Keep the operation moving!"

Walid exhaled once he was safely inside the Kia in the condominium complex's covered parking. He started the ignition and backed out of the parking slot. He already knew where to go. A location that he had kept secret from everyone. Getting to the secret location had always been part of his plan, but now he would be heading there before the attacks began. *It is actually better this way*, he told himself. The cabin nestled in the Washington wilderness would offer total safety, if he could get there without being discovered or arrested. Once inside the cabin, Walid already had all the forged documentation necessary in getting first into Canada, then to Egypt.

Yes! he thought to himself. *Nothing has changed for me!*

Walid still hoped the attacks were successful, but if not, he would still be free to fight another day. Either abroad or in America. It didn't matter as long as he was part of the fight against the oppressive West.

Walid Nadir never even saw the black SUVs parked outside the entrance to the condominium complex. Within seconds they had the Kia boxed in on the road. Men in bulletproof vests armed with assault weapons jumped from their vehicles, their rifles aimed at him from crouched positions behind their opened doors.

Walid raised his hands from the steering wheel as they barked orders to him from a loudspeaker. Within seconds he was jerked out of the Kia and thrown facedown on the pavement with his arms and legs spread wide.

As Walid was being handcuffed, he saw the armored vehicles surrounding the condominium complex as SWAT members began getting into position for the raid. *At least I'm still alive,* he told himself, knowing that most in the condo would never be taken alive.

After being placed in the backseat of a sedan and driven away, Walid could hear the faint reports of gunfire behind him. The raid had begun . . .

EPILOGUE

One Year Later

*B*ash adjusted the settings on his Marshall half-stack guitar amplifier and returned his hand to the fretboard of his vintage '68 Fender Stratocaster, the guitar Trent had given him. "Okay, sorry, he said. "Let's try it again."

Ricky counted in the song. Along with a huge cymbal crash, Bash and Terry hit the downbeat with a thick, rich chord before proceeding into a high energy instrumental showcasing Bash's fast hammer-on and pull-off style of one-handed playing. He had one of Jonni's elastic fabric hairbands attached around the neck of his guitar near the first fret, preventing any open strings from making extraneous noise due to the hard hammer-ons and high input gain of his amp settings. He had developed a few one-handed tricks—like raking the strings of small chords with his pinky finger while using his other fingers for the chord—but mostly all sounding of notes were done by hammering on and pulling off his fingers on the strings, without the aid of a right hand to pick or strum the strings. Bash smiled while attacking the guitar's fretboard, experiencing more peace than even before his accident. He truly appreciated his gift now, unlike before his accident when he took it all for granted.

Bash was still amazed that he had never thought of adopting this style of playing after losing his arm. There were many videos on the internet of one-armed guitarists using similar methods but he had never searched for them. When Terry suggested that Bash try a one-armed method for drums, using Def Leppard's one-armed drummer for example, Bash never thought of applying the idea to the guitar. It wasn't until a month after the ordeal with Khalid and Ishaq that he accidentally found the business card the college students gave him the night of the party at Rock Bottom. When he finally searched the YouTube address written on the back of the card and saw several examples of one-armed guitarists attempting to develop a playing style, he marveled that he never thought of it himself. *Too busy feeling sorry for myself, I guess.*

Jonni entered the cabana-style building near the cozy little house she and Bash owned, purchased with a small part of the large inheritance she had received from her foster parents after their deaths. The one room building was perfect for small band rehearsals and the entire property stood a good distance away from neighbors, allowing them to practice within reasonable hours of the day. Hanging from the ceiling of the room was a large mirror ball with a laser light box aimed at it from a mount on a wall nearby—a housewarming gift to Bash and Jonni from Ricky.

The trio finished the song and Jonni approached Bash to give him a hug and a peck on the cheek. "You sound awesome," she said. "How's my superstar husband today?"

"Better now," Bash said before extending his lips for a real kiss.

Ricky stood from his drum set and stretched his back. He cleared his throat loudly. "Uh, excuse me!" he announced in a loud voice. "You guys know what happened to the Beatles because of Yoko, don't you?"

Terry grinned but Bash and Jonni seemed oblivious as they finished their kiss.

"I have lunch ready in the kitchen for everyone," Jonni said. "For everyone except Ricky, that is."

"Uh-oh," Ricky mumbled. "I guess Ringo's in trouble."

"Thanks, Jonni," said Terry. "I'm starving."

"You're always starving," Bash said while turning off his guitar amp.

They left the cabana and walked on a limestone path toward the main house. Inside the kitchen, Bash and his band sipped on fresh mint iced teas at an antique oak table in the breakfast nook, discussing their song list while waiting for Jonni to bring lunch.

Their conversation turned to current news events when Terry said, "I heard there was another hearing today regarding a trial date."

"Yeah, me, too," said Bash. "I still wonder if Walid will somehow wiggle out of this."

"I don't think so, Bash," Terry said. "Everyone is very tired of all this Islamic terror business."

Bash shrugged while staring at his glass of iced tea.

"I haven't been following the news lately," Ricky said. "Deliberately, I guess."

"I understand," Terry said. "I'm sure we'll be hearing from the Federal Prosecutor again soon enough. At least I will."

"You heard from Shadya lately?" asked Bash.

"Not since February," Terry said, "but I imagine she is still dealing with the same issues she had back then."

"What do you mean?" Ricky asked.

"She wants to come back home to America," Terry explained. "She hates living in Egypt but if she comes back she's afraid she will be forced to testify."

"They can make her do that?" Ricky asked. "Testify against her own father?"

"I don't know," Terry said in a dismissive tone. "The laws seem to be different when it comes to terrorism."

Jonni brought lunch to the table. She took a seat at the table. "Let's say Grace."

After a prayer led by Terry, they began their lunch: Boar's Head ham and Havarti cheese on ciabatta bread with bowtie pasta on the side.

"What did you guys think about the church service Sunday?" Ricky asked.

"I thought it was great," said Jonni.

"What about you, Bash?" Ricky asked in a nonchalant tone.

Bash knew Ricky was curious about his opinion of the church. "I thought it was good," Bash said. "Except for that drummer in the worship band."

Ricky made a face toward Bash. "Ha-ha. You are so witty."

"So what did you really think about it?" Jonni asked Bash.

"I was surprised," Bash said. "I guess my idea of church was outdated. I expected a robed choir and some little old lady playing piano."

"You knew I played drums there," Ricky said. "What did you think? That we played old hymnals with only drums and piano?"

"Yeah," Bash said with a mischievous grin. "You and some old lady jamming together on *Amazing Grace*."

This drew chuckles from around the table.

"Seriously," Bash said. "I guess I had a stereotype in my head regarding churches. But everyone at this church seemed so normal. Just regular people. Not the pretentious, holier-than-thou crowd with their fancy prayers and 19th-century music. I guess church has changed since I attended when I was a kid."

"When did you ever go to a church?" asked Terry in a surprised voice.

"I went with Jake and his family once," Bash said.

"Jake?"

"Yeah. Remember that freckled kid that lived next door to us in Tarrytown?"

"Oh, yeah," Terry said after remembering.

"Many churches have changed since then," Ricky said. "And many folks of the old guard hate the changes. They say it's bad that worship music has turned into loud rock and roll."

"There are many churchgoers who believe that," Jonni said, joining into the discussion. "Most of them are older folks, though. Tradition seems to outweigh the need to reach people with the message in many people's thinking. You mainly find this strict adherence to church tradition in the major denominations."

"What do you mean, Jonni?" this time from Terry.

"Major denominations meaning: Baptist, Methodist, Lutheran, Catholic, and so on," she said. "Division among Christians is all I think about it. I also believe God detests anything that divides his followers."

"Amen to that," said Ricky.

"So does that mean these denominations are bad?" asked Terry.

"I believe the denominational thing is bad because it divides Christ followers," Jonni said, "but there are many strong Bible-believing Christians in denominational churches. It doesn't mean those churches or their members are bad. It means they are imperfect. Like we are all imperfect. Many have accepted the traditions of their fathers and grandfathers as being more important than the word of God. Then they hand these traditions down to future generations, which keeps the division continuing onward."

"Well said, Jonni," Ricky agreed. "Show me a perfect church and you'll know you're in heaven because they don't exist here on this planet."

"Or," Jonni said, "find a perfect church, then attend it, and you'll find that it's not perfect any longer."

Ricky nodded with a smile.

"But using modern music in church that young people can relate to," Jonni continued, "seems a no-brainer to me. God's message has never changed but the style in which it's delivered has always changed. I believe God encourages those changes to reach as many people as possible through the course of time. Especially with the youth of each generation. The older churchgoers who don't like the changes should look deep inside themselves, beyond their own preferences, and tolerate the changes because of the more important issue of reaching young people with the Good News."

"It always needs to be delivered as *good* news," Ricky added. "Not *old* news."

"I like that," Jonni said before pausing to take a bite of her pasta. After swallowing her bite she asked, "So what did you think about the pastor's sermon, Bash?"

"It was pretty good," Bash said. "Lots of quotes from the Bible. I scribbled down the scripture references as fast as I could but I still don't write well with my left hand, you know. But I wrote them down so I can check them out for myself later. Isn't that the way we're supposed to do it?"

"Yes," she said. "The Berean approach."

"What do you mean?" Terry asked.

"The Berean approach, where Luke described the trip the Apostles Paul and Silas took to Berea," Jonni explained. "They thought highly of the Berean Jews who accepted their message with eagerness but later examined the scriptures themselves to see if what Paul was saying was true. You'll find it in Acts 17: 11."

"Thanks for another scripture to look up," Bash said with a mock frown.

"I'm glad you're curious," Jonni said with a smile.

Bash smiled back at her. "I'm glad you're glad," he said, "but can we change the subject now? I got a feeling everyone's going to break into a chorus of Kumbaya any moment now."

Jonni giggled before returning her attention to her lunch.

Bash tried to play down the spiritual awakening he had been experiencing the last few months. After the traumatic events at Rock Bottom,

Bash had kept his promise to God. The promise of getting to know him, or what Ricky called *diligently searching.* Bash didn't have a problem now with believing in the existence of God, but the whole Jesus thing had become quite a stumbling block to him. He understood and accepted that mankind had been spiritually separated from God by disobedience, and he even understood that this spiritual separation had been passed down to all generations, like a disease in our DNA. *But why was it necessary for God to send someone else to redeem us? Why couldn't God, in a huge voice from the sky, just tell us, "Okay, you all are forgiven now!" Why did he have to send Jesus of Nazareth to die here in order to free everyone?*

Bash did what Jonni suggested he do: He prayed. He prayed for God to answer the question. He prayed the prayer for days but no answer came for months. When the answer finally arrived, it came in a very unexpected way.

Not long after marrying Jonni, Bash had been taking a stroll in a small park near a medical facility while waiting for Jonni to finish a routine examination at a doctor's office. He saw a white-haired elderly man sitting on a park bench nearby. The old man had accidentally dropped his eyeglasses onto the ground next to the bench and was having difficulty leaning over to pick them up. The timing was perfect. Bash approached the bench and leaned over to retrieve the eyeglasses before handing them to the old man on the park bench.

"Thank you, son," the old man said while placing the eyeglasses on his face. He noticed the loose sleeve where Bash's right arm should be but he didn't say anything. "That was very kind of you."

Bash saw the Bible in the man's lap. "Reading the good book, I see."

"Yes, but I can't read without these darn things," the old man said while adjusting the eyeglasses on the bridge of his nose. "Getting old is not for sissies."

Bash grinned.

The old man patted the Bible in his lap. "You ever read it?"

"Well," Bash answered, "I started not long ago. I haven't finished it, though."

"I don't think we ever finish it," the old man said with a warm smile. "Have a seat, son."

Bash wasn't planning on sitting but for some reason he did.

"You said you've been reading the Bible," the old man said. "Learn anything yet?"

"Yeah, a few things," Bash said. "Actually, a lot of things. But I'm still struggling with a few matters."

"Aren't we all," the old man said. "I think that's the way it's supposed to be."

"Really?"

"What I mean is," the old man said, "maybe struggling to understand something is the only way we can actually learn."

Bash nodded. "Yeah, maybe so."

"For years I had a real problem understanding any of it," the old man said. "I eventually quit trying and went on with my life. It wasn't until I was about fifty that one particular issue eventually became clear, even though I had quit trying to understand it decades earlier."

"What was the issue?"

"The reason God would have to send his son, or anyone actually, to us here on Earth," the old man said. "I couldn't make sense of it. Or get my head around it, as many folks put it. Until I got an answer to that question, I would never be able to understand the most important part: that bit of foolishness about Jesus shedding his blood on a cross in order to make us right with God again."

Bash was more than surprised. Here was an old man, a stranger in the park, describing the very issues Bash was struggling with. "How did it become clear to you?"

"It became clear to me because of a story about a man in the newspaper business," the old man said. "Care to hear it?"

Bash knew Jonni would be in the doctor's office for a while. "Yes, I would."

"This newspaperman had started off as a reporter for a small town weekly paper," the old man said. "He'd worked his way up the ladder and eventually became the owner and editor of one of the largest newspapers in the midwest. On one particular Christmas Eve, while celebrating the holidays with his family in their luxurious cabin in Minnesota, the newspaper man was sitting in his favorite leather chair near a roaring fire in the fireplace while a major snowstorm raged outside. His wife and kids had finished dressing and were ready to head to a church nearby for its annual Christmas Eve service. This routine had been going on for years, ever since his kids were little. But something had been bugging the newspaperman for the last few years. He had started feeling like a hypocrite for attending the Christmas Eve services since he had convinced himself that the entire Christmas message was just a bunch of baloney. His main beef over the matter was: Why would God have to come to us through a human vessel, in this man called Jesus? Why not just speak to us directly? You understand, son?"

"Yes," Bash said, perfectly understanding the newspaperman's dilemma. "I do."

"So anyway," the old man continued, "the newspaperman told his wife he wasn't going to the services that night. She was very surprised and asked him why he was breaking their family tradition. He just told her he didn't feel like dealing with the snow blizzard, and that they shouldn't drive in it, either—just excuses to avoid telling her the real reason he didn't want to go.

"So after her and the kids left, the newspaperman settled into his favorite leather chair by the fireplace to read a novel. A few minutes later he heard a loud bang on the large picture window near his chair. He looked to the glass and saw nothing but darkness outside. Then it happened again. And again. He got up from his chair and turned on an exterior light so he could see what was hitting the window. He saw clusters of large snowflakes blowing against the window; a virtual whiteout caused by the Minnesota blizzard. Then another bang. He saw it this time. A little bird. Maybe a sparrow. It was obviously trying to escape the blizzard, seeing light and sensing warmth on the other side of the large windowpane. The newspaperman stood close to the window, trying to shoo away the little bird from colliding with the glass by waving his arms in big arcs. But his hand motions only seemed to frighten the little bird, making its attempts to get through the glass even more frantic. He now saw tiny smears of blood on the window where the bird was colliding with the glass.

"The newspaperman put on his hat, boots, gloves, and heavy parka, before grabbing a flashlight and heading outside toward the large picture window. As the bird fluttered near the window, still smashing into it to escape the blizzard, the newspaperman used his flashlight beam and his waving arms to try to stop the bird from flying into the glass. The little bird really became frightened now. It was chirping loudly as it continued to collide into the windowpane.

"The newspaperman got an idea. He trudged through the snow toward the barn which stood fifty yards in the distance. He opened the barn door and switched on its interior lights, then left the barn door cracked open before returning to the cabin, hoping the little bird would *see the light* from the barn and enter into its warmth and safety. But the little bird didn't seem to notice the opened barn door. It kept flying into the glass. The window was now smeared with blood. The newspaperman was now frantic himself. He stood outside the window, his arms flailing, trying to coax the bird toward the barn. The little bird only became more frightened from the monster waving its arms at it. The newspaperman had reached a point of total frustration, realizing that the little bird didn't understand that he was trying to help it and not hurt it. He said to himself, *If I could only convince it that I want to help! If I could only communicate with it in a way it would understand! I wish I could be a bird for just a moment and tell it I'm trying to save it from destruction!* The truth hit the newspaperman harder than the little bird was hitting the glass."

The old man paused his story to take a sip from a bottled water. He glanced at Bash to see if he was still listening. Bash had already caught the meaning of the story. He understood now. It was like a bright light had been turned on inside his soul.

"You see," the old man continued, "we are like the little bird. God, in his vastness, is imperceivable to us, just like the newspaper man appeared to that little bird. God loves us and only wants to save us from an existence without him. So God came to us in a form we could perceive, the form of a human, Jesus Christ, just like the newspaperman wished he could turn himself into a bird so he could communicate with it and tell it he only wanted to help it and not hurt it."

Bash fought back tears welling in his eyes. The truth of the message overwhelmed him. He cleared his throat before asking, "So what did the newspaperman do?"

"He left the cabin and drove his other vehicle through the snowstorm to join his family at that Christmas Eve service," the old man said.

"He accepted God's gift of redemption on the spot. His life was never the same afterward."

"Whatever became of him?" asked Bash. "Is he still around?"

The old man smiled while locking eyes with Bash. "You're looking at him."

Bash stared back at the old man. He could only think of one thing to say. "Thank you."

"I hope that story helped you in some way," the old man said while rising slowly to his feet. "I've got to head back home now. It's time for my lunch and some medication the doctors have me on. God bless you, son."

Bash watched the old man walk away from the park. A moment later he realized he had never introduced himself or asked for the old man's name. When Jonni finished her examination at the doctor's office, Bash thought of telling her about the old man and his story of the little bird, but he did not. Somehow, the revelation he received seemed private—a personal message from God, for him and him alone.

Now, while eating his lunch with Jonni, Terry, and Ricky at the oak table in the breakfast nook, Bash smiled when thinking about his time with the old man on the park bench. He still wished he had gotten the old man's name, but he also realized that maybe God wanted it that way. Bash would just remember him as *the newspaperman.*

"Guess what, baby?" Jonni said after swallowing some pasta.

"What?" Ricky said quickly, beating Bash with his response.

Bash gave Ricky a look. He kept his eyes on Ricky as he asked Jonni, "What, baby?"

After a short giggle, Jonni said, "Someone's building a house on the site."

"What site?"

"Where Rock Bottom stood," she said with a twinkle in her eye.

Bash thought for a moment before saying, "I wish them luck."

"Maybe someone should warn them," Jonni said.

"Warn them of what?" Bash asked. "The house is gone."

Jonni didn't answer but she kept her eyes on his. She had actually gotten her paranormal healing website up and running months earlier, and had already helped four families with their *paranormal problems.* But she was still working alone. Two potential coworkers had come forward to join her ministry, both women, but they didn't last long because neither were convicted with enough faith to handle the trauma associated in dealing with the dark spiritual world. Jonni knew that God would eventually send the right person or persons to join her in these endeavors. But it would happen in *his* time, not hers. Until then she was satisfied to handle the cleansing by herself.

"I mean," Bash continued, "whatever was there is gone along with the house, right?" He bit off another bite of sandwich while staring back at Jonni.

Ricky and Terry also waited for her response.

"Not necessarily," she finally said.

"But we cleansed it," Ricky said. "I mean, *you* cleansed it."

"We were never there long enough to know," she said, amused by their reactions.

Terry didn't comment on the subject. He had learned little from Bash about the *spiritual happenings* at Rock Bottom, before the crazy events with Khalid and Ishaq, but he did not know what to think since he had not witnessed anything paranormal himself. Also, Bash did not elaborate much when he recounted the story of the attic to Terry. He never even told Terry about his dreams of seeing him hurt in the shack. All those events had been too much for Bash to process. *Maybe one day I'll tell Terry all about it.*

"It's not our problem, Jonni," Bash said, "so it doesn't matter."

"But we can help," Jonni said in an imploring voice.

"How?" asked Bash. "You think they will believe you when you tell them about the *unclean spirits* that haunted the previous house and its occupants?"

"I discovered some new details," she said casually. "Actually, *old* details."

"About the fire in the 1800s?" asked Ricky.

"What fire?" Terry asked.

"The original house on the site burned down," Ricky explained. "The family living there died in the fire."

Terry raised his eyebrows in surprise.

"That's one theory anyway," Ricky added, deciding to let it go.

"Actually," Jonni said, "I'm talking about much later. In the early 1970s."

This got everyone's attention.

"The owners of Rock Bottom back then had a twenty-year-old son named Robert Halliday," she explained. "His parents lived out of state while he lived alone at the house. According to newspaper articles from the time, his parents let him live in the house to get him out of their hair. He was . . . troubled, to say the least."

"How troubled?" Bash asked.

"He was a rock musician," Jonni said with a smirk.

"Ha-ha," replied Bash.

"In 1972," Jonni explained, "Robert committed suicide inside the house after Austin Police Department homicide detectives closed in on him. The disappearance of nearly a dozen missing persons had been connected to him, leading to a search warrant of the house and surrounding property. When the police arrived to serve the warrant, they discovered multiple shallow graves near the house; graves of young men, all of them local musicians gone missing. Then they found Robert's recently deceased body. Guess where they found his body?"

Ricky and Terry shrugged.

"In the attic," Bash answered.

"That's right," Jonni said. "With a self-inflicted single gunshot wound to the head."

Bash said nothing, although he could have.

"Apparently," Jonni continued, "Robert Halliday lured young musicians from bars and nightclubs around Austin and took them out to the house with the promise of drugs and alcohol. One report claimed he offered to form a band with many of them to get them to join him out at the house. Anyway, once isolated at the house, he drugged them before ritualistically torturing and killing them with a knife."

"Wow," said Ricky. "That's awful."

"A serial killer," Terry offered.

"A sadistic serial killer," Ricky added.

Jonni nodded solemnly.

"What kind of rituals was he involved in?" Bash asked.

"One of the newspaper articles stated that he was involved in rituals connected to ancient Indian cultures from Mexico and Central America."

"Like the Maya," Bash said.

"Yes," she said, knowing what he was thinking.

"So you think we were dealing with this Robert dude the night you did the cleansing?" Bash asked. "Or his spirit?"

"It makes sense," Ricky said. "The music. The attic. Everything."

Jonni weighed her words carefully before answering Bash's question. "I think," she began, "that Robert Halliday opened a doorway to the demonic. And those demons used Robert in the sordid activities at the house while he was alive, and used his *likeness* afterward when he was not alive."

Bash didn't know what to think about this new news concerning this Robert Halliday sicko. A month after Rock Bottom burned to the ground, Bash had learned from the forensic investigation that the explosion had been caused by a pressure cooker bomb detonated by the remains of a cell phone apparatus found in the kitchen. He already knew this but one question still plagued him: *Why did Khalid have the bomb detonated by Walid or whoever when he knew we had escaped the house?* Bash usually answered that question with: *Maybe it went off accidentally.*

Lately, another possibility began entering Bash's thoughts. *Maybe Walid never made the call that triggered the explosion,* he thought. *Maybe someone else made that call. Or maybe not someone else, but something else.*

Bash stood from the table. "I think we should change the subject," he said in an upbeat tone, "and let's go finish our rehearsal. Our first gig is only a week away!"

"I know!" Jonni said in an excited voice. "I can't wait!" She reached for Bash and he responded by leaning down for a kiss.

"Here we go again!" Ricky said while standing from the table and carrying his plate to the sink. "Come on, Terry. Let's go make some music before Yoko shows up!"

Jonni threw her napkin at Ricky. She turned to Bash, "Are you going to let him talk about me like that?"

"What do you mean, Yoko?" said Bash.

Jonni punched him in the arm.

"Careful!" Bash said. "That's my only arm!"

Terry laughed and took his plate to the sink before following Ricky out the door.

Once they were alone, Bash told Jonni, "If you want to contact the people building on the site, it's fine with me."

"Thanks, sweetie," she said, "but that's ancient history."

Bash smiled, not really surprised. "And what did they say?"

"Nothing," she said. "But I'm quite sure they thought I was out of my mind."

"Told you so."

"It's okay," she said. "If nothing is there once they move in then it doesn't matter. But if the problem returns, the people can give me a call. I left them my number and email and web address."

Bash gave her another kiss. "I love you, Mrs. Nadir."

"I love you, too . . ."

† † †

to be continued . . .

CPSIA information can be obtained
at www.ICGtesting.com
Printed in the USA
FFOW02n2024020418
46123930-47162FF